MCPINE

LOVE AT THE HIGHEST LEVEL

D.B. CRAWFORD

McPine

D. B. Crawford

This is a work of fiction. All characters, events and locations are the product of the author's imagination or are used fictitiously.

McPine, Copyright © 2021 D. B. Crawford All rights reserved.

No part of this book may be reproduced, stored in a retrieval system or transmitted in any form or by any means without the prior written permission of the publisher, except by a reviewer who may quote brief passages in a printed or online review.

Description: First U.S. edition. First International edition.

Identifiers: Library of Congress Control number 2021904703

ISBN: 978-1-7776274-0-9

Ebook ISBN: 978-1-7776274-1-6

Subjects: Austin, Cameron (fictitious character) – Fiction.

GSAFD: Romantic suspense fiction.

BISAC: FICTION/Romance/Family Life/Politics.

First U.S. Edition: April 2021

First International Edition: April 2021

DBC

For Meghan and Haley

CHAPTER ONE

The old lady had a knack for getting under his skin, Cameron contemplated. Her frankness, often disarming, was becoming irritatingly bold, and her blunt words at their weekly dinner just a few hours earlier had made him cringe: "To say nothing of your emotional and sexual needs which are not being met," she had told him. "It has to affect the performance of your duties. Unless of course you pay for it, but that would not fill your emotional needs, would it?"

Surely few — if any — women talked to their sons that way.

Seeing that he was annoyed, she adopted her Rose-Kennedy-esque stance. "I've changed your diapers, Cameron. That fact alone gives me some rights that no one else can ever have." He had almost burst out laughing because he doubted that his mother, Grace Winfield Austin, had ever changed a diaper. Hell, if she ever had to identify the cloth diaper from his day from a line-up of tea towels, serviettes and bidet cloths, he was certain she would fail.

There were so many people about in the Austin household as Cameron was growing up on the outskirts of Baltimore that it seemed servants had their own servants. Each of the four Austin children had a nanny who relieved Grace of the need to be involved in things as mundane as diaper changing. Not that she was not a model parent. She was close to her children from the moment they came into the world. As a child of wealth, she simply relegated the less-pleasant duties to the servants. Outgoing by nature, young Cameron made friends with all these people - something his mother encouraged. "We must treat everyone with respect, no matter their lot in life or the color of their skin," he remembered her saying often.

That had resulted in some ire from her own mother, Cameron's grandmother, who considered herself at least one step above other mere mortals, and who, if she had had her way, would have forced servants to crawl on their bellies in her presence. Cameron Austin was thankful that his mother had inherited her father's good sense, or was it the servants' good sense? After all, she too had been raised by nannies.

Grace Winfield was barely twenty-one when she married George Austin, older by more than a decade and well established in the family business. In an old newspaper clipping Cameron had read, the marriage had been reported as an amazing union of wealth and was accompanied by a black-and-white photo of the intertwined *G*s of the couple's names, designed for the occasion. The monogram appeared on many of the wedding gifts which had been showcased on a long table covered with a crisp linen cloth, and photographed for those who could only dream of such materialistic excess. The debate in old stuffy clubs as to which family had actually been the richest was never won. The mesh of companies which combined the accumulated fortunes of the Winfields and the Austins was today overseen by Cameron's two younger sisters and their husbands.

When Cameron Austin heard a comment that his mother was the cream of the crop, he was not sure what it meant, so he asked his grandmother to explain. "Cameron, it means that you are very fortunate to be the son of a woman who is not like everyone else."

Today, Cameron Austin could only agree that Grace Winfield Austin was indeed a rare breed who in her mid-seventies still wielded a great deal of influence. And not solely because of her wealth. She had immense personal strength gained from a reality no amount of money could have changed when the eldest of the Austin boys, Terrence, barely out of his teens, had been killed by a drunk driver as he crossed an intersection.

In the years that followed, Grace Austin became a model for grieving parents everywhere as she fought for tougher laws against drunk drivers. She was eventually able to influence legislation as well as societal views, and now her efforts were being aimed at broadening the meaning of driving under the influence to include all manner of drugs.

Grieving at a very personal level, George Austin had been stoic after his son's death, while Grace explained to her remaining children the need to surrender to a higher power. Crying was a must, she told them, but only when they were together as a family so as to be an example of courage to the outside world. She arranged for the three of them to vent, in turn, their very personal feelings about their devastating loss to a distinguished therapist. Cameron was still grateful to his mother for recognizing that those sessions had been needed, especially in his case because it had afforded him a unique opportunity to also come to terms with his America which was involved in a war he was far from convinced it had the right to wage.

While serving in the Air National Guard, he was to be deployed for the Gulf War but his involvement was short and sweet—something that was still occasionally the butt of late-night television comedy routines—because of an emergency appendectomy.

The whole tumult convinced Cameron that he had a role to play in being of service to his country. When he expressed his views at dinner one evening, his father was clearly disappointed that his only living son would not go into the family business. Nevertheless, he and Grace were thrilled at their son's goal to enter politics. "You'll be the pride of the Austins."

Cameron realized early that his mother's determination had had a positive effect on his goal. "You cannot give up simply because your nomination seems out of reach, Cameron," she told him when he was facing strong opposition in his first bid for the Maryland legislature. "It's all part of the learning process."

Earlier, at their dinner, his mother had challenged him for losing sight of his ultimate goal. Not just his goal. The whole family's goal. Grace Winfield Austin's goal, the one she had supported and influenced all these years. "It is a fact of life that you cannot get there if you are not married."

"Mother, may I point out that you did not remarry after Father died."

"That's quite different, and you know it. I'm an old woman. You are a man in the prime of life with needs and a very precise goal. You owe it to your supporters who want you as Thomson's replacement in three years."

Cameron was painfully aware that a widowed presidential candidate did not carry the same weight as a man with a charming wife and poised children at his side, but what woman in her right mind would marry a fifty-something man who still mourned the loss of the woman he had so loved, a woman who had been unable to give him children.

"I know that you are not even looking, Cameron."

Those words had especially irritated him. What in hell did she expect? He was the Vice President of the United States. He couldn't simply run an ad in the *Washington Post* or join an online dating service: *SWM, 6'2", 185 lbs., black hair and eyes, considered attractive, in position of power, looking for an intelligent soul mate with whom to spend very little time;* or join a Washington singles club. His options were limited.

"Come," Cameron said in answer to a soft knock on the door. He kept his eyes closed and his head against the back of the wide comfortable leather seat.

"Sir, we've entered Canadian air space over the lake," Lonsdale, one of the men in his secret service detail informed him. "We'll be landing shortly."

The pilots of Air Force Two brought the plane to a stop on a runway at the Canadian Forces base just north of Lake Ontario shortly before nine-thirty in as smooth a landing as a duck touching down on the satiny surface of a calm lake. By design, it was the only aircraft in the area at that hour. It taxied to a stop and a nondescript black minivan smoothly glided to a stop as the door of the craft opened and steps were positioned. Two agents exited in the moonlit spring night ahead of the Vice President of the United States who was wearing casual khakis and a brown leather jacket. He was followed by the two other men in his detail. All four men were dressed in black suits.

The driver of the minivan, a tall lanky man with a lined face, got out and went to shake hands with Cameron Austin. "Welcome back to Canada, Mr. Vice President."

"Thank you, Harold. How have you been?"

"Just fine, sir. And you?"

"No complaints, but I'm glad to have nothing to do but rest for the next few days." He smiled. "You don't think I'll be shot, do you? With all this tension between our two countries."

"Of course not. It might be a different story if your President…" At that moment, Harold, a faint smile on his lips, saw fit to cut his remarks short.

Cameron Austin chuckled. "Don't worry, I won't report you."

As the two men watched the luggage being loaded into the minivan

Harold spoke a little more somberly. "To tell you the truth that war of words between Washington and Ottawa has me a little scared."

"It's not going anywhere, believe me. You don't really expect our two countries to end their diplomatic relations over this, do you? Canada and the U.S. are best of friends. Just a little annoyed at each other right now, that's all. It'll pass."

"My wife says she wouldn't be surprised if the U.S. simply decided to grab us and turn us into one giant state. Then where would we be?" Harold asked, not expecting an answer.

About to comment, Cameron Austin turned his head at the sound of a government-issue car which came to a brusque stop a few feet from the Vice President. Two agents rushed to it. A tall man wearing the uniform of a Canadian Armed Forces colonel stepped out from the front passenger side, saluted and then approached Cameron Austin.

"Good evening, Mr. Vice President. Sorry to be late."

"Good evening. Late for what?"

"To officially welcome you to Canada," he said, extending his right hand.

Cameron Austin remained unmoving for a few seconds before shaking the man's hand. "We asked that there be no official notice of my visit to your country since this is strictly a personal trip."

"I simply wanted to let you know that we are honored to have you in our country and that the area is extremely secure."

Cameron Austin's voice was friendly but firm. "Thank you, but I would be very grateful if no one outside the personnel on duty here now knew of my visit."

"Of course, sir," the colonel replied.

"Good evening," Austin said hastily, seating himself in the front passenger seat. Harold, who had opened the door while the two men were talking, now closed it. The four agents piled into the back of the minivan and soon it was being driven away, leaving the colonel to his thoughts. The crew of Air Force Two went back on board, latching the door.

The minivan traveled the smooth two-lane paved road dotted with farm houses that would take them to their destination. Sometime later, the minivan which Harold guided effortlessly on roads he knew well slowed when a sign indicated that Green Lodge was coming up. After the short drive on a road cut from a dense forest where the moonlight could only pierce with dappled jerky spasms, the car stopped in front of a locked wooden gate. Light shone on the unmistakable logo on the right from which hung a notice that the lodge was closed.

A young man in his early twenties appeared behind the gate flooded by the minivan's beams. He unlocked the gate and pulled it open until the minivan had passed. Slowly Harold drove over the gravel driveway. A few seconds later the lodge, a rustic structure of rich maple syrup-stippled logs bathed in light, appeared. It had large windows facing the lake on the first floor and two other floors with dormer windows. Roomy white rattan chairs were ready to receive the weary and tired on the wide porch which spread the length of the building. A few yards to the left, the calm water of the lake shimmered lightly, and in the moonlight a corridor the color of polished silver brought the surface to life. There was a short pier with a couple of motorboats bobbing so softly as to appear still, and a couple of canoes were spread upside down near the water line.

Cameron Austin stepped out of the car and had just enough time to take a satisfying deep breath so his lungs could be renewed by the fresh country air when a man with a full head of graying hair and a pleasant face, opened the front door and approached at a fair pace despite the noticeable limp. The two men embraced warmly.

"Welcome to Canada, Mr. Vice President."

CHAPTER TWO

Steve Marsh led Cameron Austin to the warmth of the country refuge he proudly called home. The four secret service agents followed, scanning the darkness for possible enemies while helping Harold bring in the luggage.

To the right of the entrance and the wide wooden staircase facing it, the dining room was in semi-darkness. On the left, the focal point of the large room was a floor-to-ceiling fieldstone fireplace in which a log fire was roaring. The country-style furniture was inviting, and on the white stucco walls above the pine wainscoting hung a collection of photographs of anglers and hunters posing with noteworthy catches which added warm charm.

The Vice President sat near the fire, while Steve Marsh settled across from him and invited the four other men to find seats. Harold, the driver, slipped out the front door almost unnoticed. Marsh identified himself and offered drinks. All declined.

"Let me introduce my team," Cameron Austin began pointing to each in turn, identifying only their family name. All were tall with short-cropped hair and in their thirties. Agent Jacoby had black hair but the short cut did not hide the fact that it was curly, while Agent Bradley's hair was dark blond. Agent Dunlop, the shortest of the four, had a stocky physique and his brown hair was thinning. Agent Lonsdale whose skin was the color of warm chestnut had features so sharp that his face seemed to have been chiseled. None of them smiled.

"Nice to meet you, gentlemen," Steve Marsh said. "Since it's your first time in this neck of the woods, why don't I explain a little how things work around here and give you a little history. That'd make things easier all around. Your Vice President and I have been friends for a lot of years, ever since we were roommates in college. I'm a Canadian whose father was employed by a large North American company. When he was transferred to the headquarters in New Jersey for a few years I was a teenager so naturally I went too. That's how I ended up at Yale with your Vice President. After we graduated, I stayed on in your country even though my father had returned to Canada. One of the reasons is that Mr. Austin wanted to go into politics, and I felt I could be of service. We worked together for what? Fifteen years?"

The Vice President nodded.

"Then a car crash severely damaged my hip and leg. I was out of commission for a long time because I needed several operations and a lot of physical therapy. My wife and I had to redefine our future. During one of our trips to Canada, we saw this place, fell in love with it, bought it and moved back to Canada where my hip and leg had a chance to heal as much as they ever will. We've never regretted our decision because we've been happy here; however we do miss old friendships, so your Vice President comes to visit once or twice a year when he can manage it. Of course, things were not as complicated when he was simply Governor Austin of Maryland. Ever since he's become Vice President, his visits require shall we say a little more attention. That's what I really want to talk to you about."

The four men continued to listen attentively, their eyes darting at Steve Marsh's face.

"The lake in front of you is called Green Lake, but you won't find it on maps, or at least not identified as such. The reason is that it's a private lake. The property is huge and takes in the lake, so it is a safe haven for Mr. Austin because there are no cottages or houses around it."

"But what about that house up there?" Agent Dunlop asked, pointing to a light to the east that seemed to be hanging above the lake.

"The property here extends mostly to the west and north of the lodge and ends at the bluff on the eastern side. The light you see is Laurie Cosner's house which was built on that bluff. It's the only property that can be seen from this lodge. She's a widow who writes and cultivates roses. Clearly, she doesn't pose a threat, if that's what you're worried about."

"We only have your word for it," Dunlop continued.

"Yes," Steve Marsh replied amiably, "but you must understand that I know everyone around here and can vouch for them."

"Steve," Cameron Austin put in, "I hope you appreciate that my men are concerned about terrorism and are not too pleased that no security check was conducted prior to our arrival."

Marsh smiled briefly. He and Austin went through the same verbal dance every time new agents were assigned to accompany the Vice President on his vacation. Truth be told, both men enjoyed these exchanges.

"Gentlemen, this is a very secure area. There's no need to worry. The town of McPine— some people call it a village—with a population of three thousand or so is on the eastern side of the lake. This is farming country; the town's claim to fame is a large dairy which is the economic hub of the region along with a facility that freezes all the farmers' vegetables. Everyone in and around McPine is aware of the Vice President's visits, but it's a subject that's not discussed with outsiders. That has always been a sort of badge of honor for people around here.

"To give you an example, an enterprising young reporter from Toronto who had heard a rumor that Vice President Austin's plane had been seen landing in this part of the world got a taste of that badge of honor. He went into our local post office to inquire as to Mr. Austin's whereabouts. Annabelle, our local postmistress, looked him straight in the eyes and said, 'You're one of them city folks that smokes those funny cigarettes, aren't you, boy? Pray tell, why would the Vice President of the United States come to McPine? To taste our cheese? Now get out of here, I've got mail to sort.'

He left and tried again to get information from Roger McTavish, a local farmer who was walking down the sidewalk on his way to his truck. Roger looked at the young man. 'No Austins around here, boy. And I know everyone.' No other reporter has been back since. However, I suggest that you get rid of the black suits during your stay, otherwise you'll stick out like sore thumbs and attract the attention of any media types who might dare to sniff around again."

His friend's verbal dissertation made Cameron Austin smile.

"What else should I tell you? At the moment, beside myself, the people on the property are my wife Esther, my daughter Leslie, and my son Mac, whom you met when he opened the gate to let you in. My wife and daughter will prepare and serve the meals with my son's help.

My duties for the next few days entail keeping your Vice President happy while he relaxes. We do a lot of fishing together. Harold, your driver, is a local farmer and a very dear friend. Driving long distances is very tiring for me because of my leg, so he takes over when needed. He has gone home, and will come in if we need him."

Steve Marsh went on to tell the agents that the patrons of the lodge were mostly outdoorsy types who came in for the fishing and hunting, depending on the season. These people came back year after year, but none was aware, Steve emphasized, that Vice President Austin ever stayed at the lodge.

"If you decide to go into McPine when you're off duty, you might be disappointed. It's not exactly Washington, D.C. We have a tea room where the local ladies gather in the afternoon to exchange gossip, recipes or whatever else over a cup of tea. We have a local deli that serves decent soup and sandwiches, a couple of restaurants, and we have a bar where you can watch almost any game you fancy. Of course we have churches, a library, a couple pharmacies, a couple of food stores, and a post office.

"We've got a satellite dish so we get lots of stations," Steve said, indicating the large television set in a corner of the room. "If you're looking for something more lively, you'll have to travel some fifteen miles down the road to Medford. That's where the children around here go to high school. It's a town of about thirty thousand which has a movie theater and a variety of entertainment spots. Any questions?"

The lodge's stone fireplace was double faced so that it could also be enjoyed by patrons in the lounge area which Cameron Austin was doing seated at one of the stools at the richly varnished bar. Steve Marsh poured each of them a brandy and joined his friend after assuring himself that agents Jacoby and Bradley in the next room were out of hearing range.

"So, tell me the truth, Cameron," Steve Marsh began, "What's REALLY behind this whole rigmarole in Washington? I know our new Prime Minister can be a little wacky, but I think President Thomson and your media are maligning us."

"I'm sure it will die down in time. President Thomson used a poor choice of words—words that were said privately, not meant to be overheard—on a very bad day." Austin lowered his voice. "Between us, after a fight with his wife."

"Really? They seem so happy!"

Austin smiled briefly. "The President and Mrs. Thomson are both strong natured. It makes them prone to flaring up at each other."

Steve Marsh said softly, "Like a lot of other people."

"Exactly. So Andrew Thomson was not in a good mood, and quite tired. He was not in a frame of mind to face the press, but he wanted to let the world know about the anti-pollution bill of which he's very proud, and with good reason. He should not have considered taking questions from the media, but he did. When the reporter asked how he would deal with the increasing criticism of the United States' overtures to your government to establish a defense base in your far north during his upcoming trip up here, the President was noncommittal. The problem is that he was a little too curt in his remarks afterwards which, as we know, were overheard."

"Curt? Hell, he said that the Americans shouldn't have to ask permission of anyone, especially a woman, to set up that base," Marsh commented. "Never mind that it's our territory, our country, and that we consider that a woman has every right to be Prime Minister of this country even if he doesn't."

"Unfortunately," Austin said, "by the time White House staff attempted to put a positive spin on Thomson's faux pas, it was too late. The Canadian media had jumped on the remark and it didn't take long for your Prime Minister to make her views known."

"If I recall, Prime Minister Roy said that the U.S. cannot expect other countries to play dead while it continues to act like a bully. It was time to rebel."

"Again, very poor choice of words, but the real problem is that it was a slow news day. I think that after the recent pandemic and terrorist attacks, the media was generally bored, so they played it up for all it was worth on both sides of the border. Suddenly it became an open rebellion against the United States of America, a rebellion led by a woman no less. Our citizens were outraged, of course. We Americans are always right, don't you know," Austin concluded.

Both men chuckled.

"At least now I hope Americans can find Canada on a map!"

"I know the Americans' reputation for ignorance of Canadian affairs, but we are also very patriotic, something we have certainly proven in recent years. And your Prime Minister's unfortunate comments about our President hit at the core of what we believe."

"Cameron, we both know she's trying too hard to carve a reputation for herself. I know that calling President Thomson 'Angry Andy' pissed off many Americans given his current rate of approval. And I suppose I don't blame your networks for featuring it as the top news of the day."

"And now everything our two countries have ever disagreed on seems to be open for discussion, from fishing rights to the never-ending lumber dispute. But we as a nation are especially concerned about your new-found hardcore stance relative to the North."

"It's the same on this side of the border," Marsh commented. "Not everyone agrees with our Prime Minister's views."

"Yet she continues to push in that direction."

"As I said, she's desperate to carve a name for herself in the history books in addition to being a female Prime Minister. She will no doubt listen to the voices of the people and make it impossible for President Thomson to have his way, although we are small potato next to you. Many years ago, a former Prime Minister compared Canada's position as that of someone sleeping next to an elephant, and that no matter how friendly the beast may be we are affected by every twitch or grunt. Yet, we've always managed to be on good terms, so why does it feel like we're ready to shoot each other now?"

Cameron Austin took a sip of his drink. "You're correct when you say it *feels* as though things have shifted, but they have not. We simply have a President and a Prime Minister who need to upgrade their diplomatic sensitivity, and a hungry media ready to kill for THE story, whatever that happens to be. As you know, we're in a dry season now that the presidency has long ceased to be fodder for news networks and comedians. Another factor, of course, is the fact that the President was forced to cancel his trip to Canada soon after your Prime Minister's remark."

"Many people feel that you should have gone to represent Thomson at the funeral in Paris. That's part of your job description, isn't it? To stand in for the President at such functions?"

"We had a long discussion on exactly that point, but the President was not simply attending the funeral of the President of France, he was attending the funeral of a man he considered a dear friend, a man who has long been considered a peacemaker. He wanted to be there to personally offer his condolences to the family. It's quite unfortunate that Canadians felt slighted. However, Andrew Thomson is rescheduling a visit here very soon."

Austin took another sip before continuing. "We can only hope that by that time some disaster or other will keep the media busy."

"You put a lot of the blame for this current state of affairs on the media."

"I do. It is not the first time leaders of both our countries have uttered unfortunate remarks, yet this time the media has masticated them beyond recognition, to the point of using the word 'war' freely. It's stupid considering what we've all been through in recent years, and at some level, a little scary," Austin replied.

"More so for us than for you. America has proven its military might. This is no longer 1812. This time Canada would definitely be unable to fight the Americans on three fronts."

Cameron Austin chuckled again.

"Look at it this way, Cameron," Marsh added. "You're away from Washington and the media. Your only worry now is the size of the trout you'll catch tomorrow."

"I like the sound of that," the Vice President said with a smile.

CHAPTER THREE

Sleep was still lingering in Laurie Cosner's body like the last warm effect of a relaxing drug as she came down the stairs of her home wearing a time-worn white terry robe, her five-year-old golden retriever dutifully at her heels. They turned right and proceeded along the short hall to the kitchen at the back. She opened a sliding door for the animal, grabbed a jacket hanging on a hook, draped it over her shoulders and followed Brandy onto the recently redone deck from which she towered over Green Lake. She pulled the jacket around her neck to keep out the cool morning air as she watched the dog make its way down the steps and begin its routine of a morning reconnaissance around the property.

An almost invisible mist, which seemed to be spewing from the bluff in front of her, hung above the lake, distorting it somewhat. The large black mass deep all around the lake would not metamorphose into pines of rich green and blue hues until the rising sun behind her had arched high enough. She went back inside, turned on the radio and went about preparing breakfast.

The song ended and the morning man's voice from the station in Medford filled the room. "Well, folks, another gorgeous spring day here in pine country. The air is still cool, but isn't the promise of summer just grand after the long winter? You're going to need a sweater this morning, no doubt about it, but who cares when you live in God's country, right? Well, folks, on the international front, it would seem that our neighbors to the south are still of the opinion that we are a bunch of frozen country hicks who have no business criticizing their leader. America, America, and all that. Know what I think? We should organize a boxing match between President Thomson and Prime Minister Roy and let the best man or woman win. Since Roy is what? Almost six feet tall and a black belt, and Thomson shorter, we Canadians might just have the last laugh and end this stupid show. What do you say? Let's fax, e-mail or phone our Prime Minister to show her we are behind her all the way. And why not? I've had enough of Angry Andy's tyrannical approach. If he had his way, he'd make us all Americans and just erase the forty-ninth parallel."

Laurie Cosner turned off the radio and once more wrapped the beige jacket around her shoulders, the sleeves flopping about her as she stepped outside with a bowl of cereal. She sat on the long bench circling the deck. The mist was burning off quickly and she saw a small craft making it way to the eastern side of the lake. Although she could not make out the faces of the two men on board, she knew Steve Marsh was taking U.S. Vice President Austin out for a spot of trout fishing. As was the case most mornings, the lake was polished emerald where the sun had succeeded in making its presence known, and was undulating lightly in the light morning breeze. She could only agree with the radio morning man: pine country was indeed God's country.

The sweet sounds of Mendelssohn's *The Evening Star* echoing from the piano in the front room and reverberating through the partially closed sliding door brought her out of her *rêverie*. Brandy had come up for his breakfast, and as always was waiting in front of the door. Laurie stepped inside and fed the animal before noiselessly making her way into the living room. At the white baby grand in the front corner, her daughter's fingers were effortlessly traveling the keys sending melodic notes dancing into the air toward the photograph displayed next to a vase of pink roses. Laurie sat in an armchair a few feet from Sarah in awe as she always was at the girl's marked talent, not detecting one false move.

At fifteen, Sarah was a pretty girl with a sweet face still immune to the worries and pains of life. She momentarily smiled at her mother, her full head of dark curls bouncing with her every movement. She was wearing a pair of faded jeans and a red tee, but was barefoot on the pink carpeting. It was a tradition—an obsession her aunt Rita teasingly called it—that she always removed her shoes before sitting at the instrument.

The piece ended, and Laurie clapped enthusiastically. "Just great, Sarah. Perfect."

"No, it wasn't. I still mess up just before the end."

"Well, I certainly didn't catch anything."

Sarah smiled faintly, her dark eyebrows going up ever so slightly, a look Laurie knew was saying her mother would never be able to tell the difference between an E sharp and an F if her life depended on it.

"You're always so hard on yourself."

"I want to get it perfect before the concert."

Laurie rose and came to put a kiss on her daughter's forehead. "I know you will. How about some breakfast?"

As mother and daughter ate, Laurie asked, "Are you all packed?"

"Yeah. I'll bring my suitcase down before I go. 'You sure Aunt Rita's going to stop by here before picking me up at school?"

"Of course. She's coming to have lunch with me. By the way, she said to tell you she got tickets for that piano concert at the University of Toronto."

"Great!" Sarah exclaimed.

"It's going to be lonely without you for three whole days."

"Come on, mom," Sarah said, her uncomplicated happy face looking at Laurie. "You're glad to have time to yourself, admit it."

"Maybe," Laurie said looking at the clock on the stove. "Better get going or you'll miss your bus."

A few minutes later Laurie was looking at her daughter sauntering along the curving driveway as she descended to the road, a red backpack over her denim jacket. Sarah turned and waved at her mother standing in the open front door just as the yellow bus stopped and the door folded open. Laurie sighed. This weekend was just the beginning, was it not? Little by little she would have to let Sarah go to set her own pace in the world. It was a thought she found quite distressing.

The sun was warming everything in its glow very nicely by the time Laurie walked down the gradually sloping path to the greenhouse several hundred feet to the south of her house, Brandy in tow. A discreet oval sign on a post announced: *Only Roses Inc.* She took time to inspect the large outside garden where the company's rose bushes, a large part of their trade, appeared happy in the still-rising sunlight.

"You know what they say, spring weekends bring out the gardener in everyone," Bernie Wesson told Laurie as she stepped inside the wooden structure that served as an office and storage facility near the entrance to the large L-shaped glassed building.

"I'm all for it as long as they want roses," Laurie replied. "How's it going?"

"Couldn't be better. When you said you wanted to grow only roses, I didn't quite agree as you recall."

"Didn't agree? You as much as told me I was a lunatic!" Laurie said smiling.

"Well, you were certainly right. Take a look," Bernie invited. He was a tall man in his early forties whose long lined face bore witness to an outdoorsy lifestyle. He proudly pointed to the computer screen. "I told our customers that orders had to be in by five this morning if they wanted them for Saturday. Lots of people want to plant rose bushes this year as you can see."

Laurie was amazed at the number of orders that had gotten confirmed overnight on their website.

"And that order for twenty-four dozen red roses? Well they've doubled it!"

"Wow! We don't have enough!" Laurie said, a touch of alarm in her voice.

"Never fear, dear lady. Actually, just. Luckily I sold them on white for half the order—red and white roses to signify unity—otherwise we would have had to call up one of our competitors."

"What in the world would anyone want with forty-eight dozen roses?"

"It's some sort of hifalutin wedding in Toronto," Bernie told his partner.

"Do you need any help?"

"No. Everything's under control. With Ed here, I should have everything ready to go in an hour or so, then I'll be on my way. I want to be in Toronto well before rush hour which seems to start at two on Fridays. You sure you're going to be okay handling things this weekend? I won't be back until late Monday afternoon."

"No problem. If any rush orders come in, I'll get Ed to take a drive."

Together they stepped inside the warm humid air of the large greenhouse and were greeted by what appeared to be a small forest of green dotted with flecks of red, pink, white, yellow and peach. The narrow aisles crisscrossing the expanse in front of them and on the right were almost invisible among the green. Ed, their part-time employee, was expertly guiding the rose-harvesting machine, gathering bouquets and placing them on a small table set on casters. Laurie guessed that he had almost half of the day's orders of long-stem roses already picked.

She walked to one corner of the main greenhouse where she grew fresh herbs and a few varieties of lettuce for year-round use for herself, Bernie and some friends. Also in the area several dozen geraniums in small green pots were beginning to show off velvety red blossoms. Above them, healthy begonias in hanging baskets were praising the sun from their perch. This was the corner grown especially for the people of McPine. *Only Roses* stepped outside its wholesale business in the spring by filling orders for the people in and around the town.

Laurie walked back, inspecting the roses as she went, bending from time to time to take in the heavenly smell into her lungs. She loved this place and what it represented. She loved that here she felt Robby's soul which he poured so lovingly into the plants he grew and nurtured all his life. He'd been gone five years now, yet thoughts of him still made her struggle with emotion because it seemed like only yesterday that she had said her last goodbye.

"How about it?" she heard Bernie Wesson ask.

"What?"

"How about dinner next week, Tuesday?"

"Sounds great."

Her reply had been less than enthusiastic, and Bernie immediately regretted having asked her out while in the greenhouse. This was Robby's domain and that hadn't changed in the last few years. He, Bernie, would always be second fiddle here. Nothing would ever change that.

Bernie Wesson and Robby Cosner were both local boys who had hit it off in first grade and remained friends until Robby's death. When, in their last year of high school, Robby talked to Bernie about going into business together growing plants and flowers to sell in the city, Bernie had had reservations. McPine was too far from Toronto to be competitive, he argued, but Robby, who had plotted long and hard, was convinced it was easily feasible. Medford was not far away after all, and there were good delivery companies in the town. Besides, Robby could not imagine ever leaving McPine like most young people his age were doing. It was his home. Bernie had himself thought about leaving, but as an only son he knew he would inherit his dad's large and profitable dairy farm someday, and he did enjoy the outdoors. Why go to the city to work in a stuffy office?

After studying horticulture, the two friends went into business together. The first years were lean, but they soon managed to turn a steady profit. After Robby died and Laurie inherited his share, she and Bernie had long discussions about the future of the operation. Laurie felt the company did not have a clearly defined focus, and suggested that they abandon time-consuming retail sales. Bernie had wanted to buy Laurie's share and she had been tempted to sell, but in the end she convinced Bernie of the benefits of a wholesale operation specializing in roses. Reluctantly he had agreed and they had been working side by side with little conflict ever since. She oversaw the financial end, and Bernie took care of the roses. He was the expert.

The problem for Bernie was that he wanted his relationship with Laurie to grow beyond their friendship and the arrangement of occasional carnal encounters they had fallen into in recent years. For Bernie, it was a constant struggle to try and convince her to share more of their lives. The hurdle, of course, would always be his wife, Clare, who had lost her hold on reality. Their marriage had died long ago and she was constantly in and out of mental facilities, coming home when all appearances pointed to a recovery, but these periods were always short-lived. She had now been away for over a year, and he had little hope she would ever come back home, yet in his heart he couldn't let himself divorce her. Guilt, no doubt, he contemplated, sighing. But then again he had vowed: in sickness and in health. He had meant it. He owed her.

But did it have to mean he would spend the rest of his life alone?

CHAPTER FOUR

The train of words on the screen kept getting longer and longer as Laurie Cosner's agile fingers sped across the keyboard. She was gaining momentum as another chapter of her latest novel *Beads of the Sea* was being contrived. Her long fingers could hardly keep up with the plot of her imagination. Brandy's bark—a low and joyful effort announcing a friendly arrival—failed to interrupt her train of thought. Still typing, she stretched her neck to look through the window of the front room she used as an office from which she could view the curving driveway. Rita Payne, her sister-in-law, was getting out of her mustard-yellow mid-size sedan. The newest color on the market she had said when she bought it, but Laurie had and still considered the shade more suited to a school bus. Rita knocked briefly before walking in just as Laurie was turning off her computer.

Born a couple of months apart almost forty years earlier, the two women were the same height, taller than most women, and both still had figures that belied their age. An auburn tinge brought Laurie's shiny hair, the color of field wheat, to life; she kept it short because she had little talent when it came to handling a hair dryer and brush. In contrast, Rita's jet black hair fell neatly to her shoulders, obviously totally docile to her expert handling.

The two women had become friends while studying writing in Toronto more than two decades earlier and had remained close over the years. But there was more to it. They were related. Laurie was the widow of Rita's older brother Robby. Laurie who had been born and raised in Medford now lived in McPine, while Rita was true McPine stock with an ancestry going back to the founding of the region. She and her family now lived in Medford where the Paynes owned Medford's newspaper and radio station. That was where Rita put her writing skills to good use.

The two women embraced warmly and brought each other up to date on the goings-on in each of their lives as they moved into the kitchen and Laurie brought out the salad and sandwiches she had prepared earlier.

"Are you sure having Sarah along this weekend's not going to be a problem?" Laurie asked. "I mean she won't spoil your time with your daughter? I'm asking because I got the feeling Sarah did sort of invite herself."

"No, she didn't. Emily wanted her along. She thought it'd be more fun than being with her mom all the time. Go figure!"

"You don't mind stopping at my mother's do you, so Sarah can pay her a visit? She invited all three of you for dinner on Saturday, but I told her I wasn't sure of your plans."

"I'd love to eat there. Such a lovely home," Rita commented as her well-defined lips easily went into a smile, making fine lines more discernible. Happiness lines, she always called them. She transferred some of the Caesar salad from the bowl to her plate.

"Well, that's what happens when you marry money," Laurie said. "Just call her when you get to Toronto. She'd love to have you."

As the two women began eating, Rita asked: "Have you heard from Mike lately?"

"No. Why? You know he doesn't come around here unless he's looking for something, usually money. Being a revolutionary of sorts doesn't come cheap, you know."

"Well, he was in Medford this week," Rita said.

"Really. What for?"

"Don't know. Someone saw him having lunch at April's place."

"Oh, boy. Trouble ahead! April has a way of building just enough of a spark under Mike's ass to detonate it."

"I thought he had settled down with a good job at the power company," Rita commented before taking a bite of her sandwich.

"Yeah, after my mother pleaded with her husband to find him something, anything. As far as I know my dear brother's still there, but if he was in Medford on a weekday he must have quit."

"You don't know that for sure, do you?"

"No, but I know Mike. He's got to be bitchin' about something or he's not happy. April must have convinced him of her latest cause and he couldn't resist. I think she actually gets periods of insanity instead of regular periods like the rest of us."

Rita let her friend vent her frustration. She knew Laurie loved her younger brother, but that oftentimes his involvement in public protests of one kind or another could be a source of anger and embarrassment for his sister, especially when he got himself sent to jail, something he somehow relished. It especially angered Laurie when Mike gave little or any thought at all to some of the causes he championed, because she felt some were dubious at best.

Now, April was an all-together other matter. Laurie disliked the woman, and nothing could and would ever change that. April McLaren was the antithesis of Laurie—loud with the ability to use foul and vulgar language at the most inopportune time. Besides, her hair was dyed so light that black roots, the color of her heavy eyebrows, always seemed to show through.

Mike had met the woman, many years his senior, at the diner where she worked in Medford, a popular hangout owned by her aunt and uncle, which everyone knew would one day belong to April. In the years since, the pair had marched, protested and participated in sit-ins to bring attention to a variety of causes from seal hunting and globalization, to the legalization of marijuana and gay rights, not that either of them was gay. The cause was always the rationale. They had been arrested numerous times in the process.

"All I can say, Laurie, is let it go," Rita suggested. "Nothing you can do will change your brother, and God knows you put in a decent effort."

"You're right, of course. But you'll let me know if you hear anything about their plans?"

"Don't I always?"

After Rita left, Laurie went back to her writing. She had been at it for a couple of hours when, as was her routine, she activated the voice mail for both the business and her own land line. She then went for a bike ride, a daily workout for herself and Brandy.

There were only a few puffy clouds in the sunny sky, and the air had warmed up nicely. She pedaled at a good pace toward Main

Street, Brandy keeping up behind her until they reached the post office. Leaning her bike against a wooden post and admonishing the dog to stay and wait for her—which the animal always did—she stepped inside the small brick structure with the unmistakable rectangular dark blue logo on a red background seen on the facade of all Canadian post offices.

"Hi, Annabelle. Anything interesting today?"

"Well, looks like you finally got a check from that magazine up in Vancouver for your article," the woman of about sixty with a more-than-healthy interest in local gossip and goings-on began, handing Laurie a sealed window envelope, "and I hope you don't mind that I read your article in this issue about setting up a garden. Very interesting."

"Thanks, Annabelle. Anything else?"

"That's all the mail, but Harold told me you-know-who arrived yesterday."

"I figured as much. He was out on the lake with Steve this morning."

"Trout should be great right now. I wish we could see him, you know, just to say hello, welcome him."

"That would defeat the purpose of his incognito visits, wouldn't it? See you tomorrow, Annabelle."

Tossing her mail into her backpack, Laurie got back on her bike, and she and the dog continued down Main Street, waving at the few people she encountered. At Bridge Street she turned right making her way to her favorite spot, the ancient covered bridge that spanned the lazy Pine River just outside the town limits. She was musing that small towns everywhere invariably called their streets Elm, Church or Bridge, but that the McPine town fathers should change the name of this particular street to Memory Lane. It was after all where Robby Cosner had proposed to her, by the bridge where she was now stopping. She watched Brandy make its way to the river's edge while her eyes pierced the clear water in an effort to remember every inch of Robby's face, a quest which was becoming harder and harder with each passing year.

She had the impression that he was fading from her mind, slipping away from her like water being absorbed by the soil, unless his photograph was in front of her. Perhaps Bernie was right. Perhaps she was trying to hang on to a past that had after all been short-lived. She had to look to the future. But to what exactly? She was happy enough in her life, although the thought of spending the rest of her life alone was not especially welcome. There certainly was no one in McPine that could steal her heart. Bernie was great, but he was simply there, even if he had convinced himself that their relationship could become the kind of romance that make hearts flutter.

She got back on her bike calling the dog to follow her across the narrow wooden bridge. Her eyes had trouble adjusting to the sudden darkness as the tires of her sturdy mountain bike traveled the long ancient planks. She was almost across when she saw a newer-model silver sedan, bathed in sunshine, approaching from the other side. She pressed faster on her pedals to make it out into the light before the car reached the bridge. She knew from experience that a car took up most of the space inside the structure. Seeing her, the man at the wheel applied the brakes.

"Hi there," the friendly voice said through the open window.

"Hello," Laurie replied, coming to a stop near the car.

"I was wondering if you could help me. I seem to be lost. I'm trying to find my way back to the lodge by the lake, but for some reason I can't find the road."

Laurie was looking at the pleasant face of the American Vice President. He had removed his sunglasses to reveal fiery dark eyes. He definitely had what she considered a sensual mouth if one were to go by the rules she and Rita had established a couple of decades earlier to define sexy lips. Gray showed through the black curly hair, but the fine lines around his eyes and mouth bore witness to a lineage of men who aged well.

"That's probably because the sign's down and hasn't been put back up again. In winter the plow often manages to knock it down." Indicating with her hand, she added, "You go straight to Main Street, turn left, go south through town, then right just past the Opera House."

"The Opera House? There's an opera in this village?"

"Town. We prefer town," Laurie chuckled. "Not quite. We, the locals, call it the Opera House. It's just a large hall where we hold bazaars, dances, that sort of thing. No one seems to know exactly where the name originated. The wood sign in front says McPine Hall."

"I was there. I was everywhere, to tell you the truth. I turned around in the parking lot at the hall but I certainly didn't see any road."

"It's a few hundred feet south, sort of hidden by trees, so you have to really look not to miss it. Would you like me to show you?"

"Don't disturb yourself. I'm sure I can find it with your directions."

"If I may be so bold, why are you traveling alone . . . I mean without your secret service people?"

"You recognized me I see."

"Well, the world doesn't end at the border between our two countries. We do have computers, newspapers and magazines up here, and we can actually read. We also have a new invention; you may have heard of it, it's called television," Laurie said with as straight a face as she could muster.

Cameron Austin chuckled. "Touché. But you're hard on my fellow countrymen, Ms . . . ?"

"Cosner. Laurie Cosner. It might have something to do with the fact that last night I heard a newsman on one of your networks commenting on the current, shall we say, unpleasantness between our two countries," Laurie said without a trace of harshness in her voice, "as a sad state of affairs between Canada and the largest country in the world. Don't you people go to school? The average Joe may not know that Canada is larger than the U.S., but a newsman?" Her lips went up into a pleasant smile.

Cameron Austin continued to look at her, impressed by her forthright approach. He had read similar comments from the media in Canadian newspapers — which he perused daily — but to hear it directly from the mouth of a person on the street, or rather a country road in this case, painfully pointed to a need for a more global view south of the border. He was also impressed by the honest face. That woman would tell it like it was no matter what.

"He might have been referring to the population. We are bigger than you in that sense, aren't we?"

"Of course, by many country miles, but there are countries with more people than the U.S. Sorry, Mr. Austin. I didn't mean to be impertinent."

"You were not," he commented, and the rest of the words were out of his mouth before he could study possible ramifications and change his mind. "You candor is refreshing. Let me buy you a drink or a coffee to show my gratitude."

"Mr. Austin, or perhaps it's more proper to say Mr. Vice President, do you really want people to see you in a public place?"

"Everyone around here knows I stay at the lodge, don't they?"

"Of course."

"Even though I haven't met them personally, I consider the people of McPine my friends. I consider you my friend."

Laurie couldn't look away. There was something in those dark eyes, an intelligence she had rarely seen. They were attracting her like a refrigerator beckons fancy magnets. And Cameron Austin, Vice President of the United States of America, certainly didn't seem in any great hurry to get back to the lodge.

"Well, friend," she said at last, "here's a better plan. Come up to my house. I make a mean cup of coffee. Certainly as good as what you're used to in Washington."

He smiled warmly. "Very well. Lead the way."

She pedaled back toward Main Street, turning right at Hill Street towards her house, the dog in tow, the sedan following some distance away, and all the while wondering what in the world had come over her. She had to be going insane. Maybe she had a brain tumor. What other reason would there be for her to invite the American Vice President to her house when she didn't even remember if she had put the lunch dishes away, or if the living room rug needed vacuuming?

Too late, you fool, she told herself.

CHAPTER FIVE

Standing on a two-step ladder, Laurie brought out her best cups from the top shelf of the cupboard above the refrigerator, the ones her mother had given her for Christmas a few years back, and that she used only when the older woman came to visit. Laurie was aware that they were of exquisite English bone china, the same kind the Queen used her mother had said, but now as the coffee slowly dripped in the machine on the white countertop, she wondered if the cups were too delicate for today's occasion and perhaps better suited to a tea party.

What in the hell kind of china was one supposed to use when the Vice President of the United States dropped in for coffee in a rather impromptu fashion, anyway? She finally directed her attention to a lower cupboard where her everyday mugs were, inspecting them closely, and finally choosing two after making certain they were perfectly clean—the dishwasher did leave some specks behind from time to time.

Returning to the living room she saw Cameron Austin looking at the photo on the white piano which, on the pink carpeting, contrasted nicely with the flower splashes of the upholstered furniture.

"That's my husband Robby with my daughter Sarah when she was young. She's now fifteen. My husband died when she was almost ten years old," Laurie explained.

"Sorry to hear it. I know what that feels like."

"If I remember correctly, your wife died shortly after you took office."

"Forty-two days into our first term," Austin replied, still cringing deep inside at the unfairness of his situation. "A brain aneurysm, and there was nothing anyone could have done. She had retired to her private room at our official residence in Washington, and I found her when I came home."

Laurie could sympathize with his pain. "How awful for you. Please sit down," she invited, anxious to change the subject. "I'll get the coffee."

She brought the filled mugs on a little square golden tray—part of an ensemble with a matching carafe—someone had given her and Robby as a wedding gift. She had arranged a few grapes and pieces of cheese on a small plate.

He graciously took a piece of cheese and a steaming mug. "You're right, this is great coffee."

"What did I tell you?"

"Are you the pianist?" he asked, pointing at the Steinway.

"My daughter is. She's very good for her age."

"Does musical talent run in the family?"

"My mother played the piano professionally when she was younger and taught it for years. It skips a generation, I guess."

He smiled, and broached the subject she wanted to avoid. "What happened to your husband?"

"Leukemia."

He knew her short reply signaled her desire to avoid lingering on the subject. He quickly turned to another avenue. "What kind of work do you do?"

She was happy to elaborate on her career as a freelance writer and the author of two books. Both had been on the market for a few years, and while they had not been instant bestsellers, they did however continue to sell. She was working on a second novel, which was difficult to describe, she said. Then she went on to the details of *Only Roses Inc.* for the benefit of the Vice President.

"Growing flowers and plants had never been in my plans, I must say, but life threw it on my lap. I enjoy it and it is a steady source of income which allows me to write. Despite what you might have heard, not all writers are rich."

Cameron Austin smiled as he sipped his coffee, and she was trying to assess his reaction. What sort of interest could the man possibly have in her financial situation? She had read the articles, and she was aware of the extent of his wealth.

As if taking a cue, he said, "I take it the roses on the piano are yours?"

"Of course."

"They are simply beautiful. Do you know that the rose is the official National Floral Emblem of the United States?" the Vice President asked.

"Actually, I did," she replied. "And we owe that fact to President Reagan."

"I'm impressed," Austin said, "but I bet you don't know who the first rose breeder in the U.S. was."

"I know roses, sir. It was George Washington."

"Now I'm truly impressed," he said, smiling at her.

She wanted to change the subject. "To come back to my earlier question, Mr. Austin, what are you doing out driving Esther Marsh's car by yourself? Doesn't a man in your position have to be shielded at all times especially in the current international climate?"

"Yes, but at some level it does get annoying. I'm on vacation and I simply wanted to get out and feel free for a short while. I hadn't driven a car in ages."

"Felt good?"

"Mighty good, I must say."

"Aren't those supposed to be guarding you going to notice you're missing?"

"Probably, but they know this area is safe."

"Safe because we Canadians don't all carry a gun or have one under our pillow?"

Austin stared into his cup for a moment before responding. "That's certainly part of it, yes. I do feel safe up here, but in all fairness you do realize that some of us in positions to make a difference are working toward changing gun laws in the United States."

"But the gun lobby and all that." She sipped her coffee, then asked, "Do you know the definition of a Canadian?"

"I dare not guess," he said smiling.

"It's an unarmed American with healthcare who apologizes a lot."

He chuckled. "You can't change attitudes and habits overnight," the Vice President commented.

"I'm sure, but why does almost every American feel it's their duty to own a gun? Okay, not everyone, but certainly a high percentage."

Before Austin could answer, Laurie added with a touch of passion in her voice, "And don't tell me it's a right guaranteed in your Constitution. I doubt the architects of the document meant that people should have guns to shoot anyone who pisses them off!"

"This really bothers you," Austin said, somewhat astonished.

"I have to tell you that going to the United States now makes me nervous. You just never know when someone's going to shoot you."

"Come on, Laurie, things aren't that bad. People are not out in the street shooting each other."

"Maybe not, but we hear of a new mass shooting every week, it seems."

He knew she had a point. He tried another tactic. "You do have guns here in Canada, don't you?"

"Of course. What I'm saying is that outsiders can feel less secure in your country, especially those who hail from a close cocoon-like society like McPine," Laurie said. "I must sound quite provincial..."

Brandy's barking made her stretch her neck to look outside. A tall black man and a stockier white male, both casually dressed, were looking over the silver sedan, the dog making its annoyance known a short distance away. "You've been found out, Mr. Vice President."

Austin got up from the comfortable easy chair and made his way to the window as the two men were coming up the walk.

"You're in for it now!" Laurie said with a touch of mischievousness in her voice.

"I suppose so," he replied, and went to open the door before the two men could knock. "Come in, gentlemen, please."

Not moving, Agent Dunlop said, "Mr. Vice President, how do you expect us to do our jobs if..."

Cameron Austin had put his hand up, standing squarely in the door. "I appreciate your position, and I apologize, but I simply wanted to drive around the countryside for a while. I intended to return to the lodge before you had time to miss me, but I got lost." Moving in a little and pointing with his hands, he said, "This is Ms. Cosner. Laurie Cosner."

Both men nodded curtly.

"She was kind enough to give me directions and we were simply enjoying a cup of coffee. Gentlemen, you must realize that this is McPine, not some rough, largely Republican area, where I could be in trouble. It's quite safe."

"Sir, with all due respect," Agent Lonsdale began, "any number of people could have seen you. This will make our job that much more difficult."

"We've been through all this. Everyone in this area knows of my visits," Austin said, annoyance in his voice. "The fact that I came out of my cage for a moment is not going to turn them violent!"

Cameron Austin, the even-tempered Vice President who had a reputation for counteracting President Thomson's fits of bad humor, had shocked himself. For a second he wondered why, although he knew the answer. His men had interrupted a pleasant conversation he wished could have gone on much longer.

"Please wait for me in the car," he said, having noticed the lodge's black minivan, "I'll be out in a moment."

He closed the door and turned to Laurie. "Thank you. I really enjoyed your company."

"Even if I was a little rough on you?"

"I enjoyed the honesty. I wish I could see you again before I leave."

"Why can't you?"

Austin smiled. Again the disarming forthrightness. "I'd have to come with my men…"

"So? They can wait outside. The weather's nice."

The Vice President smiled. "I'd like to take you out for dinner at a nice restaurant, unfortunately that would be too much of a logistics problem for my men."

"Why? You could simply disguise yourself. You do it from time to time, don't you?"

He was totally taken aback and momentarily speechless.

"Think about it. I did enjoy your visit, Mr. Vice President," Laurie said, extending her hand.

He took it, put his left hand on top of hers, and smiled. "I will think about it. In the meantime, how about dinner at the lodge tonight? I caught a nice-sized trout this morning. You do like trout, don't you?"

Laurie thought she would truly enjoy getting to know the man better, but then again privacy would be non-existent at the lodge. Should she dare invite him to dinner at her house? She quickly took a mental inventory of her pantry, and although she could get supplies in town, she decided against it. Cameron Austin was certainly used to fine cuisine, and although she was a reasonably good cook, a cordon bleu she was not. On the other hand, Esther Marsh was a whiz in the kitchen, and Laurie mused that she hadn't had fresh trout in some time.

"What about it?" Cameron Austin asked again when he didn't get a reply.

"It would be nice. Thank you."

"Great," the Vice President said, his voice leaving no doubt that he was very pleased. "Should I send one of my men?"

"I'm a big girl. I know the way."

He smiled. "Six-thirty?"

"I'll be there."

Through the window she looked at him walk to the car while one of the two agents slipped into the passenger seat. Cameron Austin drove the circle of the driveway down to the street followed by the black minivan.

Was it wise to have agreed to see this man again, she wondered? There certainly was no future here even though she couldn't deny the attraction, which she knew instinctively was mutual. He would be gone in a few days, but on the other hand it had been a while since she had had an interesting date. Not that Bernie Wesson wasn't a nice guy but there was no excitement in their relationship. Certainly having dinner with Cameron Austin would be more stimulating. She was still young, and she needed some spark, however brief, in her life.

Now, what was one supposed to wear to have dinner with the Vice President of the United States?

At six-fifteen, for the umpteenth time, she examined herself in the long mirror fastened on the back of her bedroom door. She had decided on her most classic outfit, the one she wore whenever she went to Toronto to meet editors: a well-cut navy linen pant suit with a classic white silk blouse. Her only jewelry was a pair of gold studs in her pierced ears, and she had applied a minimum of makeup. She had always felt the look could take her anywhere, and now she was certain it was perfect for dinner at the Green Lodge with Cameron Austin. She could feel a twinge of nervousness in her stomach, and she wished she could have called Rita to discuss all this, but that would mean that Sarah could overhear. Better restrain herself.

Downstairs, she turned on a lamp in the living room and the fluorescent over the kitchen sink as she always did before going out, then checked her face one last time in the small mirror in the hallway before stepping out. She walked down to the side of the house where her car, a medium metallic blue sedan, was parked. The air had not yet gotten cooler, and she could see the sun, a fiery red ball, slowly being eclipsed by the huge pines across the lake as it was going down into hiding, but not before offering the promise of another sunny day in the morning.

She drove slowly, wondering how many people already knew of her date. Certainly Steve Marsh and his family, but they were the soul of discretion. Luckily she didn't see anyone on the road to the lodge. When she turned into the lodge's wide entrance she saw that Agent Dunlop was waiting for her. She smiled. Without acknowledging her or nodding, he proceeded to pull the gate open to let her pass. She drove in and parked next to the minivan at the front of the building. She was checking her hair in the rearview mirror when, without having seen him approach, Agent Lonsdale was at her side, opening the door.

"Good evening," she said pleasantly.

"Good evening. Vice President Austin is waiting for you inside," Lonsdale said, without a trace of emotion.

"Thank you," she said, stepping out.

Cameron Austin was not inside. He was standing on the large porch, a tall slim figure in an off-white sweater over dark slacks. Smiling, he stepped down to greet her. She smiled back.

"I was hoping you wouldn't change your mind," he told her.

"Now, why would I do that? After all I was only tempted about a dozen times."

He chuckled, putting a long arm around her back to guide her inside.

Laurie had been inside the lodge many times over the years, yet she was impressed anew by the warm country atmosphere. Cameron Austin pointed to the dining area and they sat at one of the round tables near the front window. It was covered with a crisp linen cloth on which rested two place settings and a crystal vase containing a single pointed peach hybrid tea rose. She remembered that Steve Marsh had come around the greenhouse a couple of days earlier while Bernie was inside. Of all their blooms, this was her favorite. It was a good omen.

"I take it this is one of yours," Austin commented.

"Yes, indeed. It's a tea rose. It means I'll remember always."

"Appropriate," he said, as he pulled one of the captain's chairs for her and got comfortable across from her, "although I must say I know little about roses or flowers in general. What would you like to drink? Steve has some white wine cooling. A nice Chardonnay which I happen to like."

"Sounds good."

Steve Marsh approached quietly. "Good to see you, Laurie. How are you?"

"Just fine, thanks. You?"

"Couldn't be better. The only way people around here are going to know you came around is if you tell them," Marsh said, smiling.

"I appreciate that, Steve."

"We'll have the wine, and I'm ready to eat. What about you, Laurie?"

"Certainly."

"I'm starved after spending most of the day outdoors," Austin said, "but if you prefer to wait a while..."

"No, I could use some food. I wasn't able to have my regular afternoon snack today," she said, smiling at Austin.

He definitely liked that quirky mind.

CHAPTER SIX

*P*repared by the expert hands of Esther Marsh, the trout—the one he had caught with his own hands that very morning—could only have been described as pure pleasure. The pink flesh melted in their mouths. Outside, the sun had disappeared, and the dark blanket that was spreading was lightened by silver rays dancing on the softly undulating surface of the lake. Laurie felt contented as she peered at the calm view. Her earlier nervousness had totally vanished.

Steve Marsh had served the wine and Esther had been in charge of the food, both of them appearing and disappearing as quietly as mice. Laurie knew the secret service men were about, but didn't see them except for the back of one head protruding over the back of the sofa in front of the large television set in the next room. The dinner and the conversation had been delightful, and she was pleased to see that the Vice President seemed to be enjoying his break from the mundane worries of high elected office.

In answer to her questions, much of the conversation had centered on the history of his family, a tale Laurie had found fascinating. Or was it his sweet voice? She knew she could go on listening to it for hours. He had talked about his mother—conveniently omitting to express his irritation at her frequent remarks on the state of his personal life—and about his late brother. He had talked briefly about his wife, praising her dedication on his behalf during his years in public life.

Esther Marsh, a no-nonsense lady with a full head of graying hair which gave her a distinguished appearance, approached. "How was everything?"

"My dear Esther, you outdid yourself," Austin said, briefly kissing the arch formed by the thumb and index finger of his right hand.

"It was great, Esther," Laurie added.

"Coffee?" Austin asked Laurie.

As they sipped their coffee, the Vice President switched to telling her about his political life and his work. She soon realized she was getting a brief education on the workings of American politics even though she didn't quite understand all the intricacies.

"In other words, the vice-presidential running mate is chosen because of the area he represents. You being from the east balances out President Thomson who's from the northwest."

"It's not quite that simple, but in essence, yes."

"You knew President Thomson before you joined his campaign?"

"We have been friends for a while. I consider him a great leader."

"But don't you find it a wee bit embarrassing when he says things that can offend allies like Canada?"

"Andrew Thomson is a man history will judge kindly. He is dedicated, hardworking, and fair. Certainly, he can be a little curt, but those close to him know that it's a flaw that has a plus side because it can be quite valuable when tough decisions have to be made."

"But in essence he said that Canada—and its female leader—should accommodate the will of the United States. That's far from fair."

"Agreed," Austin said, "but you must understand that it was a private remark made on a very bad day. It was a poor choice of words, and I am certain things will calm down."

"You're defending him!"

"Of course. He's a good man. His record speaks for itself. No one is perfect, Laurie, and when you live in a glass house, as the President does, or I, to some extent, any imperfection is magnified. It's something all of us in public office have to live with," he concluded, pushing his empty cup away from him. "It's a beautiful night, how about a walk?"

"I'd love that," she replied.

They walked slowly near the lake, and Laurie was aware that the man who had been sitting in the shadows on the front porch as they had come out was now following at a distance. It made her feel uncomfortable.

"Does he have to follow us?" she asked Austin.

"I regret to say that it's his job. Don't let it get to you."

"Are you ever alone?"

"Of course. When I'm at work in my office, they stay outside. The same at my home. If you're worried about any gossip, rest assured they are discreet."

"Still...this is McPine. Did they get on your case when you left my house?"

"It was made quite clear that if I ever dare to pull a similar stunt again, they would quit *en masse* and leave me to fend for myself."

"Really?"

"Not quite, but the message that I could have put their jobs in jeopardy was clear. Secret Service has a long and proud tradition, and I felt I had to apologize again. Of course, if I hadn't gotten lost, they might not have found out, but then again, I wouldn't have met you," he said, reaching for her hand.

She smiled. It felt good to be holding hands in the moonlight.

He stopped. "May I see you again? Tomorrow?"

"I'd love that," she replied, "but I wouldn't feel comfortable coming back to the lodge. I hope you understand."

"Completely," he said, his voice showing disappointment as they continued walking hand in hand.

She had to ask. "What's your girlfriend's name?"

"Girlfriend? I don't have one."

"But who's the lady who's often at your side in official pictures?"

"Oh, you mean Marjorie? She's my cousin, on the Winfield side. She accompanies me at official functions at the White House when my staff tells me it is imperative that I have someone with me, often because dancing's on the program. Marjorie is married to a lawyer who has been confined to a wheelchair for half-a-dozen years because of a shooting incident. I know what you're thinking, and you're right of course," he said, briefly putting up a hand. "In any event, she doesn't often get the chance to get out and dance. Plus she enjoys mingling with the Washington political elite, so it benefits both of us."

They were silent for a moment, then Austin asked, "What about you? Anyone special?"

"Yes and no."

"I regret to say, dear lady, that I have no idea what that means."

"My partner in *Only Roses* and I often go out. We're good friends."

"I see," Austin said, although what she actually meant was quite unclear to him. Was he intruding in her life? Earlier in the afternoon it had never occurred to him to ask if she was involved with anyone. At the time, all he knew for certain, as he did now, was that he wanted to spend more time with the attractive woman who was not the least shy in frankly expressing her views. He had to admit he rather enjoyed that trait which at first had surprised if not mystified him.

She stopped and looked at him in the dim light. "Let me make it clearer. Bernie and I do enjoy each other's company and do date from time to time. He's married. His wife is in an institution, probably for the rest of her life."

"I see," the Vice President said simply.

But she knew he didn't, and she was not ready to tell him all the small details of her life. She would have to let him infer whatever he wanted. She led the conversation in another direction. "How about eating lunch or dinner at my house tomorrow? Your men could stay outside, couldn't they? Without being too visible?"

"That could be arranged. We could make it for lunch."

"Great. What do you like to eat besides freshly caught trout?"

"I'm certain whatever you prepare will be perfect. Don't go to any trouble. I'm a man of simple taste."

"I'm sure you don't have just a tuna salad sandwich for lunch."

"I've been known to. I do like a good tuna sandwich."

"Very well. Tuna sandwich it is. Will I also have to serve your men?"

Cameron Austin smiled briefly. "To be as facetious as you, I could ask them to join us if you insist."

By the time he walked her to her car, he knew he truly liked this woman, but unfortunately it was rather unlikely that he could continue seeing her after going back to Washington. He sighed secretly, intent on making the best of the days left.

"Thank you very much for the lovely dinner," Laurie said.

"My pleasure," he replied, bringing her hand to his lips. "I look forward to tomorrow."

She drove back slowly toward McPine, a bittersweet mood enveloping her. No one had stirred deep feelings in her since Robby, yet she knew there was no hope of exploring any possibilities even resembling a relationship with Cameron Austin. Having known perfect love with Robby, she could never settle for anything less.

Now that she had experienced the warmth and intelligence of a man who had lifted the veil of her self-imposed limiting world, a man who could, she felt, make her discover perfect love again in the bargain, she felt defeated before getting onto the playing field.

As soon as she had parked her car, Brandy expressed its joy at her return by coming to rub against her leg. She took time to caress the back of the animal's head, and together they sauntered to the back deck. The lake was a large blue-black expanse because clouds were now covering the moon, however the lights of the building she had just left shone brightly in the night. She sighed deeply. Cameron Austin was probably in the large upstairs room, the one with the porch, phoning someone in Washington, maybe the President. He had told her he kept in touch on a daily basis with the goings-on in his country.

"Well, my dear," she told the dog, "it looks like I'm revving with nowhere to go."

In her dream, Laurie was trying desperately to find a ringing telephone as she dug deeper and deeper into the soil until she opened her eyes and realized that the sound came from the instrument on her bedside table.

"I hope I didn't wake you," her mother, Eileen Danfort said over the phone. "I know you always get up early. Rita and the girls are coming over for dinner tonight. Why don't you get in your car and join us? You could stay over and go back tomorrow."

"Sounds tempting, Mom, but I can't. Bernie's away for the weekend and I have to take care of business."

"And here I was thinking that you run a wholesale nine-to-five sort of operation."

"Sure, but you know how people are."

"Is something wrong, Laurie?"

"Not at all. On the contrary." Pulling the comforter off, Laurie sat on the side of the bed stretching her legs as she spoke. "I have a date."

"Anything serious?"

"Not so far. Please don't tell Sarah or Rita, okay?"

"Sure, if that's the way you want it. Anyone they know?"

"That's just it, they don't know him and they'll be asking all sorts of questions that I can't answer just yet."

"Very well, dear. Hope you have a great time."

"Thanks, Mom. I'll go down for a weekend soon. By the way, have you heard from Mike lately? Is he still with the power company?"

"I haven't seen him, but he called this week. He had a couple of days off as payment for some overtime. Said he was going to visit friends. Why are you asking? He hasn't done anything, has he?"

"No, but I heard he was in Medford during the week. Now I know why."

"You know I would be the first to be informed if he messed this one up after all the trouble I went through to get him the job."

As she was hanging up, Laurie realized that she had overslept, something she rarely did. It didn't surprise her, however, because she had trouble falling asleep after trying to put together a luncheon menu for the Vice President. She had perused her recipe books in an attempt to be inspired to provide a creative yet tasty menu, even though she had no idea what types of food Cameron Austin liked or disliked, or if he had any food intolerance. In the end, the simpler the better won out. She knew her final choice was perfect.

Going downstairs to let the dog out and make coffee, she peered through the glass of the sliding doors and saw the boat anchored on the lake. Cameron Austin and Steve Marsh were again trying their luck with the fish, and she wondered what they talked about although Austin had intimated the previous evening that he felt blessed to have the ear of someone out of the Washington loop. She pulled herself away. There was no time to lose. She ate breakfast, got dressed and drove to the grocery store.

Shortly after eleven-thirty, Laurie examined the table in the dining room and was pleased. Instead of covering with a tablecloth the antique monastery-style table she had found at an estate sale in Medford, she used two placemats part of a set of four her mother had given her shortly after *Only Roses* had become a reality. Laurie had always appreciated the gift not only because her mother had hand-embroidered the mats herself, but because each featured a lovely red rose displayed on the left side. The matching glass coasters and napkins were adorned with embroidered rosebuds.

She had pulled out her best crystal glasses and the silverware she rarely used. For the middle of the table, she had arranged half a dozen red roses in a low crystal vase. For a moment she wanted to take a photograph of the table to perhaps accompany an article she could write for a style magazine. The idea fizzled as quickly as it had appeared. She was going back into the kitchen when she heard Brandy advising her that someone was approaching. In a moment she was opening the front door for Agent Lonsdale.

"Good morning, ma'am. I need to search your house before the Vice President's arrival."

Lonsdale was dressed like a man at home in the country in a pair of faded jeans and a matching jacket over a white T-shirt. He was not smiling.

"You're kidding, right?" she said.

"No, ma'am. It is my duty to ensure the Vice President's safety, and I intend to do my job. Another man is checking the grounds and the greenhouse."

Laurie felt momentarily annoyed. "I hope he doesn't break the door down since I have the key to the greenhouse."

As she kept busy in the kitchen, she heard Lonsdale going through her house, opening and closing doors. For reasons she could not fathom at that moment, it made her feel insecure although the reverse should have been the case.

When he finally appeared in the kitchen and looked over the food, she refrained herself from asking if he feared she was going to poison Cameron Austin. She simply gave him the key to the greenhouse.

"I take it you've investigated me."

"Yes, ma'am, we have."

"I assume I passed."

"Your brother could be a problem if we were to be staying here for any length of time."

She looked at him, her mouth falling agape. *Thanks Mike for embarrassing me one more time,* she thought.

As Lonsdale turned to step outside using the side door, Laurie rallied and said, "Please don't make yourself too obvious. I'll have to continue living in McPine once you're gone."

Lonsdale's chiseled features remained indecipherable, but he did nod ever so slightly.

CHAPTER SEVEN

I never determine a person's worth based on their job description or material criteria, Eileen Danfort, Laurie Cosner's mother, was fond of saying. The fact that the woman had chosen to marry a wealthy and influential man little more than a year after Laurie's father had died made the statement all the more ironic. But Laurie had to agree that the woman had kept her feet squarely on the ground in her newly found status. She never forgot that for twenty years she had been the wife of a good man—the best, everyone said— who had been happy seeing to the insurance needs of the people of Medford while she devoted herself to teaching music to the young artistic minds of the region. That was always a privilege for me, she had told her daughter.

Today, keeping an eye out for the arrival of her powerful and wealthy guest, Laurie could only think that, like her mother, the title and the money of the man did not impress her. The kindness and the dedication were the impacting factors.

It was noon on the dot when Cameron Austin drove up her driveway alone in Esther Marsh's vehicle. Laurie thought suddenly that the visit would be more feed for the village gossip mill. Earlier in McPine Groceries, while cutting Laurie's order from behind the deli counter, Adele had remarked, "I saw that Esther Marsh paid you a visit yesterday." Laurie quickly replied that the lodge needed fresh roses. Now, from her vantage point at the window, she wondered if she was fooling anyone. The people of McPine had eyes, and they watched out for each other. Adele and others could very well have seen Cameron Austin and his two agents yesterday just as they were seeing him now driving Esther's car. No matter, Laurie thought, she would answer their questions when the time came.

Brandy, who had been lying outside the front door as if sensing a visitor was expected, responded to the arrival with a low joyful bark, getting to its legs and moving to welcome the man, its tail wagging. Laurie opened the door, surprised that she couldn't see any of the agents.

"Good morning," Cameron Austin said cheerfully as he approached, taking time to pet the animal.

The sun was high in the sky, the air was dry and the temperature was what she considered perfect: warming without being hot. And the handsome Vice President was on her doorstep. Laurie contemplated that this was as good as it could get for her. She smiled as she invited him inside.

"I don't see your men," Laurie said.

"I told you they were discreet."

"They investigated me, I understand."

"Sorry I didn't discuss it with you, but surely it didn't come as a surprise that you would be the object of a background check," Austin commented. "It's part of the game. What if you were a criminal?" he concluded, smiling mischievously.

Laurie invited him to sit down. "I assume I passed with flying colors, but I'm told my brother didn't."

Austin detected annoyance in her voice and didn't like it. "You understand that my men had to look into your family as well, but I don't consider your brother's interest in protesting what he believes needs to be brought to the attention of the public at large, as dangerous behavior."

"But your men do?"

"Not necessarily, but they would like a closer look at his record to satisfy themselves that there is no terrorist proclivity."

"My brother may be outspoken, but he certainly is not a terrorist," Laurie said a little more passionately than she would have liked.

"No one is saying that he is. And since he's not here, his activities shouldn't even be discussed," Austin said.

Laurie decided that she wouldn't let Mike ruin her day. She was the master of her ship after all, even if her brother often sailed less-than-calm seas. "You know, if your men's investigation had gone back far enough, they would have seen that I come from American stock."

"Really?"

"My ancestors on my father's side were Loyalists. They came to Canada at the time you Americans decided the only way to gain your independence was to wage war. I know, it wasn't quite that simplistic, but don't you think that the fact that we Canadians are overall non-violent is probably due to a trait inherited from Americans?"

Seldom had Cameron Austin been at a loss for words. At that moment he was. That was certainly a new take on the Loyalists.

She laughed. "Interesting fact, isn't it? How about a drink while you mull over my reasoning? I have white wine cooling, a Chardonnay, or anything else you want."

"I rarely drink during the day. A glass of your pure fresh water would be great for now, if you don't mind."

Returning from the kitchen with two water-filled crystal glasses, Laurie asked, "I saw you were out fishing again this morning. Catch anything?"

"Actually, I caught a nice trout again, but catching fish is not the object of the game. It's being away from it all, breathing in pure fresh air, being free, and relaxing completely. You're fortunate to be living in this part of the world."

"I do love it, of course," she agreed, "but we don't get the excitement, the rush of living in the middle of action in Washington, D.C. I did get the firm impression last night that this is something that makes life worthwhile for you."

"Of course. Politics was my choice."

"And if we can believe the political analysts and pundits, you're being touted as this century's Kennedy, the Democrat's choice for the presidency when Thomson's second term ends."

He sipped his water for a moment before commenting. "There is a push in that direction, yes, but I have not made up my mind yet. There are some roadblocks."

"What sort of roadblocks?"

He looked at her, his dark eyes intelligently enticing. "If you don't mind, I would rather not discuss that sort of thing today. I'm on vacation, and I want to concentrate on more pleasurable pursuits like having lunch with you."

"I take it that means you're hungry."

"Here in the fresh air of McPine I seem to be forever famished."

"Good. Lunch is ready."

She was glad she had kept the menu simple. Because she lived some distance from many friends and relatives, it was the type of meal she often served out-of-town visitors. It was a no-fuss solution, and always welcome.

Once the Vice President was seated at the dining room table, she brought out the first course: freshly made cream of carrot soup—an easy recipe she had long mastered—garnished with a dollop of plain light yogurt and served in her best china. Austin praised her cooking ability and accepted a second helping. She was elated.

For the main course, she brought out a plain salad of green and red lettuce leaves from her greenhouse drizzled with raspberry dressing, and a large tray with an assortment of cold cuts, slices of onion, avocado, hard-boiled eggs and tomato, with green and black olives all presented around a bowl of tuna salad. Cameron Austin chuckled.

"You said you like tuna."

"You're simply delightful."

"Bread?" She offered him a basket of deli rolls baked fresh by McPine Groceries earlier that morning.

He took one and went about building what Laurie thought was an interestingly tall sandwich which he attacked with gusto.

"This is just great, Laurie. Thank you," he said between bites.

She ate her own sandwich, but the pleasure he seemed to be deriving from her efforts was the most delectable. The meal ended with the mango, orange and strawberry salad she had prepared earlier. Cameron Austin was again very generous in his praise.

Pointing to the red roses in the middle of the table, he asked, "And what do those roses mean?"

"The red rose symbolizes respect," she replied, omitting that it also stood for love, and momentarily wondering why she had chosen red.

Later she was touched that he helped her clear the table then sat at the kitchen nook while she put the food away, happily chatting and asking questions.

She took him through the sliding doors to the back deck, and he was impressed with the view of the lake and the lodge. "You have a better view of those pines than I have from my room."

"Beggars can't be choosers," she retorted gaily.

He returned the smile before turning again to the vista before him. "It's easy to see why the village is called McPine."

"I'll have you know it's officially a town, not a village."

"Sorry."

"I'll let it go this time," she said, smiling.

He loved that smile.

She continued. "As you may already know, this area was originally settled by Scots, many of them with Mc in their names. They simply combined that with the pines they saw all around."

"Steve Marsh kept inviting me up here after he and Esther bought the lodge, and I must confess that when I finally came, I fell in love with this area the first time I saw it. It's so pure, so real."

"No argument from me."

"How much property do you own?" Austin asked.

"Let me walk you around."

"What a wonderful aroma," the Vice President exclaimed as they walked into the glassed greenhouse after she had shown him the extensive outdoor gardens. "And the color of these roses! This is impressive."

"Sometimes when I hit a block in my writing, I come in here and walk up and down. It never fails to inspire me."

"I can see why," Austin told her.

She took him through the various aisles explaining how roses for the commercial market are grown, multiplied and harvested, the need to control the air and feeding inside a large greenhouse, the problems that can arise in a cold climate, the vigilance needed to avoid possible disease, the capital required and other tidbits.

He was impressed by the operation and told her so.

As a retort, she asked, "When are you leaving?"

He stopped in the narrow aisle to look at her. "I wish it could be longer, but I'm leaving Monday, late in the day."

"I'll send a rosebush to the lodge for you to take as a souvenir of McPine. Have someone plant it in your garden. You do have a garden at your official residence?"

Cameron Austin was touched. A fresh ice-packed trout was the only thing he had ever taken away from McPine. Now he would have a concrete reminder of the time spent with the lovely lady. "What a lovely thought. Thank you," he said. "I know exactly where I'll have it planted on the property."

"What color would you prefer? Pink, white, red, yellow, or peach?"

"I want to remember. Definitely peach," he said.

She smiled. "Good. My favorite."

The clock in the kitchen indicated four-thirty when Laurie went in to boil water for tea. She could only be grateful for the sense of total well-being that was sheltering her from everything and everyone in the world. Cameron Austin was stretched out on her white sofa, a couple of flowered cushions under his head, reading the manuscript of her novel *Beads of the Sea*. He had insisted. To Laurie, it was as if he belonged there even if he was in fact but a fleeting entry in the journal of her life. She didn't care, she was happy and determined to live the moment to the fullest.

"This is great reading so far," the Vice President said as she came back into the room with a filled teapot, two mugs and a plate a cheese and crackers.

"Thank you. I think this one could fly."

"How do you know so much about harvesting pearl oyster beds? Have you ever been to the Indian Ocean?"

"No, but I did a lot of research on the business."

"Fascinating. I wish I could read all of it," he said, straightening himself up to accept a mug of tea. "But that would mean I would have to stay here all night and tomorrow by the look of the thickness of this thing," he added, pointing to the piled pages on the coffee table.

"When it's published, I promise to send you a copy. A signed copy. But don't hold your breath, it might take a while."

They sipped their tea in silence for a moment.

"This is really nice, Laurie, enjoying the simple pleasures of life in the company of a lovely person."

"I'm enjoying it too, Mr. Austin."

"Please...my name is Cameron. We are friends, aren't we?"

"I hope so, Cameron."

"We are," he stated firmly. "And I am glad. I have many friends in Washington, but I can only discuss political problems or strategies with them. I have few friends with whom I can talk freely about other things. Steve Marsh is one, of course. And my cousin, Marjorie, another. But these contacts are limited. With my mother and my sisters, the conversations always seem to focus on family. And I suppose that's the way it should be. What I am trying to say is that since I met you, I've come to realize that we could have a close friendship, if you are willing to have me in your life."

"Cameron," she began, "there's nothing I would like more, but may I remind you that I am not a political person and that I am a Canadian."

"That's what makes you so special; you have no agenda of any sort. Together we have a clean slate, no history or baggage. I like you a lot, and I believe it could become a great deal more."

They were sitting at opposite ends on the sofa, looking at each other. Both knew the truth of the words and the import of those words.

Cameron Austin put his mug down on the coffee table and came closer to Laurie. Looking into her dark green eyes, stirred by long-neglected emotions, the Vice President of the United States bent down and kissed her willing lips for a long instant.

Then it was Laurie Cosner's turn to put her mug on the table. She had no intention of avoiding the inevitable. As naturally as if they had been born for this moment, their arms reached for each other.

It was some time before Laurie, her mouth near his ear, whispered, "Mr. Vice President, are you trying to seduce me?"

"Would you object?" he asked.

"Not in the least, but you do realize that this can only be a transitory thing. I mean you are going back to Washington on Monday, back to your exciting world of politics and high-level achievements. I'm fully aware that the only room for me in your life has to be here in McPine."

"That's not the way I see it. We don't live so far from each other. And there is a new invention, you may have heard of it, it's called an airplane."

She chuckled. "I remember reading something about it, but the reality is that you're a busy man, Mr. Vice President. I doubt that you would have the time to fly up to McPine for a tuna sandwich a few times a week."

He tried to ignore a sad internal twinge. She was right, and they both knew it. Did he really have the right to ask her to come to Washington to spend time with him when she had her own life here among the pines?

"You know what they say about summer romances, Cameron. They peter out pretty quickly once the vacation is over."

"Do you really think this is a summer romance? It doesn't feel like that to me."

"But the reality..."

"My reality, you mean. The reality of my busy life..." He felt there was no need to continue. The roadblock was much too high.

"But that doesn't mean we can't enjoy the time we have at our disposal, does it?"

He smiled. "What did you have in mind?"

"A simple dinner, a lot like lunch actually, to start."

He smiled warmly. "Then?"

"Then we could go dancing in Medford."

"You know I can't do that."

"You did think about what I said yesterday, didn't you?"

"Yes, but I have never disguised myself. It would be…"

"It would be what? Are you thinking that it would be unbecoming to your office, Mr. Vice President?"

"I am thinking that if I'm ever found out, it could prove quite embarrassing."

"Who in the world's going to find out? Let your hair down, literally, why don't you?"

He pierced her eyes, once more astonished at the way her mind worked, wondering why at some level he was opposed to the idea while finding the proposition quite exciting on another level.

He was no stranger to difficult decisions, and when you looked at it closely this one was certainly a no-brainer. He had earned the right to enjoy himself.

He did not reply immediately, but he did kiss her again and again.

CHAPTER EIGHT

The music and vocals emanating from the lounge in the ancient Medford hotel were soft and inviting. A couple walked into the hotel lobby. He was tall with dark blond hair and a matching mustache, and wore beige slacks with an open-neck white shirt under a light tweed jacket. His date was wearing black slacks and a white jersey top under a light white cardigan. Mr. and Mrs. Everybody out for a bit of dancing.

Passing a mirrored column in the lobby, they both took a quick peek at themselves and smiled. Laurie had been right, Austin thought. Who could possibly recognize him?

In casual attire, agents Jacoby and Bradley on duty this night followed shortly behind. Although they had not openly said so, Austin had felt their objection when he informed them of his decision to go out in disguise. He could still feel their disapproval as he and Laurie stopped at the entrance to the room to look around and the two agents walked past them to settle on stools at the bar. A heavy-set man whom Laurie recognized as one of the owners of the hotel approached, and Austin made certain they were given a table as close to his agents as possible. He did have an obligation to simplify their lives to make up for the unorthodox evening. But he did console himself that this had to be more pleasant for them than sitting out on the porch at the lodge staring into black nothingness.

Austin looked around the nearly-filled room, glad to see that most patrons were over thirty. The singer was a blond woman of around forty, and the soft music was provided by a keyboard, a guitarist and a sax player. A middle-aged waiter made his way to their table. All the people who worked at the Medford were seasoned and experienced. It was part of the hotel's promotion and special charm.

"What will it be, folks?" A waiter asked amiably, placing round coasters in front of Laurie and Austin.

"I'll have a glass of white wine," Laurie replied.

"What about you, sir?"

"A beer will be fine. Thank you."

"What kind? Canadian? Imported?"

"Whatever's on tap."

The waiter nodded and left to take another order.

"You are aware," Laurie commented, "that Canadian beer actually has taste compared to American beer."

Austin smiled. "Oh yeah. It's one of the things I look forward to on my visits."

"So, what do you think?" She asked. "About being out like this?"

"Actually, I must confess that it's a lot of fun," he replied looking about the room. "Liberating. And the music is certainly enjoyable."

"Good," Laurie said, pleased that he seemed at ease in the environment she had chosen and that the accouterment Austin wore was indeed becoming. When the thought of the Vice President disguising himself had briefly entered her mind, she knew she had the solution right in her own house. The previous Christmas, her daughter Sarah had been asked to play one of the Magi in the school's annual holiday play because she was tall and her home-room teacher insisted that all the children have their turn on stage as an exercise in self-confidence. Laurie had bought a good-quality wig, mustache and matching beard in Toronto while Christmas shopping with her mother. In the end the items had remained in their box because Sarah decided that a crown made of gold-colored paper adorned with glued-on stones looked better over her own dark hair. When Laurie had shown the wig to Austin he deliberated for a time, but after stretching it over his own hair he had looked at himself this way and that way in the mirror in her hallway, objections fading as if pushed away by a gentle warm breeze.

He did, however, refuse to try on the beard. Looking at him now, Laurie felt that it had been a judicious choice.

"Are you questioning my look, dear lady?" He asked, his eyes reflecting his inner sense of joy.

"Not at all. Just admiring my handiwork."

The waiter returned with their drinks, and deposited the bill on the table near Austin's hand who looked perplexed for a moment.

"Why don't I get it," Laurie said.

"Sorry, but I seldom carry money," he said, and she smiled at his embarrassment.

"I owe you anyway," she said, reaching for her purse and pulling out ten-dollar bills with their intricate mixture of design and plump hues. The waiter made change, put it on the table and left.

"Owe me for what?" Austin asked.

"For agreeing to come out like this."

"I'll pay you back with real green money," Austin said, winking at her.

"I still say our money has always been more interesting than yours even if you're starting to jazz up the greenback."

He chuckled. "I love of the sound of this group. Want to dance?"

She took his proffered hand and he gently led her to the highly polished dance floor where a few couples were already moving gracefully.

It was a slow song and he held her close. Laurie had the impression that their two long bodies meshed together perfectly. How nice it was to be in his arms. If only it could last! When the music ended and she opened her eyes she saw that agent Bradley was on the dance floor with an attractive thirty-something year old blonde.

"Wonder what he's saying he does for a living," Laurie asked. "Condom salesman?"

Austin laughed heartily. "It wouldn't surprise me."

Cameron Austin and Laurie Cosner stayed on the dance floor for the next two songs until the trio took a break. As they were getting back to their table, a couple in their fifties appeared.

"Hi, Laurie," the attractive woman said. "How have you been?"

"Just fine, Janet," Laurie replied. "And you?"

"Great. It's our twenty-third anniversary, so Ted's taking me out."

"How nice! Congratulations. Oh, this is my friend George Bucci."

The Vice President got to his feet, extended his hand and congratulated the couple.

"Well, we'll let you enjoy your evening," the woman said as she and her husband found their way to their table.

"Is this going to be a problem for you?"

"Why should it? Tongues will wag, of course, as they try and figure out who you are, but I don't mind. No Bucci in this area that I know of."

"I meant for Bernie."

"I told you, Bernie and I are just good friends."

Her answer had been a little too swift and curt for his taste. There was probably more to her relationship with the man than she was willing to discuss, but he let it drop. After all, it was none of his business.

The moon was still round, bathing trees and fields in silver as he drove her back to McPine. She was at peace. Evenings like this one had been rare indeed in her life of late which, when she thought about it carefully—something she tried to avoid—was rather dull and predictable. The unexpected appearance of Cameron Austin had changed the landscape. He had made her come alive and she was ready to forget the past.

"Are you okay?" he asked.

"Great. I had a wonderful time this evening. Thank you."

"Thank you, Laurie. You forced me out of my methodical existence and showed me that life can be spontaneous and fun, something I had forgotten. For that, I am truly grateful," he said, reaching for her hand and bringing it to his lips.

In her driveway Austin turned off the motor of Ethel's sedan, and the beams of the minivan which had been following went dark several feet behind.

"Do you want to come in?" she asked.

Rather than answering, he got out and went to her as she was slipping out of the car. "It might be a mistake," he said simply, taking her hand.

They walked to the door and Laurie slid her key into the lock. Austin followed her inside, and as soon as the door closed, his long arms went around her and they once more melted into each other as easily as cake batter to a mold.

It was some time before they could manage to break apart.

"Don't you think that the disguise has served its purpose?" she asked.

He smiled and pulled off the mustache and wig, handed them to her and combed his own hair with his hands. "I was unaware that I was still wearing them. Totally amazing. Please keep them for me.

They might come in handy again next time I come up to this neck of the woods."

"I hope so," she replied.

When he left several minutes later, a bizarre sensation which had settled in her stomach shot up into her throat. She had had a wonderful evening, yet she felt sadness encircling her, nearly choking her.

"So, what's the problem?" Steve Marsh asked Cameron Austin as they ate breakfast alone in the dining room of the lodge the next morning. "Laurie's a fine woman. Bright and a lot of fun."

"Perhaps you didn't hear me. I said that I haven't felt this way in a long time."

"And I repeat," Marsh said, heaping marmalade on a piece of toast, "what's the problem?"

"The problem is that I want to spend more time with her, but I cannot give her the sort of attention I would like to because of my work, because of the distance between us. Also her life is here in McPine. I cannot ask her to come to Washington. She has her business, her daughter."

"If you want my opinion, Mr. Vice President, you're looking for excuses," Marsh commented. "When life hands you a curve ball you have to be dynamically prepared to catch it."

Austin chuckled at the memories the words brought to mind.

"What was the name of the girl in college who kept repeating that?" Marsh asked. "I know it was unusual."

"Pier."

"That's it. She had the greenest eyes... and she was totally in love with you as I remember."

"Until I told her I was planning to go into politics! Perhaps she had the right idea. Being married to a politician can't be easy," Austin concluded.

"Have you discussed any of this with Laurie?"

"She seems to feel the same way. I mean that we're doomed before we ever get out of the gate."

"That's a first," Marsh said. "I've never known you to be a defeatist. Give her a couple of plane tickets. I mean, you can afford it."

"Of course, but the reality of the situation... Steve, I never expected to meet anyone here in McPine, of all places. I rather thought that the First Lady or the wife of one of the senators would introduce me to a widow from their circle of friends and that we would settle into a pleasant arrangement."

"What you really mean is that after Jean you never expected to fall in love again."

"I don't believe it has gone quite that far," the Vice President commented, staring into the mug of coffee in front of him.

"Not from where I sit," Steve Marsh said simply.

Puffy white clouds were concealing the sun at intervals, but Cameron Austin didn't notice as his sports shoes hit the ground with every step. He was walking back to the lodge after running most of the way around the lake. In Washington the air wasn't always as fresh and pure as it was here in pine country so he exercised on a treadmill.

Two agents were keeping up with him, but he was unaware of them. His thoughts were on finding a way to solve his current dilemma.

He knew his mother was right in that he was a man who did not bear being alone with grace. His life with Jean had been too good. Hell, he still reached for her in his sleep only to wake up to the reality of the loneliness of his life. He also knew that his friend Steve Marsh was probably right. He had to concede that he was in love, or at least falling quite quickly and unable to change this unexpected course in his life. It was indeed somewhat scary, but he had not reached the second highest office in his country by being afraid. The facts were clear. He wanted Laurie Cosner and he needed her. The question was: how deep were her feelings for him?

And there would be other problems to face, none the least of which would be his mother. He could hear Grace Winfield Austin question the wisdom of having a Canadian at his side as he ran for the presidency, especially someone from a country some Americans felt was less than supportive when it came to America's goals. And, as he had told Laurie, to some extent he did live in a fish bowl, and Laurie would join him in that bowl. He wondered how the independent and disarmingly frank writer would feel at having her every public move dissected by a hungry media. Could he really ask her to give up her independence, to leave the cocoon that was McPine? And if she did, would she be happy?

But then again was he not getting ahead of himself? If they got to know each other better, was it not possible that they could come to the conclusion that they were indeed hopelessly mismatched?

One way or the other he did owe it to himself to find out.

CHAPTER NINE

From the kitchen Laurie heard the unmistakable sounds of Debussy's *Claire de Lune*. He had not mentioned that he played the piano, yet when she came into the living room Cameron Austin was seated at the baby grand, his long fingers handling the keys with the aplomb of experience. She put her hands on his shoulders and gently kissed the top of his head. He stopped playing.

"Don't stop. You play well," she told him.

"I have to confess that I need sheet music in front of me for that piece or any other for that matter. This instrument is great though."

"It was a gift from my mother to Sarah for her fifteenth birthday last year."

"Quite a present!"

"It made me wonder what she'll give her for her sixteenth birthday. Sarah was so pleased she cried when she saw it."

"Not too many kids have their own baby grand," Austin commented.

"No," Laurie said, sitting on the bench beside him, "but I was very happy for her. She definitely has talent, and my mother encourages her any way she can. She can afford to. She married a very rich man."

"Are your parents divorced?"

"Dad died when I was nearly eighteen. He was hit by lightning on the golf course."

"Really?" Austin said, more as a statement than a question.

"Really. It was a first around here. I suppose it was his time to go."

"When did your mother remarry?"

"Just a little over a year later. At the time I thought my mother was being disrespectful of my father's memory. What can I say, I was a snotty teenager. I had it in for her for a while, but she held no grudge. Eventually I understood what a good and giving person she is. When my husband Robby was in the hospital in Toronto in the last months of his life Sarah and I stayed with my mother and her husband. Sarah was young then, and my mother was always happy to take care of her, and her husband couldn't have been kinder to the both of us. Nothing like a tragedy to make you appreciate people, those who really count," Laurie concluded.

"How true," Austin commented. "Since Jean died, I make it a priority to see my mother and my sisters and their families on a regular basis. Life is so short, we have to grab every moment."

"No argument from me there."

Austin put an arm around her shoulder. "You and I have to grab the happiness that is knocking at the door," he said kissing her cheek. "I have been thinking that we owe it to ourselves to get to know each other better, find out if we could stand each other outside the confines of McPine."

She stood up. "Nothing I'd like better, Cameron, but we both know it's impossible."

"We could try," he said, looking up at her with intensity in his eyes. "You could fly down to Washington from time to time, and I would make an effort to get away to McPine more often. I think it could work if we both wanted it."

She had hoped he would make the suggestion—even if she had serious doubts that she could ever be accepted in Washington. But a bigger worry was how she would explain it all to Sarah. Would the girl feel as betrayed as she herself had felt when her mother remarried? Yet Laurie had to admit that Sarah hardly remembered her father, while Laurie had been daddy's girl for nearly eighteen years. The situations were very different.

He stood up. "The question is do you want it?"

"I've never wanted anything more in a long time, but you know—"

He had put a finger across her lips. "We could stand here and fill a basket with reasons to just go back to our lives as if nothing happened. I simply cannot do that. I want you in my life. We both know this is more than a summer romance."

"But how are you going to feel when your friends, including the President, want to know if you left some of your marbles behind in McPine? Surely everyone expects you to find a charming American who knows her way around politics, not an intruder in your world, and a Canadian at that! President Thomson might well pick up a gun and shoot me himself!"

The Vice President laughed. "I swear to jump in front of you and take the bullet."

Laurie smiled and her arms went up around his neck. "Until then, how about some dinner? Linguini with shrimp and pesto made with home-grown basil?"

Did she actually expect him to refuse?

Brandy had been shooed away from its usual sleeping spot, more surprised than dismayed. The animal had gone to sleep alone on Sarah's bed missing the presence of a warm body with which to cuddle. It was time to rectify the situation. The dog jumped off the bed and trotted along the second floor hallway to the door leading to his mistress's bedroom. Pushing with its long nose, the animal was surprised that it didn't open but was not defeated. The effort was repeated until the door finally eased open from the ill-adjusted latch. Brandy took a few steps inside then stopped. No one was putting up a fuss, so the animal jumped on the bed and stretched out in the middle cuddling close to its mistress's legs while also touching another leg. That felt good. The dog closed its eyes and was soon joining the soft snoring of the two bodies in deep sleep.

In the east a slight pinkish light was beginning to furrow the white blue of the horizon. Another day was on the brink of making itself known, promising to again be sunny. Rather than driving up the circular driveway in front of Laurie Cosner's house, agents Lonsdale and Dunlop went to park the black minivan near the greenhouse next to her sedan where trees provided cover from possible prying eyes. Carrying a thermos of fresh coffee, the two men dressed in jeans and sweatshirts walked up the incline to the house. Agents Jacoby and Bradley were on the back deck.

"Anything?" Lonsdale asked.

"Not a sound. How anyone can live here all the time is beyond me,"

Jacoby commented. "Well guys, have a good time in this exciting atmosphere while we get some sleep."

"The keys are in the ignition," Lonsdale said.

Jacoby and Bradley nodded and walked away.

"He's right, you know," Dunlop said to Lonsdale. "I'd be so bored living here I think I'd kill myself."

"Some people like the quiet of the country," Lonsdale commented as he poured himself some coffee from the thermos bottle. "Want some?"

"I'd better take a walk around the property first."

"Whistle if you come across any cute girls," Lonsdale said in a low voice as he watched his partner go down the steps.

Dulop was back in a few minutes and sat on the bench edging the deck, accepting a cup of coffee.

"Look at it this way, we've got less than a day to go," Lonsdale commented.

"Can't come soon enough," Dunlop said. Pointing to the second floor of the house, he added, "Well, at least our man got it on."

"Can't blame him, can you? He's had a mighty long dry spell," Lonsdale said.

"I suppose. What if this thing continues? What then?"

"You mean if she comes to Washington?" Lonsdale asked.

"Yeah."

"I dunno. It's been a while since a President or a Vice President dated while in office."

"You mean while they were actually single."

Both men laughed.

When Cameron Austin woke from a deep satisfying sleep, his hand reached for the warmth near his lower body. He touched hair and momentarily wondered in what position Laurie slept, but when he raised his head, his eyes met those of Brandy which were looking at the Vice President as if questioning his presence. Then the dog put its head back down and closed its eyes. No point getting up until the lady of the house was ready to start her day. After all, it was their routine.

Good thing dogs can't talk, Cameron Austin thought as he smiled.

With Laurie still fast asleep, he eased himself from under the white comforter, reached for a terry robe she had supplied the previous evening and made his way to the washroom, the dog's eyes now open following his every move.

Several minutes later Cameron Austin came back into the bedroom with a tray on which rested two mugs of steaming coffee, a couple of kiwi fruits and a plate of buttered toast which he deposited on the night table near Laurie. He was surprised that they had slept in, something he rarely did, but again there had been no need to get up at the crack of dawn especially since his body needed to recoup after the exertion of the previous evening—a welcome exertion he had almost convinced himself he would never again enjoy.

The sun was already bathing pine country with warming rays. He went to the window where he turned the white blinds under the lace curtains ever so slightly to let some of the daylight in. Laurie stirred and he went to her, sitting on the side of the bed.

"Good morning," he said, kissing her mouth as soon as she opened her eyes.

"Good morning," she replied, smiling. "How did you sleep?"

"Better than anyone has a right to," he replied, kissing her lips again.

"What will your men say?"

"Nothing, and they'll keep their thoughts to themselves."

She lifted herself up to rest her body against the padded headboard displaying a colorful pattern of small flowers. "Do I smell coffee?"

"Right here," he said, indicating the tray.

"You prepared this?"

"I have been known to fend for myself once in a while, you know."

She smiled as he gave her one of the mugs. How lovely she was, even in the morning, and even after a night of generous abandon when they had become one as easily as two long-time lovers anticipating the other's needs and hidden cravings. The green striae in her eyes seemed to beam with new vibrancy.

"I am going to miss you, Laurie Cosner," he said.

"And I you, Mr. Vice President."

"You will come to Washington in two weeks?"

She smiled. "I'd better if I don't want to go crazy missing you."

He bent down and let his lips linger on hers for a moment then said, "You don't have anything urgent this morning, do you?"

"No. Not really. What did you have in mind?"

He put his mug back on the tray, and reached for her. "Making up for lost time."

Her hand went to his chest. "If you feel you must, Mr. Vice President, then you must, but Brandy needs a walk."

"I'll take care of it," he said. Pointing a finger at her, he added, "Don't you go anywhere."

When called, Brandy followed Cameron Austin down the stairs and to the back of the house. Barefoot and in the white terry robe, the Vice President slid the patio door open to let the dog out while taking a quick look around. He didn't see Lonsdale and Dunlop now sitting near the deck on a rock overlooking the bluff. The dog went down the steps of the deck ignoring the two agents while the door slid back and was locked.

A moment later, Lonsdale said to his companion, "Great day in the morning! He ain't done yet!"

"When are you expecting your daughter?" Austin asked sitting on the side of the bed lacing his sports shoes.

"Early afternoon," Laurie replied as she finished buttoning the white cotton shirt she had donned over a pair of jeans.

He looked at his watch. "It's after ten. I'd better get out of your hair." He stood up. "Are you going to tell her about us?"

"Of course. She has to know sooner or later. But don't worry, I'll be kind and focus on your good points."

Cameron Austin smiled broadly and came to her, putting an arm around her shoulders. "I've always loved coming to McPine. Now I'm leaving my heart here."

"I'll take very good care of it, Mr. Vice President."

When they finally broke their embrace many minutes later, Laurie asked, "At what time will you be leaving?"

"As soon as it gets dark. I want to attract as little attention as possible."

"Then I won't see you again," she said, walking away. "I have to go to the greenhouse. Remember I promised you a rosebush. I'll see you downstairs."

He heard her making her way down the steps and felt a tightening in his throat. This was it. He was now convinced that this woman was the only one who could complete him and make his soul sing anew, yet he would not see her again for at least two weeks, maybe longer. He sighed silently. How sad and difficult his life could be at times. He went to the window where, through the laths of the blind, the ancient pines towered over Green Lake. What a beautiful sight. They would be part of the memories of a vacation that would, he knew, always bring joy to his bitter-sweet reality.

Lonsdale followed Laurie inside the greenhouse. He was again impressed by the feast that assailed his eyes and nose although he did not speak. He waited while she went to a corner where he could only see green. She went to a corner of small bushes with their roots wrapped in mesh, chose one and brought it to a work table near the door. There she wrapped it in heavy paper.

"Please tell Mr. Austin that it should be planted as soon as possible."

"Certainly," Lonsdale replied.

"Would you be willing to do me a favor?"

"What sort of favor?"

"If I give you something, can you make sure it's on the Vice President's desk first thing in the morning?

He hesitated for a moment, then replied, "Of course, Ms. Cosner."

"Good," she said, and taking a pair of yellow-handled shears, she walked with determination to an area where peach roses were beginning to show their colors. She chose one, cut it off and brought it back to the work table. She took what looked like a small vial from a compartment on the small shelf above the table, filled it with water at the sink in the corner, capped it with a rubber lid with a hole in the center, and then slipped the long-stemmed rose into it. She reached for a long narrow white box on one of the shelves along the wall, lined it with a sheet of white silk paper and lovingly, Lonsdale thought, put the rose inside. She put the lid on the box, wrapped it in paper and handed it to Lonsdale.

"This is what I would like to deposit on his desk so he sees it first thing tomorrow."

"Certainly, Ms. Cosner," he said. After a moment he asked, "Don't you want to include a card?"

"None is needed," she replied simply.

CHAPTER TEN

*I*t was shortly after seven-thirty on Tuesday morning when Cameron Austin, a spring in his step arrived at his office in the west wing of the White House.

"Good morning, Mrs. Winterburn."

"Welcome back, sir. I trust you had a nice vacation."

"As usual, it was great," he said walking into his office, his secretary following. He saw the long white box on his desk, opened it and brought the rose to his nose.

"It was delivered this morning, sir. There was no card," Shirley Winterburn said. "Would you like me to find out where it came from?"

"It won't be necessary. Thank you. Please put it in a vase on my desk, and could you please ask Oliver Rogge to come and see me this morning as soon as you can rearrange my schedule to free up ten minutes or so."

"Certainly, sir."

Oliver Rogge, a shortish man in his late thirties who looked a few years younger, had a full head of reddish-blond, somewhat straggly hair and intelligent light brown eyes. He was wearing a dark blue jacket over beige pants, and seemed uncomfortable as he waited on a straight chair a few feet from Shirley Winterburn's desk. This was the first time the Vice President had ever asked to see him, but he knew why he had been summoned this morning. He had come prepared. He had the file in his hands.

After meeting with President Thomson, Vice President Cameron Austin walked back to his office, and as soon as he saw Oliver Rogge he invited him to step inside. The door closed behind them.

"Please make yourself comfortable," Austin said, indicating a dark red leather wing chair. Rogge obeyed, and Austin sat in an identical chair across from him.

"I'm sure you know why I wanted to talk to you," the Vice President began. "I understand that last Friday one of my men called you with a request to run a background check on a certain lady."

"That's correct, sir."

"I see you have a file with you, so you anticipated my question."

"Yes, sir, I did."

"Good. You check people, that's your specialty?"

"Yes, sir. People the administration wants to know more about, that sort of thing. And I also do research."

"What sort of research?"

"Any topic the senior staff requires," Rogge replied.

"You're good at what you do?"

"I believe so, sir. Yes."

"What's your background?"

"Navy intelligence, sir."

"I would like you to tell me every detail you found out about Laurie Cosner. Please don't leave out anything," Austin said, preparing himself to listen attentively.

"Certainly, sir," Rogge said and opened the file. "Laurie Cosner, née Gilbert, was born in Medford, Ontario, Canada, on January 1—"

"On January 1st? Really?" the Vice President asked.

"Yes, sir. At fifteen minutes past midnight. She missed out on being the first baby of the year in the province, but she was the first baby of the year in her hometown. Her picture appeared in the local paper at the time."

The Vice President nodded and Rogge continued.

"She comes from a middle-class family. Her mother taught piano and her father was an insurance agent. She has one sibling, Michael, born three years later. Both children were raised in Medford where the family moved when they were young. The father died when struck by lightning while playing golf. The mother remarried a year later and moved to Toronto bringing the children with her. After getting a degree in journalism and writing, Ms. Cosner—Gilbert then—went back to Medford and worked at the local paper. Fifteen years ago she married Robby Cosner, a horticulturist and farmer from McPine, and they had one daughter, Sarah."

Oliver Rogge stopped and looked briefly at the Vice President whose fingers, resting on his chin, were touching to form a triangle.

"Something wrong?" Austin inquired.

"No, sir, but I would like to make a parenthesis here," Rogge began, looking again at Austin. "Sarah was born a little over six months after the couple married. The baby weighed eight pounds."

Without moving, Austin said, "I appreciate you telling me, Oliver."

Rogge resumed his report. "Since her marriage, she has been writing for newspapers and magazines, and has published two books, a novel and a handbook on roses. Both are still being sold in Canada and in the U.S. Her husband, Robby, died of leukemia a little over five years ago. She inherited his share of a nursery business, which she and her late husband's partner, Bernie Wesson, also a horticulturist, run together, although they now only grow roses. She is a quiet sort of person, but people in the region seem to like her."

"You talked to people in McPine?" the Vice President wanted to know.

"A few, yes. I had to because the information was needed so quickly. I passed myself off as a reporter from Toronto doing a piece on Laurie Cosner for her upcoming book."

"You know that she is writing another book?"

"I simply assumed, sir."

Oliver went after what he wanted, Austin thought briefly. "Anything else?"

"Not really, sir. Everyone in McPine seems very fond of her. If I were a prospective employer, I'd hire her on the spot."

"Nothing else?"

"I ran a check on her brother, Michael. Do you want to know about that?"

"Very much so," Austin replied.

"Very well, sir. For the past dozen years or so, he has been active in the protest movement. He has traveled across Canada and the U.S. protesting a variety of causes from the slaughter of seals in Newfoundland to globalization conferences. There does not appear to be a special focus in any of these activities, although he was very much involved in the demonstrations aimed at the last administration. He has been arrested and thrown in jail six times. Once he was arrested after he chained himself to the fence outside a prison in upstate New York with other protesters who wanted death penalty laws changed."

"So, he has been in jail here in the United States?"

"Yes, sir. Twice."

"What happened?" Austin asked.

"Nothing, really. As it usually happens in such cases, he spent a few hours in jail then was released when his bail was posted. His mother is the one who puts up the money. Then he appeared before a judge and was fined. That's about it. He was never charged with a felony of any sort. He seems to have remained very quiet in the last year or so, and now works for the local power company."

"Has he ever been married?"

"Yes, he married ten years ago but was divorced two years later. He has not remarried since. I have not yet been able to find out anything about his wife," Rogge concluded.

"That won't be necessary," Austin said. "With his record, can he get into the United States?"

"Yes. The charges against him were minor, and do not prevent him from obtaining a Canadian passport. He is free to travel to the United States."

"I see," the Vice President said. "Anything else?"

"No, sir," Rogge said. "Do you want me to continue digging?"

"No, that's all the information I need. This will be kept confidential, I take it?"

"Of course, sir."

"Good," Cameron Austin said, getting to his feet, Rogge doing the same. "The reason my men asked you to conduct this investigation is that I met Ms. Cosner when I was in McPine, and I intend to continue seeing her. Socially I mean."

"I see," Rogge said simply.

"At the moment, only you and my men know. I will impose upon you and ask you to keep it that way until she comes to Washington and is seen in public with me."

"Certainly, sir. You can count on my discretion, and may I offer my congratulations, sir."

"Let's wait for that, Oliver. I only just met her," the Vice President said, smiling. "But, of course, you never know where it will lead."

Although Austin was unaware of it, Oliver Rogge had more of an interest in the Vice President than other people on staff in the

Thomson administration. Rogge was mindful of the source of that interest. He was long-term strategist and he knew that Austin would most probably be the next President. After just missing being considered as press secretary in the present administration, Rogge was planning his career to be at the heart of the Austin White House. That was one the reasons he had worked particularly meticulously in the Cosner affair, as he referred to it in his mind. Cameron Austin needed the information, Rogge was there to serve. He had done his duty well and had been very pleased to be able to inform the Vice President himself, and although he had suspected the reason for the request, Austin's last comment had nevertheless left him surprised.

Oliver Rogge did however manage a bright smile.

Laurie Cosner looked at the sky. Overhead, thin semitransparent clouds were moving in front of the sun, dimming its rays, while further to the west long thin stratocumulus clouds were presaging some precipitation. She pedaled toward Main Street, Brandy in tow.

"Hi, Annabelle," she said entering the post office. "What's new?"

"Just some bills today," the older lady said, handing Laurie two envelopes, "but I should be the one asking you what's new."

"What do you mean?" Laurie asked, her suspicions now confirmed.

Annabelle spoke softly. "What's he like? As nice as they say?"

"How did you find out?"

"Adele, Charlie and me saw him go in or come out of your house... on different days!" Annabelle said in a low voice. "But don't worry, we're keeping it to ourselves."

"You're not going to discuss it with anyone else?"

"No, but other people might have seen you."

Laurie sighed deeply. She had expected the revelation, yet she was very disappointed. She was wondering how she would respond to the curiosity that would be the object of more questions.

"How did you meet him?" Annabelle wanted to know.

"On my bike. He stopped to ask a question."

"Really!"

"And I invited him to my house for coffee, then lunch, and then dinner."

Annabelle was looking at Laurie with the intensity and wonder of someone who might have just seen God Himself.

"He's gone now, so that's it," Laurie concluded.

"You're not going to see him again?"

"Perhaps next time he comes up to the lodge."

"He's such a handsome man, and you need someone in your life, Laurie, so I was, you know, hoping——"

"Annabelle, I'm not exactly in his league."

"Still…"

Both women turned as McPine's barber, Charlie Lamb, an ancient man with hair as white as fresh snow, walked in.

"Laurie," he began, "nice to see you." In a lower voice, he added, "Our man's gone, I take it. You two get along okay?"

"Fine, thanks Charlie."

"You know we won't say anything."

"I'm holding you to that because Sarah doesn't know. Nor Bernie."

Annabelle was surprised. "You're not going to tell them?"

"I don't see that there's a need to do so. Sarah will ask too many questions."

Annabelle and Charlie exchanged glances.

"You ashamed or something?" Charlie asked.

"No, Charlie. I just want to protect my daughter. I've got to go. Bye," Laurie said, abruptly stepping outside. She doubted Annabelle and Charlie would keep what they knew to themselves. It was after all a most juicy piece of gossip in a world where boredom was always casting a misty net over lives. She knew she had to have a tête-à-tête with Sarah, but had wanted to wait. Now she couldn't.

Laurie was at the window when the yellow school bus stopped below to let her daughter out. As was the routine every school day, Brandy had gone to greet her and get a pat as they walked together towards the house.

"Hi, Mom," Sarah said, stepping inside.

"Hi. How was school?"

"You know, school's school. When's dinner? I'm starved," the girl announced.

"I'm having dinner with Bernie this evening…"

"Cool."

"But your dinner's almost ready. I'll feed you before I go."

"Mom, I can take care of myself. You don't have to f-e-e-d me, you know."

"I know, but I want to talk to you about something."

Sarah eyed her mother. "Oh, oh."

Laurie smiled. "Don't worry, it's not anything negative. I'll call you when dinner's on the table."

Later when her mother deposited a salad in front of her, Sarah asked, "So what did you want to tell me?"

Laurie sat across from her daughter at the kitchen nook. "I met someone this weekend."

"Really! Anyone I know?"

"Not exactly."

"What does that mean?" the girl asked, bringing a forkful of greens to her mouth.

"I met Vice President Cameron Austin." It was out and she felt immediately relieved. Why had she been making such a fuss in her mind about it?

Sarah chewed her food and scrutinized her mother.

Laurie continued. "He was over for lunch and for dinner, twice. I really like him."

"Wow!" Sarah finally exclaimed. "That's so cool. Someone finally met him in person after all the years he's been coming up to McPine. Wait till I tell my friends!"

"That's just it," Laurie said cautiously. "I don't think it would be a good idea to talk about it just yet."

"But you are going to see him again, aren't you?"

"I plan to, yes."

"Then what's the problem?"

"Sarah, the problem is that people are not going to leave you alone, the media I mean. Once this gets out, they'll want details on anything and everything, and that truly bothers me. I don't want to place you in a position you're sure not to like until I am certain that Mr. Austin and I decide we can make a go of it. Which might not happen, you know. We're from two very different worlds."

"It's so romantic," the girl commented. "The handsome Vice President of the United States and my mom!"

Laurie sighed. "Sarah, promise me you won't talk about it."

"Sure, Mom, if that's what you want," the girl replied, a touch of annoyance in her voice.

"A few people around here saw him come to the house, but I'm pretty sure they won't talk, just as no one ever mentions his visits to anyone outside McPine. I'm simply asking the same courtesy."

Sarah looked at her mother for a long moment. "You always find a reason not to get serious about any man, Mom, so this will probably not be any different. Don't worry, I won't say a word."

Her daughter was putting her own spin on things, and why shouldn't she? But then, how could Laurie explain that for years she had been searching for love, only to find it—or at least getting as close to it as she ever would—in the least expected manner?

CHAPTER ELEVEN

Bernie Wesson held up an umbrella over Laurie's head as she settled in the company van, then went to sit behind the wheel.

As he turned the key, Laurie said, "I'm sorry, but it won't be a late night for me."

"Not feeling well?"

"You could say that. I'm having my period and lots of cramps lately. Must be the beginning of old age."

"Come on, Laurie. You're a young chick!"

Laurie looked at him in the dimming daylight. "A young chick?"

"You know what I mean," he said. "Anyway, if you want to make it an early night, let's just have dinner and skip the movie."

"I appreciate that, Bernie."

He smiled briefly, and they drove in silence for a time on their way to Medford, the windshield wipers swishing the rain away rhythmically.

Laurie broke the silence. "How's Clare?"

"No change. Had no clue who I was."

"What do the doctors say?"

"They can't do any more for her now than they could when she first went in. It's so frustrating. She was such a lovely, vital woman."

"I'm sorry, Bernie."

He shrugged his shoulders, the way he always did when there was nothing else to say about Clare.

Laurie could sympathize with her friend, but as usual she had nothing to offer that could ease his pain. She turned the conversation to business matters.

While coffees were put in front of them after dinner, Laurie decided she could no longer avoid broaching the subject. "There's something I want to talk to you about, Bernie."

"What is it?" he asked, his lined face questioning.

"I met Cameron Austin on the weekend, and he had dinner at my house."

"Really?"

"Yes. I thought I should tell you since a few people saw him, and you're sure to hear about it."

"So, what's he like?"

"Very nice. I must say I did enjoy his company."

And a lot more, girl!

"Are you going to see him again?"

"Maybe next time he comes up."

"Did he invite you down to Washington?"

"Yes, he did. And I haven't yet decided if I'm going."

"You two must have hit it off, then."

Bernie was looking into his partner's eyes and was realizing what he had failed to acknowledge when he had seen her the previous evening. There was an unmistakable spark in the green of her eyes. But, of course, meeting the handsome beloved Vice President of the United States must have been quite exciting for her, he thought. It was understandable and surely could not be anything more.

"It was nice." *Nice is not quite the word for it, girl!*

"Well, that's quite something," Bernie said. "What did you two talk about?"

"Lots of things. Sarah, his work, our business, that sort of thing. Bernie, I would really appreciate it if you didn't talk to people about this. I mean, I wouldn't want the media coming around here to 'find' a story, if you know what I mean. I wouldn't want Sarah to be caught in all this."

"You know me enough to know I'd never do that."

"Thanks, Bernie," she said, briefly touching his hand across the table.

"You didn't fall in love or anything like that, did you?"

She laughed briefly, awkwardly. "Now, why would you say a thing like that?"

"Well, he's intelligent, handsome, rich. My sister in Toronto was telling me she read in some rag or the other that he regularly gets marriage proposals."

"What?"

"Yeah, apparently lonely widows and divorcées write to him, telling him their life stories and hoping he'll want to marry them."

"I don't believe that!" Laurie said, a little too firmly for Bernie's taste.

"Well, it's not the first time I've heard it."

"Why were you talking to your sister about Cameron Austin? Does she know he comes up to McPine?"

"No. Of course not! I was over at her house for dinner on Sunday. Her husband was going on and on about that thing between Ottawa and Washington of late, and my sister just wanted to change the subject I guess. It worked to some degree," Bernie said, smiling, "because her husband then started on how stupid some women can be, yada, yada, yada."

Laurie smiled back.

Grace Winfield Austin was renowned for her fashion sense which had not abated with advancing years. This Thursday evening, tall and straight in her impeccably cut navy silk suit which contrasted neatly with the blond tint covering her white hair, she opened her arms to welcome her son, the Vice President of the United States. They embraced warmly.

"You look well, Cameron. Your little vacation seems to have done you a world of good."

"As always, Mother, it was most restful and enjoyable."

"That pleases me. How about a sherry?"

"Let me get it," he said, going to the carved sideboard while his mother sat in her favorite easy chair in the living room of her impressive Georgian-style mansion.

Cameron Austin handed a glass to his mother and sat on the love seat next to her chair, the way he always did on his weekly visits. They both sipped.

"Thank you for the lovely trout, Cameron. It was superb."

"Glad you enjoyed it."

"How many did you catch up there in...what's the name of the place again?"

"McPine."

"Yes. McPine."

"Quite a few actually."

"Your sisters were not able to join us this evening unfortunately," Grace said. "They will all be coming for dinner on Sunday the fifteenth. Do you think you'll be able to join us?"

"Probably not, Mother. I have plans that weekend. Personal plans."

Grace Austin's ears perked. Could he be talking about a woman? At last! "Will you be away?" she asked.

He eyed his mother, knowing exactly what she was going for, and what she wanted confirmed. On the drive down to her house he had decided to tell her about Laurie. There were many reasons for that decision. Mostly he thought Grace Winfield Austin a wise woman who, because she expressed her opinions frankly, had often helped him see situations, both personal and political, more clearly. He knew she would have reservations about Laurie Cosner, but he had decided to get them on the carpet at the onset.

"No. I will be at home entertaining a lady."

Grace smiled again. "Indeed!"

"You mean at last, don't you, Mother?" Cameron remarked, his lips forming a naughty smile Grace remembered from his youth.

"You know I'm very happy for you, Cameron. Who is she?"

"Her name is Laurie Cosner. She is a writer who lives in McPine. She is a widow and the mother of a fifteen-year-old daughter. I've invited her down on the weekend of the fifteenth."

"She's not an American then?"

"No. Canadian. A very lovely Canadian. I know this probably disappoints you, but..."

"Why should it? I'll reserve comment until after I've met her. How long have you known her?"

"I met her last weekend."

"Just last weekend? And you already invited her to your residence? Are you telling me that you fell in love with her at first sight?" Grace said, incredulously.

Cameron Austin twisted the elegant crystal glass in his hands for a moment before replying. "All I know, Mother, is that I am extremely attracted to her. I invited her down because I want to know her better, I want her to see my world, and we'll see where it leads."

Grace looked at Cameron and could not avoid seeing the many problems ahead for her son were he to get serious about a woman who was not American. She knew that many people—mostly stubborn old men—would object to backing a presidential candidate not married to an American although there was nothing in the Constitution prohibiting it, or was there? And what about the voters? This would be a first in American annals, as far as she was aware, and she knew her history well. How would they react? Many would probably think it was some type of treason. But wasn't she getting ahead of herself? Cameron had invited a lady for a visit. They were not planning a wedding! Not yet, at least.

"When will I meet her?"

"If we decide to continue seeing each other, I'll bring her around next time she visits," he replied. "That's the best I can do."

"Very well. Does Andrew Thomson know?"

"No. It's not something that needs to be discussed with the President at this point."

"I was simply thinking that he might blow a gasket if you were to introduce her publicly in Washington considering the way our relations with Canada now stand."

Cameron smiled. "You know he has scheduled a trip to Ottawa. I'm certain fences will be mended and we will be able to get back to more important matters."

"Let me repeat, Cameron, that I am very happy for you."

"Thank you, Mother."

"Now I know why you look so well!" she said, and Cameron Austin did not the miss the devilish hint in her voice.

"You know, Mother, Laurie is a very forthright person. She tells it like it is, and she was not shy about pointing out the many foibles of Americans. You two should get along tremendously well. Or perhaps not," he concluded, momentarily patting Grace's hand.

Grace Winfield Austin was tempted for a moment to chuckle but she did not. Part of her would not allow it. She had wanted to see her son happy again, and he was probably embarking on a satisfying journey, but the dream she had dreamt was not unfolding as she had envisioned. Not at all.

Not at all this romantic.

Later, alone in his bedroom, Vice President Austin stretched out on top of the richly patterned beige-and-brown comforter on the bed and reached for the telephone on the bedside table. He pushed a series of numbers, now etched in his memory, and the signal was received in McPine.

"Hi," he said simply after she answered.

"Hi. How was your day?"

"Fine. I had dinner with my mother this evening and told her about you."

"And you're still alive to tell the tale?"

He laughed a magical laugh that erased all cares, political or otherwise, then spent the next twenty minutes talking to the woman in pine country. The late-night calls were a blessing he looked forward to many times during his busy days, and he wondered how he ever managed without them.

CHAPTER TWELVE

Rita Payne seemed irritated. "You mean to tell me I'm the last one to hear about this?"

"You told me you'd be busy all week."

"Yeah, but if I had known what it was about I would have gotten unbusy!"

"Rita, the only people who know are Sarah—I had to tell her—and Bernie, well, I felt I owed him, and the three people who saw Cameron come to my house. I wanted to tell you when you drove Sarah home on Monday, but—"

"Laurie, I'm teasing," Rita said, smiling as she lightly punched Laurie's arm. "So give me all the details and don't you dare leave anything out, like if you were a teenager would your acne have cleared up?"

Laurie smiled. "Definitely!"

"Nooo! Really? After you just met him?" Rita commented, now totally excited. "What am I saying? It's great! How did it all happen?"

The two women were having lunch at Rita's house so they could talk privately. Laurie recounted the highlights of the weekend for her sister-in-law who listened intently, her expression one of pure joy.

"I can't tell you how glad I am, Laurie. It's about time you met someone. It's been much too long. My brother made you promise you'd remarry again, remember?"

"Yes, I remember, but who's talking marriage?"

"Well, my dear, there's no use arguing. It's clear you're in love."

"Rita, I just met the man. I like him, yes, I enjoyed our repartees, yes, I found him very attractive, yes, we made love because I simply couldn't help myself, yes, we talk on the phone every day, yes, but I still don't know him well and a new day has dawned. I'm certainly in deep like—deep lust perhaps—but love? That's something that takes time, even years, and I know from whence I speak as you know."

"Me thinks the lady does protest too much," Rita commented.

"There's no talking to you is there!"

"Okay, maybe not love but it could become love, and you know it. Are you going to see him again?"

"I'm planning a trip to Washington next week, but I don't mind telling you that I am scared. I won't fit in. I'm simply from the wrong side of the tracks, or in this case the wrong side of the border. And there's Sarah to consider."

"What about Sarah?"

"If Cameron and I were to become an item, as they say, I couldn't ask her to leave her life here behind and move to Washington."

"And, pray tell, why not? I mean McPine ain't exactly a teenager's dream spot for meeting cool guys," Rita emphasized.

"Did Sarah tell you something?"

"No, but I hear her and Emily talk. They're dreamers, like we were, like all teenagers in fact. They want to be where the action is," Rita said, drawing large quotation marks in the air with her fingers. "And the action is not McPine."

"Sarah never said anything," Laurie commented, disappointed.

"Of course not, you're her mother. Besides, Sarah dreams of being a concert pianist, and she certainly has the talent. Don't you think that moving to the States and having a celebrity for a mom might open the right doors for her? It might be quite cool actually," Rita concluded.

Laurie had failed to consider this point of view. Focusing much too much on the negative fallout of a possible relationship with Cameron Austin without allowing herself to concentrate on its enchantment. She had missed an obvious benefit for her daughter.

"You might be quite right," she finally said.

"Of course. I always am," Rita retorted without shame. "Now, what are you going to wear to go to Washington?"

"I know what you're going to say. That my navy pant suit might be fine around here, but that—"

"Actually, it'd be just fine. You like it and you're comfortable in it, so go for it. Of course, if you want some help shopping for something new...heavens, what am I saying, you haven't bought anything new in years."

"Okay, I get your point, but being self-employed in McPine I certainly don't need a new outfit every month!"

"Try every year," Rita retorted, smiling at her friend. "I could make myself available for a shopping trip this weekend."

"You're on."

A zoo. That's how Agent Lonsdale qualified it in his mind as he watched people come and go in all directions. Standing tall against a wall in a light beige windbreaker over an open-neck white shirt and beige pants, an ensemble which praised his chestnut-colored skin—no sunglasses—he was the image of aplomb. He was a man like any other waiting for a friend or relative to arrive. His first reaction had been one of irritation when the Vice President asked him to meet Laurie Cosner at the airport, but now he was considering that he should have been flattered to be chosen. After all it was a personal nod from the man himself. And the lady was not so bad. In fact, he had to acknowledge that she had an endearing way about her.

A light drizzle was falling in the Washington area when the Air Canada jet landed at Dulles International Airport after the short flight from Toronto. Comfortable in the wide seat in the business-class section of the aircraft as it taxied to its assigned gate, Laurie Cosner could see rivulets of rain dripping like tears against the window. It reminded her of what her mother had said while they lunched together at the older woman's home before the trip to the airport.

"I'm so happy for you, Laurie. It's more than time for you to leave the tears behind. Robby would want you to be happy," she had said, gently patting her daughter's hand. "You grieved for a long time and that's okay. We're all different. I know how long you resented me when I remarried until you realized that the person you were angry at was your dad, for leaving you, and since you couldn't be angry at him, I was the target. I had dared to live. But, you know, I think that being happy is the ultimate praise for dear ones who have gone."

Indeed, Laurie thought. She would forget all the red lights that kept popping up in her mind and enjoy the weekend. Make it count.

Wearing her linen navy pant suit, she followed other passengers into the terminal, pulling a black wheeled weekend bag behind her. Agent Lonsdale saw her and waited until she got closer before approaching. She was wondering where to go when the tall man appeared at her side.

"Welcome to Washington, Ms. Cosner."

"Thank you."

"Let me take your bag."

"It's okay. It's easy to pull."

"Ms. Cosner, I have my orders and I'll have to continue living here once you're gone," Lonsdale said, no emotion showing on his chiseled face.

Laurie smiled and was touched that he remembered their exchange in McPine. She let him take the bag and he directed her out of the busy terminal to a waiting limo. She sat in the back while Lonsdale joined the driver in the front, a thick glass separating them, and she wondered if this was the car in which Cameron Austin was usually chauffeured around town.

The traffic was heavy and the drizzle did not afford an appropriate view of the city which she had seen only once years earlier when she and Rita had driven to Florida. She did not know if the route the limo took was the most direct one, or if Lonsdale was treating her to some of the most famous landmarks in the city. She recognized the Capitol Building on its hill, the White House from across the south lawn, and the Washington monument. Other buildings which seemed important she did not recognize, but she was certain she would get a proper tour during her short stay.

Traveling in fashionable northwest Washington, the car crossed the bridge above Rock Creek Park and proceeded to the grounds of the United States Naval Observatory. When it stopped under the portico of an impressive three-story Queen Ann-style home, Lonsdale got out and opened the door for her.

Laurie was ushered into the house and introduced to Millie Spock, a middle-aged housekeeper, who welcomed her and smiled warmly. Soon Laurie was shown to a large room on the second floor and was immediately properly impressed. As was the case with the other rooms she had been able to glance at, the decor was a statement of elegance and tradition while being warm and inviting.

"Would you like me to help you unpack?" Millie asked matter-of-factly.

Laurie offered her best smile. "Thank you, but it won't be necessary."

"Please make yourself comfortable. The bathroom is through that door," Millie said, indicating with her right hand. "The Vice President is expected around seven. Would you like some tea and something to eat in the meantime?"

"That would be very nice, thank you."

The woman nodded and disappeared, closing the door behind her.

Laurie looked around the room, and when she saw her reflection in the long mirror near the closet, she was appalled at the state of her suit. The humidity had dealt her a dirty hand.

She had showered and was putting on the white terry gown she had found hanging in the bathroom when Millie came in with a tray which she deposited on a round table in front of one of the windows.

"Can I do anything else for you, Ms. Cosner?" the woman asked.

A moment later she was leaving with Laurie's navy suit which she promised would be pressed and returned by morning.

Laurie poured herself some tea and had a couple of small tasty sandwiches with the crust cut off as she watched the soft rain. Having slept poorly the previous night at the anticipation of her trip, like a child excited at the prospect of a visit from Santa, she felt weary. The thick mattress of the four-poster bed was inviting. After finishing her tea, she stretched out on top of the comforter and was soon asleep. She never heard the soft knocking at her door sometime later.

His ear pressed to the door, Vice President Austin detected no noise of any kind after having knocked twice. He decided to let himself in and found Laurie still in the arms of Morpheus. He approached the bed softly and was watching her, unable to deny the surge of happiness he felt. Soon, as if feeling he was scrutinizing her, she stirred and opened her eyes slowly. After a moment when she appeared to be determining where she was, she smiled at Cameron Austin. He sat on the edge of the bed and, without either uttering a word, their arms reached for each other.

"I make a point of coming home early and I find you asleep. Not the best for my ego," he said.

"This trip has been stressful!"

"Stressful? Why?"

"I told you that coming to the States is always stressful for me. Even more so today."

"Was there a problem with your flight?"

"No, Mr. Vice President," she smiled. "The whole idea of trespassing in your world stresses me."

"Why should it? You know I don't bite," he said, his fingers lovingly caressing her face.

"No, not you, but perhaps others in Washington."

He pulled her to him. "We'll take it very easy so it won't be much of a culture shock, I promise. How's everything in McPine?"

She pulled herself gently away. "Just as you left it. Except some people saw you come to my house so I was bombarded with questions, but I managed to refrain from going into any great detail as to what we did."

"I'm glad," he commented, his face full of joy.

"And my daughter thinks that it's quite cool, you and me."

"Does she now? She's not alone. So do I."

She reached for a long narrow box on the bedside table. "A gift for my host."

He lifted the lid and saw the single long-stemmed peach tea rose and smiled warmly at the woman who was adding a welcome new orb to his life.

CHAPTER THIRTEEN

"Is it true that women regularly write to you to propose marriage?" Laurie asked. She was seated on the Vice President's right at the long mahogany table in the dining room of his official residence. They were sharing their first meal together in Washington.

"Apparently so," he replied after swallowing a spoonful of lobster bisque. "But Shirley Winterburn, my secretary, handles that sort of thing."

"What do you mean, handles? Don't you at least read them?"

"I've read a few at random, but since I'm not about to marry anyone who writes to propose to me, Shirley sends out a kind letter to thank them for taking the time and so forth."

"But it must be terribly wonderful for your ego. I mean it must make up for all the Americans who don't support the current administration."

Austin eyed her, wondering where she was going with this, but he replied truthfully. "In a way, I suppose you're right, but on the other hand it can be quite unsettling to think that there are so many lonely women out there who are ready to offer themselves to a man they know nothing about."

"I remember you saying in McPine that you live in a glass house. These women know a lot about you from seeing you on the news and hearing you make speeches and they like what they see."

Cameron Austin wiped his mouth with the large serviette. The conversation was making him self-conscious. "Perhaps we should talk about something else."

"Of course," Laurie said simply. Looking around the room, which she found stunning with its exquisite furniture and many paintings of historical figures and events, she asked, "Don't you have a smaller room for casual dining? I mean this is a little overwhelming for me after McPine. It's almost like being in a museum."

He chuckled. "I'll see what I can do."

And on Saturday and Sunday, they ate their meals in a smaller room off the kitchen where the furniture was of warm pine and the walls a combination of yellow and bright wallpaper with small flowers. She didn't ask, but she knew Jean had left her mark in the room.

Saturday morning the rain had not let up. Cameron gave her a tour of the house, and Laurie couldn't have missed the large framed photo of Jean on the bedside table in his bedroom. Neither commented, but she couldn't fault him could she? She too kept Robby close by.

Austin took a couple of phone calls, but he and Laurie spent some time in his office den talking and reading the many newspapers, just as they did the next day, that had been stacked up on a small table near one of the leather sofas in the room. Many editorials still managed to concentrate on the war of words between Canada and the U.S. because of President Thomson's impending visit to Ottawa. It seemed that everyone wondered how the President and the Prime Minister would be able to have a successful meeting while the irritating edge of uttered words still hung in the air.

"The President must mend fences, but it's something he's quite skilled at doing," Cameron Austin said in reply to Laurie's question about the visit.

"You mean because he's done it so often?"

Austin smiled. "He is first and foremost a diplomat. I'm sure the visit will be a resounding success all around."

By dinner time, the skies had cleared, and as soon as it was dark, Austin took Laurie on a tour of Washington. They traveled in a nondescript black town car with tinted and bulletproof windows with a chauffeur and Agent Lonsdale in the front seat. Another nondescript car followed. Cameron Austin was proud to show her his city in all its lit glory on a perfect spring evening, giving her a brief history of some of the buildings, but he did talk at length on the Senate, its history and his role in its democratic process.

As they were traveling near the Mall, Austin signaled the chauffeur and the car stopped. "It's a nice night for a walk," he invited.

When she seemed hesitant, he put on a pair of large black-rimmed glasses which he pulled out of a breast pocket, and donned a baseball cap with the logo of the New York Yankees. "Just another tourist out for a stroll," he said, taking her hand.

The rain had cleansed the air. She breathed deeply as they walked slowly hand-in-hand and she was able to see the pink petals from the last spring blooms of the Japanese cherry trees in the water of the Reflecting Pool. There were many people about, but no one was giving them a second look. Agents were following discreetly, but this night she did not mind. She could even ignore their presence. She was just a tourist like all the others out for a stroll, except that unlike the people who were taking pictures, she could not have a picture of her man on her digital desktop.

Strolling along the Mall, a two-mile strip of greenery and fountains stretching from the U.S. Capitol to the Lincoln Memorial, Cameron Austin told her how the Mall had been conceived as a grand avenue by Pierre Charles L'Enfant, a man who fought under George Washington during the Revolutionary War. Austin was proud to point to the obelisk Washington Monument, the FDR Memorial Park, the Jefferson and Lincoln Memorials as well as the Vietnam Memorial. He explained that the area had been set up to honor the country's heroes with monuments, memorials and many museums. He pointed to some of the buildings making up the Smithsonian Institution. Later, back in the car, he pointed to the lights of the John F. Kennedy Center for the Performing Arts reflected on the Potomac. She was impressed by the city and felt privileged to have had the ultimate tour guide.

As was his habit, on Sunday morning Cameron Austin attended services at a small Anglican church. In reply to her question, he said, "I never do anything simply for appearances. Whatever I do is out of conviction."

Laurie Cosner wished she could have attended with him, but saw the wisdom of declining his invitation. She stayed behind and phoned Rita's house where Sarah was spending the weekend only to get voice mail. She did not leave a message.

Before Laurie knew it, Sunday afternoon was in its last stretch and she was finishing packing for her flight back to Toronto. How quickly the weekend had gone by. They had laughed and loved as easily as if they had known each other forever, and there was no doubt in her mind now that she wanted the man in her life. That she needed him. She could adapt to a changed lifestyle. She would adapt. It was merely a question of setting her mind to it.

She could be at the Vice President's side in public and still have time to carry on with her life as a writer. Bernie Wesson would be devastated, of course, because he kept hoping for a progression of their relationship, but a clean-cut break would be a tremendous relief as far as she was concerned. He had offered to buy her share of *Only Roses* once, and would no doubt jump at the chance now. She hoped.

She carefully folded the two outfits Rita had helped her choose, a long-sleeved ecru shirt with matching flowing pants, and a classic raw-silk black dress she had worn with a light black woolen cardigan and pearls Robby had given her years earlier. Both had been perfect.

She took a last look around the bedroom and was zipping up her suitcase when Austin knocked softly and walked in.

"Agent Lonsdale will take you to the airport. I think it's better that way."

"Of course."

"Here," he said, giving her a small white box. "This is a souvenir of your visit."

She lifted the lid and saw a gold pin in the shape of a long-stemmed rose.

"It's beautiful," she exclaimed. "Thank you."

He took it from her hands and lovingly attached it to the lapel of her navy jacket. "You will be back for the dinner for the Russian President? You won't back out on me or anything like that, will you?" he asked, smiling, an arm around her shoulders.

"I'd better not. I have a feeling you'd send your men to McPine to fetch me!"

"That I would," Austin replied.

"You realize that choosing the right outfit is going to be a problem," she said.

"Why should it be? You saw the photos I showed you of the First Lady at such functions. It should give you a good idea…"

She put an index finger to her cheek, interrupting him. "I know, I'll get a slinky gold little number and really give the media something to fuss about."

"Why not?" he replied embracing her.

Her eyes were moist when Agent Lonsdale held the door of the limo open for her under the portico. She waved at the Vice President who was standing in the doorway. Part of her wanted desperately to run back inside and never go back home again.

At the airport Agent Lonsdale again opened the limo door for her.

"I'll take you to your gate," he said as the chauffeur handed him her bag.

She nodded, and they made their way into the busy cavern of the airport.

"I love your pin," Lonsdale said as they walked among the crowds.

"Thank you. Did you shop for it?" she asked.

"No, ma'am. The Vice President chose it himself. May I ask if you will be returning to Washington soon?"

She smiled and looked at Lonsdale. "Yes, I will. I hope you're not too disappointed."

"No, ma'am. I'm glad," he commented, his face showing only the slightest hint of a smile.

She asked, "Would you be willing to do me another favor?"

Mike Gilbert was watching television in the den at his mother's house in Toronto while sipping from a coffee-filled mug. Eileen Danfort was busy in the kitchen when the doorbell rang. She went to answer and smiled widely at the sight of her daughter.

"Laurie, how was the weekend? No need to tell me," she said closing the door. "I can tell you'll be seeing him again."

"I intend to," Laurie Cosner replied as the two women embraced briefly.

Eileen smiled back. "Good for you. Your brother's here. He came for dinner. By the way, did you eat?"

"I'm fine."

The two women came into the den and Mike Gilbert barely glanced up.

"Hi, sis. How's it hanging?"

Laurie disliked this style of greeting with a passion. "I'm fine," she managed to reply while putting an index finger across her lips for her mother's benefit. The less Mike knew the better for all concerned, she had told her mother before heading down to Washington. Both women sat down.

"Mom says you went to Washington for the weekend. Has to be a guy in the picture, right?" Mike asked.

"I was visiting friends," Laurie replied evenly. "What about you, Mike? What are you doing these days?"

"Well, you know, same old, same old."

"You like your job?"

"It's okay. Actually I enjoy it, so you two ladies must be very pleased."

"I hear you were visiting April McLaren in Medford recently," Laurie said.

Mike laughed. His eyes, the same gray as his mother's, were as usual full of mischief, Laurie thought. One never knew what to expect. "I forget sometimes how provincial people in small towns can be and that you can never go unnoticed. Yes, I went to see her. We're friends," Mike said, adding, "actually more than friends. I've asked her to marry me."

He seemed to enjoy the look that went from Laurie to his mother and back again.

"What?" Laurie exclaimed.

"Why didn't you tell me? Do I know her?" Eileen Danfort asked. "The name seems familiar."

"Mom," Laurie began, "that's because they were arrested together on more than one occasion and you put up the bail money for both of them."

"I see," Eileen managed to say.

"Mom, I was waiting for Laurie to get here so I could tell you both at the same time," Mike explained.

"It's always nice when people who marry have common interests," Laurie said.

"I know you don't like April, Laurie, but that doesn't mean she's not a nice person. I think she's perfect for me," Mike retorted.

"Isn't she a lot older than you?"

"Nine years. So what? Women marry older men all the time, so what's wrong with the reverse? The fact that she's mature is a plus, don't you think? A lot more stable than my ex-non-lamented wife! And since there's enough people in the world, I certainly don't want to have children."

Eyeing her mother, Laurie quickly saw that the older woman was disappointed at the prospect of not having more grandchildren.

"He could be right, Mom. Mike and April seem to be cut from the same cloth," Laurie said. Turning to her brother, she asked, "Where are you going to live? I mean you have your job in Toronto and April has the diner in Medford. How are you going to work that out?"

"We're working on it. I'll probably move back to Medford. It would be the sensible thing to do."

"And quit your job?" Eileen asked, a touch of panic in her voice.

"Mom, don't get on your high horse," Mike said. "I know your husband got me that job—and I'm grateful—but handling customer complaints is neither a high-profile nor a high-paying job. I could do just as well managing the diner in Medford, but we're not going to get married for a while yet. Not before next year. So things might change."

Laurie thought her mother was going to cry.

"Are you sure you love this woman," Laurie asked her brother, "or is it a convenience thing so you two can more easily plan your rounds of protests?"

"You never could understand, could you, Laurie? What we activists do is important. Canadians are famous for sitting on their asses and bitching about whatever, but they don't do much to change things. People like April and I are the reason change happens. As a concrete example, it's because of us and people like us who were willing to get involved, and to call for change that large lumber companies are no longer destroying the rain forest in British-Columbia while cutting trees. They had to listen to the protesters. They're still cutting but not destroying."

He took a sip of coffee before continuing. "I'm not like you, Laurie, content with the status quo. You have a daughter, you should be concerned with what's happening to our world, with the way a few rich corporations are dirtying our air and mutilating the environment, with the way some governments have been trampling on basic human rights in the name of fighting terrorism. What kind of world is she going to inherit? I, for one, intend to leave the planet a better place than I found it. My aim has never been to just make money. Of course, you two ladies think that I should have been a little more concerned with the nuts and bolts of earning a living over the years, but you know very well that the jobs I lost or was unable to get had everything to do with how people perceived my social conscience rather than my abilities or desire to work. That in itself is an outrage."

Laurie eyed her brother for a moment, envying his passion. She knew that he had been instrumental in affecting change in many areas. People like him and April McLaren were important in the scheme of things, but did they have to make it the purpose of their lives? She might not have been as vocal as her brother, but he was wrong when he said she did nothing. She may not have joined marches in the street as Mike did, but she did call or write companies and government representatives when she felt it was warranted. Aloud she said, "Mike, it's one thing to protest injustice, but it's another to be violent while doing it."

"I've never once been violent. Some protesters are, I'll grant you that. But I, personally, have been arrested for the simple reason that governments and big companies get embarrassed when people like me speak out. They want us out of the way ASAP, so they have us arrested. It's that simple. I've never been violent nor will I ever be."

"You've not been in trouble for a while," Laurie stated. "What's your next target?"

"If you must know, President Thomson's visit to Ottawa. Why should we Canadians simply lie down and let the Americans go ahead with their agenda to control the world?"

CHAPTER FOURTEEN

When the small, almost weightless package arrived at the White House mailroom, it raised a flag for the staff: it came from Canada and was addressed to Agent Lonsdale. Agents seldom, if ever, got mail from the outside, especially another country. They did get mail from other government departments and buildings, but these were delivered by pouch. Lonsdale was advised of the anomaly, but not before the package was carefully scanned by machine.

After assuring the staff that its content and source were secure, he unwrapped the long narrow white box. Although he was certain it would contain only a single long-stem peach rose, no card, he ascertained nothing else had slipped in under the white tissue paper and then proceeded to Shirley Winterburn's desk.

"This has just been delivered for the Vice President," he told her matter-of-factly.

"Again!" she said after opening the box. "Do you know who sends these roses?"

"Probably a fan."

"No card. The last time I got the feeling that Mr. Austin knew who the sender was."

"Maybe he does," Lonsdale said as he shrugged his shoulders and turned on his heels.

Shirley Winterburn retrieved an appropriate vase from a cabinet behind her desk, filled it at the water cooler in the corner and went to deposit both on Cameron Austin's desk. She was returning to her desk when the Vice President and an aide came in. A minute later the President and his Chief of Staff followed.

Cameron Austin was placing the rose into the prepared vase when Andrew Thomson walked in. "Don't tell me. Ladies are no longer content with writing letters, they now send roses."

The Vice President smiled, but did not comment.

The President eyed Austin for a moment and was suddenly certain that the Vice President was no longer a lonely man without female companionship. "Anything you want to tell us?" Thomson asked.

"Not at this juncture, Mr. President," Austin replied amiably.

The group sat down in a circle of comfortable chairs around a round table.

"Here's the thing," the President began. "When I go to Ottawa, I want to have as much ammunition as possible. You've been vacationing in Canada for years. You have friends there. Anything you think would be important to include in the speech or in my private conversations?"

"First of all, while on the surface Canada appears to be just like the United States, that is an illusion," Cameron Austin began. "It's quite different in many ways. I would say that Canadians are increasingly different from the U.S. in political culture, for instance, with what many people consider daring policies. Despite this, they remain a people who tend to be more self-conscious and definitely less violent than us. There is an old joke that puts it into perspective. How do you empty a bar in the United States? The bartender takes out his gun. How do you empty a bar in Canada? The bartender asks people to leave."

Seeing no change of expression in the three faces in front of him, Cameron Austin continued. "On the whole, in Canada, people are more reserved and restrained. While we say: 'Give me liberty or death', in Canada it's more along the lines of: 'Give me liberty...if that's okay with you.' It's not just by chance that their armed forces act as peacekeepers in the world's trouble spots rather than being combative."

"Forgive me a moment," the President said, "but isn't that because their military might could almost be qualified as laughable?"

"I don't think that's the way we saw it when Canada supported our efforts in Kuwait, Afghanistan and in the Gulf during the Iraqi crisis," Austin replied. "They don't have our military power, certainly, but we must give them credit for doing their share of peacekeeping on the world stage despite limited resources."

"Maybe, but they do rely on us to protect them. That's always been the case, yet they have the nerve to tell us they don't want an American base on their territory? It's going to be built by Canadians, and it's going to help their economy for godsakes. They're crybabies if you want my opinion," the President concluded.

"They're opposed to the project because of ecological concerns in the North," the Vice President stated. "They don't see us as being as concerned with the environment as we should be."

"We have a better environmental record than the last administration," Thomson said.

"I believe they wonder why this administration has not been more aggressive in its environmental policies."

"We can't change everything overnight!" the President charged.

"I am simply telling you what I see as being the Canadian position. With their low population base, they see us as the big shot next door and consider us self-important. We need to be more conciliatory in our approach."

"You mean forget the base? Everyone—Republicans and Democrats alike—agrees that it is the only answer at this time."

"What I mean, Mr. President, is that we should look at all possible options with the Canadians. They are concerned not only with the ecological ramifications in the North, but also because they think we'll strong-arm them and eventually steal their resources. We must find a way to convince them that it won't happen," the Vice President stressed. "Perhaps that's what you should emphasize on your visit to Ottawa, that our two countries could work together to find a solution everyone in Canada can live with. Invite suggestions and proposals. Perhaps you could hint at the possibility of incentives in other areas of common interest. For example, an offer of the renegotiation of lingering disputes would certainly be welcome. I believe it's the only way at this time."

"Next you're going to tell me to be generous in my praise of our neighbor. When I offered my congratulations to Prime Minister Roy by phone on her recent victory at the polls, she found it necessary to belittle me soon after. That to me makes it clear she has little respect for this office. I'll probably never live down the 'Angry Andy' moniker!" Andrew Thomson concluded, passion in his voice.

"Perhaps it would be best to simply skim over the incident. Refer to trivial differences between two leaders of the North American family, just as it happens between any other siblings," Cameron Austin offered.

"The question is will the media on both sides of the border let it die? Some still blame me for starting the whole thing, when they in fact ran with a ball that should, out of respect for this administration, have remained exactly where it was."

"You know my position on that point," Austin said.

"Do you think I'll be met with protesters in Ottawa?" the President asked.

"No doubt about it at all, sir."

"Won't be the first time nor the last," Thomson said as he stood up, the other men doing the same.

"May we have a moment?" Cameron Austin asked his aide and the Chief of Staff.

The men exited, closing the door behind them.

"What is it, Cameron?"

"I just wanted to let you know that I will have a lady other than Marjorie on my arm at the dinner for the Russian President."

"Good for you!" Thomson said truthfully. "That answers my question about the rose. Anyone I know?"

"I'm afraid not. She is not from Washington."

"Well, the First Lady and I will be looking forward to meeting her."

Laurie Cosner let a self-assured middle-aged saleswoman zip up the back of the floor-length black gown. The lace bodice had a modestly plunging scalloped neckline and the shortest of sleeves over a semi-flowing silk skirt. It fit Laurie like a second skin.

"Now, this one was made for you. Classic elegance," the woman exclaimed as Laurie examined herself from all angles in the three-sided mirror of the fitting room.

"I don't know," Laurie commented.

The woman obviously born with a talent for anticipating the doubts of the boutique's clientele said, "Why don't we ask your friend?" She opened the door of the small room inviting Laurie to step out.

Rita Payne who had been sitting on a settee in the anteroom at the back of the store got to her feet. "Oh my! Oh my!" she squealed, putting a hand to her face.

"What did I tell you?" the saleswoman asked Laurie.

Laurie spun around, letting the skirt flow around her as she saw her reflection in the mirror that covered most of the back wall.

"And you don't really need any jewelry with this dress," the saleswoman continued. "Perhaps just diamond studs."

Diamonds? Of course. Her mother had a pair of rather impressive studs she might be convinced to lend her daughter and thus help relations between the United States and Canada.

Rita examined her friend in the front, in the back and from the sides. "That's definitely it!" she finally said.

"Did you see the price tag?" Laurie asked in a low voice.

Rita dismissed the remark. "You can afford it."

"Of course, but I'm probably going to wear it only once."

"Well, that's what you get for hanging with the wrong crowd," Rita laughed.

"It's certainly not fair, you know," Laurie began. "Men only need a well-tailored tux and they're in business for all their social duties, while the world still expects us women to be dressed to the nines and pay for it."

Rita was about to comment when the saleswoman leapt into her pitch. "You were looking for something spectacular yet classic. You can't get more classically spectacular than this dress. We got it in only two days ago and I told myself that it would be gone in a week. Since it's perfection itself on you, we might be able to offer a discount."

"Go for it!" Rita exclaimed, "Be your own woman while the men all look like penguins."

"Well, I've just blown my clothing budget for the year!" Laurie said, a large white garment bag over her arm as she and Rita walked to their parked car.

"More like the next five years, the way you never buy anything," Rita chimed in. "But, you'll be the belle of the ball and the envy of the Washington women."

"I wouldn't go that far. The First Lady has her own designer."

"Yeah, but is she going to be wearing a classically spectacular gown?"

Both women laughed, and it helped Laurie relax. After spending hours going from one store to another and being offered an array of gowns—from the backless and almost frontless to the truly ostentatious—she had almost lost hope of ever finding a suitable dress until they entered the last boutique on their list.

"Thanks for coming with me, Rita. I really appreciate it."

"What are you talking about? I wouldn't have missed this for the world. When you're famous I'll have a nice tale to tell the people in Medford."

"You wouldn't?"

"Hey, why do you think I've been hanging around you all these years?"

CHAPTER FIFTEEN

"Do you think they'll show the reception on TV?" Sarah Cosner asked her mother.

They were in Eileen Danfort's bedroom where Laurie was putting her mother's diamond studs through her pierced ear lobes in front of the mirror over the impressive cherry wood dresser. "I don't know. Maybe on the news. The Russian president is an important person."

"Well, everybody'll be looking at you," Sarah said. "Your dress is really bad!"

"What are you saying, Sarah?" Eileen Danfort reproached her granddaughter. "Your mother could not have chosen a better dress."

"Mom, that's exactly what Sarah means, that it's great," Laurie replied, pulling back her short blondish hair around her ears so she could appreciate the jewelry.

"Really?"

"Yes, Grandma," Sarah emphasized from her sitting position on the large bed.

"You should give me a dictionary of some sort so I know what you kids are saying these days." Eileen commented. To Laurie she said, "The earrings look lovely on you. Wear them with my blessing. How about the matching pendant?"

Laurie turned around. "Thanks, but I don't need it. I'll be wearing the gold rose."

"And well you should. It's so lovely."

"Thanks, Mom," Laurie said, bending to kiss her mother's cheek.

"I'm so glad you're happy, Laurie. I pray it all works out."

Laurie only smiled. She found it impossible to confide in her mother that each passing day made her feel more and more uneasy. And she knew that her impending visit to Washington was not the only reason. Certainly part of her was a tad frightened at the prospect of leaving the cocoon of her ordered existence to rub elbows with the American political elite, but she was confident that, with Cameron Austin at her side, she would easily conquer those fears.

Her feminine intuition was telling her that something else was in the offing that would cause her grief, yet she couldn't do anything to prevent it. Her brother Mike and April McLaren would be among the protesters when President Thomson visited Ottawa in a few days. How badly would they embarrass her, she wondered?

"Well, your brother should be here soon. Why don't we all go downstairs?" Eileen invited. "Dinner should be almost ready."

Sarah jumped off the bed and preceded her mother and grandmother down the wide stately stairs. "Nanna, is it okay if I practice a little until dinner?" she asked.

"Of course, dear. Go right ahead," Eileen Danfort replied.

Sarah almost flew down the last steps to rush to her grandmother's classic time-worn but much-loved piano in a corner of the large living room. Laurie and her mother went into the den across the hall where soon the melodic sounds of a piece Sarah had written herself reached them. She was vocalizing softly.

"She's getting so good," Eileen said. "I'm not just saying that because she's my granddaughter, you know. How about a drink?"

"Thanks, Mom. I'll wait and have wine with dinner."

"So, how are you really feeling? About this whole trip?" Eileen asked her daughter, settling into her favorite easy chair.

Laurie sat on the edge of an antique settee. "A little nervous, I suppose, but a lot more calm than I expected. I've decided that if President Thomson and the others don't like me, it's their loss. I'm going to be happy with Cameron."

"Good for you," Eileen replied, just as the doorbell chimed.

"I'll get it," Laurie said, getting to her feet.

In a moment she was coming back into the room with her brother Mike who bent down to kiss his mother's cheek.

"So, how's everything?" he asked, and not waiting for an answer, added, "Why are we having this family dinner in the middle of the week, anyway?"

"Because I've got something to tell you," Laurie put in.

"What?" Mike asked, letting his lanky body fall on a leather sofa. His light brown hair had been cut shorter than usual, Laurie thought.

"Would you like a beer?" Eileen asked.

"Before she starts, you mean? Must be important," Mike said. "Sure. I'll get it."

As he came back into the room, Eileen asked, "How was your day?"

"Fine, Fine. So, what's this all about?"

"Mike," Laurie began, "I have to tell you that I'll be in Washington next week."

"Again? A guy, right?"

"Yes."

"I knew it," he said eyeing his sister for a moment, the piano sounds from the other room dancing softly around the room. "You look different. Is it serious?"

"Could be," Laurie replied.

"I see. You and me could have a double wedding then," Mike said, taking a swig from his beer bottle.

Dismissing her brother's remark, Laurie said, "Mike, what I want to tell you is that the man I'm seeing is Cameron Austin, the Vice President of the United States."

Mike was lifting his beer bottle toward his mouth. His arm momentarily stopped in midair. "What? Where would have met him?"

"I won't go into the details of how we met. I wanted you to know that I'll be at

Cameron's side for a state dinner for the Russian president next Monday."

"You mean your picture's going to be on the news and in all the papers?"

"Possibly, but what's important here is that you keep me in mind when you protest President Thomson's visit to Ottawa next week and that you don't do anything stupid that'll get you arrested."

"What you mean, my dear sister, is that you wouldn't want the media to make the connection between the two of us. You don't want to be connected to anything potentially socially embarrassing."

"I'm simply asking you to keep a low profile. That's all. Don't get carried away."

Mike took another sip from his bottle.

Laurie continued. "I respect your right to protest, Mike, even if you don't believe that I do. All I'm asking is that you make an effort to not be too visible."

"In other words, allow Angry Andy to swing his mighty sword to let everyone know that America is somehow better than the rest of us? That it has all the rights? Let the Americans destroy our land with their—"

Laurie interrupted boldly. "That's only your perception because the media has blown the whole thing out of proportion."

"You mean what Thomson said was not the way he really feels?" Mike asked, his voice rising. "I see they've already converted you!"

"Mike, people say things in the heat of the moment all the time that don't necessarily reflect how they really feel. I'm sure President Thomson and Prime Minister Roy will find a middle ground that's acceptable to everyone."

"And, as usual, Canada will lose," Mike said. "We're wimps when it comes to international relations. How much do you want to bet that Roy caves in to Thomson?"

"What do you mean, cave in? The proposed base would be good for Canada. It'd create lots of jobs and stimulate the economy. We just have to make sure certain concerns are addressed," Laurie concluded.

"Yeah, the American concerns. You're talking like you're already an American. Makes me want to puke," Mike said, his voice once again loud.

"And you have a one-track mind," Laurie rebuked. "You want to protest next week? You want to get arrested? Go ahead. Be my guest. It's a free country, but I thought that you would want to take my personal concerns into account since I have been generous with you in the past."

"So that's it, is it? I owe you."

"Please stop it both of you," Eileen interrupted firmly.

At that moment the maid appeared at the door of the den to announce that dinner was served. "Will you be waiting for Mr. Danfort?"

"No, Marie. He can join us when he gets here," Eileen Danfort said. Once the maid had gone, she added, "Mike, Laurie asked you for courtesy. That's all. So let me make myself quite clear right now. If you and that girlfriend of yours get arrested, I will not be putting up the bail this time."

Mike stood up and eyed Laurie then Eileen. "Women stick together I see, but how do you know I'll get arrested?"

"You usually do," Laurie put in.

"Now, let's have a nice dinner," Eileen invited as Sarah came into the room.

"Hi, Uncle Mike," the girl said as she went to kiss his cheek.

"Hi there, Pumpkin. You're better all the time. I like that song you were playing."

"Thanks. I wrote it myself."

"Wow, that's great."

"Mom told you?"

Mike nodded.

"Maybe soon I'll be playing for the President at the White House."

Mike Gilbert unwittingly flinched.

"And you, dear brother, will be invited. You wouldn't want to disappoint your niece, now, would you?" Laurie asked.

CHAPTER SIXTEEN

Millie Spock, the executive housekeeper at Cameron Austin's residence, was making Laurie nervous as she hovered about in the bedroom.

"My orders are quite clear, Ms. Cosner. I have to make certain you have everything you need," she said, hanging the long white garment bag in the closet.

"I'm all right, I assure you," Laurie replied.

"May I look at the dress you'll be wearing to the reception in case it needs some attention after your long trip?"

"I'm sure it's okay," Laurie said patiently.

"If I seem to be meddling it's only because I'm quite excited," Millie explained.

"Thank you, Ms. Spock, but..."

"Call me Millie, please."

"Thank you, Millie, but why don't you give me time to get unpacked, then I can try on the dress? Come back in about thirty minutes, if you don't mind."

"Certainly," Millie said, disappointed at having to exit.

Laurie sighed deeply. She was certain the woman only wanted to help, but little did she know that Laurie who wore jeans more often than not was somewhat overwhelmed at the thought of having another human being helping her dress. Millie was used to people wanting things done for them. When Laurie wanted something done she did it herself. A clash of two worlds! Looking at the immaculate grounds beaming in the bright afternoon sun through the window, Laurie suddenly wondered where her rosebush had been planted. On her previous trip to Washington, she had never gotten around to finding out.

Laurie took time for a warm shower then opened the long bag in the closet. The black dress seemed none the worse for wear after her trip from Toronto. She pulled it out, spreading it on the bed just in time for Millie's knock.

"Oh, Ms. Cosner, what a beautiful dress," Millie exclaimed as she came in.

"You have experience in these matters, Millie. Do you really think it's an appropriate choice?"

"More than appropriate. I know the Vice President will love it."

"Were you here when Mrs. Austin was alive?"

Laurie saw that Millie hesitated for a moment. "Yes, I was. She was a lovely person, although I didn't know her for very long. She—"

"I'm aware of what happened," Laurie said softly. "But tell me, what kind of clothes did she wear? Would she have chosen something like this?"

Laurie was not sure what type of answer she expected nor the reason for the question.

"Mrs. Austin usually wore bright clothes. She loved red."

"I see. In other words this dress is a little too somber."

"No. It's classy. Very chic. Everybody'll be looking at you, I assure you," Millie said, trying to reassure Laurie.

Not because of my dress but rather because I'll be the new woman on the arm of the Vice President, Laurie thought sighing. After a moment when Millie did not move or comment, Laurie added, "Why don't I try it on?!"

"Let me help you," Millie offered.

After Laurie had slipped the dress on, Millie pulled up the back zipper then went around examining what seemed to be every inch of the silk skirt as Laurie stared at her reflection in the long mirror, fighting feelings of doubt about her choice.

"There's a little crease here in the back. I can have that pressed for you in no time," Millie said.

Turning around to see what the housekeeper had detected, Laurie was not convinced it needed attention. "That won't be necessary. There'll be other creases I'm sure once I sit down."

"It'll only take a moment."

"It's okay, Millie. Do you like it?"

"I think you look like a model, Ms. Cosner."

Laurie chuckled. "I wouldn't go that far."

"I would," the strong male voice said. Both women turned to see Vice President Austin standing in the open doorway. Neither had heard him. "You look sensational."

"Thank you," Laurie said, smiling.

"Excuse me," Millie said, closing the door behind her as she left.

Cameron Austin approached. "I want to kiss you, but I don't know if I should."

"You should," Laurie insisted.

Many minutes later, when he eased his embrace, Laurie asked, "I know my plane was delayed, but aren't you home early? Slow day at the office?"

"Not exactly. On my way back from the Capitol I decided on a detour to welcome you to Washington. Actually, I wanted to make sure you had arrived and that you hadn't changed your mind."

"I gave you my word, didn't I?" Laurie said, smiling. "In fact, I'm actually looking forward to Monday."

"Good. I was afraid you might be nervous."

"With you at my side, why should I be?"

He smiled at her and acknowledged, totally without reservation, that the woman in his arms had not only captured his heart, but his spirit as well. There was no turning back.

Laurie had spoken the truth when she told Cameron Austin that she looked forward to the dinner for the Russian president. She had willed her nervousness away over the past two weeks having decided that if the price for being at Cameron's side was to appear in public, she would pay it. Willingly. Happily.

However, she had failed to add that meeting Grace Winfield Austin was a totally different matter.

Wearing the classic black silk dress she had bought for her previous visit to Washington, she was putting pearl studs through her ear lobes to match the simple necklace around her neck and wondered what made her so apprehensive about having Sunday dinner with the older woman. Perhaps it was the personal nature of the meeting, and the fact that she, Laurie Cosner, would not only be assessed but also compared to the previous Mrs. Austin. There was no avoiding that element of family dynamics, something that would not enter the equation when she met Cameron's friends and political colleagues, even the President. They would barely give her a second glance after the initial meeting. Of that she was certain.

They would, of course, be pleased that the Vice President had someone in his life once again, wish her well, and go on to more important matters. When it came to Grace Austin, Laurie knew that she needed to charm the woman and wondered if she was up to it this beautiful spring Sunday. A knock on the door interrupted her thoughts.

"Hi," Austin said. "You look great. I like that dress."

"Thank you, Cameron. I didn't think you'd notice such things."

"And why not? I have good taste. Are you ready?"

"As ready as I'll ever be."

"Don't let meeting my mother worry you," he said, pulling her to him.

"I wouldn't exactly say it worries me, but rather that the thought causes me to hyperventilate."

For a moment he was lost for words.

"I'm kidding, Cameron," Laurie said smiling. "I'll reserve comment on your mother until I meet her."

Austin pulled her to him and kissed her cheek loudly. "My mother doesn't bite, you know."

"I assumed as much, but she might decide to rally the forces and drive me out of town!"

Austin chuckled. "I'll get my own forces and fight her!"

Laurie picked up a long white box from the dresser and slipped her arm into his as they stepped out into the hall. "On another matter, Cameron. You never showed me where the rosebush I gave you was planted."

"I'll do it now," he said.

They walked out together through the main door into the warm sunny spring day. Austin gestured to the agents waiting near the limo and, taking Laurie by the arm, directed her to the right. They walked over the impeccably maintained lawn until they reached a small mount near the house that she saw had been set aside especially for the rosebush not far from a variety of colorful perennials.

"I was told this was the perfect spot for it," Cameron commented.

"It looks a little lonely now, but you're right. It should grow well here."

"No one ever gave me a rosebush before. I'm looking forward to seeing the peach blossom," Austin said.

"Shouldn't be too long."

Holding hands, they made their way to the waiting limo in silence.

First Lady Barbara Thomson—affectionately, not pejoratively, known as Barbie because of her slim figure and rosy complexion—came into the den of the first couple's residence on the second floor of the White House. The President, seated on a comfortable sofa, was watching a baseball game on television. He didn't seem to notice that his wife had joined him.

"Andy, what would you prefer for dinner? Chicken or fish?" she asked, sitting on the opposite end of the sofa from her husband.

"Whatever. I don't really care," the President replied, not looking at his wife.

"Andy, when is this going to end?" she asked, a frown replacing her famous public smile.

"What are you talking about?"

"You know darn well!" Barb Thomson replied, anger in her voice.

President Andrew Thomson turned to look at his wife. "I'm going to be civil to you when I'm done being angry, Barb, that's when. Okay?"

"Andy, how many times do I have to tell you that I didn't mean it when I said I should never have married you? I was angry. That's all."

"That's not what I think," the President commented as he returned his attention to the game.

"Fine, if that's the way you want it. Did you ever think that maybe I was simply looking to get some attention?"

"For heaven's sake, Barb. We've been married for more than thirty years. I would think you would know by now that I'm not the type of guy to leave little notes on the pillow. My time is taken up by somewhat more important matters," he concluded, passion in his voice. "You knew the deal going in."

"Sure, but I guess I didn't count on being always last on the totem pole," she said getting to her feet. "I'll tell the staff we'll eat chicken," Barb Thomson snapped, making her way to the door.

"By the way," the President said, his voice more conciliatory. "Cameron told me he'll be with a woman at the reception tomorrow night."

The First Lady smiled. This was good news. "Who is she?"

"All he said was that she's not from Washington."

Well, well, Barb thought. Someone new to pal around with would be fun. And the First Lady was in an excellent position to warn the poor woman of the cost of high office on a marriage.

CHAPTER SEVENTEEN

*C*ameron and Laurie traveled to Maryland on a perfect day. The sun illuminated the newness of spring while Austin offered a historical perspective of the area.

Whenever he traveled to his mother's house he usually used the time to catch up on reading in the back of the limo as it sped on its way. Today, it was so much more pleasant to take the time to enjoy the afternoon and appreciate the beauty of his home state. He had made certain that the limo avoided I-95 so Laurie could see for herself what the area had to offer. The car drove a short distance from his house—his estate really if he were to be truthful—and for a moment he thought of showing it to her, but soon dismissed the idea. He would reserve that surprise for another trip, a weekend when nothing else was on the agenda.

When the Austin family mansion appeared on the right and the car traveled the long driveway, he knew Laurie was impressed.

"Wow," she said. "That's where you grew up?"

"Yes."

"Boy, are we from different worlds!"

He put a hand on her shoulder. "A real home has nothing to do with size."

"If you say so."

The door was held open and, stepping out, Laurie eyed the property and guessed it was comprised of at least three acres. The Georgian mansion stood on an impeccable jade lawn, manicured with utmost care. Around the house itself, the bushes and flowers had also been tended to by expert hands. There was a three-car garage to one side and tennis courts beyond it. Laurie was certain there was a swimming pool hidden by the three-story home.

"I'm absolutely amazed," Laurie commented. "Your mother lives here alone?"

"Not quite. Part of the house is used as a hotel of sorts. Because of what happened to my brother, mother makes rooms available in her house for children whose parents are injured by drivers under the influence while they recuperate."

"Very noble," Laurie commented, "but there can't be that many."

"You'd be surprised. But she also shelters children with parents in the hospital for a variety of reasons."

"She does it all herself?"

"She has people who handle the day-to-day details, of course," the Vice President replied, "but she does oversee things."

"Then your mother is probably not as much of a stuffed shirt as I presumed."

Cameron Austin was smiling as he took Laurie's arm and directed her inside.

"Mother," Cameron began after they embraced, "I would like you to meet Laurie Cosner. Laurie, this is my mother, Grace Austin."

Laurie smiled and extended her hand to the woman who, she decided, looked much younger than her years. No doubt a combination of good genes, expert pampering and the designer beige suit. "I'm very happy to meet you, Mrs. Austin."

"Thank you, my dear. At last Cameron has seen fit to introduce us," Grace said as she took the proffered hand. "Welcome. Please sit and make yourself comfortable."

Laurie thanked her and handed her the long white box she had been holding. "This is for you, Mrs. Austin."

"What is it?"

"Just a little gift from my greenhouse."

"Oh," Grace said opening the box to reveal a rose of such a deep red as to be the color of cherries. "It's beautiful. How thoughtful. Thank you."

"I'm glad you like it. It's a hybrid I've been toying with," Laurie said.

"Flowers are a hobby I take it."

"Not quite," Cameron said. "Laurie operates a wholesale rose business."

"But you told me she was a writer!"

"I am, Mrs. Austin," Laurie put in. "I combine the two."

Grace Austin eyed her guest for a moment and Cameron knew that she was impressed. His mother had never worked for money, but she was in awe of women who owned businesses. "Very commendable, my dear. Please sit while I take care of this beautiful rose."

"Let me do it," Cameron offered, taking it from his mother.

"Tell Lucia to put it on the dining room table," Grace told her son.

"Certainly," he said and disappeared.

Unknowingly Laurie chose to sit on the love seat Cameron called his own whenever he visited his mother, and gave the room a quick glance. She whistled secretly. The furniture was antique classic, and the walls were covered with impressive paintings. Knowing nothing about art, she didn't even dare an internal comment.

"So, Laurie," Grace Austin began after sitting in her usual chair, "how do you like Washington so far?"

"I love it. It's such a beautiful city."

"Like all the great capitals," Grace commented. "At least what the tourists see. The ugly secrets are hidden deep beyond the noteworthy buildings. I understand you live in a small community."

"McPine is a small town, yes. I adore it. The air is pure and people watch out for each other."

"And that's where your rose business is located?" Grace asked.

"Yes. My first love is writing, but I inherited the business from my late husband who was a horticulturist. I run it with his partner."

"I see," Grace said. "Coming to Washington must be quite a culture shock."

Laurie's lips went up into a half-smile. "Not really. I do travel."

"I'm sure," Grace said, suddenly well aware that the woman in front of her would not be intimidated, not by the Washington power elite and certainly not by the Austins. "However, seeing a city and living in it are two different things, aren't they?"

Laurie smiled before asking, "Without being impertinent, Mrs. Austin, are you trying to ask what my intentions are as far as your son is concerned?"

Grace Winfield Austin smiled back, not letting the fact that she had just been taken aback show. "Not at all, my dear. All I am saying is that

Washington is a city like no other, a city where politics are always front and center."

"Not today," Cameron Austin said as he reentered the room. "Laurie, what will you have to drink?"

Everyone agreed on wine, and the Vice President did the honors. He sat on the sofa facing Laurie thinking that this day she was absolutely radiant.

"Cameron loves to go up to your town but I regret to say," Grace began, "that I have never been to Canada, and I am a little ashamed of it. I nearly went once, years ago, when my husband had business in Toronto. However, the evening prior to our departure my mother suffered a stroke and I had to stay behind."

After taking a sip of her wine, Grace continued. "My friend Dorothy Mercer goes to Toronto regularly. Her daughter married a Canadian she met on vacation and now they have two lovely daughters, so Dorothy makes it a point to visit as often as she can. When she returns she tells me all about it. Dot and I have been friends since our school days," Grace found necessary to say. "She loves Canada and Canadian people. A few years back she recounted a rather amusing tale. Dot was visiting her daughter when she heard on the radio that the expected high for the day was twenty degrees. Dot began to panic because she only had light clothes with her until, of course, her daughter pointed to the fact that Canada uses the metric system."

"Using two different systems is certainly a bit of a problem for two countries who share so much," Laurie commented. "Americans not familiar with metric who drive up to Canada are a bit taken aback when they see that our speed limit for the most part is a hundred, until they realize it's not a hundred miles per hour. Just like the temperature does not change by forty degrees at the border."

"Having two different systems is especially problematic when it comes to doing business," Cameron Austin put in. "The conversion of pounds to kilograms for exporting to Canada can be an aggravation I hear often. The United States is one of the last holdouts in that area, and although I believe we should follow the rest of the world, realistically I think that moving away from the imperial system is still a long way away, even if some soda bottles are now sold by the liter. When we tested the metric system years ago all we ended up with was discarded signs. It's difficult to change public opinion about such an ingrained thing."

"Is our system a problem when you come into the U.S.?" Grace asked Laurie.

"Not really, because I remember the days before Canada switched to metric. Of course, many older people like my mother, for example, still think the old way, and since they account for a large portion of Canadians who travel to the States in the winter in search of a warmer clime, it's not a problem."

"You have been in our country many times before, I assume," Grace remarked.

"Oh yes. I drove down to Florida with a friend after college and we took many side trips along the way. I ended up staying in Florida for a while."

This was the first Cameron heard of this. Rogge made no mention of this in his report. He was suddenly curious and about to inquire further when Laurie continued.

"And after my husband passed away, my mother took me on a trip of the southwest, Las Vegas, California. I enjoyed it very much.

The maid announced that dinner was served, and Laurie let herself be guided into the elegant dining room where her dark red rose was displayed in an exquisite silver vase, no doubt replacing the centerpiece originally planned, she thought.

Soon Grace Austin was asking, "Are you aware, my dear, that Cameron is a favorite of the Democratic Party to replace Andrew Thomson when his term ends?"

"Yes, ma'am, I am."

"That would mean that if you continue to be at my son's side, you would be expected to share in his political life," Grace said before eating a forkful of tender greens.

"Mother, why don't we just wait and see what happens," Cameron said.

"I realize, of course, Cameron, that you have not been seeing each other very long, but one must always keep a watchful eye on the future," Grace replied amiably.

"I take it, Mrs. Austin, that you are worried that my being a Canadian would not be particularly well received," Laurie said.

"It's not the fact that you are a Canadian, my dear. Americans are fond of Canada and its people, even now with the war of words going on, but—"

"Mother," Cameron interrupted in a gentle voice.

Grace Winfield Austin smiled softly even if she was momentarily annoyed at her son. The subject needed to be discussed at the onset. The poor girl had to be made fully aware of the possible mountain of problems that her being from another country would bring to Cameron's campaign for the presidency. It was not something to be left to chance, and certainly not now that Grace was convinced her son was deeply in love. Others might miss the subtle signs, but she didn't. She had known him too long for that. Nonetheless, she would let the matter drop for now. There would be other days.

Laurie spoke. "I am aware of my lack of political experience, but if Cameron and I do live in the White House, it won't be the first time a Canadian does."

"You mean Chester Arthur, don't you?" Grace asked.

"Yes."

"I'm impressed by your knowledge of American history," Grace said.

"I did warn you, Mother; Laurie is not just another pretty face."

"Few Americans are aware of the real story there." Grace began. "Chester Arthur was born in Canada and not Vermont as records show. When the family moved to the U.S. he took on his dead brother's identity who had been born here."

"Of course, records in the 1800s were not what they are today," Austin said.

"Still, he was not American-born as your Constitution requires," Laurie put in.

"It is of little importance at this point in history," Grace said. "Besides, Arthur was only supposed to be the Vice President. The Presidency was thrust on him after James Garfield died after being shot."

"I realize that this couldn't happen today, but just for the record, I have not been lying about my background," Laurie said, smiling. "Since you've never been to Canada, Mrs. Austin, why don't you come visit McPine sometime, maybe next time Cameron comes up?"

"That's a splendid idea," Grace replied.

"I agree," Cameron said, unable to hide a sly smile. He could almost see his mother's surprised look as she went traveling down the main street of McPine. That's it? she would say. He decided to get the image out of his mind. "Mother, do you know that Laurie's daughter, Sarah, is a gifted pianist?"

"Really? How nice!" Grace replied enthusiastically. "I used to play myself, but these arthritic fingers," she added, briefly showing one of her hands, "won't let me. One of the pleasures of getting older. I'd love to hear her play."

"Perhaps someday," Laurie said, eyeing Cameron.

"Perhaps next time you come down," Cameron said hopefully. "I'm sure she'd love Washington."

"I'm sure she would," Laurie replied.

"Then we can look forward to your next visit," Grace said.

And that comment worried Cameron. His mother had probably already made up her mind that the daughter might be a good source of information of the type her son would not or could not share with her about Laurie. He loved his mother, but she could be cagey. He needed to warn Laurie, although he was pretty certain that she had already made up her mind about Grace Winfield Austin.

CHAPTER EIGHTEEN

Sitting in the back of the black vice-presidential limo, Laurie wondered if her decision to wear black this evening had been judicious. Although the sun had not yet begun its descent into the blackness of the universe, she was floating in a sea of black. The leather seats and everything else in sight in the luxurious vehicle was black including, of course, Cameron Austin's new silk tuxedo ordered specifically for the occasion. It was of the richest ebony.

While she loved her elegant perfectly fitting gown, Laurie had the impression that she was somehow almost invisible in black. She contemplated that perhaps the late Mrs. Austin's taste for bright colors had been acquired rather than innate.

"Are you okay?" Cameron Austin inquired. "You seem far away."

"I realize how little I fit into all this," she said with a sweep of her arm.

He took her hand. "Would you rather turn back? I would certainly understand."

"No, it's just that I wonder, for instance, what I can contribute to the dinner conversation sitting at a table with three senators whose combined political experience probably totals two hundred years."

"Senators have been known to talk about things other than politics," he said, squeezing her hand. "Besides, their wives will be there, and I know for a fact that all wives of senators have a God-given talent to steer any political exchange to more pleasant topics," he added smiling. "These people are all good friends of mine, and I am certain that conversation will not be a problem."

"What worries me is that I know so little about the U.S. and its history compared to most people in Washington. I probably know the names of most of your presidents over the past thirty years or so, but I would have trouble identifying the points of contention between democrats and republicans, for example. I consider myself reasonably well versed in your geography, but I would have problems naming all your state capitals."

"And why do you see this as a problem? I can assure you that you won't be subjected to a pop quiz! Remember what you said when we first met in McPine?"

"I said a lot of things, Mr. Vice President!"

"That Americans know little about Canada. That is the case even for some politicians. Believe me, everyone tonight will be terribly impressed by your overall knowledge of our country. I know I was."

Laurie smiled at him. He always knew what to say to make her feel better.

Soon the limo drew to a smooth stop under the north portico of the Executive Mansion, and Agent Lonsdale got out of the front passenger seat to open the back door as other agents slipped out of the escorting car. Vice President Austin took time to smile at Laurie. "Ready?"

"As ready as I can be."

"Did I tell you how stunning you look this evening?"

"Yes, Mr. Vice President, you did, but thank you again," Laurie said, smiling.

Austin stepped out of the vehicle and held out his hand. She emerged into the warm spring air smoothing the long silk skirt of her dress. She looked around briefly and saw that the late-day spring sun covered the grounds in a rich blanket of golden hues. A perfect setting for an outdoor reception, she thought. She would have so much preferred being outside where it would be easier to avoid the limelight spot. Or maybe it was just wishful thinking. With a sweep of his arm Cameron Austin invited her to step up and make her way inside the White House for the first time.

There was no going back now.

Cameron Austin felt proud of entering with Laurie at his side, but he also felt a little sorry for her. He knew it was a courageous act for the woman of McPine to step into his world of official receptions and all the attendant undertones. He tried to distract her a little.

"Do you know that this building was officially proclaimed as the White House by Congress in 1902?" he asked. "Of course it had already been its popular nickname for a number of years."

Laurie smiled nervously as a reply. Once inside she was surprised to see a small crowd in evening attire. "White House staff," Austin whispered under his breath. Laurie immediately recognized the White House Press Secretary who always appeared so self-confident and efficient whenever she had seen him on television. Laurie smiled as she heard Austin reply to the many "Good evening, Mr. Vice President," knowing full well that everyone wanted to be among the firsts to see for themselves who the Vice President had favored to be his official guest. Laurie knew that the Vice President's office had issued a simple memo to the White House staff informing them that he would be accompanied by a Canadian writer by the name of Laurie Cosner. "That's all they need to know for now," Austin had remarked as he had kissed her.

In a moment Austin was guiding Laurie up the stairs. "Doing okay?" he asked warmly, taking her hand and putting it on his arm.

She nodded and smiled.

"Good. Let's have a glass of champagne."

Together they stepped into a reception room in the private quarters of the first family where conversations were subdued. Laurie immediately recognized President and Mrs. Thomson talking to guests. Luckily no one seemed to have noticed the Vice President. Just yet, anyway.

Suddenly Laurie heard the distinctive voice. He was approaching.

"There you are Mr. Vice President," the President said as he came closer, the First Lady beside him. Addressing Laurie, he extended his hand. "Good evening Ms. Cosner. I'm Andrew Thomson. Welcome to the White House."

Laurie took the proffered hand. "Thank you, Mr. President. It's an honor to meet you."

"This is my wife, Barbara," Thomson continued.

"Good evening, Laurie. It's a pleasure to meet you," the First Lady said with a bright smile. She was dressed in a flowing off-the-shoulder ecru moiré gown which, Laurie thought, did look a bit like one of the outfits in the Barbie doll collection her daughter still clung to. "We must get together for a chat," Mrs. Thomson was saying as Laurie took in the huge single diamond that hung on a gold chain around the First Lady's neck.

"It would be my pleasure, Mrs. Thomson."

A waiter appeared putting a tray of filled champagne glasses in front of Laurie and Cameron Austin. Each took one.

"Cameron tells me you're a writer," the President said. "Are you famous?"

"Hardly. I have written a couple of books, but I write mostly magazine articles and I'm part owner in a rose business."

"That explains the beautiful brooch you're wearing," Barb Thomson commented.

"Oh," Laurie said, suddenly remembering the gold rose on the black lace of her dress. "It was a gift from Cameron."

"Nice," Barbara Thomson commented.

"I understand you're not from Washington," President Thomson said.

"No, sir. I'm from Canada."

Cameron Austin momentarily enjoyed the quick glance that went from the President to his wife and back.

"I assume you two met while Cameron was up there fishing," Andrew Thomson was saying. "What's the name of that place again?"

"McPine," Cameron Austin replied. "A beautiful area where the pines are majestic and the people wonderful."

"I'm sure," the President said. "Well, Ms. Cosner, it's always nice to welcome Canadians to the White House. Don't believe everything you read or hear on the news."

Laurie smiled. "I'm relieved. I was afraid you might consider me an enemy, Mr. President, and ask that I be removed at once."

"We're great friends of Canada, Ms. Cosner. We are both part of the great North American family. Nevertheless, occasionally family members have differences of opinion that need to be brought out into the open and discussed. And that's exactly what will happen when I meet with your Prime Minister this week. The United States has no intention of bullying anyone. After all, recent history—the one dictated by another administration—did teach us that trying to stand alone without our allies is a poor way to achieve our goals."

Sometime later, after Laurie had been introduced to members of the political elite on hand for the occasion, she realized that most of the women and some of the men in the room were glancing at her from time to time, smiling as soon as Laurie noticed.

"You realize of course that their interest is on high alert because you are the most beautiful and best dressed woman in the room," Cameron Austin told her.

"Most of these women are wearing exclusive designer gowns. My dress is off the rack."

"My point exactly," he retorted. "Good taste has nothing to do with money."

She beamed at him, glad that all this was happening. The nervousness she had felt earlier on was all but gone. She was happy. She was with Cameron Austin.

Before she could realize what was happening, Laurie was on Cameron's arm following the President of the United States and the President of Russia and their wives as the party made its way to the sumptuous state dining room with its gold-and-white decor. She could see that cameras were recording the event for posterity, and she was very much aware that she would be the object of comments all over North America within the next few hours. Just a few weeks earlier the thought would have been totally asinine, however now with Cameron Austin at her side, it seemed a very small price to pay indeed. She smiled her brightest smile.

Once seated around one of the impeccably set tables, she was thinking that the many American women who wrote to the Vice President offering to be his mate would be terribly disappointed, if not crushed. And the irony was that any of them would probably have felt more at home and prouder in this White House environment than she, a Canadian, ever could.

"I think Andrew Thomson likes you," Cameron was whispering in her ear.

Until he finds out I have a brother ready to take on the Americans, she thought briefly. Luckily she had no time to linger on what might happen in the next few days. She was introduced to the other guests at the table and the conversation took on a life of its own as the Russian-inspired meal was served. Laurie was pleased to answer questions about Canada and her rose business, and everyone seemed to hang on to her every word.

Later, after the President and Mrs. Thomson and their guests of honor danced, Cameron Austin and Laurie Cosner were in the limelight on the dance floor. "You realize of course that people are whispering about us," she told the Vice President, "probably wondering if I am good enough for you and if we've slept together."

Austin chuckled. "With such an overripe imagination, it's no wonder you write fiction. All they want to do is tell their friends tomorrow that they saw the belle of the ball."

"But they're also asking themselves if a Canadian is a wise choice for the Vice President of the United States."

"Let them."

"You don't mind what your peers think?"

"In politics, yes. I must take a variety of opinions into account, however when it comes to my personal life, that's another matter entirely."

"What if my presence here makes the Party reevaluate whether or not you are the best candidate to replace Andrew Thomson as President?"

"Some may, but I doubt it will have much weight one way or the other," Austin replied although he was not certain it was the truth. He would face that hurdle in due course.

On their way back to his residence at One Observatory Circle, Cameron Austin bent down to kiss Laurie's cheek. "Thank you for being at my side this evening."

"The pleasure was mine. I did enjoy myself."

"You wouldn't lie to me now, would you?"

"No, sir. It was an enlightening experience, and I got to see you on your home turf."

"Then you won't mind doing it again?"

"It would be an honor, although I hope it's not every week!"

He smiled at her. She was so frank and so charming. Would she ever consider being his wife, he now wondered?

Mike Gilbert and his fiancée, April McLaren, were enjoying a cup of coffee in her diner in Medford. "So, you're sure Thomson's arriving at eleven o'clock?"

"Yes," Mike replied. "They said on the news last night that he was coming in only in the afternoon, but that's just a ruse, the way things are done now to protect the President. That's what my buddy in Ottawa told me. Anyway, it doesn't matter since we're going to Parliament Hill. Thomson won't be there until the afternoon."

"There's going to be a hell of a lot of security people. We won't be able to get close to any of the action. I wonder if we should even bother going," April commented.

"Shit, April, what are you saying? I took time off so we could be in Ottawa as we've been planning. Did my sister call you?"

"No. You know Laurie doesn't like me. Why would she call me? Besides, she's been busy in Washington. When's she getting back?"

"I've no idea."

"I must say she looked beautiful in the picture in the paper. And what a beautiful dress! Is she going to marry him?"

"How should I know?"

"What the hell's wrong with you today, Mike? I only asked a simple question."

"Sorry, April. I've got a lot on my mind these days."

"What exactly besides our trip to Ottawa tomorrow?"

"Lots of things."

"I know what this is all about!" April exclaimed. "Laurie asked you not to protest in Ottawa tomorrow, didn't she?"

"What if she did?"

"I know you, Mike. That makes you want to go even more, doesn't it?"

"Yes it does, so please don't say you don't want to go," Mike said, his voice calmer.

"I was just thinking aloud," April said. "Of course we'll go. Everything's in the car; the signs, the masks."

"Good," he said, but he wondered if his mother had been serious when she said that she would not put up money for his bail if he got arrested. He and April would have no one else to turn to. But, Mike considered, she was his mother and she had made the threat before only to go back on her word.

The difference was that this time he had a nagging feeling in the pit of his stomach that the old lady had meant it.

CHAPTER NINETEEN

Neal Landau was enjoying a glass of ice tea on the shady lanai grateful for the warmth of another Florida day. A sixty-foot yacht was slowly gliding by on the Intercoastal waterway making him wish he could be on board instead of vegetating in his home day after day, no longer able to expand the physical exertion that would be needed. His doctor kept telling him not to lose faith, that new drugs were being tested all the time and that a real breakthrough which could save him was probably just around the corner, but Neal didn't believe the rhetoric anymore. He knew in his bones that he was sinking quickly and that the cocktail of drugs he had been taking for years now, adjusted from time to time by his physician, was no longer effective. AIDS was gaining ground and soon he would be just another statistic.

The thought of killing himself was crossing his mind more and more often these days. There was nothing to look forward to anymore. His family—two brothers—were rarely in touch. They were of the opinion that he had brought this predicament on himself, and they had their lives to lead and their own families to care for. As for his friends and colleagues, well they had disappeared into thin air when the music and the parties had ended. Who could blame them, Neal thought. Nobody wants to stand around and watch somebody else die.

And, worst of all, it had been so long now since he had last tried to write a song. He was unable to focus long enough for any inspiration.

What a tumble for a man who had written songs for the top vocalists in the country. It all seemed so long ago now.

He knew exactly how he would kill himself. The problem was that, no matter how dismal life was, the survival instinct could put up quite a fight as it had the previous evening. His doctor's words had flashed in front of him. Maybe there was a little bit of hope. And then he considered that he was more fortunate than many others in his condition. With the royalties from his songs, some of them now classics, coming in regularly and his insurance coverage which, thanks to Marty his shrewd manager, had included a disability clause, he was in a position to continue enjoying his home and the simple pleasures of looking at expensive crafts lazily making their way on the water.

Maybe tomorrow after he talked to his doctor, Neal told himself. Maybe then he would find the courage to end his worthless life. Right now, his wretched body told him he needed to lie down for a while.

Slowly, he made his way inside through the patio doors to the den that was now his bedroom, and at length, painfully, stretched out on top of the white coverlet on the hospital bed. He caught a glance of himself in the mirror and contemplated that he looked as if he could break like a dry twig if the slightest force was applied. The effort of going outside had tired him and he waited a few moments until his breathing stabilized before reaching for the television remote on the bedside table. There was always something on the tube. Maybe he could find a good movie that would distract him for a short while until Marty came. He was the only regular visitor these days. Of course he was paid for his efforts, but nevertheless it was nice to have a visitor.

Neal pressed a button and on the screen at the foot of his bed a talk show was just beginning. He decided to watch until the line-up of guests was announced. On previous occasions he had seen former buddies, now successful artists, being interviewed. Knowing that his songs had helped make them famous gave him a small measure of contentment.

The hostess was babbling on about everything and nothing for a while. Neal half listened as his eyes were closing.

"So what's the question everybody is asking today?" she inquired rhetorically. "Of course, there's only one question: Who was that lady on the arm of our handsome Vice President last night at the reception for the Russian president at the White House?" A picture of Cameron Austin and Laurie took up the whole screen. "My spies tell me," the hostess continued, "that the lovely lady's name is Laurie Cosner, and that she is a Canadian writer."

Neal Landau's eyes opened and he stared at the picture. Could it be? Hard to say. Same first name though. In a moment the picture had disappeared and the host was back on the screen. "My spies tell me that this could be the one! Wouldn't it be funny if they got married? I mean as far as I know it would be the first time a Vice President married a Canadian. I think it's so cool!" Neal turned off the set.

"Rosita," Neal called out as loud as he could. "Rosita."

"Yes, Mr. Neal. What can I do for you?" Rosita, a Mexican-American with a heart of gold who took care of his daily needs, replied as she came into the room.

"Can you get me the paper? I want to see something."

"Si. It's in the kitchen."

Rosita was back in a moment. "Look at this," she pointed out. "The Vice President's new girlfriend. It's nice, no?"

"Yeah. Nice. Thank you, Rosita."

Rosita left noiselessly and Neal stared at the large picture of the smiling Laurie Cosner on the front page on the arm of the Vice President. Could it be the Laurie Gilbert he had known so many years ago now? The lady in the picture was more mature, but it did look a lot like the Laurie Gilbert he remembered. He had thought about her lately while assessing his life, wondering and sort of hoping.

For now he would wait and see. There would certainly be other pictures of the pair in the media as time went on.

CHAPTER TWENTY

Sarah Cosner could hardly contain her excitement as she listened to her mother recount on the phone the highlights of the reception at the White House.

"I don't know about the other dresses, Mom, but you had to be the best looking," the girl said truthfully.

Laurie was touched. "Thanks, but as I warned you, people are going to ask you all sorts of questions at school. Do you think you can handle it?"

"Of course. I'll just say I don't know you."

"F-u-n-n-y! The media only knows that I am a Canadian. They don't know where we live, so they shouldn't bother you. Not yet, anyway, but you have to be ready."

"Mom, you worry too much."

"It's my right as a mother!" Laurie exclaimed.

"Okay. Well, I've got to go or I'm going to be late for school. Auntie Rita's hovering around. Talk to her," Sarah said.

"I'll be home tomorrow morning, so take the bus to McPine after school tomorrow."

"Okay. Bye," the girl concluded, handing the phone to her aunt.

"Start talking," Rita told her sister-in-law after bringing the receiver to her ear, "and don't you dare leave out a thing."

Laurie smiled. "I wouldn't dare. What exactly do you want to know? And can't it wait until I get back?"

"No," Rita replied emphatically.

Okay, Laurie thought, and proceeded to summarize the previous evening as best she could, including the fact that she had been impressed by the First Lady. "We're having lunch today," Laurie added.

"Really? Where? The White House?"

"No, actually she's coming here."

"Wow. You must have made quite an impression!" Rita exclaimed.

"Not necessarily. She might just want to get out of the house, if you know what I mean."

"The House! I get it! What about the President? What's he like?"

"Nice, actually. I was sort of expecting him to flip when he heard I was Canadian, but he didn't. Very diplomatic."

"So, what do you think's going to happen about that base?"

"Your guess is as good as mine."

"You'll tell me all about your lunch tomorrow?" Rita asked.

"Do I have a choice? By the way, did you see Mike around Medford lately?"

"He comes down most weekends these days, as you know, but no I haven't seen him. Why are you asking?"

"No reason. Just curious," Laurie lied.

"You figure he's going to be in Ottawa when President Thomson visits, and that worries you."

"Of course it worries me, but I can't do a damn thing about it."

"I'm sure he'll behave himself," Rita said halfheartedly.

After hanging up and calling her mother to share her happiness, Laurie sat back down on the large bed. Cameron had left some time earlier and would be busy all day, but he had promised to be home early so they could have a last night together before she left in the morning. Now she had to worry about the First Lady's visit. Laurie found it odd that Barb Thomson wanted to lunch with her. Perhaps, Laurie considered, it was part of the Washington protocol for the First Lady to size up Vice Presidential girlfriends.

There was a knock at the door and Millie Spock came in at Laurie's invitation.

"I would like to discuss the menu for your luncheon with Mrs. Thomson, Ms. Cosner, if it's convenient," Millie said.

"Of course. But you have more experience in these things than I do, so I'll leave it up to you. Is that okay?"

"If you wish, Ms. Cosner, but tell me, do you think a nice salad followed by a plate of salmon and fresh asparagus will be appropriate?"

"That sounds great, Millie. Thank you."

"For desert, how do you feel about a fresh fruit cup and a selection of cheeses?"

"Perfect."

"Thank you, Ms. Cosner," Millie said, turning on her heels.

"Excuse me, Millie," Laurie said, "but did Mrs. Thomson ever come for lunch here? I mean when Jean Austin was alive."

"Not that I recall."

The First Lady had made it quite clear that the lunch was to be an informal affair, so Laurie asked the housekeeper to set the table on the screened patio overlooking the garden. It would afford privacy while making it possible to enjoy the beautiful spring weather. Barb Thomson was obviously delighted with the decision.

"This is just great, Laurie. It's so seldom that I have a chance to eat informally outdoors," the First Lady said as she sat down. "It only happens when Andy and I can get away to our farm, and that's not very often."

"I'm glad you're pleased, Mrs. Thomson. Would you like a glass of wine?" Laurie asked, noticing men in black suits patrolling the grounds.

"That would be nice, thank you."

Millie did the honors. She had told Laurie it would be simpler if she took care of the service and Laurie had agreed.

"Cameron told me last night that you have a daughter?"

"Yes. Sarah's fifteen."

"I only had boys as you know, on their own now, but I think I would have liked a daughter. Girls are closer to their mothers than boys, aren't they?"

"I know I'm close to Sarah."

Lunch was served, and as they ate Barb Thomson asked, "So what do you think of Washington so far?"

"I love it. I was lucky to have a very knowledgeable guide explain the historic significance of the various buildings and monuments," Laurie said smiling. "Of course, I don't know many people yet."

"Washington is a one-industry town, my dear. Everyone eats,

breathes and dreams politics. It can be difficult for an outsider to fit in."

"In other words, I am bound to find it almost impossible," Laurie observed.

"All I'm saying is that it's the nature of the beast. Don't get me wrong, Laurie, I like you. I just think it could mean hurdles ahead for you and Cameron. As you may be aware, I have known Cameron for more years than I care to remember. I like him. He's a good man."

"No argument from me there."

"I was looking at him dance with you last night and I can tell he's in love. And I'm sure everybody else in the room reached the same conclusion. So, to get to the point, I simply wanted to warn you about two things. First, being married to a man who can only devote a limited amount of time to his wife is not always easy. Not that I'm complaining, but it can be a lonely proposition at times. As long as you know."

"I certainly appreciate your concern, Mrs. Thomson. That a relationship with Cameron is far from conventional goes without saying, but I'm a big girl. I have been a widow for a number of years now, so I certainly can handle being on my own. Also, since I'm a writer, I'm used to spending a lot of time by myself." Laurie took time for a sip of wine before continuing. "But, I have to point out that Cameron and I have been seeing each other for only a very short time. We are certainly not planning on getting married."

"Maybe so, but you have to be ready to face the facts head on, my dear," the First Lady said. "Cameron's work is bound to put a strain on any personal relationship, which you might find difficult should you decide to marry in the future."

"Forgive me, Mrs. Thomson, but I get the feeling that you are trying to dissuade me from dating Cameron."

Barb Thomson was taken aback. The woman in front of her would not be easily deterred whatever her plans. It was definitely to be admired. The First Lady rallied. "Not at all, my dear. I'm simply saying that it's a fact of life that a relationship with the Vice President of the United States would not be as simple as a relationship with, say, a horticulturist. I want to spare you grief."

"Again, I appreciate it. May I ask what the second point you wanted to make is?" Laurie asked amiably.

The First Lady smiled briefly. "If Cameron decides to seek the Party's nomination for the presidency, let me assure you that the campaigning is no picnic, and ideally the woman at his side should be well versed in the history and political landscape of America."

Laurie's lips went up into a half smile to hide her mounting annoyance. "I must tell you, Mrs. Thomson, that Cameron and I have not discussed his future plans. He may simply decide to leave politics behind and hide in McPine."

"Where?"

"The town where I live in Canada."

"I see. Do you mean to tell me that's a possibility?" Barb Thomson asked, a hint of alarm in her voice.

Laurie smiled. "I only meant to point out that nothing has been discussed or planned at this time."

"I understand," the First Lady said, "but I trust you appreciate that I only have your and Cameron's best interest at heart. I would hate to see him unhappy now that he has put the tragedy of Jean's death behind him."

So that was it, Laurie thought. She was being compared with the first Mrs. Cameron Austin, an American of formidable political acumen—if gossip of the previous evening was to be believed—who, from what Laurie had read, had been a great asset as Cameron had climbed the political ladder.

The White House was worried that a Canadian unfamiliar with the ins and outs of daily life in Washington might hurt the Party. Laurie considered that Barbie Thomson had been sent by the President and/or his advisers to find out what plans were in the offing, and perhaps gently scare her away so as to not upset the exclusive clique of the Thomson administration. No wonder the President had appeared to be the diplomat par excellence! He let his wife do the dirty work!

Screw all of you, Laurie thought. To Barb Thomson, she said, "Do you prefer tea or coffee, Mrs. Thomson?"

"Unfortunately, I'll have to pass on coffee because I have to get back for a meeting at the White House. I hope you'll forgive me," the First Lady said with a bright smile.

"I understand, of course."

"Laurie, it was a delightful lunch. Let's do it again soon."

Let's not, Laurie said to herself.

Long after her guest had gone and the lunch table had been cleared, Laurie was still sitting on the patio trying to determine whether or not she had been too harsh in her assessment of the First Lady's motives. It could very well be that the President, who had more important matters on his mind, had been totally unaware of his wife's lunch plans. Out of concern for the new kid on the block, Barbie Thomson may simply have wanted to caution Laurie that she was stepping into a totally different world and that she had to expect people would be keeping as close an eye on her as they would on a dog inside a church. And that was exactly what she was, Laurie considered. Entirely out of her element. It was bound to make Washingtonians nervous. If she continued to see Cameron Austin, could she find herself unable to support him in his aspirations?

Of course, there was the other side of the coin to consider. She was in love with the Vice President, that was no longer open to discussion, and therefore she was not prepared to let him go to spend the rest of her life alone in McPine. She had found love for the second time in her life, surely there would be no third. Sitting once more at the exquisite banquet of love, she could not simply get up and leave.

Every relationship has its challenges, she thought, *but they can be managed if those involved are ready to work hard. Just look at Robby and me. We didn't exactly start out on the right foot, and yet we certainly had a most successful marriage any which way you look at it.*

What she needed to do was to remove or at least lessen some of the hurdles on the road. She was a fairly intelligent woman; she could make up for her lack of knowledge by taking crash courses on the history of the United States and on its political process. And, the wives of the Senators she had met the previous evening seemed very eager to offer help in any way they could. They could be an interesting source of information with a welcome perspective.

And then there was Barbie Thomson. *Get to know her more*, Laurie thought. *Find out what's really going on. And wait to see where the chips fall*, she admonished herself, *before judging her and discussing any of this with Cameron.*

CHAPTER TWENTY-ONE

The temperature had been climbing nicely, but by late morning the charcoal-gray skies over Ottawa hinted at rain within the next few hours. A crowd of protesters of assorted ages, mostly youngish, was slowly gathering on the grounds of the Parliament buildings under the watchful eyes of a large elite force of armed security personnel, some standing behind a recently erected barrier, both camps eyeing each other suspiciously. Dressed in their eye-catching red uniforms, some Mounties on horseback were circulating around the area keeping a careful eye on the crowd. As many of the protesters were settling in with an array of equipment, from blankets and tarpaulins to gas masks and large banners decrying American intimidation, several cameras were recording their movements.

Both dressed in jeans and T-shirts, Mike Gilbert and April McLaren did not stand out in the growing crowd as they inched forward, chatting along the way with fellow activists they had met before or were meeting for the first time. There was always a marked spirit of camaraderie among the protesters, and today was no different. Some in the group, who had traveled from as far away as the west coast, were being praised repeatedly as news of their dedication spread. Mike shook hands with a couple of mature men who had left the U.S. for Canada at the height of the Vietnam War controversy and still considered the leaders of their country of birth untrustworthy.

After much fraternizing Mike and April finally settled on a spot close to the fence, just a little to the left of the main portal of the Parliament Building. That was where President Thomson was expected to be ushered in to address the House of Commons in the afternoon. April spread a blanket on the grass and pulled a thermos out of her large bag. Soon she and Mike were enjoying warm coffee and sandwiches as they settled in for a long wait.

After being accompanied on its trip from Washington, D.C. by two fighter aircrafts, Air Force One landed in Ottawa as planned at eleven o'clock. The American President emerged to be officially met on a red carpet by the Governor General of Canada, a handsome middle-aged man in a wheelchair, the tall and lanky fiftyish Prime Minister, Patricia Roy, and the gray-haired American Ambassador to Canada, as well as other top government dignitaries. A half-dozen Stars and Stripes were flying alongside red and white Canadian Maple Leaf flags.

Soon, a formal cortège of limos fitted with bulletproof windows was traveling to 24 Sussex Drive where the President and the Prime Minister were to have a private luncheon at her official residence. It was almost mid-afternoon when the two leaders emerged to face the media and make themselves available for photo ops.

The first question from a Canadian television reporter had been expected. "Madame Prime Minister, do you feel the United States is ready to acknowledge Canada's sovereignty over its own territory?"

"I believe," Prime Minister Roy replied, "that the United States has always respected our rights as a nation. Today, President Thomson and I have begun the process of looking at all possible options so we can work together in harmony. We have not reached any definite agreement, but by continuing to work hand in hand, I have no doubt that our two countries will find solutions to the issues now confronting us."

The next question came from an American journalist. "Mr. President, do you think that Canada should officially apologize for the verbal abuse to which the Americans have been subjected lately?"

"Canada and the United States are more than friends. We are part of the great North-American family," President Thomson began, "and as in any other family, there are bound to be differences of opinion. Words have been uttered that may have been misconstrued and exaggerated by the media," he emphasized with a short pause, "but make no mistake, relations between Canada and the United States have never been stronger. In the upcoming weeks we intend to work closely together to investigate every choice at our disposal to benefit both countries."

"A lot of words that mean almost nothing," Mike Gilbert commented to April McLaren as they listened to the press conference on their phones as many of the protesters were doing.

"Thomson's blowing a lot of wind up Roy's skirt," April said. "He wants to appease Canadians today, but he'll get his way as soon as he can shove his plan down our throats."

"Have you agreed on any sort of deadline to reach a decision?" an American reporter was now asking.

"No," President Thomson replied "because we don't know at this point where discussions between our two countries will lead."

"Bullshit," April commented out loud.

"Mr. President, can you tell us," a Canadian reporter asked, "how you feel about your Vice President dating a Canadian?"

Thomson chuckled. "I have no opinion on that. It is, after all, a personal matter between the two parties," the President replied.

Laurie Cosner smiled at the reply. She had just returned from Washington and was watching a news channel on the television set in her bedroom to see for herself how things were progressing in Ottawa.

Soon the two leaders were on their way by car to Parliament Hill. It was a cue for the protesters who had been waiting patiently to spring into action. Banners and signs condemning America for its autocratic vision went up. Television cameras were now beaming shots of the group, and Laurie scanned the picture looking for her brother's face. There were so many people that it was impossible to recognize anyone.

Police personnel, some in riot gear, who had also been waiting patiently, got ready. They had their orders. Canadians were free to protest, but the demonstration was not to get out of hand.

As the motorcade approached slowly, the activists became more vocal. The limo bearing the American flag rode up slowly behind uniformed policemen on motorcycles, and the fervor of the protest increased. The group began pushing forward against the barrier, but the Mounties on horseback on the other side made it clear that anyone trying to cross would do so at their own peril. The crowd stopped pushing but continued to shout as Secret Service personnel got out of a plain sedan ahead of the limo and circled it as President Thomson emerged. His arm went up in a wave to show Canadians he was not afraid of a little protest even if the noise was tumultuous.

Then, in a split second the shot was heard loud and clear. It had come from somewhere at the front of the crowd which began to scream as people fell to the ground. At that moment, as if the shot had perforated the clouds, a hard rain began to fall.

Secret Service agents pounced on President Thomson and pulled him away to safety inside the century-and-a-half-old structure that was the seat of Canadian government, while Prime Minister Roy was somewhat brusquely drawn inside by the security men in her detail. To their relief and that of other dignitaries milling about, both leaders were unharmed as were the special agents guarding them. As far as they could tell the bullet had gone astray.

The Canadian Prime Minister was full of apologies. "Mr. President, I deeply regret this incident, but I must point out that they may have been aiming at me."

President Thomson could only hope that was the case.

Outside, a special force of American and Canadian marksmen on hand for such an eventuality had been watching the crowd closely, paying special attention to the protesters nearest to the fence. Those in the front always seemed to be the most fanatical, the ones who could incite the crowd. As soon as the shot resonated, the men drew their weapons, scanned the front rows for any sign of the gun and moved forward jumping the barrier. All they could see in the rain was the fear that had taken hold of the crowd as people screamed and hid under jackets and blankets.

Like most of the protesters, Mike and April fell to their knees as soon as the shot was heard from very close by, pulling a blanket over their backs. April held on to two gas masks in case the police decided to use pepper spray on the crowd, something that could always be expected. The pair remained face down for a moment until Mike saw Al's wet face on the grass a few inches from his. Al had claimed a spot near Mike and April for the past couple of hours, and they had chatted about anything and everything. Truth be told, Mike saw Al as a little frightening, expounding at length as he did on the many ways the President and the Prime Minister could be killed. Mike had finally decided it was all bullshit.

"I did it," Al was suddenly proud to whisper.

Mike's and April's eyes widened in disbelief. "What? Are you nuts?" Mike retorted in a low cracking voice.

"Didn't aim at anything. Just wanted to scare the crap out of everybody," Al replied smiling widely as the rain hit his face. "Here's a gift," he said, slipping the gun out of a pocket and pushing toward

Mike who, before he could realize what was happening, had grabbed it by the barrel. "See ya," Al said, crawling away.

Mike and April looked at each other for half a second, totally stunned. Mike quickly shoved the gun under a corner of the blanket just as he saw menacing black police boots a couple of feet from him.

Not looking up, Mike whispered, "Let's get out of here."

In a low voice, April said with some alarm, "Your prints are on the barrel!"

Mike looked around. In the bedlam, many protesters were getting to their feet, shoving each other as they attempted to move away from the police. Mike moved his rear end to the corner of the blanket and, as well as he could manage with a hand under him, rubbed the barrel of the gun through the blanket. As one, Mike and April got halfway to their feet and followed the sea of protesters rushing away from the area, leaving the blanket behind and the police frustrated.

Laurie Cosner was now on the edge of her chair scanning the crowd on the screen of her TV set. She couldn't make out much of anything. People were running away, and the camera mostly caught the wet backs of exiting protesters. She had not seen either Mike or April, a good sign she tried to convince herself.

"It's now official," the announcer now on the screen said. "The bullet did not, I repeat did not, touch either the President or the Prime Minister, nor anyone in their entourage."

Laurie Cosner sighed deeply, realizing she had not been breathing since hearing the shot.

CHAPTER TWENTY-TWO

*V*ice President Cameron Austin, who was meeting with two senators, was interrupted by his secretary and advised that Roger Lancia, the White House Communications Director, was again on the phone. The first call an hour earlier, which had reached the Vice President less than two minutes after the shot had resonated in Ottawa, had been succinct in its description of the events. Cameron Austin now wondered if something else had happened.

"Sir," Roger Lancia told the Vice President, "to keep you informed of the events here in Ottawa, the police have recovered what they think is the weapon used in the attempt on the President's life. It was hidden under a blanket left behind by one of the protesters. They're running the prints on the gun and they're looking at the video of the crowd to determine who was standing in that spot."

"I appreciate being kept informed," the Vice President said.

Soon after the gun shot in Ottawa, Eileen Danfort called her daughter in McPine. "What do you think?" she asked as soon as Laurie answered. "Mike couldn't have done this, could he?"

"No, Mom, he's not that crazy and he doesn't own a gun. I wasn't able to spot him in the crowd. Did you?"

"No," Eileen answered. "There were just too many faces, but I had my PVR on so I could tape it and watch it again."

"You did? Did you look at it again?"

"No, but maybe next time you come down we can look at it together."

"Sure, Mom, but don't worry. Mike's never been violent," Laurie said, wondering if for some reason things had changed. Could April have suggested shooting the President of the United States? Nah, Laurie thought. That would have required more brains than the woman could claim.

After the call, Laurie walked down to the greenhouse, and found Bernie Wesson busy on the computer.

"Hi, there," he said. "I didn't hear your car. When did you get back?"

"A few hours ago."

"Saw you on the news. I guess you and the Vice President are an item now!"

"Well, we'll see where it goes," Laurie replied, aware of Bernie's disappointment.

"You did look great. Everybody's talking about you in town. You should have a press conference or somethin' so they stop calling and asking me questions," Bernie commented a little sarcastically.

"Bernie, let's put our cards on the table, okay?" Laurie said gently. "We've been friends for a long time, but it's never been serious between us, you know that."

He looked away for a long moment then said, "I guess I just wish things were different."

"I know, but you will meet someone who's right for you, and then you'll want to divorce Clare," Laurie said.

"What do you mean? That you weren't interested because I didn't divorce Clare?" Bernie asked, incredulous.

"I'm saying that you're the one who's never been quite interested enough in me to take that step. If you think about it honestly you'll see that I'm right. You couldn't commit fully to a relationship with me because it was nothing like the love you and Clare shared. I don't doubt for one second that you like me, but you don't love me even if you wish you did. That's what you've got to accept."

"Since when did you become a psychologist?" Bernie asked in a harsh voice.

"Feminine intuition, Bernie. Don't be mad at me. I'm only verbalizing what we both know is true."

"I'm not mad at you. You may be right, but then again you could also be wrong," Bernie said. "Anyway, I hope that thing with the Vice President works out for you. I mean that sincerely, and I know Robby would be pleased."

"Thank you. Now, how's business?"

Later when Laurie went to town to stock up on groceries in McPine, she was met with a barrage of questions from everyone she met. *Maybe Bernie had the right idea when he talked about a press conference,* she thought. Meeting people all at once would be easier, so she began to tell people that she would be at the tea room later to answer questions. "What a great idea," Annabelle, the postmistress, said. "I'll tell everybody."

And Laurie was certain she would.

As usual Sarah Cosner was met by Brandy barking with joy as she got off the school bus with her black duffel bag. The girl patted the animal's head and they walked up to the house together. Laurie was waiting at the door and the two embraced.

"So, how was school in the last couple of days?" Laurie asked.

"School was fine. If you want to know if people asked me questions, the answer is no."

"Really?" Laurie was both pleased and somewhat disappointed.

"When she saw you on the news, Aunt Rita cried! You did look great."

"Thanks. What were they saying about me?"

"I dunno, something like 'All eyes last evening in Washington were on the U.S. Vice President's girlfriend, Canadian Laurie Cosner.' Oh yeah, they said you live in Toronto and that the two of you met while you were vacationing in Washington."

"Well," Laurie exclaimed, "it certainly proves that you can't believe everything the media says!"

"My English teacher and the principal must have seen you because they asked me if it was really you."

"What did you say?"

"I was going to tell them no, but I figured they'd find out anyway. They said it was nice."

"Nice?"

"That's what both of them said. None of the kids asked me anything. I guess they don't watch the news. What's for dinner? I'm starved."

Laurie was back to her reality, and family life was resuming as simply as it always had. No claim to fame here, she thought, her mouth going up in a naughty grin.

Summer was approaching quickly and the evening air smelled of nature's newness as Laurie, her dog Brandy in tow, walked down to the tea room, leaving Sarah practicing at the piano. She laughed at herself as she walked, expecting that probably one or two people might show up to ask questions. This was not after all a White House press conference, but she realized how wrong she was when she opened the door to Adele's Tea Room. People from McPine were crammed in like green peas in a can, some sitting at the small tables, the rest standing. They began applauding as she walked in.

Laurie couldn't help blushing as she was greeted by the owner, a middle-aged woman of Irish descent with graying hair and the brightest of smiles. "I think ya do well to sit here," she said indicating a lone stool near the cash register. "That way everybody'll catch sight of ya."

Laurie couldn't believe her eyes. She had expected that a few of the women she knew best would show up, but this was a little ridiculous. Now that the stage was set, she had no choice but to give the people what they had come for. She sat down on the stool and quickly scanned the crowd, amazed to see that Bernie was sort of attempting to be inconspicuous at the back and that Esther Marsh of Green Lodge was sitting at one of the tables in the front. No doubt her husband Steve had talked to his friend the Vice President, but she obviously wanted the real skinny with the woman's point of view.

"I want to say," Adele began, "that speakin' for everybody here we're s-o-o-o happy for ya. And darlin' Robby, God bless his soul, must be smilin' up in heaven," she concluded, her eyes momentarily glancing upward. Everyone in the room applauded and Laurie felt like an idiot. But, she quickly reminded herself, these were kind people, generous people, even if they lived for anything that would bring excitement to their otherwise mundane lives.

Adele continued in her self-imposed role as master of ceremonies.

"How should we do this?" she asked then answered her own question. "Laurie, why don't ya start by tellin' us how it all happened, and when you're finished people can ask questions. Okay?"

Laurie nodded. She did not have a choice.

She knew that people were mostly interested in how and where she had met Cameron Austin, so she described their encounter near the covered bridge and her ensuing invitation to her house. She could see that people were hanging on to her every word. "Of course, I ask you to keep this tidbit to yourselves. It might prove quite embarrassing to the Vice President if it became known that he was driving alone without anyone guarding him in this day and age. And not understanding what kind of people live in McPine, the Americans might feel he should be removed from office for putting himself in danger. That would ruin his life. So please," Laurie implored, "don't discuss it, just like you don't discuss his visits up here."

There was a general muttering of: "Of course," "Goes without saying," and so forth.

"If, later on, anyone from outside asks you how Cameron Austin and I met, just say I never told you but that you know I took a trip to Washington earlier this spring."

Again the muttering. "Sure," "Good idea."

Then Laurie continued her description of the events that followed — skipping over the private details — ending with the reception at the White House earlier in the week. "And that's it," Laurie concluded.

"But you are seeing him again?" Esther Marsh asked.

Laurie smiled. "That's the plan, yes. He might come up for a weekend soon, but that's not sure yet."

"Are you going to get married?" Annabelle asked.

"Not even a thought at this point," Laurie said firmly. "We live so far apart! A long-distance relationship is always difficult."

"But you are in love?" Annabelle insisted.

Laurie smiled. It was time to be crafty. "I have to admit I like him a lot. That's the only thing I'm sure of right now."

Bernie who was looking at her from the back of the room had, she knew, seen through her lie. That was fine, she told herself. After all, it was more than time for him to move on.

"He's so handsome!" Chris, a forty-something second grade teacher, commented.

And there was group consensus on that point.

Laurie answered a few more questions that satisfied everyone. They could now go home, pleased in the knowledge that they knew exactly what was going on because they had heard it from the horse's mouth, so to speak.

As McPiners were slowly filing out of the tea room, Bernie approached. "You know I was only kidding when I said you should have a press conference."

"Must have been a great idea, you're here," she pointed out.

His mouth went up into an easy smile. "Got to know what goes on around here. Good night," he said, bending to kiss her cheek.

It was eleven on the dot when the telephone on her bedside table rang. "Got home okay?" Cameron Austin asked.

"Just fine, thank you. How are things in Washington? I mean after today's incident in Ottawa."

"As you can imagine, people were upset for a while, but everyone is now noticeably calmer."

She had to ask. "Do they know who did it?"

"I understand the police did recover nice fingerprints off the gun and have identified the owner. I'm told he has been arrested several times at similar rallies."

Laurie was no longer breathing.

Austin continued, "It's certainly only a matter of time before he's captured."

Laurie took some air into her lungs, and said, "Just so you know, Mike did go to Ottawa today," she said.

"I figured he would. He has a right to voice his discontent with this administration."

"That's very generous of you, Cameron."

"Not at all. I firmly believe that to be effective, the government has to be challenged so it can look at itself clearly, even if the challenge comes from your brother."

"I must say you seem more accepting of Mike today than you were when we first met," Laurie said.

"When we first met my men investigated quickly and warned me that your brother had been arrested and in jail on more than one occasion. Not having all the details, I was cautious. That was then, this is now."

"Cameron," she said, "I'm very sorry a Canadian attempted to kill the President."

Gone were the smart repartee about gun control. She was acknowledging that evil can show up anywhere at any time. "I will pass on your message to the President personally," Vice President Austin said.

CHAPTER TWENTY-THREE

When Laurie heard a car driving up her long driveway, she peered through her office window and was stunned to see her brother Mike. She quickly ended her phone conversation and rushed to the front door.

"Could I talk to you for a minute?" he asked after greetings were exchanged and he had petted the dog.

She offered him coffee, but he declined. His body language told her that whatever he had to say was difficult to put into words, so she took the lead.

"I take it you were in Ottawa yesterday when the commotion broke out?"

"Yeah. I went with April."

"Did you see who shot the President?"

"No, we didn't."

"So what's the problem, Mike? You're not the one who fired that gun, are you?"

"Of course not," he said, offended. "You know I don't like guns."

"I know."

"Here's the thing, Laurie," he said, looking at his hands for a moment. "I swear to you I didn't see the shooting, but seconds after it happened, when everybody got down on their knees, this guy, his name is Al, he was beside April and me all the time, said he had done it. He took the gun and gave it to me."

Laurie felt a momentary odd spasm somewhere in the region of her heart.

"I took it by the barrel and shoved it under our blanket. I tried to smudge my prints through the blanket then April and I hightailed it out of there. We left the blanket behind." He was looking at her squarely now. "You understand that I had nothing to do with the shooting. This idiot just shoved the gun towards me because he didn't want to be caught with it. I don't know how successful I was at smudging my prints."

Laurie felt suddenly quite frightened.

Mike continued. "I wanted to tell you exactly what happened because of the cameras on the Parliament building. The police may see us near this idiot."

"They can't arrest people just because they were standing near the guy."

"In principle, no, but what if they don't know who he is?" Mike asked.

"I do know they got good prints off the gun. I just don't know if they were yours or your friend Al's."

"How do you know this?"

"I have sources in high places," she replied smiling faintly.

He smiled back nervously. "I was mad at you when we were at mom's place, but you know I'm happy for you. That you found someone, I mean."

"Thanks. But what are you going to do now?"

"D'you think I should go to the police? I mean, I want to do the right thing, but is there any point in putting myself out there?"

"I don't know what to tell you," Laurie said, wondering if the media would find the family connection were he to go to the police. And, as he had pointed out, since in reality he was only a bystander, was there any reason for her brother to bring attention to himself until they could both find out whose prints had been identified?

Mike was also pensive for a long moment then said, "I would prefer not saying anything at this point, and April thinks whatever we say wouldn't help the police anyway. It would just complicate things. What d'you think?"

"I tend to agree," Laurie replied. "Of course, if you go repeating this to all your friends, the police may want to talk to you."

"We didn't say anything to anyone. April's actually quite scared that we could be charged as accessories to the attempted murder of the President or some such thing."

"If you haven't done anything, they can't charge you."

"With all the laws that were passed to fight terrorism, who knows! I mean, attempting to kill a head of state is a serious offense compared to what we've been arrested for in the past. Hell, we're pacifists. We don't go around harming people no matter how much we disagree with them."

"I know. Let's not lose our heads here, Mike," Laurie said. "Keep this thing under wraps for now and let's wait and see what develops. Just don't talk about it. I'll try and find out where the investigation stands and I'll let you know. Okay?"

"Okay," he said sighing slightly.

The lead story on the all-news channels that night was the shooting in Ottawa which was examined and explored from every possible angle with footage of the American President and the Canadian Prime Minister being rushed away, and shots of the chaotic crowd scene chronicled seconds after the gunshot. Unfortunately, the clarity of the picture was limited by the rain. This, as expected, was followed by an analysis from a variety of law and security experts. At one point a representative from the Attorney General's office discoursed on the problems the assassination of an American President on foreign soil could generate for that country. All the while Laurie was hoping to be able to locate Mike and April in the sea of people in front of the Parliament building, but she did not succeed. The camera shots were generally too wide and the fence hid the faces of some of the people standing close to it.

She was about to turn off the set when a news bulletin came on. "We have just received word," the anchor began, "that a man has been arrested in the attempt on the President's life in Ottawa today as he was crossing the border into the United States. He has been identified as Alan Needham, a thirty-five-year old man from Buffalo, New York. The statement indicates that he is an American citizen and a veteran with a history of mental problems. No other details are available at this time, but we will keep you informed as the story develops."

Laurie sighed, deeply relieved. She called April's diner in Medford. Mike answered.

No, he told her, he had not been listening to television.

"You no longer need to worry," she told her brother, and proceeded to relate the news bulletin. Mike and April could now breathe easier. She could breathe easier.

She smiled as she hung up. An American was the culprit! That meant she could continue to hold her head high in the company of the elected elite of Canada's neighbor to the south. And that was the point she made later to the Vice President when he called.

"Even if a Canadian had fired at the President, why would anyone have blamed you?" Austin inquired.

"Perhaps not personally, but by association they could validate the contention that a Canadian invading the high echelon of Washington society can only mean trouble."

"Why have you got such a complex?" the Vice President asked.

"I don't have a complex."

"Seems to me you do," he said lovingly. "You're always making excuses for the fact that you are not an American."

"I didn't realize I was. All I'm saying is that if a Canadian had fired the gun in Ottawa, the Americans would have been pretty pissed off. In a way, I'm glad that this criminal act came from someone on your side of the border."

"So what you're telling me is that it proves your theory about Americans being violent."

"Easier access to guns, Cameron, that's all. Being deranged and mean knows no boundaries that I'm aware of. By the way, do they know where this fellow, Al, got his gun?" Laurie asked.

"Apparently it was his gun. And knowing how you think, I can only agree with you. He should never have been allowed to own a firearm. By the way, I expressed your regrets about the incident to President Thomson on his return to Washington. He was touched. Now, let's talk about more interesting things, shall we?"

"Let's," she echoed.

CHAPTER TWENTY-FOUR

Sarah Cosner could have been an advertisement for happy teenagers everywhere. School was all but out for the summer and her fingers were dancing on the white and black keys of the piano as she fine-tuned her own lively composition barefoot, as was her habit. The notes and the lyric transported her to a world without limits where creativity and joy reigned.

The sounds reached Laurie in her office and her ears perked up. The song being rehearsed was spirited, and Laurie could only hope that one day her daughter would be recognized for her special ability to marry notes and vocals. That was in the future. For the moment Laurie was proud that Sarah would be displaying her talent at a school concert the following day. Teachers had arranged the evening to give gifted students the opportunity to be showcased. The program indicated some young people would, among other things, sing, dance, recite poetry they wrote, play guitar, and the piano. Sarah would be the last performer of the evening. "Perhaps she will be asked to give an encore," Mrs. Bradley, the school's music teacher, had told Laurie with assurance. If it were the case, Laurie knew that the song she was listening to now would be given its first public audition.

The music ended and Laurie joined Sarah in the living room. "I like that song more and more, Sarah."

"Thanks," the girl said as she slipped her feet back into her sandals.

"All set for tomorrow?"

The girl shrugged her shoulders. "I suppose, but I'm a little nervous about performing in public."

"You've done it before," Laurie remarked.

"Sure. In front of the class. That's not the same as a whole bunch of people."

"If you want to—"

The girl interrupted. "If I want to be a serious pianist, I'd better learn to play in public! I know, Mom. They say all great artists are nervous before a performance so I'm just normal. Or great!"

"That's the spirit!" Laurie commented, pleased at her daughter's levelheadedness. "I just got off the phone with your grandmother. She and John will be in the audience. Your uncle Mike's not sure he can make it, but he said he'd try to get off work early so he can drive down."

"Good. Is Grandma going to stay here?"

"No. She wants to visit old friends in Medford, but she'll be coming for lunch on Saturday."

"Can you teach me to drive?" Sarah asked suddenly.

"What brought this on? You're only fifteen," Laurie pointed out.

"Yeah, but I'll be sixteen in a few months. I should start learning."

Laurie eyed her daughter, understanding her desire to be independent. She knew that if Sarah could drive she would jump in the car and drive to Medford to be with her cousin, Emily, and other friends from school instead of spending evenings at home with her mother. McPine had been a great place to raise a girl, but now that she was gracefully maturing into young adulthood, Laurie wondered once more if it was not time to give her a chance to be part of a larger world. How would she feel about living in Washington? Was it too soon to discuss that point with Sarah? Better start with driving lessons.

"You're right. We'll try a short ride this weekend," Laurie said.

"Thanks, Mom," Sarah said, stopping to hug her mother before flying up the stairs to her room where she would no doubt be on her phone for a while.

Laurie had wanted to tell Sarah about the possibility of Cameron Austin being at the concert if he could manage to get away early and spend part of the weekend in McPine, but it was only a possibility at this stage so why make the poor girl more nervous than she already was.

The concert was scheduled to begin at eight o'clock on Friday evening, the last day of the school year. Laurie was to meet her daughter in Medford by late afternoon and treat her to dinner, but by mid-afternoon she was dawdling around the house hoping to get a call from Vice President Austin. He had promised to let her know what, if anything, he could arrange for the weekend by calling her at home. He did not want to call her cell phone because it might be a lack of security, he had said.

Now she was a little baffled since he had failed to call the previous evening. She wondered if anything was wrong and wanted to call even if it intruded on affairs of state, but reason prevailed. The only thing she could do was wait, a part of the relationship that was not especially ideal. After checking the time on her watch one last time she decided she could no longer tarry. Her daughter now took precedence over everything else.

After dinner, Sarah changed into a plain short black skirt and a short-sleeved white top interwoven with discreet shimmering silver threads. With the full head of black curls, Laurie thought her daughter looked like an angel. "You look great," she told her proudly.

"Thanks. See you in a bit," the girl said hurrying out the door with her cousin to be at the school in plenty of time for the concert.

"I hope you're proud," Rita Payne told her sister-in-law as she poured two cups of coffee at the kitchen table.

"That I am."

"So, is he coming this weekend or not?" Rita asked.

"I guess not. I mean he hasn't called. He has other things on his mind and I simply have to accept that that's the way things are going to be," Laurie said a little sadly.

"But you two make up for it when he's around, don't you?" Rita asked smiling, momentarily touching her friend's hand.

It made Laurie think that Robert Frost put it best when he wrote that happiness makes up in height what it lacks in length.

That evening the parents of those who would be performing had reserved seats in the front. After noting exactly where the piano was on the stage, Laurie chose to sit at the end of the second row on the right, some distance from her mother, Eileen Danfort and her husband, John, who had claimed seats smack in the middle. Laurie wanted to have a clear view of Sarah's face rather than her hands on the keys. Rita Payne was in the next seat.

Soon the lights dimmed and the evening's entertainment was

underway. Mrs. Bradley walked on stage to offer words of welcome before proudly introducing the first performer, a teenage boy with an obvious talent for the guitar which he played with the gusto of youth. As his song ended, the audience burst into applause as it did for the other talented teenagers that followed, each taking a first step toward artistic excellence.

About midway through the program, there was a short break to allow time for the school's choir to properly assemble on stage. Both impressed with the quality of the performances, Laurie and Rita were discussing their favorite so far when Laurie recognized Agent Lonsdale's face at a side exit door that had opened slightly. She stopped talking mid-sentence.

"Someone you know?" Rita whispered.

Laurie nodded. "One of his agents."

"So he did come after all. Go," Rita urged. "I'll be okay."

"Don't say anything, please," Laurie said.

"I can keep my mouth shut," Rita said, feigning being insulted.

"Good evening, Ms. Cosner. He's in the back of the hall and would like you to join him," Lonsdale said simply after Laurie had stepped out into the corridor.

Laurie's lips went up into a bright smile.

"We'll wait until the choir begins to sing," Lonsdale was telling Laurie as they approached the door at the back of the hall. A few people were going back in and eyed Lonsdale a little suspiciously.

"Not too many non-Caucasians in this part of the world, I'm afraid," she whispered.

A few moments later they heard the voices of the school choir, and Lonsdale held the door to the hall open, pointing to the right. Agent Dunlop who was standing against the back wall nodded ever so slightly. Then she saw Austin listening to the choir from the second seat of the back row and smiled at the blond wig and short matching beard. She approached and quietly slipped into the aisle seat. Vice President Austin smiled, took her hand and brought it to his lips, then held it firmly as if afraid that she would fly away. The voices of the choir were superb. *All is right with the world*, Laurie thought.

As the audience applauded, Austin asked, "How long before Sarah comes on?"

"She'll be the last one. I like the look," she whispered.

"Thank you. I had a good teacher," he said smiling briefly, then added, "I would prefer not hanging around here too long once the concert is over. I was thinking of slipping away and meeting you back at the lodge."

"You talked to Steve Marsh and didn't call me?"

"I wanted to surprise you."

"You did," she said. "Can we meet at my house?"

"If you prefer," he said, squeezing her hand.

Before long Sarah Cosner was introduced and walked on stage. Cameron Austin was struck at how much she resembled her mother, except for the black curly hair. The girl sat at the piano and waited a moment for the audience to go totally silent. She slipped her feet out of her sandals, and her fingers began to play the notes of Mendelssohn's *The Evening Star* with mastery and passion. Cameron Austin was speechless as he took in Sarah's obvious talent. Beside him, Laurie wondered how she could ever feel prouder of her daughter.

The applause was thunderous. Sarah slipped her sandals back on and stood up to take several bows. The audience, including Cameron Austin, showed no sign of weaning, so Mrs. Bradley came out again. "Ladies and gentlemen," she began as she signaled for people to quiet down. "We're all very proud of Sarah, and I know that as a special treat she would like to perform a song she has written herself. So, ladies and gentlemen, once again, Sarah Cosner."

As the new applause subsided, the girl sat down again, this time forgetting about slipping off her sandals. She pulled the microphone that had been resting on top of the piano to a proper level and her fingers sprang into action. In a moment she had the audience mesmerized with the notes and vocals of her ballad. The Vice President held Laurie's hand in his while she read the happiness on her daughter's face. Motherhood did have some tremendous rewards.

When it ended and the crowd resumed its roaring applause, Cameron Austin got up and slipped quietly away with his men. Laurie didn't look back as she continued to clap. She then began moving towards the front but was stopped many times along the way by other parents and acquaintances who wanted to congratulate both her and Sarah. One of them was Bernie Wesson who was full of praise. Laurie thanked him and invited him to her house for a little celebration.

When she was finally able to meet up with Rita and her mother and stepfather, the group went backstage where they found Sarah in quiet conversation with a tall lanky boy who was, Laurie remembered, a member of the school choir.

Mother and daughter embraced amid congratulations from everyone in the party. "You were just awesome," Laurie said.

"Thanks. Mom," Sarah said, "this is Neil McTavish."

"Hello, Neil," Laurie said, extending her hand. "Any relation to Roger who owns that large farm on route 10?"

"He's my uncle, Mrs. Cosner."

"So you know where McPine is then?"

"Of course. I go there all the time," the boy replied, sneaking the fastest of looks in Sarah's direction.

Laurie was a little taken aback as to why she wasn't aware of this.

"As a matter of fact, I'll be working on my uncle's farm this summer," Neil was saying proudly. "Better than flipping burgers."

"Certainly is," Laurie commented although she was not sure she liked this turn of events.

Rita Payne embraced her niece warmly. "I'm so proud of you. Just as your dad would be. I'm sure he was watching."

Sarah thanked her aunt and introduced Neil all around. Then Eileen Danfort said to Sarah, "My dear girl, we have to talk about finding you the best music school in the world, nothing less will do."

Sarah smiled broadly. "Thanks, Nana, but I think mom wants me to finish high school before making music my life."

"You've got that right," Laurie added. "But right now we have to celebrate. Let's go to my house. You too, Neil."

The boy was quite pleased.

"Thank you, Laurie," Eileen Danfort put in, "but it's been a long day for John, and since he drove here, I don't think he wants to go all the way to McPine. I thought we could go to a restaurant here in Medford."

"Mom, things have changed and it's less than a half-hour drive," Laurie pointed out.

"What has changed?" Eileen wanted to know.

Laurie took her mother's arm and pulled her aside. "How would you like to meet the Vice President of the United States?"

"He's here?" Eileen said, incredulous.

Rita approached. "I'd be very pleased to drive you and your husband to McPine and bring you back. I don't know about you, but Emily and I don't want to miss out on the fun."

Eileen Danfort smiled a contented smile. "What are we waiting for? Let's go!"

CHAPTER TWENTY-FIVE

Brandy was wondering what all these people were doing at the house at the same time. The animal was ready to crash for the night and oddly everyone appeared to be in a party mood. After enjoying being petted by a bunch of different hands the dog went to lie under the piano in order to keep an eye on things.

Sarah was helping her mother prepare drinks in the kitchen. "So, what do you think of Neil?"

"He seems very nice. Anything serious?"

"Mom, I'm fifteen. We're friends."

"Why didn't you ever tell me about him?" Laurie asked.

"Because there was nothing to tell. Let me get that," Sarah offered, taking a tray of glasses from her mother.

"Sarah, Cameron was very impressed with your performance."

"You already told me in the car."

"Well, it bears repeating. However, to get back to Neil, he knows he can't brag about meeting the Vice President, right? I mean you discussed it with him?"

"Yes, Mom, he's cool. He won't say anything."

Just then the doorbell rang. "Well, here comes our guest of honor."

But it was not. Agent Lonsdale was standing in the doorway. "May I have a word? Outside."

Laurie stepped down, closing the door behind her, aware that all eyes inside were darting in her direction. "Problem?"

"The Vice President is confident no one in there poses any sort of threat."

"Of course not, they're my family," Laurie retorted a little stiffly.

"I'm only doing my job, Ms. Cosner. A man came in a short while ago. Who is he? Your brother?"

"No, Mike isn't here. That's Bernie Wesson, my partner in the rose business."

"I see."

"Agent Lonsdale, may I repeat what I said to you before. This is McPine. There are no terrorists here. And may I point out that only the people inside know that the Vice President is visiting. As you are aware, I made certain the media believes I live in Toronto. I know you work in a world where you must anticipate danger at every turn, but please relax while you're here."

"My thought exactly," Cameron Austin said as he approached, the collar of his white shirt open under a light-weight blue blazer. He had removed his disguise and Laurie thought he looked relaxed.

"Agent Lonsdale, please feel free to join us inside," Laurie invited.

Agent Dunlop stepped from the darkness into the glow of the porch light and, with Lonsdale, followed Laurie and the Vice President inside. Dunlop remained by the door, and Lonsdale made his way to the kitchen as the guests watched.

"I'm sorry about that," Austin told Laurie once the door closed.

"Not a problem. Are you in the mood to meet people?"

"Of course."

The group in the living room had stopped talking as they waited. Upon entering the room, Laurie took the floor. "As you all know this is Cameron Austin, the Vice President of the United States. He attended the concert this evening, but stayed in the back of the room for obvious reasons. The two men there," Laurie said pointing to Dunlop and Lonsdale, "are Secret Service agents charged with protecting our guest, and there are more men outside. Now, let's get to personal introductions."

Laurie introduced Sarah first. "You are one talented girl," Austin told her. "I have a feeling this is only the beginning."

Sarah blushed. "Thank you, sir."

"I would like to arrange for you to play for the President and Mrs. Thomson when you come to Washington. What do you say?"

"That'd be cool," was all Sarah could manage to say as her color deepened.

One by one, Laurie's guests were introduced to the Vice President who demonstrated his social charm with a special word for each. He praised Eileen Danfort on her family, and she was so delighted that Laurie thought for a moment her mother might faint. When Bernie Wesson was introduced, Austin was full of compliments for *Only Roses* and the rosebush now growing on the grounds of Admiral House, the first Bernie heard of that. And when Rita Payne shook Austin's hand, Laurie was amazed that her friend seemed to be giggling like a school girl meeting a rock star; quite a contrast to the two teens, Neil and Emily, Sarah's cousin, who both appeared in total control as they shook hands with the Vice President.

Soon everyone began to relax and the conversation was easy. John Danfort talked to Austin about some of the high-profile Americans he knew because of his many business interests, and the two men were mutually impressed.

"How long will you be here?" Eileen Danfort asked Austin.

"Just until late tomorrow. Unfortunately I have to be back in Washington for Sunday morning."

"Pity," Eileen said. "I would have loved to have you dine with us."

"How very kind. How about a rain check, perhaps the next time I come up?" Austin asked amiably.

"Cameron, you know that my mother lives in Toronto," Laurie put in.

"That's where you live as well, is it not?" the Vice President asked winking at Laurie, and everyone laughed.

Later Sarah approached her mother, pulling her aside. "That man in the kitchen keeps looking at me in a funny way."

Laurie chuckled. "Lonsdale's just very impressed. He saw you play tonight."

"I don't like him. Neil and I are going for a walk."

"An agent might follow you," Laurie said.

"What! Why?"

"Sarah, I'm sorry, but it's all part of the game. Why don't you stay here? It'd be easier."

The girl was clearly annoyed. "Are these men going to be around all weekend?"

Laurie could only reply, "Afraid so. You like Cameron don't you?"

Sarah replied sincerely, "He's nice."

"Well, he's quite taken with you, and you know that I care deeply for him. I spent a lot of time debating with myself the cost of my relationship with Cameron on you, and when we talked about it you seemed ready to accept all these little inconveniences," Laurie remarked.

"Yeah, I know. It's just…"

"Just what? You didn't think it would be so…real?"

"Something like that," Sarah said.

"You know, when you come to Washington with me in a couple of weeks, there'll probably be an agent with you all the time," Laurie said, although it was doubtful.

"Really? Me?"

Laurie put an arm around her daughter's shoulders. "Think about it, it's kind of cool, isn't it? I mean who else do you know who's in the same boat?"

Sarah smiled. "If I can't go for a walk, can I at least go and stay at aunt Rita's tonight? I'm sure you'd prefer being alone."

"So you can spend more time with Neil?"

"It's a fair trade," the girl said.

I suppose it is, Laurie thought, lifting an eyebrow.

Cameron Austin was admiring the vista spreading before him like an exquisite carpet. Despite the early hour, the golden sun of early summer was beaming warm rays on the countryside, and the waters of the lake below him appeared to be a rich mixture of blue and green amid the tall pines. On a rock protruding out of the water not far from the shore, a lone great heron, immobile in a statuesque pose, was waiting to prance on an interesting prey.

The Vice President contemplated that he could be tempted to leave his busy governmental world behind for a simple effortless life where time was not a seldom-experienced luxury but rather a sweet fruit savored daily in the bounty of nature.

Carrying a pot of freshly brewed coffee Laurie Cosner joined him on the deck and filled the two mugs resting on the round table shaded by a bright green umbrella. She was wearing navy shorts and a white T-shirt with a large pink rose on the front. Austin liked the look.

"Thinking about your past sins?" she asked.

"Not quite. I was admiring the view."

Laurie sat on one of the padded plastic chairs. "Wish you were fishing?"

"No," he said turning to her, "I came to see you."

She smiled at him. How handsome he was, how kind and loving. "It's so nice to have you here to myself like this without all the pomp and circumstance of Washington."

He took her hand. "You much prefer this life here, don't you?"

"Cameron, I'm a country girl at heart, but I don't say no to new things."

They sipped their coffees in silence for a moment, then he took her hand again. It was now or never. After long thought he was certain that, by bringing Laurie into his life, fate had shown him the only road ahead while the amazingly ever-increasing fervor of their love-making had vanquished any lingering restraint. As for his political future, he could overcome any obstacle with Laurie at his side, of that he was certain.

"I know how great a sacrifice it would be for you to leave McPine," he said, "but would you consider becoming my wife?" He was thrilled to see her face immediately radiate with pure happiness.

"Are you quite sure?" she asked in a tender voice.

"As sure as I have ever been about anything," he replied.

In an elated voice she said, "Then, Cameron, the answer is a resounding yes."

They embraced for a long moment then he kissed her warm lips. "I am so very happy. I was worried that you would decline."

"And why, pray tell, would I want to do that?"

"All the pomp and circumstance, for one thing."

Winking a radian eye, she said, "I'll adapt. I don't have a choice, do I?"

He put his hand in the pocket of his beige trousers and brought out a small wine-colored velvet box and handed it to her. "Hope you like it."

With hands that trembled ever so slightly, she slowly opened it to see the largest diamond she had ever seen set on a plain gold band. Her hand went to her face. "Oh, Cameron, it's so beautiful…and huge!"

"You deserve the best. Do you like it?"

"Like it? What's not to like!"

"Let me," he said. Gently he took the solitaire and slipped it on the ring finger of her left hand. It fit perfectly.

"I'm glad the size is right. I could only guess."

"Did you go shopping for this? I mean, does the media already know?"

"Not to worry, my dear. I was discreet. The shop came to me, or rather at my mother's house. It was the only way to avoid attention."

"So, obviously, Mrs. Grace Austin is well aware of your plans."

"Yes, and she is happy."

"Are you quite sure? I mean doesn't she feel that you'll be marrying outside your caste?"

He smiled. "You need to get to know my mother better. She is without a doubt the most egalitarian person you are ever likely to meet. She was quite taken by you and approves of our union."

"You mean you asked her permission," Laurie teased.

"Not quite but she is a wise old bird, and I value her opinion."

"Don't tell me she's not disappointed that I am not an American!"

"She feels there certainly will be problems, but that it is time for a new vision in our stuffy Party. I am certain she has already begun her own campaign to change old ideas."

"You mean that she accepted our engagement because she had no choice, and now will take to the street to defend you?"

Austin chuckled. "All I know is that I agree with her that change can be extremely positive," he said, gently kissing Laurie's cheek.

With her hand extended in front of her she was examining the nearly two-carat stone from every angle. When sunlight beamed on it, it sparkled like a bright star in a velvety sky.

"Cameron, I do hope the old guard is not too disappointed, although I must say I'm too happy to care at this point," she said, and her long arms went to him.

Her reaction was adding to the sense of euphoria he never thought he would experience again in his lifetime. However, all was not perfect. "What about Sarah?"

"I've been thinking that it's time for her to experience a larger world than the one she knows here. She'd miss her friends I'm sure, but she's young and I think she'll thrive in a new environment."

"I was quite serious last night when I said I would arrange for her to play for the President when you two come down."

"Very generous, Cameron. She'll be thrilled beyond words," Laurie said. "When she comes over this afternoon we can both tell her the news. The exciting news."

Laurie had fantasized about a marriage proposal from Cameron Austin, and now that it was a reality, all her doubts were melting away like butter in sunlight. All was well with the world even if in her fantasy the proposal came a year later. The sooner the better, no doubt at all.

From his position in the shade of a tall maple in Laurie's yard, Lonsdale had, from time to time, darted his eyes in the direction of the sundeck ever since the Vice President had stepped outside. In the last few minutes, his glance had lingered and when he saw Cameron Austin give Laurie the ring, he had smiled ever so slightly. He liked the woman and he was happy for the Vice President. Then he contemplated that their trips to McPine would soon end. He took a deep breath. He would definitely miss the tranquility of pine country.

"Anything?" Agent Dunlop asked as he returned from a walk around the property.

"Perhaps," Lonsdale replied. "He has given her a ring."

"Really?" Dunlop exclaimed in disbelief, his eyes moving to the sundeck. "Well, I'll be. That he would meet someone in this Godforsaken place was the last thing I expected."

"I wonder how the news will be received at the White House," Lonsdale considered.

CHAPTER TWENTY-SIX

On Saturday afternoons in the summer Oliver Rogge often met buddies for a round of golf. This day, however, he was seated in his office in the West Wing of the White House reviewing one more time the tapes of the demonstration in Ottawa which had culminated in a gunshot heard across the border. There was no work-related reason for him to study the tapes, but he had a personal need to satisfy. He knew Laurie Cosner's brother had been there because he had recognized him and the bleached-blond woman at his side from the photos he had added to his Cosner file soon after his meeting with the Vice President. The photographs had been easy to get since both had been arrested on several occasions.

On the monitor in front of him Oliver was again seeing Mike and April McLaren make their way through the crowd as people congregated on Parliament Hill that ill-fated morning. Little by little the pair reached the front only to be hidden from view by security people keeping an eye on things. Rogge felt frustrated. Several cameras had recorded the crowd, but no matter the angle, Mike and his girlfriend could not be seen just before, during or after the shooting. However, Al Needham, the man who had been accused in the shooting, and had since confessed, could be partially seen from time to time when he moved about. Oliver had stopped the video and was now looking intently at the frame, wondering who Al was talking to as he gestured in such an elaborate fashion. Oliver zoomed in, but the other person or persons would forever be unidentified.

Oliver had been intent on proving that Mike Gilbert had been near the shooter, something he believed in his gut, because if that were the case, the Vice President would need to be informed now so he could be prepared for any possible embarrassment in the future should Ms. Cosner continue to be a major player in Austin's life, something that seemed all but assured at this point, Oliver thought. And he, Oliver, wanted to be the one giving the Vice President the information because it would be one more positive step towards his future in the Austin administration.

Laurie Cosner had decided that it was time for a little pampering. And why not? She was after all engaged to the Vice President of the United States. She had spent most of the week answering questions right, left and center, and now needed time to herself. She was driving to Medford for a manicure and pedicure which was to be followed by a trim and perhaps highlights to rejuvenate her hairstyle. All the while she was reviewing what had happened in the last few days. Throughout the process, she could only wonder what her life would be like once the media got hold of the news.

Sarah had appeared very happy when Cameron Austin announced that he planned to marry her mother. The girl had embraced Laurie warmly, but Laurie could tell her daughter thought things were moving too fast and that the engagement ring her mother was now wearing was ostentatious. Sarah was not attracted by jewelry, not even the array of rings and studs teenagers of all stripes wore on their fingers or their ears or their noses or other parts of their anatomy, but she did wear simple silver studs in her ear lobes and a delicate matching ring. Nothing else.

After Austin left for Washington, mother and daughter talked long into the night, and Sarah was quite excited at the prospect of moving to the American capital. Although Laurie knew that her daughter's first choice remained a music school in England she had been talking about for a long time and wanted to attend right out of high school, she was willing to look at other options in Washington. The Peabody Institute did spring into the girl's mind. Laurie told Sarah they should wait to see how things developed, but was pleased that Sarah was willing to consider an American school since the cost of a music education in London would be rather steep.

For her part, Eileen Danfort had been so happy, she had cried. Her daughter and the handsome and charming Vice President! Heaven on earth, as far as she was concerned. And the happiness she felt for her daughter was contagious. Rita Payne—and all her family for that matter—couldn't stop talking. It was marvelous. Extraordinary. Laurie deserved it after the tragedy in her life. Robby must be smiling up in heaven. And on and on.

And Bernie Wesson. Well, to her surprise he had been more enthusiastic at the news of her engagement than Laurie had expected. He was thrilled, he said, and was soon inquiring about her plans concerning *Only Roses*. Laurie was toying with the idea of selling him her share, and Bernie had smiled and said he would need to look at his finances. They both knew the approximate fair market value involved, but Laurie had reassured Bernie that after crushing numbers the final figure would be equitable, adding that she might even be willing to carry the financing. For Bernie, this was excellent news, Laurie thought, since he had always considered the business his business. No wonder he had been enthusiastic. He was no dummy. A door closes, a window opens.

And the people of McPine were all but dancing in the street as the news spread. Laurie saw the wisdom of having another impromptu session at Adele's Tea Room, but it had already been arranged before she could even suggest it, only this time, the venue would be the Opera House. The larger space afforded more people to gather easily rather than being packed into a small space like sardines.

When Laurie arrived at the Opera House, everyone began applauding as loudly as if she were a renowned singer about to give a great performance. However, she had to admit that she felt less of a fool this time having realized how important getting the proper information in a timely manner was to the residents of McPine. It was also important to her, she realized.

She answered all questions pleasantly, even managing to remain focused when it was pointed out that at the last gathering she had failed to disclose how quickly the relationship had evolved. Laurie smiled and explained that she felt it was her only option because, at the time, she was not certain that Cameron Austin was as in love as she was.

Among the many questions Laurie answered was the one about the date for the wedding. It had not yet been decided, she told them but promised to let them know as soon as it was. No, she was sorry to say, the wedding could not take place in McPine for the simple reason that it would prove too much of a logistical problem in providing adequate security for the Vice President and all the important DC bigwigs who would attend, but she promised to arrange a party in McPine where everyone could meet the Vice President in person. The news resulted in joyful cheering.

Before it was all over, Laurie did tell the residents of McPine that her daughter, Sarah, would be traveling to Washington with her within a couple of weeks. Again, everyone applauded for the simple reason that they were proud this was happening to one of their own. Proxy happiness, Laurie thought with a smile, and it added to her already heightened sense of elation. That was one of the many reasons she so much enjoyed living in McPine. There was no sense of envy here, only one of cooperation. Whatever happened to you, whether good or sad, people shared it all the way.

Now, as she reached Medford, Laurie hoped she would not be asked too many questions. Wanting to keep her engagement private for the time being she had not worn her ring, but she was nevertheless the talk of the Medford salon she frequented from time to time. Patrons smiled —some daring to ask questions—as they walked by the booth where Jackie was pampering her hands and feet. If she attracted that much attention here, Laurie thought, how would she be able to deal with the curiosity she was bound to elicit once in Washington? But then again, it would be a different matter there. For one thing, people would certainly be less overawed since they dealt with so-called important people on a regular basis, and for another, people like manicurists and stylists probably made house calls all the time.

When the hairdresser had achieved the look she wanted, Laurie stared at herself in the mirror from various angles, pleased that he had followed her instructions. She thought that the lighter blond near her face was flattering, and so did he. She would again be a striking figure in Washington next time she went down, the stylist promised. He wanted to know when that would be, and she managed to keep her answer vague much to his frustration.

After leaving the salon, Laurie walked down the sidewalk with a smile on her face. Not long ago, she had given up on ever finding happiness again, and she now marveled at how unexpected the last few weeks had been. Fully aware that life seldom works out as planned, she could only hope that nothing would mar the road to her wedding which she and Austin had tentatively agreed would be in late October. Suddenly, her thoughts were interrupted with the appearance of her brother ambling down the street in her direction.

"Being engaged seems to agree with you, Sis. You sure look happy!" Mike commented after they embraced briefly. "When's the big day?"

"Not quite sure yet, but I would like you to keep the engagement under your hat for the time being if you don't mind, Mike."

"Sure, but I don't see why. Everyone'll know soon enough."

"Of course. It's just that we want to finalize all our plans first."

"Sure." He removed his sunglasses and asked in a low voice, "Did you ever hear anything more about Ottawa?"

"There's nothing more to be heard," she replied. "Everybody's satisfied that the guy they have in custody acted alone. No need to worry."

"Good."

"Spending the weekend with April?"

"Actually I'm on vacation for a couple of weeks. We're going down to the Thousand Islands. Some cousin of April has a place there."

"Beautiful spot. Have a good time," Laurie said sincerely.

"Thanks. What about you? Any vacation plans? I mean are you going away anywhere with the VP?"

"No, but he's planning a visit to McPine in August when we'll be going to Toronto for dinner at mom's house. I'll let you know when so you can join us."

"Sure. Just me?"

"No, Mike. You and April."

"I know you don't like her—"

"Stop, please. I don't know her well. Maybe you could bring her to McPine when you get back."

"She'd like that. Maybe when you-know-who comes up."

"Why not?" Laurie said smiling, well aware that Cameron Austin would have to meet all the family, warts and all, sooner or later.

"And don't you worry, April and I will be nice. We won't embarrass you even if the Americans would like Canada to give up its sovereignty so they can feed their need to dominate the world."

"Mike…"

"We both know it's true, but I'll keep my mouth shut when I meet Austin, I promise. Maybe later when he's my brother-in-law…" Mike let the sentence hang in the air and smiled broadly. "I'll see you when we get back."

Looking at him walking away Laurie sighed. She was certain her brother would be polite when he met Cameron Austin, but she also had no doubt that he would find a way to make his views known soon enough. Perhaps it was not all negative. To some degree Mike was right. Living next door to the giant United States, Canadians had to struggle to maintain their own identity, and it would always be a work in progress requiring vigilance. It was a perspective that Cameron Austin was beginning to appreciate more and more with each trip to Canada.

CHAPTER TWENTY-SEVEN

John Danfort asked his driver to wait and take Laurie and Sarah to Pearson International Airport in Toronto for their trip to Washington. He had always had a great deal of affection for his stepdaughter and his step-granddaughter, and felt this was the least he could do, even if it meant he would have to grab a cab to go back to his downtown office. He had come home to share in the joy permeating his house as the future wife of the American Vice President —and perhaps before long, the American President—and her daughter stopped in for lunch before traveling to Washington. He was very pleased, on many fronts, at the turn of events. For one, his wife Eileen was ecstatic at her daughter's happiness, and after more than twenty years of marriage, he still found untold satisfaction in his wife's bliss. For another, his new role as almost father-in-law to the Vice President was bound to result in interesting contacts which could prove beneficial to his varied business interests.

A new excuse to avoid the subject of retirement.

Eileen kept reminding him that they should travel while they were both still in excellent health, but John Danfort was a doer who felt he simply couldn't close the door completely on his work. And as he looked at the three ladies in his life sharing in the great anticipation of the coming few months, he thought of what could have been if his son had lived. He would be older than Laurie now, and no doubt ready and eager to take over from his old man. Without him though, retirement could wait, John Danfort thought.

He was well aware of the reason for his melancholy despite the joy around him. Today marked the anniversary of the day he had come home to find his first wife and his son both dead. She had left a note giving an asinine explanation why she had drowned her infant child before taking an overdose of sleeping pills. He had been stunned at the realization that she had been depressed enough to commit such an unthinkable act. He had been so busy trying to make his mark in the business world that he had failed to listen to the warning signs of the brutality that was to come. He had been emotionally numb for years afterwards, devoting every waking minute to his work, a dedication that had paid material rewards but little else. Until he met Eileen Gilbert by chance at the house of friends. He had been captivated by her contagious joy for life despite her own loss, and had decided there and then not to let her get away.

Today, he was still amazed and grateful that she had brought him back to life.

"Are you with us, John?" Eileen was asking.

"Yes, of course, my dear."

"Then what do you think?"

"About what?" He asked, somewhat baffled that he had not heard the discussion around him.

Eileen understood the reason for her husband's wandering thoughts. She sensed the guilt that still haunted him, even though he financed many projects to encourage open discussions of the many facets of depression and to provide help to sufferers, especially new mothers. She was kind in her own unique way. "About the fact that I'm considering moving to Washington."

"What?" John Danfort retorted.

Eileen smiled. "Now that I've got your attention, Laurie wanted to know how you'd feel about giving her away when she marries Cameron Austin."

"Oh, Laurie, it would be a great honor. Yes. Thank you," he replied smiling.

"You realize of course that all those Washington matrons will have their eye on you," Laurie said.

"Don't worry," Eileen said, patting her husband's hand. "I'll make sure they know he's spoken for."

John Danfort kissed his wife's cheek. What had he done to merit such joy?

As she watched the singer on stage from the wing at Ford's Theater in Washington, Sarah Cosner found herself a little surprised that she wasn't more nervous. Waiting to go on to perform for the President and the Vice President, their families and close friends—and a TV audience—she could only hope that she wouldn't make a complete fool of herself once she went on. She took a deep breath. It was just a performance, she reminded herself, just like the one she had given at her high school. In fact, she had decided to play the same Mendelssohn piece, since she was very much at ease with it. And she was wearing the same white top with its discreet silver shimmer and the same black skirt so that there would be no surprises. She knew she was the last one on the program, and wondered what the audience would think of her effort at the piano after listening to the superb talent and voices that had been showcased thus far.

The applause was thunderous as the female contralto, a favorite of the President, took a bow. Sarah felt a twinge in the pit of her stomach, but she quickly rallied. She was being given an extraordinary opportunity. She owed it to her mother and Cameron Austin to rise to the occasion. The contralto walked off past Sarah, smiling warmly at the girl. Just then, the master of ceremonies was back on stage.

"The last performer this evening is a young girl with a rare talent at the piano, Miss Sarah Cosner."

The producer, an older man with a close-cut white beard who had been standing near Sarah nodded for her to go on, and she walked into the light of the stage. Amid applause she took a bow, and her mother's flowing white dress in the front row was the only thing she saw. She sat at the elaborate Steinway and, keeping her shoes on, took a moment to compose herself before hitting the keys with the ease and ability that only those destined for greatness possess.

As the notes filled the air inside the old hall, Laurie felt a surge of pride and a knot in her throat. Was that really her little girl playing for such a distinguished group? Cameron Austin discreetly squeezed her hand. She could only feel gratitude for the man who had made it possible for her Sarah to be finally noticed for her immense talent. Laurie took a cautious look in the direction of the President and Barb Thomson, only to see that both were totally captivated.

When she had played the last note, Sarah stood up and the sound of the applause resonated even more gloriously than the roar of the intense adulation she had imagined in her most deeply personal daydreams. She caught the eye of her mother and smiled broadly before exiting.

"Well, my dear, your daughter is a rare gem," Grace Austin who was seated next to Laurie was saying.

"Thank you," Laurie managed to say.

"I'm having a party for a few friends on Saturday. Sarah must play for them," Grace added.

"I'm sure she'd be thrilled, Mrs. Austin."

Once people stood up to leave, Laurie graciously accepted praise from the President and Barb Thomson and, as Cameron introduced her, from a slew of other people she was meeting for the first time.

Laurie and Cameron then went backstage where they found Sarah standing alone, a bouquet of red roses in her hands. Laurie smiled brightly even if the flowers Cameron had sent did not come from *Only Roses*. The girl went to her mother and let herself be embraced in her arms.

"Are you okay? You were terrific, you know," Laurie said.

"Thanks. I'm fine."

"You certainly were terrific," Cameron echoed, and as naturally as a father and daughter would do, the Vice President and Sarah Cosner embraced for a warm moment.

"Thank you for the lovely roses," Sarah said.

"It's the least I could do. You know what red roses mean, don't you?" Austin asked.

"If I didn't, I could never show my face in McPine again," Sarah replied pleasantly.

"I sent them to underscore your courage for performing tonight," Austin said.

"It was a great honor, Mr. Austin, and I appreciate this tremendous opportunity."

"Talent can't be hidden under a barrel. It has to be shared with the world. I would not be surprised if this evening led to other performances," Austin added.

"There's already one," Laurie said.

"Really?" Sarah exclaimed.

"Mrs. Austin is inviting you to perform in Maryland on Saturday. What do you say?"

"Great!" Sarah squealed.

"And my mother has some young people at her house so you can hang around with someone other than us old fogies," Cameron said. "We will be going out there tomorrow."

With his body propped up by the elevated top section of the adjustable bed set up in the den which was now his living space most of the time, Neal Landau was resting comfortably after a rather pleasant day. He considered that he might have been a bit hasty in his assessment that the decline of his body was on a swift downward spiral. It had been a good day, so good in fact that he had been able to walk on the beach early in the morning before the hot Florida sun had a chance to permeate the summer humidity. Then, with Rosita at his side, he had gone to a mall to experience the sights and sounds of life, and they had eaten lunch in a nice little deli. In the afternoon, he had paid a visit to his barber, returning home tired but happy.

Neal Landau loved Florida summers, and was now wondering if that was part of the reason for his growing sense of well-being. No matter the reason, there were now more good days than bad, something that made him want to hang on to life a little longer. Suicide could wait for a day when hope was at its lowest ebb. A little television would be nice, he thought, and reaching for the remote he began flipping through the channels, settling on a tabloid-style entertainment news program.

A piece on the break-up of a high-profile Hollywood couple ended, and the host appeared on the screen along with an inset of Laurie and Cameron Austin. "The talk of the town in Washington today is our Vice President and his lady friend, Canadian Laurie Cosner. Although it has not yet been confirmed, it is believed that the couple is engaged to be married."

As a video of Cameron and Laurie in her flowing white dress rolled, the host continued. "At a special concert for the President and Mrs. Thomson last night at Ford's Theater in our nation's capital, Vice President Austin was accompanied by Ms. Cosner who, witnesses say, was sporting a large solitaire diamond on her left hand. An official announcement is expected. In the meantime, the couple had a special reason for being on hand last night."

A clip of Sarah at the piano was now on the screen. "One of the performers at last night's gala was Sarah Cosner, the fifteen-year-old daughter of Laurie Cosner, who is reputed to be a gifted pianist. You can see the whole concert tonight on this network at eight o'clock."

Neal Landau was looking at the happy Sarah taking a bow, amazed at the pretty face. He felt frustrated that in a moment the host was back on the screen to cut to a commercial. He switched off the set.

"Rosita. Rosita," Landau called.

"Yes, Mr. Neal. What do you need?" the pleasant woman asked as she approached.

"Was there anything in the paper today about the Vice President?" he asked, regretting that he no longer found it necessary to read the daily newspaper.

"Si. They say he's engaged. I'll get it for you." And in a moment she was back with the paper folded to the page showing a large photo of Cameron, Laurie and Sarah taken in Washington the previous evening.

"Thanks," he said as Rosita walked away. He then spent some time looking at the picture.

Much later after he had listened to and recorded the Washington concert of the previous evening, Neal reached for the phone and called his friend, manager and advisor, Marty.

Sarah was a little shocked when she saw Grace Austin's mansion. She had never imagined that people could actually live in houses that big. As she entered with her mother and Austin, her eyes took in the decor as fast as they could as if afraid it might all be only an illusion. Grace Austin was happy to welcome her guests.

"Glad you could come," Grace told Sarah. "A couple of sixteen-year-old twins are staying here for a few weeks while their parents recuperate from a car accident. I thought the three of you could do something together. What do you think?"

"Sounds good."

"Ah, here they are," Grace said as two pretty red-haired girls approached. They seemed identical in every way except for their clothes. One girl wearing a white T-shirt was introduced as Julie, while the other wearing a red top was called Justine. "I can tell them apart when they wear the same clothes, but I won't tell you how just yet," Grace said. "See if you can figure it out. Hope you brought your bathing suit."

Sarah nodded. "It's in my bag."

"Good. It's been brought up to your room. Why don't you girls go and get acquainted?"

Laurie had feared Sarah would be bored to death during their stay in Washington, but now she could relax, pleased that her daughter was making new friends.

"You will stay for dinner?" Grace asked Cameron.

"Of course, Mother. Why else would we have come all this way?"

"The phone has been ringing all day," Grace said once they were all comfortably seated on the shaded patio and sipping iced tea. "Everyone wants to know when they can meet you and Sarah."

Cameron felt he should explain. "*Everyone* means the important people of Maryland."

Laurie smiled while Grace ignored the Vice President's remark and continued. "Many people will be over on Saturday for my annual garden party, and I thought it would be an opportunity for Sarah to play the piano, and for you, Laurie, to meet my friends."

"I look forward to it," Laurie replied.

"When are you going to make it official, Cameron?" Grace asked.

"Our engagement is a private affair, Mother. I certainly don't see the need to make any sort of announcement."

"Well, I disagree. The sooner people know that you are to be married, the better for all concerned."

"You mean you will be in a better position to play the crowd, don't you, Mother?"

"Someone has to do it."

"Play the crowd?" Laurie asked.

The Vice President spoke. "The crowd, in this case is made up of those with influence within the Party."

"And I take it," Laurie said, "that they need to be convinced that marrying a Canadian should not affect in any way your appeal as the next presidential candidate."

"You have to understand Laurie; we are very set in our ways" Grace said. "By we, I mean all of us Americans who have some influence on the political scene. I believe at this juncture that it is important to allay any possible negative thinking before it spreads. Nip it in the bud, if you will."

The Vice President's cell phone rang. He reached for it on the inside pocket of his jacket and stood up. "I'll be right back," he promised.

Laurie looked at him go into the house and asked, "Between us girls, do you feel that I am a negative influence on your son, Mrs. Austin?"

"I like you, my dear, and you know that I will welcome you into our family with open arms. When I see you with Cameron, there is no doubt in my mind that life is unfolding as it should. And it makes this old heart glad to see my son so happy again. However, you must not forget that when you marry the Vice President, not only the Party but also three hundred and fifty million people will be wondering why no American was good enough for Cameron. It is simply a fact that has to be faced. And that is why I believe it is important for you to be here on Saturday. People will get to know you and immediately forget that you were not born in this country. Truth be told, you are the one who must play the crowd."

"You did not answer my question, Mrs. Austin. I realize that some people see my not being an American as negative, but what about you? Do you think I'll hurt Cameron's political future?"

"I look at this from a different perspective than you. To be quite frank, there will be some negative impact, yes, but that it will be short-lived. In other words, I do not believe it will influence long-term prospects. That being said, the right cards must be played at the outset."

"You realize of course, Mrs. Austin, that I am a simple country girl with no experience of any sort in political games."

"No experience is necessary, my dear. You only need to be yourself, and people will quickly see why Cameron wants you as his wife."

"But what if I don't erase the fears of the Party's old guard?"

"My dear, there is absolutely no doubt in my mind that you will."

Cameron Austin reappeared, surprised that the two ladies in his life were no longer engaged in conversation. "Were you two talking behind my back?"

"Yes, but we were very kind," Laurie replied.

Sitting back down, Austin took her hand and kissed it.

"Cameron, I would like to again bring up the subject of the announcement of your engagement. It's important," Grace said.

"You're right, Mother. We should do it now."

Grace who had expected a dissenting riposte from her son was momentarily surprised. "What has made you change your mind?"

"My staff took an unofficial survey and they feel that waiting to make the announcement of our engagement will not be seen as positive by the average person. It will be judged as questioning my own decision which could hurt me. But, the announcement will not be a media circus." Taking Laurie's hand, he continued. "If you agree, Laurie, my press secretary will make a simple announcement tomorrow that we are engaged and that we will be married in a private ceremony later this fall."

"If you feel that's the best way to go, I certainly have no objection."

"Good," Grace said, and her shoulders relaxed. One hurdle out of the way. Life had a way of throwing curves. Survivors and winners met them head on. She could only hope that her take on the political ramifications of this marriage were on the mark, something she would worry about for some time. But, she concluded it was worth it. At last her son was a contented man now able to project the required energy into his work.

CHAPTER TWENTY-EIGHT

After enjoying a swim and changing back into their clothes, the three girls joined the adults on the patio.

"A couple of bands are giving a concert tonight at the Amphitheater in the Harbor. The three of us would like to go. Is that okay?" Sarah asked her mother.

"If I may, Laurie," Grace put in, "Julie and Justine asked me about going yesterday, and I said it would be fine. Marco will drive them and keep an eye out."

Cameron Austin spoke. "Marco has been my mother's driver for ages. You can trust him. However, since there will be a large crowd, one of my men can go along."

"Is it really necessary?" Sarah asked.

"I believe it would make us, your mother and yours truly, feel better. And it will be a good way for you to get used to having Secret Service people around, because whether you like it or not, they are part of my world," the Vice President said.

Sarah looked at her mother and her future stepfather, and smiled briefly. "Okay."

"I'm sure the three of you understand," Cameron said, "that we live in a world where we have to be on guard for the unexpected. My men are very discreet and they will not stand in the way of a good time."

Laurie didn't especially like the notion of her small town-raised daughter out on the town in a strange metropolis, something she knew

Cameron Austin understood. She was grateful he had eased her apprehension.

The sounds were a pleasant bonus this evening for agent Bradley. The band now on stage, a group which was not familiar to him, was performing songs he remembered as having been popular a decade or two earlier, but with a fresh adaptation. He was surprised to see the girls enjoying it all. The band had obviously found a way to cater to a new generation with tunes their parents could hum.

Scanning the crowd from his position behind the girls, he saw that a fair portion of the audience was in his own age range and that their hands were easily moving to the beat of the music. Marco, a man in his late fifties who was seated on the aisle seat in the row behind Bradley, also seemed to be relishing the show on stage. A pleasant evening for everyone, Bradley thought.

When the band took a short break, Sarah and a male teen seated next to her resumed a conversation they started shortly after they had been seated. Bradley listened carefully glad to see that the girl had been well advised when it came to giving out personal information. The boy with a nearly acne-free complexion was proud to brag that the last song the band had played had been written by his uncle Neal Landau.

"Really? That's so cool," Sarah commented.

"Yeah. It is. He's written lots of songs for people like Cher and Tony Bennett."

"Wow," Sarah said, and it was quickly echoed by the twins, Julie and Justine.

The boy was nudged by a friend seated next to him. After a moment he asked hopefully, "I have recordings of all my uncle's songs at my house. Maybe we could go and listen to them after the concert?"

Sarah smiled the smile of an angel, and Bradley was certain that after living in McPine the idea of getting to know anyone in the big city of Baltimore, especially a boy with obvious musical genes, was very tempting, but she politely declined.

"Do you come to Baltimore often?" the boy asked, undaunted.

"No, not really."

"Too bad. If you ever do, look for me at the Peabody Institute."

The boy had Sarah's full attention now. It was after all a world-renowned musical Mecca as any would-be serious music student knew. "You're training there?"

"Not yet. In January. I'm going to write songs, just like my uncle."

The weatherman had not dared disappoint Grace Austin. On Saturday, as the last preparations for the garden party were being finalized, the sun, lord over Maryland, combined with a soft breeze for a perfect day. Two large white tents gleamed against the sweeping immaculate emerald lawn for those who preferred to be shaded from the sun's rays. The tents had been set up adjacent to the large patio and the swimming pool, complete with temporary flooring to safeguard the heels of female guests. On a stage in a corner of one of the tents, a quartet was tuning up. Potted conifers that stood adult-height had been set up to divert attention from the poles holding up the tents.

Watching the scene through the window of the dining room, Laurie and Cameron saw Grace Austin walking about, making certain that every detail was perfect. Or perhaps a touch better, Cameron considered. "Mother's at her best right now," the Vice President commented. "She has a well-defined purpose—making certain that I am the only viable choice for the Party."

"And? Will she be successful?"

"I have no doubt, no doubt at all. One thing is certain, she will have everyone eating out of your hand. I think she's a bit disappointed that you're not an American, but she likes you and knows that we complete each other, so the challenge of selling you—quote, unquote—is terribly appealing to her. Whereas most women her age would feel overwhelmed at the prospect, it has given Grace Austin a new lease on life."

"We do, don't we?"

"We certainly do. What are you referring to?" Austin asked.

"To the fact that we complete each other. It's truly amazing when you consider that our backgrounds are totally on different poles."

"Hooray for poles," the Vice President said lifting his coffee cup in a toasting gesture.

"Mom, am I interrupting?" Sarah asked at the door.

"Not at all," Laurie replied. "Are you ready to dazzle an influential crowd?"

"They can't be more influential than those I played for the other night!" Sarah commented.

"If you mean the President, he won't be here today," Cameron told the girl.

"Then it's going to be a breeze," Sarah said, and after a moment when she seemed to be debating internally, she asked, "Mom, do you think we could go and visit the Peabody Institute while we're here? It's one of the best music schools."

"Oh, I know its reputation, Sarah, but it's summer. I doubt that it's the best time to visit."

"I'd be happy to see what can be arranged," the Vice President told mother and daughter.

"I don't mean to sound difficult," Laurie began, "but I really think we should plan in advance for that type of visit. What I mean, Sarah, is that if they know you're interested in their school—and you can't hide who you are anymore—they might arrange for a lot more than a simple tour. In the fall you might have a chance to talk to some of the teachers and some of the students."

"But you two will be married in the fall."

"So? That's one day. Fall lasts a few months as far as I remember," Laurie added.

"Okay," Sarah conceded, disappointment showing on her face.

"I'll go with you and make all the arrangements for next year. How's that?"

The girl rallied. "That's great, thanks. Last night at the concert I met a guy who'll be going to Peabody next year."

"Oh, yeah," Laurie said, more questioning than commenting.

Sarah immediately understood her mother's tone. "He was sitting beside me and we talked. That's it. He wants to write songs, like me. Last night one of the bands played some songs his uncle wrote."

"Really. Anyone we know?" Austin inquired.

"Maybe. His name is Neal Landau."

The name was familiar to Laurie, but as soon as it was recalled she let it slip back into the vacuum of discarded trivia where it had been thrown years earlier.

The Vice President held Laurie's hand as the pair came out, ready to greet guests. Servers dressed in white milled about and the quartet was in its final stage of tuning up. Marjorie, Cameron's fifty-something cousin who had so often accompanied him to social functions in recent years, had already arrived and was walking toward them, leaving her wheelchair-bound husband to enjoy a friendly tête-à-tête with Grace. Laurie couldn't help but notice the great shape and joyous face. She embraced the Vice President and he made the introductions.

"I'm so glad to meet you, my dear, although I'm a little annoyed that I will no longer be able to attend all those glittering White House affairs with Cameron," Marjorie said with a bright smile.

"I'm glad to meet you too," was all Laurie could reply.

"Don't listen to what she says," Cameron assured Laurie. "She just wants me to feel sorry for her and find her a new escort."

"But remember, Cameron, that I'm fussy."

"I'll keep that in mind."

Putting an arm through Laurie's, Marjorie said, "What do you want to know about Cameron? I know all sorts of secrets. He's not always the saint he claims to be, you know."

"Marjorie, if I were you, I'd be careful. That door swings both ways," Austin warned.

At that point guests began arriving in droves as if a gate had just opened and Laurie felt disappointed at having to end the dialogue.

With the fashions that paraded in front of her, Laurie sensed that the Grace Austin garden party was an occasion to impress and be impressed, to observe and be observed, and she couldn't help but be amazed at the new dimension of her life, a world away from where she and her friends normally wore jeans and a simple top or blouse when getting together.

Today, however, wearing an ensemble she had chosen: a short-sleeved, gently molding pale blue silk top worn with a mid-calf straight skirt in a matching shade, she felt she could compete with anyone. Sarah had gone shopping with her and, although Laurie hadn't worn blue in years, Sarah convinced her mother it was the only color that would do. Judging by the look the Vice President gave Laurie when he first saw her in it, the girl had been right.

After a while, Laurie Cosner's head was beginning to spin. It was a pleasant day all around and the sounds of the quartet were sweet, but there were so many people to meet, and so many names and faces to remember. She marched on, smiling her best smile, aware that at Cameron Austin's side as he campaigned, much more would be required of her. With a glass of water in hand, she took sips whenever she needed a moment before answering or asking a question, a trick her future mother-in-law had been happy to share. Cameron was also sipping water, proud to introduce his future wife to those who could help him in his bid for the White House.

When Grace Austin came to take Laurie away for a moment to introduce her to an old friend with limited mobility who had remained a little aside, Cameron was cornered by Senator Robert Stanton of Virginia, a man with a full head of white hair and a corpulent belly.

"Your Canadian friend seems like a fine girl, Cameron but tell me why you didn't set your sight on a nice American widow. Plenty of them around with us men having a tendency to die off before the gals."

"We never know who we're going to fall in love with, do we, Bob? I'm sure you remember how these things happen. You've been with your wife for what? More than thirty years, is it?"

"Thirty-nine to be exact. I didn't fall in love with Marion, Cameron. Our marriage was more or less, shall we say, guided. My father strongly suggested that Marion was the perfect choice for me and for our families' future. He was right. It's proven to be a most sensible arrangement moneywise, and I've grown very fond of Marion over the years. We have great kids and grandkids, and I know I'd be lost without her. You don't need to fall in love to have a successful marriage. I'm proof of that. So why put yourself through what's bound to be a sticky issue?"

"All of you in the Party will simply need to adjust to my decision to marry a Canadian. I will not be changing my mind."

"I'm not talking about anyone in the Party. We can win those people over. What I'm talking about, Cameron, is the electorate. Are they going to accept that their President lives in the White House with a Canadian the way things are right now?"

Austin was getting annoyed. "She's from Canada, for petesakes, not an alien from some faraway galaxy," he said sternly. "And as a matter of fact, she is a descendant of New Yorkers who lived in the original thirteen colonies and immigrated to Canada."

"You mean at the time of the Revolutionary War, don't you? In order words they were Loyalists! If I were you I wouldn't mention that too loudly in mixed company. I, and many people, consider that the Loyalists were, simply put, chickens. They didn't want to fight for freedom, so they fled to Canada just like our kids did during the Vietnam War."

"It's not quite that simple, and you know it," the Vice President retorted. "The Loyalists were pacifists who wanted the Colonies to effect a bloodless separation from Britain. They felt it could be done if people were willing to negotiate rather than take up arms."

"Come on, Cameron. If everyone in America at that time had been as chicken as the Loyalists were, where would we be? Still a colony of England like Canada is?" As soon as the words were out, Senator Stanton put up a hand. "Okay, I know that's not the case. I was simply adding color, something not foreign to politicians as we all know," he said, gently poking the Vice President's arm. "Who knows? The thirteen Colonies might have been able to negotiate independence from the Mother Land without bloodshed, but we'll never know, will we? Still, talking about your friend being of the lineage of Loyalists could be tricky and may alienate some voters."

"I wouldn't worry about that, Bob," Cameron told his interlocutor. "Most Americans have never even heard of the Loyalists, let alone have an opinion on the subject. Before trying to guess how the Americans are going to vote, we should concentrate on erasing the apathy that keeps them from voting in the first place."

"I'm well aware of the numbers," the senator said simply.

"It's an interesting fact that in the United States people who consider themselves very patriotic, and are, don't bother to vote. By contrast, Canadians who don't wrap themselves in the flag quite as much as we do have an excellent record when it comes to voting. As high as over ninety percent in some instances. If we had those kinds of numbers here rather than the low percentage we get, the wishes of the majority would be quite clear."

"I can only agree with you on that point."

"But you don't when it comes to Laurie?"

"As I said, she's a charming woman. I can only wish her the best, but I want to go on record as having warned you that with her at your side, the presidency may not be as easily attainable as you might think. On the other hand, with an American wife, you could be a shoo-in. You would garner the female vote for the simple fact that you've been widowed—something many women can identify with—and remarried a widow. That's what you should aim for."

"I would like to point out that Laurie is a widow," Austin said.

"Only an American widow will do, Cameron."

Neither men noticed the fifteen-year-old girl standing within earshot but hidden from their view by one of the neatly trimmed miniature pines positioned so as to obscure the poles holding up the tent.

Soon afterwards, Austin caught up to Laurie. "How are you holding out?"

"I'm starting to get into it now. It's a good thing you gave me a list of the names of the guests to study beforehand."

"Everyone's crazy about you."

"I don't know about that," Laurie commented.

Grace interrupted. "Laurie, do you know where Sarah is? It's time for her to play, but no one can find her."

"Wasn't she inside with the twins?"

"She was but she seems to have disappeared," Grace said.

"Let me look for her."

CHAPTER TWENTY-NINE

*L*aurie found Sarah sitting alone on the cool grass under a massive elm on the far side of the house. She wanted to sit down beside her daughter, but thought better of it. This was definitely not the time to get grass stains on her new skirt.

"Is everything okay? People are waiting for you to play."

Sarah was silent for a long moment then said, "I'm sorry, Mom, but I don't think I can play today."

"What's the problem? Are you feeling sick?" Laurie asked, bending briefly to put a hand on the girl's forehead.

"I'm not sick, Mom. I just don't like these people."

"Why do you say that? I thought you were in the house with Julie and Justine since we got here, so when did you meet them?"

"I was inside, but when I went to look at the piano, I heard things."

"What sort of things?"

"These people don't like you, Mom. They don't want you around."

"Some of them, yes."

"And it doesn't bother you?" the girl asked, getting to her feet.

"Not really. Sarah, you've got to understand that it's not me they don't like, it's the fact that I'm not an American. They expected and wanted Cameron to choose an American because it would play well for him and help him get elected when he runs for the presidency. It's nothing personal. I decided that having people complain about me is a small price to pay to be with Cameron."

"So what you're saying is that when I play the piano in a few minutes, they'll resent the fact that I'm not an American?"

Laurie chuckled. "Darling, you, they'll like. You have no direct or indirect influence on the Party's ambitions any which way, so they'll see you for who you are and dig you. I mean, what's not to like," Laurie said, pulling the daughter to her in a momentary embrace. "And they'll be suitably impressed with your talent. Who wouldn't?"

The girl smiled. "Okay, I'll play, but I feel sorry for you having to deal with these people."

"Don't waste your time feeling sorry for me. Most of the people here today don't care one way or the other where I come from, and they have been especially kind to me. The others, well, Cameron and I are going to change their minds in due course."

"Boy, you must love him a whole lot!" Sarah observed.

"That I do. You know," Laurie said as the pair began walking around the mansion, "when I was young, I had never in my wildest dreams imagined that I could love someone as dearly as I loved your dad, but miracles do happen."

Laurie had been right. Grace Austin's guests were enthralled with Sarah's talent and let her know by their generous applause after each of the three pieces she played. She was introduced to the crowd by the hostess, and when Sarah had sat at the piano and her fingers began traveling the keyboard as easily as the wind caressing verdant summer leaves, many miles away events were being put into motion that would significantly alter the path of her life.

The hot Florida sun was beating down as Marty Spears drove out to Neal Landau's home. Marty, a lawyer, had been Neal's manager for over twenty years, but he was also his friend. Today he was considering that he was probably the only one from the old crowd that still bothered to visit and cheer up poor old Neal. While Marty felt for his client he couldn't shake the guilt; he was after all fully cognizant that he had avoided Neal's fate but by the grace of God. He, Marty, had gone to the parties with Neal, experimenting with all manner of illicit and licit substance and had gotten so spaced out that, just like Neal, he often had had no recollection of the previous day—days in some cases. He had decided to clean up when he had awakened one night on the floor in a strange dilapidated house amid vomit which could have been his. Or not. There had been other bodies about.

Today, he didn't drink except for the occasional beer during the hot weather, and had even stopped smoking years earlier. The only remnant from those days was what his doctor called "a temperamental liver." And he had a lovely wife and son in his life. The angels had looked out for him.

He found Neal seated in the shade on the lanai. "So, how are you today, buddy?" He asked although he knew instantly that today was a good day.

"Not bad. I've been feeling a bit stronger in the last few days," Neal replied.

"Great. Need anything?"

"No, no. Sit."

"You sounded very secretive on the phone. What's up?"

"Do you remember the gang we used to hang around with?"

"Some. Why?"

"Do you remember a girl, blondish hair, a Canadian by the name of Laurie?"

"Off hand, no."

"Well, it's the same woman that just got engaged to Vice President Austin."

"Really! You sure?"

"Pretty sure."

"So what if it is? You don't want to get in touch with her, do you?"

"As a matter of fact, yes."

"May I ask why? I mean why not leave those days alone?"

"Did you see that she has a fifteen-year-old daughter who played the piano for the President the other night?"

"No, I didn't. So what?"

"You should've seen her. A real talent. I think she's my daughter."

"What!" Marty exclaimed. "What in hell makes you think she's your daughter?"

"Before she left to go back to Canada, Laurie told me she was pregnant and that I was the father. I remember it clearly. I didn't believe her then, or maybe I didn't want to. Now I do."

"You do because the girl plays the piano? I hate to disappoint you my friend, but it ain't proof of anything. Lots of people play the piano."

"Not like her! Let me show you what I mean," Neal said. "Come inside."

Slowly he got to his feet and walked into his room where he turned on the television set and pressed a button on the remote. He fast-forwarded part of the Washington concert at Ford's Theater until the section that had recorded Sarah on stage. Marty Spears watched in silence as Sarah showed off her skill, and Neal regularly checked the expression on his friend's face.

"Those black curls had to come from somewhere, don't you think?" Neal said, turning off the set. Touching his own hair, he added, "As you well know before all this gray, my hair was black and curly. Laurie's blond."

"So what? We don't all have the same color hair as our parents."

"I know, but don't you think she looks like me?"

"I don't know. It's hard to say. I think you're seeing what you want to see. For the sake of argument, let's say she's your daughter. Why would you want to meet her at this stage anyway?"

"You have your family, Marty. I lie here day after day, alone most of the time because I'm not interesting enough to associate with, and because people are afraid to catch my disease. If I have a daughter, I want to spend time with her."

"I understand, buddy, but you can't just walk into her life and say: Here I am, your dear old dad. You did deny you were the father, didn't you?"

"Yes, but that was then. I was an idiot back then."

"We all were, but you don't want to make waves at this point, do you? I mean, the girl's mother will be marrying the Vice President soon."

"I won't go public if that's what you mean. I want this to remain very low-key. I've been thinking about it a great deal and I want you to write to Laurie, meet with her and explain the situation. I just want to see and talk to my daughter before I die. Is that too much to ask?"

Marty thought it was, but he didn't say so. His lawyerly mind knew that while his buddy might be able to prove his case legally with blood tests if indeed he was the father, since he had not taken any steps in that direction in the last fifteen years, his motives would be suspect at best. Marty knew Neal needed something to lift up his spirit, but wondered if this was the way to go. Yet, what were his options? He had an obligation to do his best where his client was concerned.

"I suppose I can write a letter and see what happens," Marty said aloud without too much enthusiasm. "Do you have her address?"

"No. Couldn't you write to her care of the Vice President?"

"What? I can't do that!"

"Why not?"

"When a lawyer writes to someone, it's customary to have that person's address," Marty Spears said a little too firmly.

"Just make believe you are writing to the Vice President."

Vice President Cameron Austin was tired. He had slept poorly the previous night because of a slight cold, and it had been a long day full of irritants. All around him people had been generally uncooperative, and he had failed to make any headway in his current nisus. It was time to head for home and forget the problems that come from being the country's second in command. He got to his feet from behind his large desk just as his secretary was coming in. "Mrs. Winterburn, let's close shop. I want to go home."

"Yes, sir," then handed him an envelope. "This letter came for Ms. Cosner."

Cameron Austin took it and fished his reading glasses from the pocket of his jacket. The return address indicated a law firm in Miami which he quickly mentally noted. He was suddenly quite intrigued that an attorney wishing to contact Laurie would send a letter to his attention at the White House. Obviously the person didn't know where Laurie lived. Perhaps it was just a fan letter like the many he still got regularly from lonely widows. He asked his secretary to put it inside another envelope and mail it to Ms. Cosner.

"Yes, sir," Shirley Winterburn said, and Austin noted the name of the Miami firm in the private notebook he always kept in the inside pocket of his jacket.

He had planned to tell Laurie about the letter when he called before going to sleep, but he didn't. While Laurie waited by the phone in McPine, he was softly snoring, making up for lost sleep. He never did mention the letter to her.

CHAPTER THIRTY

*S*ummer reigned supreme on the whole North-American continent. Along the St. Lawrence Seaway which edges both Canada and the United States, the weather was especially hot and humid. It made Mike Gilbert a little cranky because he did not sustain mugginess with any grace at all. He preferred it to winter's snow and ice of course, but his internal thermostat had trouble when dampness ruled his world. He remembered his dad fighting the same villain though it never seemed to stand in the way of a good golf game.

This day, humidity was not the only reason for Mike's petulance. He was bored and worried. He and April had traveled down to the Thousand Islands where, millions of years ago over eighteen hundred islands of all sizes had sprouted in the river. Somewhat like a small company of guards, they guided the waters into the eastern mouth of the great Lake Ontario. Some of these were not much larger than a rocky formation the size of a small car while others were large enough to sustain communities, farms and elaborate golf courses. In this section of the waterway, the border between the two countries had been drawn by zigzagging around the islands in order to essentially divide them equally, and travel between the two countries was simple because they were linked by the 1000 Island International Bridge and a system of spans and island-crossing roads.

From his vantage point on the front porch of the bed-and-breakfast inn where he and April were staying, Mike could see a section of the crane-like top of the suspension bridge structure on the Canadian side, the light green contrasting with the darker green of the tree line below. In front of him lay a small quiet bay. Little else, except, of course, for the countless trees spread like a richly green cloak as far as the eye could see. His mind was thus free to worry.

The owners of the small inn were Moira, a distant cousin of April he had never heard of until recently, and her American common-law husband by the name of Shane Peachee. They operated the inn at the Thousand Islands in the summer, and a motel in Florida in the winter, each duly respecting their country's rules with regard to the number of days they could spend out of country without affecting their status as residents.

Mike Gilbert was bored because there was little to do besides walking or biking along the country road and listening to Shane's ranting. He couldn't even ply the waters all around him as the inn's twenty-five-foot motor craft was out of commission. "A part's coming from the States," Shane had said. "Should be here tomorrow." He had been repeating this for three days now.

The girls spent most of the day chatting away while April helped Moira with the day-to-day chores inside the large house. What role Shane actually played in the operation, except perhaps to chat up the guests, was still somewhat of a mystery to Mike since the workload and decision-making seemed to rest solely with Moira.

This hazy morning, seated beside Mike on one of the large comfy chairs on the verandah, Shane was working a pipe, sending smoke in Mike's direction. That fact was not displeasing to Mike; it immediately brought back happy reminiscences of his late grandfather who had seldom been without a pipe. The aroma was the same as it had been all those years ago. What displeased Mike was the tone and content of Shane's verbal dissertation.

"We have to make a strong statement. That's the only way," the tall man was saying, his long black hair moving on his shoulders as he emphasized words.

"I don't agree," Mike retorted. "I don't believe in violence. I think there's always another solution."

"Yeah. Sure. And where has it gotten you?"

Mike shrugged. "April and I have made a difference and we've never been violent." The episode in Ottawa with the gun had been a little too close for comfort as far as he was concerned. Truth be told,

Mike Gilbert was scared stiff of firearms. He was a pacifist through and through. He was a true Canadian.

"A big splash's the only way to go when you really want to get attention. And, make no mistake, I want attention."

Irritation rose into Mike's throat and he spewed out in his tone. "If you use explosives, you'd essentially be a terrorist!"

"You don't understand. The difference here's that we'll detonate when there's no danger to anyone. Terrorists set out to kill people. Our aim is simply to force Canada to apologize to the U.S. and make Americans aware that they should not vacation in Canada until then."

"You do realize that you're an American taking advantage of Canada's hospitality?"

"I'm not taking advantage. I'm working for a living, here and in the States. Just because I choose to live here part of the time doesn't mean I can't express myself, does it? There's assholes all over the world and we want you all to know in no uncertain terms that we, Americans, have had enough of being maligned—of having our president maligned. We want the message to be clear for Canadians and for the rest of the world because the world is always watching us, like they did when our president was impeached."

Mike took serious objection to Shane's claim that he worked for a living, but let it pass. The man no doubt had a gun somewhere in the house, so pissing him off could potentially be a serious *faux pas*. He pointed the obvious. "If Americans stop coming to Canada, you and Moira will be losing customers. You yourself told me you had a lot of American customers. It seems to me it'll hurt your business."

Shane's lack of response told Mike that the man, in what Mike considered less than infinite wisdom, had not even seen—let alone considered—that side of the equation. When he remained silent, Mike continued. "You say what you're planning is not terrorism, but let me remind you that since 9/11 the Americans are in no mood to put up with explosives going off, whatever the reason, whatever the intention."

Later as they were getting ready for bed, Mike put his concerns to April.

"Mike, you're exaggerating," April commented calmly.

"What? You don't believe me? That's nice to know."

"That's not what I meant and you know it," April retorted.

"Tell me something. Why did your cousin and that crazy lunatic invite you down here in the first place? You hadn't heard from her in how long?"

"A few years. What difference does it make?"

"Let me make my case here, April. They invited us down because they were looking for scapegoats. Shane wants me to help him guard explosives and keep an eye out as he puts it. In other words, if something goes wrong, I take the fall."

"It won't come to that, I'm sure."

Mike took a long look at April wondering why he'd been missing the obvious, then sat on his side of the bed, sighing. "You knew what their intentions were before we drove down here, didn't you, April?"

"Stop your mightier-than-thou attitude, Mike. It doesn't suit you. We're here to help out, that's all. Moira knew we could be trusted."

"Well, you three can count me out, and that's final," Mike said, his voice low but sharp. "Not only is it dangerous, it's against what we went to Ottawa to do: protest the Americans. They're protesting the Canadians. It doesn't make sense for us to get involved."

"And I repeat, we're only here to help."

"You know, my sister was right about you."

"That sister of yours is always right about everything! More so now that she's hanging with the Vice President all the time. I bet ya that in no time she'll have you convinced that you should not get involved in anything anymore. Or maybe you're already convinced."

"What the hell are you talking about, April?" Mike Gilbert would probably have punched himself out if it had been physically possible for him to do so. What an idiot he was for having failed to see that April had been firmly in the driver's seat in this one. Aloud, he said, "I don't do what my sister says, but I'm not about to get involved with explosives. I don't believe in violence of any kind."

"It's a free country."

"Exactly my point. We're lucky to be free to demonstrate, but I don't believe we're free to risk lives and property."

"It's all been calculated. No one's going get hurt. The only loss of property will be two old boats."

The whole idea had come to light in a very modest fashion. Like millions of people, Gerry Lefebvre, a hard-working family man who operated a farm in northern New York, had heard the comments Canadian Prime Minister Roy had uttered about the American President. He had been bowled over. How could the Canadians be so mean? And never mind trying to tell him that his family name testified to a French-Canadian ancestry. He was an American, a real American, and that's all there was to it.

At the insistence of his brother, Gerry had bought a computer three years back, and in the long cold winter nights had discovered the amazing possibilities of the Internet. Chatting with all sorts of people soon became his favorite diversion, much to the chagrin of his wife. After hearing the remark about his President, Gerry had gone online and typed away in an effort to find like-minded Americans. He didn't have to wait long for responses. Hundreds of his fellow citizens were likewise appalled, and before he had a chance to study his actions, he was being sucked in by a churning sea of action-seeking followers in the "Stay in America" movement.

Today, in the warmth of an Upstate New York summer, Gerry had become something no one, most certainly not himself, had envisaged. He was a leader. People were relying on him to guide them through this weekend's protest at the Thousand Islands, one of many all along the border. He could not disappoint them, yet as the day of the big protest grew nearer, Gerry Lefebvre's feet were getting colder. Canadians had the right to make any comment they pleased, had they not? What if some idiot decided that an orderly protest was too tame? What if things got out of hand? What if someone got hurt? Would he be held responsible? What if the police began arresting people like they did in Washington after those idiots had attacked the Capitol? What if, what if. Being a disinclined leader was more stressful than he had imagined.

Lying under the light sheet beside his ever-so-slightly snoring wife, Gerry's questioning thoughts were trotting in random directions without any definite purpose other than increasing mounting doubts, and beads of sweat began pearling on his forehead. What had he gotten himself into, he wondered, while a soft voice had trouble getting through to implore him to calm down. It finally did. These dark thoughts were not all rational, were they? Was it not true that what was planned was a simple protest? Nothing more. People—Americans—protested all the time. The worst that happened was that a few hotheads were carried away by police. Individuals were responsible for their own actions. It was up to each protester to toe the line. Silly for him to carry the weight of the world on his shoulders. He drifted to sleep.

April caught up with Mike as he was sauntering down the steps of the B&B. "Mike, please don't be such a baby. Let's talk."

The sun was still low on the horizon, but Mike knew the air would be as humid today as it had been the previous day. Nevertheless, he was planning to walk about half a mile down the road for breakfast. He couldn't stand the thought of eating at the same table as Shane, Moira and April right at the moment. He needed to be alone to think. On an earlier walk a small restaurant with an outside deck overlooking a marina had seemed inviting. He turned around abruptly to face April. "Talk about what, April? The weather?"

"If you don't want to be involved, that's okay. I'm sure Shane can find someone."

"Well, I guess that person will be an idiot."

"No one's going to get hurt, Mike."

The tone of his voice made it clear that he was tired after a night of tossing and turning. "Can you guarantee it?"

She did not respond.

"I'm going for breakfast. When I get back, perhaps you'd be kind enough to drive me into Kingston. I'll manage from there." He walked away.

"What are you talking about, Mike?" April said to his back as she began to follow him. "This is our vacation. How're you going to get to Medford for your car, anyway?"

"I'll manage," he replied without turning back.

"Who's the idiot now?" April asked.

He didn't see the point of even acknowledging the question, let alone answer that he was the idiot. He hadn't really been listening to April lately. In the shower earlier, Mike had realized that she had suggested a vacation in the Thousand Islands because her cousin needed support for a few days. From there he had let himself be led. He hadn't probed further. He had simply assumed that April had been referring to support being needed on a private or family level.

Can't blame April, can I? I'm the ass, he thought with some disdain.

CHAPTER THIRTY-ONE

The eggs on Mike's plate were excellent. Softly poached, the way he liked them, but he couldn't finish his breakfast. He had woken up hungry, but somehow during his walk, his appetite had abated. What was the problem, he wondered. The exercise in the fresh morning air? Or was it that his world was undergoing a fundamental change? All he knew for certain was that his life was whirling and he had no idea where it would finally come to a stop.

He loved April, of that there was no doubt in his mind. They had always been so in sync with one another while their differences had remained minute. As he sipped his second cup of coffee, he began questioning whether that was indeed the reality or solely his perception. After all, reality was open to individual interpretation, was it not?

They had come together as acquaintances, then as friends and finally as lovers because of their desire to change things, to make the world a better place for every living creature in it. Always within certain rules, albeit unwritten at times, but rules nevertheless. When had it all changed, and why had he been unaware of the shift?

He became conscious that someone was sitting on the stool next to his, but he didn't bother to turn to see who it was. After a moment he heard a soft voice. "Mike, how long is this going to last?" April had joined him.

Slowly, he faced her. Her brown eyes were alert and he pondered for a moment what they were saying. He saw inflexibility, he saw cunning, he saw resolve, all of which made April what she was, a determined woman who never lost sight of her goals. And Mike was suddenly shaken by the realization that he had been the follower much more than an equal in his relationship with the woman. She had set the rules more often than not, and he had simply gone along without challenging. Perhaps due to the age difference her motherly instincts couldn't be helped, he considered, although one thing was certain. The balance between them had now shifted because he had flung down the gauntlet; something she, as the mother figure, would not accept easily.

"I meant it, April. I'm not getting involved in this. I want nothing to do with anything that could hurt people."

Keeping her voice down, she retorted, "I told you. There's no danger to anyone."

"What if you're wrong? How can you rely on Shane to make certain that there's no danger? The guy's a few bricks short of a full load, and you know it."

"Know what I think? You made up your mind about Shane the very first moment you saw him, without giving him a chance. You disliked him right off because he's an American."

"What the hell are you talking about? What does his being an American have to do with anything?"

"You dislike the fact that he's a Yankee because if it were known you supported this American cause, or if you were seen in a picture, for example, it might embarrass your darling sister."

They were silent as the blond middle-aged waitress poured a cup of coffee for April and refilled Mike's cup. As he sipped quietly, April added, "You're afraid that you're being watched. You never said so openly, but I think you reckon that they, quote, unquote," she emphasized the point by making quotation marks in the air with her fingers, "are making sure you don't cause trouble for the Vice President, so this whole thing this coming weekend is making you crazy."

"Get serious April. Who'd want to watch me? I'm not exactly a terrorist," he said in a low voice. "But you're right on one count. I'm nervous as hell. The use of explosives at the border in this day and age of terrorism is stupid and dangerous. I want no part of it. And when Shane is caught—notice I said when, not if—he'll be charged with a serious crime, mark my words. The Americans are taking their security pretty seriously these days, and I certainly can't blame them."

"Okay. Fine," April finally said. "Have it your way. But at least wait for me instead of taking a bus to Medford. That'd be really stupid."

A plan had begun to form in his mind as he had eaten his breakfast, and he considered that it was worth investigating further. To April he said, "Fine. But by Sunday I'm out of here."

"I'll be ready to go by then."

"Good." He finished his coffee and put the mug back on the counter. "Right now," he began, "I'm in no mood to go back to your cousin's place. Besides, you spend your time with Moira, not with me. I'll drive you back and then I'll go into Kingston, look around, and calm down."

"Fine. You gonna come back tonight, right?" April asked with a slight note of urgency in her voice.

"Of course," he smiled his best fake smile, the one he often used in the office when dealing with especially difficult customers.

"Guess what? You have a letter from the Office of the Vice President," Annabelle said, all excited as Laurie came into the post office, her face a bit flushed from the heat.

"Really?"

"It's right here."

Laurie took the envelope and was about to open it but decided that since it was bound to be a personal note, she should open it at home. Annabelle was crushed.

"I can't tell you all my secrets," Laurie commented.

"I suppose not," the postmistress replied with a sigh. "What are you gonna do with your house? Have you decided to sell it?"

"I'm not selling. I'm going to keep it so that Cameron and I can come up for weekends whenever he can get away. I've already talked to Bernie and he'll keep an eye on the place and take care of Brandy until I can get it down to Washington."

"Good. You don't want to forget that beautiful animal."

Laurie cut short her usual daily bike ride. The letter, the first one she had ever received from Cameron, was burning a hole in the pocket of her shorts and needed to be opened. Besides, the sun was too hot for a long ride. She and Brandy would fare better exercising when the temperature had cooled off.

As soon as she reached her house, she went to sit on the back deck, Brandy dutifully following. A pair of pruning shears she had been using earlier to deadhead the red geraniums showing off in boxes around the deck now served to cut off the end of the envelope. Laurie was disappointed that there was no note from Cameron and was surprised to find the envelope addressed to her in care of the Vice President. She looked at the return name and address, but it didn't ring a bell. Slowly, again using the shears, she opened the second envelope, pulled out a sheet of paper and began reading.

Dear Ms. Cosner,

First let me apologize for sending this letter to you through the Vice President's office, but not having your address or phone number I knew of no other way to contact you.

My client, Mr. Neal Landau, with whom you are acquainted, has an important matter he wants this firm to discuss with you. Please contact this office at your earliest convenience to arrange a meeting. We would, of course, be willing to travel to Washington or anywhere else you choose. We look forward to your early reply.

The letter was signed by one Marty Spears. The name was vaguely familiar to Laurie who turned the letter over as if expecting that some note on the reverse would clear things up. There was none. Neal Landau. She hadn't thought about him in years until Sarah mentioned his name the day of the garden party, and all of a sudden he was back in her life.

But for what purpose, she wondered.

Then suddenly an intense fear gripped her as though her whole being was about to be tortured, and for a moment she felt as if she would faint. She seemed to momentarily lose feeling in her legs. She wiped her perspiring brow with the back of her hand, hoping for a moment that the summer heat might be the reason for the sudden intense feeling, but she had to acknowledge that it was not. The spark that was igniting so much discomfort in her whole being was the realization that the future she had planned and imagined while reveling in all its possibilities had just been shot a fatal blow.

The next morning, the sun was barely touching the horizon when she opened her eyes. She felt sick, she felt old, yet she was fully cognizant that it was simply an illusion. She was not sick, she was not old. She had merely spent a night that could only be described as hellish. Sleep had come in short spurts and momentarily offered reprieve from the agony that did not abate and that, she knew in her most frank personal examinations, would never fully be erased. She did not want to face a new day, but the choice was not hers to make.

"You okay, Mom?" Sarah asked at breakfast table. "You look tired."

"I had trouble sleeping. It happens when you get older." After taking several more sips of strong coffee, she put forth to her daughter the proposal which she felt would solve her problem. The only solution!

"Tell me something, Sarah. When we were down in Baltimore you seemed interested in going to the Peabody Institute. Does that mean that you've decided against going to England?"

"No. I'd prefer going to England, but since you and Mr. Austin will be living in Washington, I thought you'd much prefer me attending the Peabody."

"Not really. Like you, I think England's the better choice. We could go and visit before the end of the summer, then go from there. Perhaps you might like to stay for a term. Like until Christmas."

"What's wrong, Mom?"

"Nothing."

"Trying to get rid of me?" Sarah asked, a bit of mischievousness in her eyes.

"Why would you say a thing like that?"

"You've always drowned me with your rule that I couldn't devote myself to music until I finished high school. I haven't finished yet, you know."

"I know," Laurie replied, putting a hand on her daughter's shoulder, "but I've been thinking a lot about how much talent you have, and I've talked to people who know music. It seems that it'd be best if you took a timeout right now for music studies while finishing high school."

"But if I go to England now, I won't be here for your wedding."

"I'm so sorry sweetie. I forgot to tell you. Cameron and I have decided to postpone our wedding until next year. Early March. It fits in better with his political duties and it'll give me more time to get organized. Besides," Laurie said, making an effort to smile, "without having to worry about you, I can spend more time in Washington and really get into the groove of things," she concluded, making a sliding movement with her right arm.

"The groove?" Sarah repeated, shaking her head.

"I say it's a valid expression!" Laurie said, feeling her shoulders relax.

Sarah smiled. "Sure, Mom. So when do you want to leave?"

"I was thinking by the end of next week. What do you say?"

"I say I'm ready to go," the girl announced enthusiastically.

CHAPTER THIRTY-TWO

Marty Spears. A name from the past, a name long forgotten which was now, bit by bit, bringing back to life the years she had made such a concerted effort to forget. Hoping to nap for a while, Laurie had gone back to bed, but she was unable to shut off the avalanche of thoughts, of images.

Laurie and Rita, close friends both aiming for journalism and writing careers, decided rather spontaneously one day to travel through the United States. Since graduating from college they had worked as proofreaders and gofers at the Medford newspaper while trying to break in as freelance writers by submitting articles to every magazine and newspaper they could think of. Although they made a few sales, the response had not been as enthusiastic as they had hoped, and they were getting frustrated. They needed to expand their horizon. Besides, they needed to travel in order to evolve as they had told their respective mothers.

Neither had a car, but Robby, Rita's brother who had had a crush on Laurie "since forever" as Rita liked to say, was willing to let them have his for a month or two. No longer. He needed it in the fall when he hoped to have his horticultural business off the ground.

Lying down on her bed, Laurie momentarily saw Robby's beautiful young face as he smiled at her. "This way, I know you'll come back with the car."

But Laurie had not come back with Rita in the fall. She had stayed behind in Florida because she had met Neal Landau who was exciting, handsome, full of life, the richest man she had ever known, and who was destined to be one of the greatest songwriters of his generation. When compared with Robby, a quiet man who communicated and cared for plants as though they were his close friends, Neal was the winner as far as the inexperienced, country-bred twenty-four-year-old was concerned.

"But what are you going to do for money?" Rita had asked her friend when Laurie told her she was not going back to Canada.

"Get a job."

"You're a Canadian and you don't have a green card. Nobody's gonna hire you."

"Sure they will. Marty Spears told me he knows the owner of a local paper, and that he'll hire me under the table," Laurie had explained.

"I don't like it," Rita had commented. "You might get into trouble."

"No, I won't. Even if I do, Neal'll help me. He asked me to stay, so I've got the feeling I might be Mrs. Landau before too long."

"Your mother's not going to like that!"

"My mother remarried right after my father died. She's not too concerned about me."

"Laurie, you know that Neal's into drugs, right?" Rita asked.

"He smokes dope sometimes. Who doesn't it? Rita, we both did."

"That one time. I certainly didn't like it and I'm not doing it again."

"Me neither," Laurie said.

Rita had hesitated for a moment, then said, "He does more than smoke, you know that. I saw him do coke the other night. He lined up the powder on a glass—"

"I know how it's done," Laurie interrupted.

"Then you know he's not going to be a model husband. Addicts don't stop just like that!"

"Neal says he can stop any time. He does drugs sometimes because it helps him be more creative."

"You actually believe that, don't you?" Rita commented.

"It's the truth. He's been writing great songs in the last couple of weeks," Laurie put in meekly.

"Please reconsider, Laurie. He's not worth it."

"Are you jealous because I found someone and you didn't?"

"Please! I know who I'm going to marry. He's waiting for me in

Medford. Laurie, I'm sure Neal's got lots of qualities, but there are just too many negatives."

"Rita, I'm in love. I can't just leave."

"I think you're simply infatuated with what he does and the people he knows. We've only been here in Florida for a month. You can't know a person in that time."

"That's exactly why I want to stay. To get to know him better."

"Laurie, I think it's a huge mistake for you to move in with him. He looks like the kind of guy who'll play you as long as he can. Come back with me."

"I've thought about it a lot and I want to stay. If it doesn't work out, then I'll go back. At least I won't always wonder if I should have stayed."

Rita had left alone in her brother's car early the next morning after embracing Laurie and making her promise to keep in touch. "Don't you go and get married without telling me, you hear?"

"I hear," Laurie had replied, a tear swelling up without warning.

In the dark of her bedroom in McPine, Laurie was now remembering how scared she had been when she realized the finality of Rita driving away. The thought of her being on her own to face the future had been overwhelming, and panic had seized her soul. She had never told Rita, but a moment after the car had driven off, Laurie had tried to run after it to no avail because the blue sedan had quickly disappeared around the corner.

She stood for the longest time in the middle of the road in front of the cheap motel where they had been staying. She did love Neal Landau. At least at that moment she thought she did. How else could an insolent kid justify her rash decision?

Marty Spears had kept his word and she had been hired to write local news for a Miami paper. She enjoyed the work and always looked forward to her evenings with Neal. There were always lots of interesting people around, plenty of food and wonderful music. She wrote to Rita often to let her know how happy she was, even though she had had to face the fact that while she lived in his house and shared his bed, she wasn't the only woman in Neal Landau's life. She had often caught him passionately kissing other girls, and he had offered no apologies. He had chastised Laurie for being uptight. These girls meant nothing to him, he had said. He was simply having a little harmless fun.

Nearly a year had passed by the time Laurie decided it was time to leave Florida behind and head home. Neal had been a disappointment, but she nevertheless saw some aspects of her time with him as having been opportunities for growth. She had learned a great deal. She had experienced life. She was reasonably happy with her decision, until a week before her scheduled departure when a doctor confirmed what she feared. She was indeed pregnant. Then the future truly frightened her.

What should she do? Neal had made it very clear he didn't want children. Should she leave without telling him? Go back to Canada and listen to her mother's sermons while relying on the woman for help and financial assistance? What a mess, she had thought. Surely someone "up there" didn't like her because she had always been so careful about birth control. Then she thought she couldn't afford to feel sorry for herself. No matter what, Neal had a right to know. And faced with the reality of his being a father, he might embrace the idea. She might very well be building a scenario without foundation. He might welcome the news, he might want to marry her and straighten his life, give up the drugs. Perhaps they could make a go of it.

Or was it a schoolgirl's dream?

Only one way to find out.

Laurie was remembering how long into the night she had cried after Neal Landau shattered her psyche. He had accused her of having other lovers, of trying to trap him. Hope had disintegrated like dandelion seeds in the wind. She had packed up and left the very next day. She had never seen or heard from him again. Nor from Marty Spears. Until the letter.

And now life was again putting a complicated and messy fork in her road. But she had grown wise enough to know that no matter how much you might want to avoid the inevitable, some dreams never grow into reality. They are destined to remain solely delicate ephemeral images the soul turns to in moments of sweet and gentle phantasm. She would cry for a long time, but she would take the decisions that needed to be taken and she would survive as she had done in the past when faced with difficult options.

And if you're lucky, she mused, something great can come from difficult choices. She had a wonderful, loving daughter because someone in the great unknown did love her and had been very generous indeed.

She punched an eleven-digit number and a receptionist at a law firm in Miami answered. The woman said she was sorry, but Mr. Spears was out of the office until Friday. She promised she would contact him and give him the message.

CHAPTER THIRTY-THREE

Kingston, a historic city fringing the north shore of Lake Ontario at its eastern mouth is full of busyness and excitement in the summer, especially in the streets bordering the harbor. There are large and smaller tour boats that take tourists—Americans and Canadians alike—for a closer look at the Thousand Islands and at some of the extravagant castles built over a century ago by wealthy American business barons.

Crafts of all shapes and sizes, yachts, motor boats and sailboats, paint a wonderful scene whether docked or plying the clear water. Many of their owners are Americans who love to trek up to Canada for a little rest and recreation while taking advantage of the more often than not favorable currency exchange. They come to meet friends. To see and be seen. To enjoy life.

A gentle breeze coming off the lake was cooling the midday temperature as Mike Gilbert feasted on the parade of happy vacationers milling about while enjoying a delightfully fresh salad at a small sidewalk café overlooking the harbor. He needed to relax before putting his plan into motion, which he could only hope and pray would work. If not, at least he would have the satisfaction of knowing that he had made the effort.

An hour later he was facing a Royal Canadian Mounted Police officer across a simple gray metal desk in a small nondescript office whose door was closed. It was a most delicate matter, Mike had insisted. Complete discretion was needed. The officer was middle-aged and much taller and bigger than Mike, with a severe face, a face that made you wonder if he had the muscles required for smiling. Mike felt nervous. Why couldn't a young, cute female Mountie have been on hand to listen to him, he wondered?

While he may have been a simple farmer in upstate New York, Gerry Lefebvre was about to make a difference in the world. Or so he believed. He was to lead. A first for him. Demonstrations were scheduled all along the border between the United States and Canada the following Saturday at noon, local time, and he would be among the first in the group of New Yorkers coming from all over the cities, towns and villages in the Empire State to make a strong statement at the Thousand Island crossing point between the two countries; a statement Canada would not be able to ignore.

His wife was not impressed. She was of the opinion that people should live and let live. Besides, summer was the busy time on the farm, she said. Gerry argued that his taking a day off was not the end of the world. Their two teenage boys were there to help out and could manage on their own for a few hours. They had done it in the past.

On Thursday evening, as he had been doing nearly every evening for some time, Gerry went online and conferred with leaders of the other groups all along the border. Except for a few minor irritants, everyone seemed pleased with their own local preparations. Saturday would be a day that would let Canada know in no uncertain terms that the Americans were a proud people, a people who would not let themselves be verbally maligned.

Gerry checked for any new e-mail messages before turning in and was pleased to see one from Shane Peachee. A meeting was to take place for lunch on Friday at a snack bar on Wellesley Island, the American side of the St. Lawrence River. The final, final preparations. Gerry was getting excited.

Ryan Crowley, the RCMP officer with the unsmiling face, was listening intently to Mike Gilbert. He was taking notes, but his unflappable expression did not change. Mike told him how explosives would be used during the demonstrations at the Thousand Islands border crossing the following Saturday. The explosives would be set off in the water and were meant to bring attention to the demonstration. However, Mike told the officer that he was worried not only because of possible repercussions, but mostly because of the real physical danger to demonstrators. Mike was giving the officer these details after providing all manner of pertinent personal information.

"I'm not quite clear what your role is in all this, Mr. Gilbert," officer Crowley commented.

"I don't have one. As I said, I'm just on vacation, and I heard someone at the B&B where my girlfriend and I are staying brag about the plan to use explosives."

"That person have a name?"

Mike had long debated, but he had finally concluded that he couldn't not rat on Shane. That was the point of the whole exercise. He had, however, decided to skip over any possible kinship between Shane and himself. "Shane Peachee."

"What does he look like?" Crowley asked, and Mike obliged, as much as he could be explicit: tall, lanky, long black hair. "He's got a tattoo of a butterfly on one of his arms."

"A butterfly?"

"Well, not small like the type girls like. It's ugly and green. I think it's a butterfly, but maybe it's something else. Some sort of mystical bird maybe."

"Where did Peachee get the explosives?" Crowley asked.

"That I don't know."

"Where are the explosives being kept?"

"Already strapped to a couple of old boats. It'll be detonated by a diver, Mr. Peachee, about one o'clock on Saturday as the demonstrators block the road and prevent Americans from entering Canada."

"You say a couple of old boats. How many exactly?"

"Two."

"And where are these boats?" Crowley asked.

"If you show me a map of the Thousand Islands I'll indicate exactly where the boats are anchored."

Officer Crowley stood up and motioned that Mike should follow. In the hallway, a large-scale map of the islands hung on one of the walls, and Mike pointed to where the boats were rigged up.

"There should be more people like you, Mr. Gilbert, willing to inform the authority of planned wrongdoings. We know where you're staying. We'll be in touch," Crowley said matter-of-factly.

"I've told you everything I know, why do you need to be in touch? What I mean is…"

"Your girlfriend doesn't know about this and you'd like to keep it that way," Crowley stated.

"Exactly," Mike said, relaxing his shoulders.

"Don't worry. We can be discreet. If we need to talk to you, someone will ask you where they can rent a bike. That'll be your cue. Listen carefully to what they tell you."

"Of course," Mike said.

Through one of the front windows, officer Crowley was looking at Mike sauntering down the sidewalk and spoke to a fellow officer. "You heard?" he asked. The other officer nodded. Crowley continued. "My take is that that guy Gilbert was somehow involved in the plan and now he's ratting on his buddy."

"What makes you think that? He seemed honest enough to me."

"People don't just discuss how they're going to use explosives with total strangers on vacation," Crowley answered.

"Maybe he got cold feet."

"Could be," Crowley said. "Or they had a falling out. See what you can find out about both Gilbert and that Peachee fellow."

"Sure thing."

Mike took his time driving east along the water and made it back to the inn shortly before dinner. April who was enjoying a cold beer on the porch walked down to meet him. "You decided to come back, I see."

"What do you mean? I told you I'd be back. I just needed time by myself."

"What did you do all day?"

Mike had decided on the return trip how he would answer. "I hung around Kingston, had lunch, and then took a tour of the islands, something I'd never done before."

"Neither have I. I would have loved to go with you."

"Next time," Mike said simply.

Heavy thunderstorms during the night had drastically changed the air mass along the river. The mugginess was gone as though a giant air conditioning unit had been turned on. Mike had slept well despite the thunder and the awkwardness at dinner with Shane, obviously annoyed at him. While the inn served a buffet breakfast to its guests in the morning, they were on their own for lunch and dinner. Mike and April had therefore been the only ones at the table with Moira and Shane the previous evening. The meal had been briefly interrupted with the arrival of new guests, a couple in their early forties.

"I understand," Shane had finally said to Mike. "You're entitled to your opinion. That's what we're always fighting for, isn't it? Anyway it's all gonna be okay."

"Mike's a worrier," April had put in.

"Because I've reason to be," he had said. "Let's change the subject."

And they had, and Mike had been polite, excusing himself to go for a walk as soon as Moira and April had begun clearing the main course.

"Leaving again?" April called after Mike as he walked down to the water's edge after breakfast the next morning.

He turned, thinking that she looked pretty with the early morning sun kissing her face. "Just going for a walk. You can join me, you know," he invited.

"I've got to help Moira. Gonna be long?"

"I don't know, April."

"Is this the way it'll be 'til Sunday? You sulking and spending time by yourself?"

"I'm ready to go home now. You should too, and refuse to be involved in Shane's harebrained scheme."

"Well, I won't," she said firmly.

"Then that's the way it'll be," he said, turning on his heels and heading for the parkway bordered by a walking/cycling path. He was just about there when the couple who had checked in the previous evening suddenly appeared around a corner.

"Hi," the man said. He was tall with dark curly hair, and Mike thought that his eyes were piercing. "Do you know where we could rent bikes around here?"

Mike momentarily stiffened. The RCMP was on the case. He smiled. "No, but I can answer any other question."

The woman spoke without smiling. She was slender, but Mike knew he would lose in a hand-to-hand combat with her. Definitely in top shape. "We assume that was your girlfriend back there on the porch."

"You assume correctly," Mike said.

"Is she involved at all in the plot?"

"Nooo. She's just visiting her cousin," Mike replied a little too stiffly.

"You've come this far," the man put in, "don't falter now."

Mike could feel himself blush. "She's not involved. She might sympathize with the aim of the protest on Saturday, but that's it."

"Are you sure?"

"Of course," Mike said, flustered now. "She's not going to do anything."

"Then why are you so nervous?"

"I'm... generally nervous, that's all." And Mike could console himself that he was indeed telling the truth. The whole thing had put his nerves somewhat on edge.

"We need you to keep your eyes and ears open in case anything changes. Anything at all," the man emphasized, "please let us know at once."

"I will," Mike said earnestly.

"Just ask one of us how we like the area, and we'll take it from there," the woman said.

In an instant the pair was jogging on the path along the road. Mike followed at a slower pace. Ten minutes later, he saw them jog back towards the inn, barely acknowledging him as they ran past him.

CHAPTER THIRTY-FOUR

*L*aurie had made her decision. Not one she wanted, but the only one she could take under the circumstances. No amount of deliberation, speculation, wishing and daydreaming would alter her reality. She was, however, curious as to the reason behind Neal Landau's decision to contact her. The call would come soon enough, she told herself. She was at her desk in McPine, revising copy she had written the previous day when the phone rang.

"Ms. Cosner? This is Marty Spears in Miami," the voice said, a voice she didn't recognize at all.

"Yes," was all she could say.

"I assume you got my letter."

"Of course I did. That's why I called you."

"As I said, we would like to meet with you at your convenience."

"Why don't you get to the point right now and tell me what this is all about."

"Very well. My client is Neal Landau. I'm sure you remember him."

"Of course I remember him," she said impatiently. "I lived with him, and you, Marty, were always around so you know that I lived with him. Of course, you were so spaced out most of the time that you may not remember. What is it you want?" she asked, feeling fortunate that Sarah was at her cousin's house in Medford discussing her mother's sudden change of heart about going to England.

"Laurie," Spears said in his most conciliatory voice, "let me first say that we don't want to cause any trouble for you or interfere with any of your plans as far as Vice President Austin is concerned." Pause. She was in no mood to offer any sort of comment. After a long moment he continued. "Neal tells me that your daughter Sarah is his daughter as well."

"You know that for a fact, do you?"

"No, of course not. But we could petition the court for a paternity test."

"Why would you want to do that?" Laurie asked simply. "You know you'd lose."

Spears wasn't quite sure whether she meant that a paternity test would be denied or whether it would prove negative. He pressed on. "Neal just wants to see the girl and spend time with her. She wouldn't have to know anything. I mean, he would never tell her she's his daughter. She would just be meeting one of your old friends."

"So, pray tell, why is Neal so interested in this girl all of a sudden? Don't tell me! He saw her play the piano on TV and got it into his head that because she's talented she has to be related. If he hadn't seen her, the thought would never have entered his mind."

"The point is, Laurie, he did see her. And you can't get around the fact that she does look like him."

"Marty, do me a favor?"

"Anything."

"Cut the crap" she said calmly. "She looks nothing like him, and you know it. But, I understand why you'd say she does. Neal's paying you so you've got to stroke him. Isn't that right, Marty? You were his gofer then and I'm sure you're his gofer now. Still sniffing around to find drugs for both of you, or have you progressed to home delivery by now?" Her voice was cutting. She wasn't going down without a fight.

"We gave up drugs a long time ago," Marty Spears admitted.

"If it's true, good for you. Now, why is Neal playing this tune now?"

Spears knew that his answer was his ace in the hole. She was a woman and a mother. She would be sensitive to his client's plight. "Neal is very ill. We don't know how much longer he's got. It could be months, it could be weeks. Seeing Sarah is his last wish, and I intend to do all I can to make it happen."

Many scenarios had played in Laurie's mind since she had received the letter, but this one she had not considered. She made an effort to keep her voice even. "What's wrong with him?"

"He's got AIDS."

Laurie blanched. What if? No, she quickly considered, it was too long ago.

As if understanding her thoughts, Marty Spears said, "He found out he was HIV positive about seven years ago, now. It progressed very quickly and the meds have proven disappointing in his case."

"I'm sorry to hear this. I really am, but I still don't see the point. In other words, if Neal wasn't ill we wouldn't be having this conversation."

"Illness always changes things," Spears commented. "He wants Sarah to be part of his life for the little time he's got left."

Laurie's plan had been formulated long before she got the call. She had to take it slowly. To appear compliant. "He'd want to come up here, I suppose?"

Marty Spears smiled as his shoulders relaxed. He had gotten through to the woman after all. "Not necessarily. I'm sure a few days in the sun would be good for both of you. We'll pay your expenses, of course."

Of course. "Where does Neal live now?"

"He's always lived in the same house on Grover, near the Intercoastal. I'm sure you remember it."

How could I forget, Laurie thought. Into the phone, she said, "I'm sure you understand that I have to think things out."

"Of course, of course. Take a few days. When can I call you back?"

"Try mid next week."

As he hung up, Marty Spears consoled himself that the conversation had gone better than expected.

In her McPine home, Laurie said, "You fucking bastard," under her breath as she hung up. She had been so wrong to assume that the past would always remain in the past.

She went to stand at the window for a moment, too angry for tears. She had to let it out. "If you think you can mess up my daughter's life, you're sadly mistaken. I'll kill you before I let you near Sarah," she yelled out into the air, shocking herself.

She sat at her desk and repeated "Damn!" a number of times before being able to relax enough to continue finalizing her plans.

CHAPTER THIRTY-FIVE

Mike was not around to see Shane Peachee and April leave together in the inn's van. However, two male investigators were. One of them was one of the joggers who had approached Mike earlier in the day. The other was an FBI agent with wide experience in investigating terrorism. Neither Canadian nor American authorities were willing to take any chance that the planned demonstrations could degenerate into violence.

The two men were driving a red sports car with Ontario plates and followed at a safe distance. The female RCMP investigator had remained at the inn and had been able to read Shane Peachee's e-mail. The place and time of the meeting with Gerry Lefebvre was quickly reported by phone to the officers in the red car. In turn, the men contacted other investigators on both sides of the border.

The inn's van made its way along the 1000 Islands Parkway to the exit that would take them over the 1000 Islands Bridge to Hill Island in Canada, then on to Wellesley Island and the U.S.

The driver and the passenger in the van had no idea how many eyes were keeping tabs on them as they approached the border crossing. There were four cars ahead of them in their lane and they waited patiently, passports in hand.

When the van glided in front of the booth, Shane was happy to produce his American passport and explain that he spent part of the summer in Canada with his girlfriend, and that he would be returning to the United States the first week in September. Right now he was only going to meet a friend for lunch, and bringing April, a friend of his girlfriend, to meet this man. They might hit it off, he said smiling. The guard on duty offered no comment as he examined both passports, but said that all vehicles entering the U.S. were being inspected. Shane dutifully got out to throw wide open the back doors of the van so the guard could examine the interior.

"Not much in there," he said casually as the man looked under the spare tires in the back.

The back doors were closed and a large mirror on a low-wheeled cart was brought out to carefully examine the underside of the van. During that time, the first guard took time to take a very close look at Shane Peachee. Luckily it was summer and Peachee was wearing a light shirt and tight shorts so that it was easy to determine that he was not carrying a concealed weapon. Soon the van was on its way.

"Sometimes they put up a fuss because I live in Canada part of the year," Shane felt obliged to explain to April.

When she spoke, the subject was quite different. "You sure this guy Lefebvre can be trusted?"

"Sure. Don't worry. He's a farmer who loves his country. What more could you ask for?"

Soon Shane was parking the van on Wellesley Island close to a chip wagon, a few feet from a large sign that read: Open. Huge pictures of hot dogs, hamburgers and fries plastered all around the opening on the side of the unit testified to the all-American vacation fare. A portion of the opening, held up by a metal bar, served as sun protection while the lower portion was a shelf where plastic bottles of ketchup and mustard were prominent.

Lefebvre, a man with serious hints of gray in his brown hair and the sun-damaged skin of a farmer who never considered sunscreen, was waiting seated at one of the picnic tables nearby. Shane and April got out, introductions were made and soon Peachee went to order lunch.

"They're making it as easy as ABC," the FBI man in the red car parked a ways back said as both men scrutinized the scene through what appeared to be binoculars but were in fact listening and recording devices. The voices were coming through loud and clear.

"So, Gerry," April was saying, "everything okay? I mean you're not nervous are you?"

"A little. I mean, I've never been involved in anything this big before. Makes you think."

"Sure does," April said.

"We expect a big turnout," Lefebvre said proudly.

"That's great. Shane says it's going to be big all along the border."

They were silent until Shane returned with food and drinks. After taking a few bites of his hamburger, he told Gerry that he had come down for some last minute preparations.

"What sort of preparations?" Lefebvre asked. "I thought everything was arranged."

"We want the rally to have some punch," Peachee said proudly, "so we've rigged up some old boats with explosives."

"Bingo," the FBI man told his companion in the red car.

"What?" Lefebvre said. "That's dangerous!"

"Not the way we're doing it. We'll be pulling the boats away from the shore tomorrow morning and setting them off around one o'clock. That way a lot of people will see that we mean business and we'll get good coverage."

Gerry Lefebvre was suddenly feeling uneasy. "I don't like that," he said firmly.

"Nothing to it," Shane Peachee assured him. "It'll go off like clockwork. Now, Gerry, we don't want you to tell anyone about this, otherwise we might have some problems. The police will be keeping an eye on things tomorrow, and if they knew we're going to use explosives to make our point, they wouldn't like it."

"You're right, we don't like it," the RCMP officer in the red car said.

"They could even stop protesters from getting here," Shane was continuing. "Don't worry, Gerry. It's all gonna work out."

"I hope so," the farmer said meekly.

"After we finish our food, we'll show you exactly where the two boats are tied up so you know what to expect. Okay?"

"Okay."

"We're about to move," the FBI man said in a transmitter. "We can't lose this guy."

A short time later, Gerry Lefebvre climbed in the back seat of the van behind Shane and they were on their way. They were followed at a discreet distance by a dark battered-looking pickup being driven by the FBI man. The RCMP officer was at his side. A young female officer dressed in denim shorts and a white tee was now driving the red sports car and was soon passing the van on the narrow road. The exchange of vehicles had been quick and flawless.

The van drove only about a mile then pulled into a small marina, parking close to the water's edge. The trio got out and Shane pointed to a short pier almost in front of them.

"See those two old boats there?" Shane asked Gerry who nodded. "They're the ones we'll blow up. We'll be pulling them out about five hundred yards straight out so there'll be no danger to anyone."

"We're not anywhere close to where that guy Gilbert said the boats were," the RCMP officer commented.

"My guess is that Peachee didn't tell Gilbert the whole truth," a voice retorted on an open line. "Go figure!"

Shane was explaining to Gerry that he and April were going down to check things out and asked him to wait.

With many eyes following their every move, Shane and April made their way to the pier. Shane stepped into one of the boats. "What the hell," he yelled. "Someone's been around here." He bent down to take a closer look.

"What's going on?" April asked.

"I bet you that boyfriend of yours——"

"You didn't tell him the right spot, so it couldn't have been Mike."

Shane did not comment as he bent down from the waist, dropping both his arms into the water.

Before anyone could fathom exactly what had taken place, an explosion rocked the marina, sending flame, smoke, and debris high into the air.

"Let's go," the FBI man yelled as he got out of the pickup and began running toward the pier. Other law enforcement people who appeared on the scene on bikes were also bolting past Gerry Lefebvre who stood staring ahead in disbelief. FBI people who had been rushing to the spot in a motor boat sped up at the sight of the blast. They pulled Shane Peachee from the water. He was alive, but unconscious, badly burnt and missing an arm.

The pier itself had been blown apart and several small boats were in pieces. April McLaren's body had been thrown with such force against the mast of a nearby sailboat that she was partly hanging there in an indecent position. The FBI agent who had been monitoring the conversation from the pickup truck went to confirm the death, then slipped out of his vest to cover her. Everyone seemed to be trying to digest the import of the accident as sirens were heard in the distance.

Making his way to where Gerry Lefebvre was standing, the FBI man said, "I'm so sorry about your friends."

Gerry remained silent, his whole body shaking.

"We'll take you to the hospital."

"No...no," Gerry managed to say. "I'm okay. I've got to get my pickup."

"I don't think you're in any shape to drive," the FBI agent said.

"I've got to get home...cancel the rally tomorrow...I've got to do it now."

Gesturing to a couple to approach, the agent said, "Someone will be happy to help you with that. These people here are very nice, Gerry. They'll help you get home and do what you have to do, and then they'll take you to a doctor."

The woman put a hand on Gerry's shoulder and he turned around like a child being guided by a parent.

What the hell had happened, he kept asking himself? It was supposed to be just a peaceful demonstration.

CHAPTER THIRTY-SIX

At the White House, everyone from President Thomson on down, felt uneasy about the demonstrations planned for the following day. The President was annoyed because they would solve nothing, and would only bring attention to incidents that were best forgotten. He and the Canadian Prime Minister had conversed frankly during private talks, and they acknowledged that differences of opinions would always exist between the two countries, between the two populace, and between the two leaders. As they had long existed. They might share a continent, but each needed to aspire to particular ideas and ideals. If only the media understood that simple fact and stopped fueling problems and anger where none existed the world would be a better place, the President thought.

For his part, Vice President Austin feared that, seen on the news, the protests would work to increase negative feelings about Canada among Americans who never much thought about Canada in terms other than as a neighboring country with a cold climate. This could play against him if spin doctors working for his opponents were to stir up the perceived reason for these rallies and their imminent success. His fellow countrymen might find it difficult to forgive him for daring to find love with a Canadian. He might be seen as lacking. It could play against him.

Sitting in an easy chair across from the Vice President, President Thomson expressed aloud that he would love to be able to "sign something" and stop all this nonsense from happening tomorrow. "If I say anything at this point it's going to be seen as government interference in the free will of the people."

Vice President Austin lifted his arms up in a gesture of resignation. "If we're lucky, it will rain. All the way across the continent!"

In his small office, Oliver Rogge took a break from the file he was reading, and checked the latest news on CNN as he did regularly. He heard the anchor read a short item.

"There has been an explosion at a marina on Wellesley Island in the Thousand Islands, close to the Canadian border. Preliminary reports indicate that one person has been killed and another seriously injured. No other information is available at this time, but authorities do not believe it was related to terrorism. The investigation continues."

Rogge reached for his phone and dialed. He had assorted contacts in government and law enforcement agencies. It was vital to his job. He got nowhere with the first person he talked to, but persisting with the phone, he eventually reached the Assistant Director of the FBI.

"What's the White House's interest?"

"The explosion was very close to the Canadian border. With the rallies planned for tomorrow, we're concerned that there could be a connection."

"The official version's going to be an accident, pure and simple. A man and his lady friend went to start their boat, and somehow the gas tank exploded. That's it. Identification will take some time."

"Might I inquire as to the non-official version, sir?"

"The injured man is Shane Peachee, an American who is a part-time innkeeper at the Thousand Islands. The deceased is one April McLaren, a Canadian who lives in a place called Medford, Ontario." Rogge's ears perked up. "At the time of the incident they were being trailed by the FBI because they intended to blow up boats with explosives tomorrow during the rally. We were fortunate that Ms. McLaren's companion, a Mike Gilbert, had informed the Mounties of the plan. When Mr. Peachee went to check the boat, he noticed something was wrong and before anyone knew what had happened, the device on the boat somehow exploded. Why it did, we don't know at this point. It'll take a while to get a fix on that."

"Anything else?" Rogge inquired, intrigued.

"One of the main organizers of the rally in New York State who was on the scene at the time of the accident was pretty spooked by the whole thing. He has canceled the planned demonstration at the Thousand Islands tomorrow and has been urging other groups along the border to do the same. Our intelligence so far is that many of these other groups are canceling. Rumors spread fast nowadays with social media, and someone has been speculating that explosives were set to go off all along the border tomorrow. Demonstrators are generally non-violent, so that seems to be scaring many of them away."

After thanking the law enforcement man, Rogge said he would inform the President.

Told that the Vice President was at a meeting in the oval office, Rogge walked quickly in that direction. This was big news. Simply being the messenger could only prove positive for him. The two men were bound to be very pleased to hear of the canceled demonstrations, of that he was certain, because like in any other work environment, gossip flourished in the West Wing.

"You can go in," the President's secretary told Rogge after he waited a few minutes.

The Vice President stood up to greet him, sure that whatever it was had to be big.

"Mr. President, Mr. Vice President, there has been an important development," Rogge began. In the next few minutes he related the official and unofficial versions of what had led to the explosion in the Thousand Islands, and how it resulted in one person dying and another being seriously injured. He added that many of the Saturday rallies were being canceled.

"Rain!" the Vice President said aloud.

Rogge failed to understand the remark, but saw that the President did.

"Who were the people involved?" the President wanted to know.

"The man who was injured is an American by the name of Peachee. He will be charged as soon as he recovers sufficiently. The name of the woman who died is April McLaren, a Canadian." Here Rogge paused, then addressed the Vice President. "Sir, Ms. McLaren was engaged to Mike Gilbert."

"You mean Ms. Cosner's brother?" the President stated more than asked.

"Yes," Austin replied.

"If I may," Rogge said. "It seems that Mr. Gilbert and Ms. McLaren had a serious difference of opinion about using explosives.

He contacted the Mounties and told them of the plan. Then Ms. McLaren went off with Mr. Peachee."

"I see," Austin said simply.

"Mr. Gilbert is very much a pacifist," Rogge told the two men. "His willingness to alert the authorities certainly testifies to that."

At the inn in the Thousand Islands, Mike Gilbert was getting worried about April. Had she taken off, leaving him to worry about her as repayment for his actions of the last couple of days? Moira was no help. All she could tell him was that Shane and April had gone to get a part for the motor boat. Just across the border, she said. Maybe there was lots of traffic, she said. Sometimes the bridge got bogged down.

By mid-afternoon he went for a walk.

Making his way up the road to the Parkway, he saw a nondescript dark blue sedan slow down and stop on the shoulder a few feet ahead of him. The driver got out, and Mike immediately recognized Ryan Crowley, the RCMP officer he had talked to in Kingston.

"Hello, Mr. Gilbert."

"Hi," Mike replied amiably. "I'm surprised to see you. I thought you had other people working on the case around here."

"We do, but the thing is that there is no case," Crowley said. "Not anymore."

"I don't understand."

"Mr. Gilbert, there was an accident a couple of hours ago on Wellesley island. While Mr. Peachee was apparently handling the explosives, something went horribly wrong and there was an explosion. He was badly injured."

"That's terrible..." Mike began, then almost yelled, "What about April?"

"She was near Mr. Peachee and she was killed. I am truly sorry."

Mike stood on the side of the road staring at Crowley as if he was some sort of monster prankster. "You're lying," he yelled at the officer.

"I wish I were, Mr. Gilbert. It was a most unfortunate accident."

After a long moment, Mike yelled, "I killed her. I killed both of them."

"Why do you say that? What you told us did not make them go to the boat to check the dynamite. It was just part of their routine."

"Except it would have been me instead of April. Don't you see, she replaced me," Mike emphasized by tapping his fingers on his chest.

Because he had tried to do the right thing, because he wanted to avoid injuries, he had killed the woman he loved.

"If it's any consolation," Crowley said, "most of tomorrow's demonstrations have been canceled. Now, can you tell me who should be advised of Mr. Peachee's death?"

As he drove back to the inn in the RCMP vehicle, Mike became painfully aware that it would probably take him forever to make peace with himself.

When the phone rang in her office in McPine, Laurie jumped. Fatigue made her feel nervous and uptight.

"How are you, Laurie?" Cameron Austin inquired.

"Great now that I hear your voice. And in the middle of the afternoon at that. What a great surprise."

"Laurie, I've got to ask if you heard from your brother Mike recently."

"No, he's on vacation in the Thousand Islands with April. Why do you ask?"

"I have some bad news," Austin said, then quickly realizing that he was not going about it the right way said, "Mike is fine, Laurie."

"Good. Now I can breathe," she said. "You scared me. What's this all about anyway?"

The Vice President spent several minutes going into the details of the incident. "I'm sorry about your brother's fiancée."

"Mike will appreciate your concern. Thank you."

"Are you okay?"

"Yes... No. I never did like April very much, but I never thought she would become embroiled with explosives."

"Sometimes people do things for reasons others don't understand. Are you sure you'll be okay?"

"Yes. I'll try to reach Mike and my mother. Talk to them."

"Best thing to do. I hope this doesn't change our plans. I mean you will be coming down at the end of the month as promised?"

"Of course, Mr. Vice President," Laurie said, fighting to keep her voice upbeat.

A few minutes after she hung up, Laurie was trying to put her thoughts in order when the phone rang again. It was her brother Mike. For the next hour, they lost track of time as they reflected, examined, assessed, reexamined, analyzed, reassessed, and lulled into retrospection. With the venting of anger and regrets, the grieving process was underway as his eyes reddened and tears glistened on his cheeks.

"What are you going to do now?" Laurie asked.

"I'll make sure her remains are shipped to Medford. Her family wants a funeral there."

Laurie wished she could have been near her brother to hug him. Despite her personal feelings towards April, Mike had loved the woman. That fact alone made her a special person who deserved respect especially now that her life had been taken away so cruelly. Maybe she, Laurie, had been too close-minded to see beyond the physical details to the whole being.

A lesson to be added to all the other lessons of life.

CHAPTER THIRTY-SEVEN

"I don't understand the change of heart," Laurie's mother was saying at the end of the line. "Why's Sarah going to England now? I mean, I'm all for the Royal College of Music as you well know, but it seems so sudden."

"Mom, I can't discuss this now. Why don't we have a long talk when you come to Medford for the funeral?"

"Okay, dear. If that's what you want."

Hanging up, Laurie Cosner smiled. Her plan was falling into place. Of course, going to April's funeral could not have been foreseen, but that fact would change very little. After many phone calls to England, some of them very early in the morning to accommodate the time difference, followed by countless e-mails, her strategy was unfolding quite nicely. Everything was now in place. Mother and daughter would fly across the Atlantic in little over a week's time. Perfect, Laurie thought. It gave her time for the two side trips that would occupy most of her thoughts until they were completed.

"How cold does it get in London? I mean which coat should I take? What about boots?" Sarah was asking after flying into her mother's office.

"Not as cold as here. There's little if any snow, I understand. Tell you what. Why don't you pack light and we'll get what we need there, okay?"

"Okay. How long're you going to stay?"

"Not quite sure. Until you get settled in. I might take a short trip through Europe before coming back."

"Too bad Mr. Austin can't come with you."

"I certainly agree," Laurie said simply.

At the post office, Annabelle felt offended at not having been told the news earlier. "You mean Sarah's going to study in England now?"

"Yes," Laurie said. "It'll work out perfectly because of my book tour for *Beads of the Sea*. I'll be on the road for the next few weeks. This way I know she'll be happy."

"Seems that book got published fast," Annabelle was commenting.

"With computers today, a book can be put together in a flash."

"Good for you. What about Mr. Austin? When's the wedding?"

Laurie smiled. "Probably delayed until the spring. We still have to finalize a date, but until then I'll be going to and around Washington as often as I can during my travels."

"Good for you," Annabelle said. "Are we going to meet him before you leave McPine like you promised?"

"I'm working on it."

On Sunday, shortly after midday, Laurie Cosner deplaned and followed the other passengers arriving from Toronto into the terminal at Dulles International Airport. She half-expected Agent Lonsdale to be waiting. He wasn't, of course. No one, except her mother, knew where she was. The two women had had a long conversation, and the grandmother had agreed with Laurie that the decision was a wise one for Sarah. "But not for you," she had sadly concluded.

"I'll survive," Laurie had said.

"Maybe it'll all work out in the end."

"Mom, please don't hold your optimistic breath."

Carrying only a handbag and wearing a beige summer suit she had bought on an earlier visit to Washington, Laurie made her way outside to stand in the queue for cabs. She told the driver the general direction where she wanted to go and that she would let him know when to stop. He eyed her for a long moment in the rearview mirror, and despite the dark glasses hiding her eyes and the wide-brimmed straw hat covering most of her hair, she wondered if he recognized her. She quickly switched her gaze outside the vehicle deciding she wouldn't let it worry her.

The cab was some distance from One Observatory Circle when she asked to get out. It was a nice day, a walk would do her good.

All the men on duty recognized her as she arrived on foot to the landmark home and assumed she was expected. Millie Spock offered a warm welcome.

"I didn't know Mr. Austin was expecting you," she uttered excitedly.

"He's not. Is he home?"

"Yes. He's been busy in his office most of the day."

"I know the way. Thank you very much, Millie," Laurie said warmly.

In reply to her soft knock, she heard the familiar voice. "Come." She saw him at his desk, his reading glasses almost on the tip of his nose. He did not gaze up immediately. "What is it, Millie?"

"It's not Millie. It's me, Cameron."

The Vice President looked up and at that moment his face was frozen in disbelieving joy. "Laurie! What a wonderful surprise," he said standing up and coming to her. "Didn't you tell me you'd be busy all weekend?" He embraced her warmly with his long arms. It felt so good, she didn't want to let go.

"I have to talk to you," she began. "Can we sit?"

"Certainly," he indicated a sofa against a far wall.

She avoided his dark eyes for an instant. This was proving a lot more difficult than she had imagined in her mind's eye. Perhaps she should have taken her mother's advice and swallowed one of the tranquilizers from the little pill box the older woman had given her before her departure. "My mother, my pusher," Laurie was remembering telling Eileen Danfort.

"It'll help you relax, dear," Eileen had replied. "It's bound to be a tough trip."

Her mother had been right on the nose on that count.

"How's your brother? Is there anything I can do to help?" Cameron was asking.

"I'm the one who can help you," she said.

Austin was looking into green eyes and he was momentarily shaken. What he saw was more than pain. "Why did you come all the way down here?"

"Cameron, I'm hopelessly in love with you," she began, her hand reaching into her bag, "but I've got to give this back to you." She handed him the dark red velvet box containing the ring she had so proudly worn.

"Laurie, I don't understand. You're breaking up our engagement?"

"I'm so sorry, Cameron, but I have to."

"But you just said..."

"I know what I just said," she almost whispered, "and it's God's honest truth, but our being together is not going to work. I am a liability at your side, and that liability will only increase in the future. The media's bound to speculate about April because of her record of activism. And she was in it with Mike. They'll be saying that you're hanging around a woman whose brother could be dangerous, even a terrorist—a Canadian terrorist at that. And all this's going to hurt you in the long run," she said softly. "I can't just stand by and watch it happen."

"Laurie, no one is saying anything of the sort. Your brother's friend was the victim of an accident while on vacation. That's it. That's all the media knows and will ever know."

"Can you guarantee it? What if someone digs and finds out the truth once the man who was with her recovers enough to be charged? What then? The terrorist angle would be a lot meatier in a world where the mean, the evil and the ugly sell. Then I'd be implicated by my proximity. It'd be damaging for you."

"It is not going to happen. Besides, why would it be damaging for me?" he asked, then answered his own question. "It's certainly been proven in the past that voters accept the fact that politicians have family members they would rather not be associated with. The simple reason is that most people have first-hand knowledge of what it's like to want to avoid someone close or to be ashamed of a relative. So you see there'll be no consequences even if the worst-case scenario does present itself. But this is not what this is really all about, is it Laurie? Are you sure you love me?"

"Cameron, I will always love you."

"Then what's the real problem? Something's happened. What is it?"

Her eyes were now swimming in tears, and he could see by the short spasms of her chin that she was about to cry. He felt a vice tightening his chest.

"It's just the way things are, Cameron," she said in a teary voice. "I am a liability for you and will always be. We simply have to face facts. I will never forget your kindness, your love. I had to come down to tell you in person. I'm sorry about everything," she concluded, tears running down her cheeks.

His arms went to her shoulders and he pulled her to him. "Laurie, we can work it out."

"No, we can't," she replied pushing herself up, away from him. "I have to go. I have a plane to catch." She stood up and said, "Goodbye, Cameron," without looking at him.

In a moment the door to his office closed behind her, and he could feel the wetness of her tears on his cheek. He remained seated as if frozen in time, the shocking pain making it impossible for him to move to catch up with her. Or to think.

All he knew was that the aftershock of a terrible thunderbolt was echoing all around.

CHAPTER THIRTY-EIGHT

In the residence at the White House in Washington, DC, a televised baseball game was entertaining President Andrew Thomson. The Yankees were winning and that was all that mattered to him right at the moment. Everything else could wait. A few blessed hours on Sunday afternoons were his own, but this day his mind occasionally wondered very much outside what occupied most of his waking moments. Today, he kept wondering about Laurie Cosner and her brother. If the guy lived with a woman who had been preparing for what was in effect a terrorist act, he had to be more than a poor judge of character. Did Laurie know about it? What else did she know?

Andrew Thomson was usually very much in sync with his Vice President. He was the first to acknowledge that they made a great team and that the United States was the better for it. The problem was, the President considered, that in searching for love, Austin might have been less than vigilant. Of course, an investigation of Ms. Cosner would have been automatic, but were enough rocks turned, enough closet doors opened?

While he did want to discuss this type of concern with the Vice President, Thomson felt the need to cover all the bases so as to prevent any possible embarrassment. The only way to do this was with the right information. Knowledge was power and he had the power to access knowledge. He reached for the phone.

After finding his wife Jean dead in their bedroom, Cameron Austin had gone into shock, a state of mind which was to last some time. Accepting the cruel reality had simply been impossible on the spot. He was reliving these days once more. Only worse, he considered. He had dared to love again and the woman had in effect decided that his job was a liability, yet he knew so many other women would see his position, as Jean had, as an attractive feature in the relationship. But there was something else. He was certain it was an excuse. In effect, a lie. During her short visit, he had sensed that Laurie Cosner was running scared.

From what?

When his Jean had died, he had slowly accepted the reality of an event no amount of wishing or effort could change. Things were different this time around. Perhaps he could change Laurie's reality with the right information. Knowledge was power and he had the power to access knowledge. He reached for the phone.

In Washington, two agents were listening to their supervisor. Both felt they must have misunderstood since the operation they were asked to carry out was so outrageously outside the range of their regular service.

"When our Chief asks, we respond, so I'm counting on you to deliver. A flight to Canada has been arranged for tonight."

Once they were left alone, Jerry spoke. "McPine? What kind of name is that?" he asked, stepping up to the large map of the North American continent on the wall. "And where the hell is McPine, anyway?"

Peter, his partner in the impending exercise, also stepped up to the map. "Somewhere around here," he said, pointing to north of Lake Ontario.

"That's a mighty big area," Jerry commented.

After a moment of scrutinizing, Peter said, "Here it is." The tip of his pen on the map made the word McPine stand out.

"Watch out, McPine. We're on our way," Jerry said without too much enthusiasm in his voice.

Cameron Austin said, "I'm sorry to bring you out here on a Sunday evening, Oliver," and closed the door to his office at Admiral House.

"Not at all, Mr. Vice President. I am here to serve."

Sitting on a sofa across from Rogge, Austin began. "When we discussed Ms. Cosner shortly after I had met her, you told me that everything about her was on the up and up."

"Yes, sir. Is there a problem?"

"There might be. I'm not quite sure." Austin got to his feet and went to stand by his desk as he continued. "I believe Ms. Cosner is very much afraid of something. I do not know what exactly. Or perhaps she has been threatened in some way. It has led her to break off our engagement. I would like you to find out what exactly is going on. This will help you," the Vice President continued, picking up a small piece of paper from his desk and handing it to Oliver Rogge before sitting down again. "But it has to remain very secret for the moment. Not even the President must know. That's very important to me at this time."

"I understand fully, and you can count on my discretion," Rogge said, sympathizing with the man in front of him who no doubt wanted to mend fences in the shortest order possible. And he, Oliver Rogge, would be a part of it all. The thought was most exhilarating.

While Rogge looked at the piece of paper, the Vice President spoke. "I would suggest that you start with that law firm in Miami."

"How does this firm come into play?"

"I am not certain. I saw the name quite by accident," Austin said. "A letter from this firm addressed to Ms. Cosner was sent through to my office at the White House. Mrs. Winterburn forwarded it to McPine. The person writing, perhaps a Mr. Spears, obviously did not have Ms. Cosner's address. Don't you find that interesting?"

"Certainly, sir," Rogge said.

"Equally as interesting is the fact that Ms. Cosner lived in Florida before she was married. Some time ago, for sure. Nevertheless, I would like you to find out if, perhaps, she is being blackmailed because of something in her past. Whatever it is, I want to know what has Laurie so panicky."

"I'll look into it right away, sir," Rogge said. "I'm sorry I did not find out she had lived in Florida in the past."

The Vice President waved the remark away as unimportant.

"Did she tell you about it?" Rogge asked.

"Yes, she did, and she certainly did not appear ashamed of the fact nor of anything connected to it." Standing up to indicate the conversation was winding down, Cameron Austin said, "Again, I cannot stress enough that all possible discretion must be used."

On his feet, Oliver Rogge assured the Vice President that he was a very prudent man, then they agreed to meet again for an update the following Sunday.

Wearing shorts and a T-shirt Laurie was working at the computer in the greenhouse when Bernie Wesson stepped inside.

"Well, they're certainly not taking any chances," he said.

Laurie looked up at him. "What in the world are you talking about?"

"About the fact that the big artillery's in town."

"Huh?"

"On my way back from Medford I went to Jack's place for an oil change. These two large men were in there asking all sorts of questions."

"About what?"

"General questions about the area, the people around here, that sort of thing. They said they were writers working on a book about little-known regions of Canada, but I assure you they have FBI and CIA written all over them."

"You mean they actually have letters on the fronts and backs of their jackets like the agents carrying out raids on TV?"

"Funny! Of course not, but you can tell. One thing is their accent. They're definitely not Canadians!"

"Watched another dark movie last night, did we?"

"Don't believe me. Fine!"

"Maybe they are writers. This is an interesting region if you look at the fact that we feed a lot of people."

"I don't think they're writers. Want to know why?" She wanted to say no, but let him continue. "Because there are two of them."

"Come again?"

"Writers work alone. I mean, look at you."

"Haven't you heard of people collaborating on a book?"

"Yeah, but it seems to me one of them would write about one region, and another about somewhere else."

"It doesn't always work that way, you know. Did you talk to them about our operation? We could show them around and have free publicity in the bargain."

"That's what got me suspicious. When Jack introduced me, they said they were looking for a human angle, not a business one. I argued, of course, that the human angle of *Only Roses* was the interesting part, but they just shrugged. I just know they're government. Besides, they're big and in shape. I'm sure they could fell me like a tree with one sharp blow."

"If they're investigators, what would they be investigating anyway?"

"You? Us? All of us? They might want to make sure that before you marry the Vice President you've not been influenced by a bunch of bad guys hiding in the pines around here."

"Ha, ha," Laurie commented aloud, but inside she had a gut feeling that he was right. It frightened her. "Well, I'm all up to date. Everything's okay," she assured her partner while pointing to the computer.

"Good. Now let me get your travel plans all clear, here. Tomorrow you're away at April McLaren's funeral, the next day you're going to Toronto to spend time with your brother, and then on Sunday you leave for your book tour. Right?"

"Right. Yes. Sort of. You will remember **not** to tell people that I've gone to England, won't you?"

"Of course. But why the secrecy? Want to avoid media attention, do we?"

"It's complicated, Bernie. I just think it's better that people don't know, that's all," she said, the sharpness in her voice surprising her.

"Okay, okay," Bernie said, putting up his hands. "It's your business."

"I'm sorry. I didn't mean to snap. It's not an excuse but I've not been sleeping well. I'm tired."

"You look it."

"Thanks a lot, Bernie!"

"What are friends for?"

A while later as she made her way to the post office on her bike, she was glad that Sarah was busy until her weekend departure, earning a few dollars by working at her Aunt Rita's newspaper in Medford. One less thing to worry about, especially now with two investigators around. She trusted Bernie's judgment, but if the men were really investigating, who would have sent them? Certainly not Cameron Austin. He knew all there was to know about her. Most of it, anyway.

It couldn't be the media. She knew through her mother that they were still digging in Toronto. Had the FBI descended on McPine because of April? But why? They knew what had really happened in the Thousand Islands. Was someone worried that other possible terrorists might be lurking in McPine as Bernie had suggested? Was someone attempting to discredit her, someone who didn't know about the broken engagement?

She had little time for further perusing thoughts once she stepped inside the post office.

"Hi, Annabelle," Laurie said cheerfully in her automatic greeting before realizing that the postmistress was not at her usual spot behind the counter. She was seated at a small round table against the back wall, a table at the disposal of customers who wanted to write last minute notes or look up a postal code. Two huge men wearing jeans and dark T-shirts were sitting beside her.

"Hi, there," the postmistress said, inviting Laurie to come over with a movement of her arm. "You should talk to these fellows. This is Jerry and this is Peter," she said pointing them out. "They're writing a book about this area, among others."

"Really?" Laurie said.

"Laurie's a writer too. She's published a couple of books," Annabelle felt proud to point out.

The men nodded ever so slightly. The noncommittal nod she had so often seen. Another sign that Bernie was right, Laurie thought. "Pray tell, what makes this region so interesting?"

Jerry had stood up. The tall, muscular body, the short hair and the keen eyes reminded her immediately of the men in Cameron Austin's Secret Service detail. The pink scar on his lower left cheek told her it was recent. Acquired in the line of duty? "We're focusing on lesser-known regions of Canada, and this is one of them."

Definitely an American, the accent immediately told Laurie. "And what will you be writing about? The people? The villages and towns?"

Peter answered this time. He too was tall and all muscles with an intimidating look. "A little of both, I reckon, although you can appreciate that we're still researching."

"I see. What other part of the country will you be writing about?"

Jerry fielded that one. "We'll be including regions of all the provinces, that's for sure."

"You said you were focusing on regions that were not well known, right?" Laurie said, and both men again nodded ever so slightly. "I'm just curious because I have relatives who live in the Okanagan in B.C. Will you be writing about that part of the country?"

"Could be," Jerry said. "As Peter pointed out, we'll gather a lot of material and see how it all fits."

"I hope you do. The people out there are very proud of their region, especially their diamond mines."

"We'll certainly look into it," Peter said.

Gotcha, she said silently. *If you were Canadians, you'd know that our diamond mines are in the north, not close to the U.S. border.* Aloud she said, "Well, I wish you well in your project. It sounds fascinating."

"We might like to talk to you, if you don't mind," Jerry said.

"I'd be happy to be interviewed. Drop by later on today. It has to be today because then I'm off to the funeral of a relative for a few days."

"Certainly," Peter said.

Then we'll see who's who, Laurie thought.

While eating his lunch at his desk, Oliver Rogge was finally able to spend time thinking about the Florida problem. He was studying the website of the Spears and Spears law firm, specialists in representation for the entertainment industry, and wondered which of the partners had actually written the letter to Laurie Cosner. Not having that information made it impossible for him to simply call their office. Also, the author of the missive could have been a more junior partner since the firm had a total of seven attorneys, all with specialized expertise, the site informed him. He turned the problem in his head for a time as he chewed on take-out Chinese food which had gotten cold. He would need to travel to Florida himself, something which had been authorized, and get to know someone in the firm. Something he was good at, he considered, but time consuming. Then a thought hit him. Perhaps Ms. Cosner would herself be traveling to Florida. No harm in checking.

With the many avenues at his disposal it was child's play to find out that Laurie was booked on a flight to Fort Lauderdale in two days. This was going to be easier than he had anticipated. He felt doubly fortunate when her name appeared again—along with that of Sarah Cosner—on the list of passengers for a flight from Toronto to London the following Sunday evening.

What was the lady up to?

CHAPTER THIRTY-NINE

*I*n his office in Miami, Marty Spears reached for the phone and punched numbers. The phone rang in McPine.

Laurie picked up on the second ring. She had just come in and had been pouring herself a glass of water.

"Ms. Cosner? Marty Spears in Miami."

Laurie felt a little jolt. She had hoped to be gone by the time he called. He had said midweek.

"I know it's earlier than we had agreed to," Spears was continuing, "but I have to go to New York for a few days, so I thought I'd check with you before leaving. Have you decided how we can work out your visit?"

"I'm afraid not. I simply haven't had time. You see there's been a... My sister-in-law was killed in an accident. It's been chaos."

"Oh, I'm sorry to hear this, Ms. Cosner."

"Thank you."

"When do you think we can talk again?" Spears asked hopefully.

"This week's going to be crazy time-wise, but I promise that by Monday I'll be in a position to give you exact dates."

"That'd be great. Thank you."

And I'll be long gone, you bastard, she thought. She finished her water and made her way to the greenhouse. Bernie was busy with an order.

"You went to see them, didn't you?"

"I went to get my mail."

"Sure. Anyway, what do you think? Was I right?"

"I've got to hand it to you, Bernie, right on the nose."

He smiled smugly. "So what are they here for, anyway?"

"Don't know yet, but they're coming over to interview me very shortly."

"How did you manage that? They didn't want to hear about me."

"Poor Bernie. That's what you get for not being in the limelight," she teased.

"You mean you think they're here to find out something about you? They're not media, are they?"

"No. Definitely government issue. If you're up for it, we could have a little fun."

"I'm always up for that," Bernie replied.

Laurie and Bernie were ready and waiting when Jerry and Peter drove up. From a corner of the front window of the greenhouse office, they saw the two men slowly get out of their rented mid-size black sedan and take a very detailed look around.

"Do they really expect someone to charge them?" Bernie asked.

"Force of habit. Cameron's men have the same routine," Laurie pointed out. "Let the games begin."

Stepping out to greet the visitors, Laurie introduced Bernie. "You met him a littler earlier today, I believe. He told you about our rose business, but you didn't seem interested."

There was vacillation, if not confusion. Their strength was obviously in the physical. She thought that whoever had sent them had failed to realize how the two men were badly suited for the task at hand.

"Why don't we take you on a tour of our operation anyway since you're here? It's something different for a somewhat far-removed part of the country, don't you think? It'd make good copy."

Peter seemed to be back in control. "We wanted to talk to you because you're a writer."

"I fail to understand how my being a writer is a factor in a book about the region."

"A writer getting her inspiration from nature, that sort of thing," Jerry answered.

"One of my books is a handbook on roses, so a something on our operation would tie in well," Laurie offered.

The two men glanced at each other quickly.

"That might work," Peter put in after a second or two had passed.

"Good," Bernie said. "Let me show you around, gentlemen. This way," he said, making a broad gesture with his right arm.

The two visitors seemed appropriately impressed as Bernie explained what was involved in growing roses in the area. Many times he caught them stealing glances towards the greenhouse office at the front. They wanted to talk to Laurie, not listen to some idiot droning on about a business they couldn't have cared less about. They did, however, manage to ask some intelligent questions. One of them surprised Bernie.

"What happens to the business if one of you moves away?" Peter asked.

"Her share reverts to me or my share to her, for a price of course," Bernie answered amiably thinking that the encounter was proceeding quite well.

"Do either of you intend to move?" Jerry asked.

"Excuse me. Excuse me," Laurie was almost shouting as she walked down the middle aisle, much to the apparent surprise of the two men.

"What's up?" Bernie asked.

"There's a phone call for Peter," she said as she approached, the receiver in her hand. The two men exchanged a quick puzzled look. "I'm sure you'll want to take it. They just asked for Peter. It could be some sort of prank, but the lady sounded serious when she said it was the White House."

Peter was about to open his mouth, but Jerry spoke. "Best to see what it is."

"Here," Laurie said, handing him the handset.

The man proceeded to walk a few yards down the aisle, somewhat hesitantly, both Laurie and Bernie thought, Jerry in tow. Laurie winked at Bernie as they followed.

"There's no one on the line," Peter complained a moment later.

"They must have hung up," Laurie said innocently.

Jerry spoke. "Perhaps we could pick up this visit later," he said.

"Or perhaps never," Laurie said. "If I were you I would leave McPine right now," she added with bite in her voice.

The two men looked at her as if she were some sort of specter.

"Gentlemen, sit down while I make myself quite clear," she said. "Go ahead, sit," she insisted, indicating the long bench against the front wall. She picked up the phone on the table where Peter had left it and punched in a series of numbers. When a male voice answered at the other end, she asked for President Thomson's secretary by name and waited, eyeing both men squarely. They were staring ahead at the colorful buds sprouting out from among the green, but Laurie could feel the tension emanating from their bodies.

"Good afternoon, Mrs. Langmuir. This is Laurie Cosner. I would like to talk to President Thomson, please. It's most urgent otherwise I certainly would not dream of disturbing him." A moment later, she added, "Thank you."

Several awkward minutes had elapsed by the time President Thomson came on the line. "Hello, Ms. Cosner. How may I help you?"

"Get your goons out of McPine, Mr. President, sir," she said with the edge of her voice as sharp as Bernie had ever heard in all the years he had known her.

The outburst took the President by surprise, but he quickly rallied. No point denying what she obviously already knew. "There were some questions I wanted answers to."

"Then why not simply ask me? I would have told you anything you wanted to know. I don't appreciate being investigated as though I were a criminal of some sort. Should you feel I am not worthy of associating with the Vice President, the point may be moot. My family's in mourning, Mr. President, as you well know, and I want to be left alone to grieve with them. Thank you, Mr. President," she concluded and hung up.

The two men were staring at her, totally incredulous.

She spoke. "Get in touch with your contact man, or woman as the case may be, in Washington. I suspect you are now officially out of the *writing* business."

In the oval office, President Thomson put the phone back on its cradle. No one in the world, save Barbie of course, would dare talk to him in such a fashion, yet there was nothing he could do about it. Luckily no one had heard. The lady had spunk, he had to grant her that, which could, if expertly funneled, work out to be an asset for Cameron, he considered, but then the President wondered what she had meant by saying it was a moot point. He let the question hang in the air without resolution because he had to turn his attention to more pressing matters, not the least of which was aborting the foray into McPine.

CHAPTER FORTY

The Air Canada plane landed smoothly at Fort Lauderdale airport after an uneventful flight from Toronto. Laurie Cosner exited in step with the other passengers and followed the crowd to the bank of luggage carrousels where the red sign indicating their flight number could not be missed. She carried only a small black bag over her shoulder and was totally oblivious to the man with straggly reddish-blond hair wearing dark glasses a few feet behind, carefully watching her every move. She walked past passengers waiting for their bags and made her way to the car-rental desk where her transaction was quickly completed. The man tailing her, dressed in beige shorts and a matching polo shirt, casually stopped to pick up a folder of local attractions and unfolded it as he followed Laurie out of the terminal. No one noticed either of them. They were, after all, just another couple of tourists arriving in Florida.

It was nearly noon by the time Laurie stepped into the warm midday sun and was hit by a flood of memories. How curious, she thought, that the heat of Florida would be the trigger to her distant past life. She was far from the ocean, yet she could almost hear the constant agitation of the waves. She was nowhere close to boats, but she could almost see them glide easily on the Intercoastal. There were few people about as the sun baked the parked cars, yet the laughter of a party crowd and the piano playing of Neal Landau invaded her mind.

She was walking and checking license plates on the late model sedans parked in the rental car area when the man in the beige shorts hurried to a dark car near the exit of the parking area. He opened the passenger door and slid into the cool inside air.

"Everything's ready, just like you wanted it," the driver, an older man with dark sunglasses, uttered without emotion.

"Thanks."

"You know how to work this stuff?"

"Yeah," was the reply. "No problem. I'll leave the car here tomorrow morning. If there's a hitch, I'll call."

"Good luck," the older man said slipping out of the car.

Oliver Rogge got in behind the wheel and had to wait only a few minutes before seeing Laurie drive out in her rented white sedan.

She knew her way around this part of the world, and soon she was cruising south along route A1, leisurely taking in the sights. Some things had changed in more than fifteen years, although many of the structures along the way were just as she remembered them. The traffic was light. She turned on the radio and chose an easy rock station, almost as if she wanted to be in tune with the sounds inside the black car keeping an eye on her.

After a time she stopped at a coffee shop for a sandwich and a cool drink. Rogge was grateful because his throat was parched. He sat in the far corner of the large room, watching her eat. She was preoccupied, of that he had no doubt, but would she lead him to the answers he wanted? When he saw that she was studying a map on her phone, he paid his bill and walked out to wait in the black car.

When Laurie entered a residential area she was fairly familiar with the streets while Rogge who was not had to be extra careful not to be spotted. When she hesitated at an intersection, he quickly pulled into a driveway until she continued driving. The streets, obviously planned so that traffic would be restricted to those living in this suburb, were somewhat of a maze. The houses were not upper class, but certainly high-end middle class. They were sprawling bungalows on large lots, probably built some thirty to forty years earlier, Rogge thought. Most had high wooden fences—some hidden by hibiscus in full bloom— around the back, no doubt enclosing large clean pools.

Laurie finally found the house she was searching for, and parked across the street. She did not immediately get out, so Oliver drove by and was grateful that another street branched off to the right. He drove a short distance, turned his car around and parked it almost at the corner just as Laurie had gotten out of the car and was crossing the street on her way to a house. He reached for a piece of equipment that was a combination camera/recording device in the back seat.

A heavyset middle-aged woman answered the door.

"Hi. I would like to see Mr. Landau. I'm an old friend."

Rogge smiled. He had heard her voice clearly. Things would work out as planned.

"He could use a friend," Rosita said in her thick accent. "Please come in. People don't come around much now."

"How is he?" Laurie asked.

"Well, he has good days and bad days. Today is so so. His bedroom's set up there," Rosita said indicating the room on the other side of the large living room, "because he can see the garden. He loves his garden. Follow me."

"That won't be necessary. I know where it is."

Rosita smiled at Laurie. It was about time old friends stopped being afraid of catching his disease. "I'll be in the kitchen if Mr. Neal needs anything."

Laurie walked across the huge living room with the white grand piano in the corner. It appeared to be the same instrument she remembered. How many parties that room had seen, she wondered, when being a friend of Neal Landau, or simply a hanger-on, was something to crow about. The door to the den was open, and as she approached she saw that the sliding glass patio doors were also open. She could hear no sound, hesitated for a moment, then stepped lightly into the room.

Fully aware of his condition, she had promised herself to face it head-on without emotion. However, she was not prepared for the sight of the man lying on the bed against the far wall. Now in his fifties, he looked much older, in part because of the almost totally white hair. He was so skinny as to be but a shadow of the firm body she had embraced all those years ago. His eyes were closed. The nightstand was littered with pill bottles, and magazines had been thrown haphazardly on the floor. The large television set at the foot of the bed was turned off.

In his car, Oliver Rogge was beginning to panic because of the silence. He aimed the black tool in his hands at the front windows in turn, but nothing.

In the old days, a large oak desk had stood where the bed now was, and there had been comfortable easy chairs all around the room. It had been her favorite room in the house. It was a wonderful place to relax

244

and enjoy interesting conversations. Today it was a room on which death was undoubtedly keeping a close eye. She knocked on the frame of the door. He opened his eyes slowly, trying to focus.

"Laurie," he said at last in a weak voice. "You look good. You haven't changed."

Rogge's shoulders relaxed. The words had been clear.

"Neal, I'm very sorry to see you're ill, but please cut the crap. If you hadn't seen my picture on the evening news or in a paper, you wouldn't know me from Adam."

"I don't have the strength to argue. Marty told me he spoke to you, so I assume you're here because you're ready to do the right thing."

"The right thing? You must be joking."

"As you can see, I can't afford to joke anymore. I simply want to see my daughter before I die. It's not too much to ask, is it?" The words had been spoken slowly.

"And what makes you think that my daughter is your daughter, pray tell?"

"You told me so, remember? You said you were pregnant and that I was the father," Landau said, each word uttered as if he were in pain.

"Neal, back then I was a romantic young girl with stars in her eyes who thought she was in love with you. I wanted you to marry me, and I thought that the idea of being a father would convince you to do just that. I would claim a miscarriage soon after. How stupid I was, so stupid in fact that I didn't see that you preferred the white powder in your nose to anything else.

"Anyway, you told me it couldn't be possible. You told me you had a vasectomy, and the next day you found someone else to charm, so I went back home where I found the true meaning of love with a great guy and we had a wonderful child. I can't see why you want to claim his daughter is yours."

"I lied to you back then. I never had a vasectomy."

"It still doesn't prove anything, does it?"

"But it does point to me. Anyway, I cut out her picture," Landau said, painfully stretching his arm to open the drawer of the nightstand, and pulling out a magazine page. "She looks just like me. You can't deny that."

"She looks nothing like you and you know it. I want to know what your scam is."

His face contorted into a grimace. "No scam. I just want to see her. She...wouldn't need to know anything."

"Of course not, because there is nothing to know."

"Then where did she get her talent for the piano?"

"As I recall, you never took the time to find out much about me—even if you had you wouldn't remember much after all the drugs—but my mother's side of the family is very musically inclined. That's where my daughter gets her talent."

Neal Landau closed his eyes. She was unable to interpret the gesture. Was he thinking or was he just too weak to keep them open?

"Neal," she said calmly, "There is no reason for my daughter to see you, and I came to tell you it just won't happen. I won't put her through this. Tell Marty Spears. I don't want him to call me anymore."

He looked at her from under heavy lids. "I'm going to fight you as long as I am alive."

"But why?"

He didn't reply.

"Let me guess. You took a close look at your life and you want to score some brownie points with the guy upstairs before you meet Him face to face. Or is it about money?"

"Money? When did I ever mention money?" he said, his voice now a bit stronger. "My income more than takes care of my needs."

"Then leave me and my daughter alone."

"I still have friends and I can easily contact Mr. Vice President. I'm sure he'd be interested in what I have to say."

"I'm sure. He's always so keen to listen to the ranting of a brain ravaged by decades of booze and drug abuse. Besides, it would be of little use since he and I no longer see each other."

"That's what you want me to believe."

"It's the truth, whether you believe me or not."

Neal Landau's eyes were piercing hers. "The way you're looking at me, I can tell that you're glad I got what I deserved."

"Neal, please give me a little credit. That thought never entered my mind. I never wished you ill, but I have to say that I'm glad that back then you dismissed me like yesterday's news. It was the best thing that happened to me."

"I'm...sorry," he whispered.

She looked at his face. His eyes were closed now and an errant tear was slowly making its way down the side of his cheek.

"I know you're sorry for your past mistakes," she said. "Please don't make any more by continuing to harass my daughter and me. Goodbye, Neal. I wish you well. I really do."

With these words she turned and left the room.

In the living room she stopped. To relieve the intense stress of the meeting, she took a couple of deep breaths, and suddenly she saw the Rosita approaching with a tray in her hands.

"Are you leaving already?"

"Yes."

"I'm bringing him some tea. Why you no join him?"

"Thank you, but I have to go. I'll find my way out."

Laurie welcomed the pleasant outside air as eagerly as the first warm day of spring in McPine. She was grateful the ordeal was over.

Oliver Rogge lowered his equipment. His mission couldn't have gone better. He had recorded every word, every damn word, yet, as his brow burrowed, he knew he hadn't learned the truth beyond a reasonable doubt.

Laurie started her car and drove away. He remained in his. He had decisions to make.

CHAPTER FORTY-ONE

  Tired of being idle in his car while observing absolutely no activity for over an hour at the home of Neal Landau, Oliver Rogge drove to a neighboring mall he had noticed earlier. At an establishment bedecked to look like a genuine English pub he had a beer, then a second, while absent-mindedly munching on a mixture of nuts placed in front of him. He was attempting to decide on his next course of action, but nothing was clear.

  He was aware that only Laurie Cosner knew the identity of the father of her daughter. Yet, if Landau was not the father, why had she taken such drastic measures as to break up her engagement to the Vice President and come down to Florida to tell Landau off? She could easily have done that on the phone. There had to be some truth to the allegations. Not some, but the whole truth, he mused.

  Perhaps Laurie didn't want to risk having Sarah find out about her wild youth. Perhaps she was ashamed, or perhaps she had wanted to simply bury the past. And the Vice President? Surely he would be disappointed even if such actions as conceiving a baby out of wedlock no longer carried the stigma it once did. Perhaps she feared it would hurt him politically down the road. So many perhaps. And she was going to England with Sarah in a few days. Why? To make certain the girl was very far away in case Landau made good on his threats to tell the Vice President and the media? Summer would be coming to an end soon, and perhaps Laurie had decided her daughter should attend a school abroad to further her music education. He would have to look into that as soon as he got back.

Were it not for Neal Landau, Laurie and the Vice President would be happily looking forward to their wedding as planned, Oliver acknowledged. However, the man who was dying had, with his claim, altered history. Vice President Cameron Austin would not be marrying the lovely Canadian. And if the rumors around the West Wing were to be believed—there was always some outrageous gossip floating about—President Thomson was not thrilled about the possibility of a Canadian living in the White House, which meant that these latest developments played right into that narrow vision.

The thought did nothing to raise Oliver Rogge's spirit. He had decided it was his duty to repair the damage caused by Neal Landau by making certain the man put his allegation to rest. Since the man was at death's door, perhaps the problem would resolve itself. The question was, how long would that take? Oliver ordered another beer and a club sandwich.

The night had been rendered toneless by the heavy cloud cover moving inland from the sea. When Oliver Rogge drove back to Neal Landau's house, the atmosphere had been altered. A sunny summer day had turned into gloom. It suited his mood.

Parking his car a block away, he made his way to Landau's house on foot, thankful for the inky quality of the darkness because he was certain that night walkers were not a common site in the area. Earlier he had spent some time assessing the house and its surrounding property, and he was confident his plan would work. He would not, could not, let himself back away at this point. The man was half dead anyway. It was the only solution, he kept reminding himself.

His trained, agile body quickly made it over the fence and, thankfully, landed on soft grass. The light from Landau's room was tracing a wide path across the lanai to the blue water of the pool. Except for that path, everything was as dark as an underground cave. He moved silently until he could see inside through the partially opened patio door, and was surprised at how small and sickly Neal Landau looked. His eyes were closed and his head was pushed back against the slightly elevated top portion of the hospital bed. The sounds emanating from the television set were soft. Rogge wondered if his prey was asleep or just resting. He decided to wait to make certain that sleep had taken over, otherwise it would be impossible to do the deed.

He sat down carefully on one of the chairs on the patio.

Nearly one hour later Rogge was still hesitating as he kept an eye on Landau, wondering why the man did not budge in his sleep. He had not seen him move a muscle. Suddenly, the housekeeper, somewhat dolled up Rogge thought, probably returning home after a special night out, came into the room. She turned off the television set and went to the bed. She picked up an empty bottle from the top of the coverlet, looked at it then her hand went to Landau's neck. She uttered words in Spanish as she made the sign of the cross and reached for the phone. In a moment she was almost yelling into it that she needed help quickly.

Remaining in the dark shadows, Rogge saw the paramedics attempt to revive Neal Landau a short time later before taking him away on a stretcher. In a moment, the spiraling yellow light from the ambulance was cutting through the darkness outside as it sped away. The housekeeper came back into the room, knelt on the floor near the bed, made the sign of the cross again and began praying.

It was time for Rogge to go.

He had just cleared the fence when a quick rain shower rushed him. He was glad for the large drops hitting his body because he needed to be cleansed, to be expunged. Would he really have done it? Would he really have killed the poor man, he wondered?

When everything was considered, probably not.

The decision to eliminate Neal Landau had been taken after alcohol had taken over his reasoning. Now that the buzz had completely disappeared, the action seemed somewhat ridiculous. And the fact that he had considered such an action made it more than a little scary. As he ambled along in the summer rain, Oliver Rogge did what he hadn't done in ages, he prayed. He asked for forgiveness.

The Air Canada airbus lifted smoothly as it made its way above the clouds, leaving the Florida heat behind. Laurie Cosner relaxed and made a point of listening to the latest news on the small screen in front of her. She adjusted her earphones, glad to be able to catch up with what had been happening in the world in the last few days, but soon her attention began wandering. She thought of poor April.

The memorial service had been simple and dignified, and extremely well attended. People of all stripes who knew her from the diner had filled all the pews, and latecomers had to stand in the back. Laurie had tried to be all but invisible in a side pew, and had stood aside as much as she could afterwards. From what she overheard, April was well liked and everyone could only sympathize with Mike for losing his fiancée under such tragic circumstances. Laurie thought her brother held up well, knowing what he knew that other mourners did not. Mike had removed the card from the flower arrangement sent by the Vice President because, as he told his sister, too many people would ask questions at a time when April's family needed all the attention and the sympathy.

Laurie came back to reality suddenly as a picture of Neal Landau appeared as an inset on the screen. The voice of the anchor was clear. "The music industry is today mourning the passing of legendary songwriter and performer Neal Landau at his home in Miami. During a colorful career that spanned decades, many of the songs he wrote for top artists became standards. Landau, who never married, died at the age of 55 after a lengthy illness."

Laurie who had been holding her breath, released it. How uncanny that he died so soon after she had seen him. Except for his housekeeper, she was probably the last one to have seen him alive. She felt suddenly very sorry for the man, but mixed with that feeling was a measure of remorse for the wasted years of her youth, and for her failure to help him give up his drug habit. But, truthfully, back then he could be an arrogant s.o.b. on whom she had little if any influence. When the cloud of drug abuse had finally lifted, how often had he thought about his child, she wondered. Probably a great deal in the last years, and deep down she could understand his desire to acknowledge that his life had been about more than his songs.

But, he had been the one to give up fatherhood. He had selfishly chosen his own pleasure over a family. She couldn't and wouldn't feel guilty for that, and neither about the fact that his passing was her liberation. Her daughter's liberation.

She wondered briefly if plans should be adjusted. She knew she could not disappoint Sarah again so soon by not following through on the trip to England. She'd go and assess the situation with her daughter in a few months.

With a cup of coffee and a cookie on the small table in front of her, Laurie was remembering the last time she had flown from Florida to Toronto. She was, by her account, about six weeks pregnant at the time and scared out of her wits. She hadn't told anyone she was coming home, and throughout the flight she wondered how she was going to break the news to her mother. The woman strongly believed that people should live together only after marriage and that unmarried girls should not get pregnant. Even if her mother had the ability to remain calm in the face of trouble, Laurie had feared the worst. Yet things developed differently.

After she had gotten her luggage, Laurie had walked around the airport, somewhat aimlessly, trying to decide what to do. She had left Florida quickly without properly planning how her life would unfold once she was back home. She had little options. She had some money that would carry her through a few months, but what would she do then? There were a lot of things to buy. Babies were expensive. The thought of having an abortion had passed through her mind, but only like an unexpected gust of cold wind. There was no way she could kill her child. Somehow she would make it.

She had finally stopped at a bank of payphones and called her mother.

Eileen Danfort had been thrilled to hear her daughter's voice, and when she pulled up at Pearson International Airport driving a brand new red sedan she was smiling from ear to ear. The woman had not aged one bit, Laurie thought. Marriage was obviously agreeing with her. She embraced Laurie with great warmth. As they drove away, Eileen had wanted to know everything. "Don't leave out anything, you hear?"

The frightened daughter had blurted out, "I came home because I'm pregnant."

Eileen had kept her eyes on the road, stealing a look or two in Laurie's direction when the heavy traffic allowed. She had said nothing for some time.

"Don't you have anything to say? Like I deserve this after living in sin."

"Why don't we wait till we get home and then we can discuss this calmly?"

And they had. Eileen confessed that she had feared Laurie's Florida escapade would not end like the fairytales of her youth, eventually resigning herself to the fact that at times youth had to learn the realities of life the hard way.

"What about the father?" Eileen asked. "That fellow you lived with?"

"When I told him I was pregnant, he didn't want anything to do with me. Aren't you going to tell me I told you so!"

Eileen Danfort stood up and, going to sit next to her daughter on the comfy beige sofa, put an arm around her shoulders. She knew how badly her baby was hurting. "No, I'm not. We'll get through this together. What are your plans?"

"I'll try to get work with a newspaper."

"Where are you going to live?"

"I was hoping to be able to live here for a couple of weeks while I look for a place. Or I might move in with Rita in Medford and get a job at the paper there."

"Rita's getting married, as you must know," Eileen told her daughter.

"Yeah, but not for a couple of months."

"If you want to live in Medford, it's up to you," the soon-to-be-grandmother said, disappointed, "but I could help you a great deal more if you stayed in Toronto."

"Thanks, mom," Laurie said simply.

Two days later Rita Cosner and her brother, Robby, had come to see Laurie in Toronto. Time and distance had made Robby's heart go fonder as far as Laurie was concerned.

"He's been worshipping you from afar all the time you've been gone," Rita told Laurie.

"Doesn't he know I was living with someone?"

"Of course, but he didn't believe it'd last."

"How's he going to feel when he learns I'm pregnant?"

"He'll probably want to marry you," Rita retorted jokingly, yet it was exactly how the drama had unfolded.

Looking at the puffy mist outside the small window as the plane now began its descent into Pearson International Airport, Laurie was remembering how Robby had invited her to come and see the plant business he and his partner Bernie had set up in McPine. She had been terribly impressed that he had had the wisdom to plan his future; quite a contrast to her flighty Florida adventure which had left her sad, beaten and disappointed in herself.

Later, when they had gone for a walk by the old covered bridge, Robby had surprised her totally by extracting a small blue box from the pocket of his jeans and showing her the ring inside, its blue gem glistening in the sunlight. "I've been carrying this around with me for over a year. I knew you'd come back. Will you marry me?"

Instead of answering or commenting on the beautiful sapphire adorning the ring, she asked why.

"Because I love you, silly."

"Rita told you I'm pregnant, didn't she?"

"Yes, and I think it's great that we're going to have a child so soon."

"It doesn't bother you that someone else's the father?"

"You don't have to be the natural father to love a child and make a family."

Twisting the crisp blue stone she still wore on the third finger of her right hand, she was now remembering how long she stared at Robby that day, unbelieving. Finally, she had said, "You're very sweet, Robby, but I can't marry you. I'm not in love with you."

"And I bet you thought you were in love with that guy in Florida. But it didn't last, did it? I'm not asking you to love me, just be with me."

After several more tries on Robby's part, Laurie finally agreed to marry him. The simple ceremony took place in Toronto, Eileen crying through most of it. Of sheer joy, she told Laurie.

Her first airplane trip from Florida to Toronto had taken her to an uncertain future, and so was this one.

Shortly after her arrival in Toronto all those years ago, she had been married to a good-hearted and loving man she soon grew to adore and still missed terribly at times. The best thing that ever happened to her and, in the bargain, Sarah got the best father she could have asked for, Laurie contemplated. Now, she was fortunate enough to have another man love her, yet that future was all but gone because she had wanted to spare her daughter. But had it been fair to the man?

Making her way out of the terminal at Pearson airport, Laurie was joyfully surprised to see her mother as she exited. It was exactly the welcome home she needed. The two women embraced, and Laurie delighted in the solace that was hers. Tears swelled up out of nowhere.

"Let's get you home," Eileen said. As she drove, she asked her daughter to tell her about her trip. "And don't leave out anything, you hear?"

CHAPTER FORTY-TWO

*L*ist in hand, Laurie Cosner was crossing out to-do items as she went along. Things were falling into place. Bernie would take care of the house and Brandy until her return. She suspected he was very happy about it, because if the McPine rumor mill were to be believed, he was courting the divorced mother of two boys who lived in Medford. With Laurie's house empty he could invite them to stay over on weekends.

She was rechecking what she had packed for herself when the phone rang.

"Laurie? Marty Spears in Miami."

Laurie was so surprised that all she could do was stare blankly ahead without seeing any of the pictures on the wall.

"I'm sure you've heard the news," Spears said.

"Yes, I have."

"I wanted to tell you that Neal really appreciated the fact that you came down. He called me after you left to say how happy he was to have seen you." He paused, and she remained silent. After a moment Spears continued. "I know you didn't want to hear from me, but there's a reason I'm calling. My firm handled all of Neal's affairs and I am his executor. The will is a simple one. He's left most of his money to help victims of AIDS as well as for more research. He had signed his will years ago, however, after your visit Neal called me and asked me to prepare a codicil to his will, which I did. It was a simple document which he insisted on signing right away, so I drove out and had him sign it. I suppose he had a feeling the end was near. Long story short, Laurie, the codicil made you an heir."

"What?" She sat down on her bed.

"In this codicil Neal left you, and I repeat you, no one else is mentioned, without proviso, the sum of three-hundred-thousand dollars."

"I find this joke in very poor taste."

"Why would I lie? That's what Neal wanted, Laurie. The money is yours, for the girl." When there was no response, he continued: "Of course, liquidating an estate always takes time. We'll need to sell his house and other assets, but we will work efficiently so you can get your money as quickly as possible."

Long after Marty Spears had hung up, Laurie sat, phone in hand, almost in shock. Neal had wanted to do the right thing by his daughter, and it had been prompted by her visit. Studying music abroad was a costly proposition—something Laurie had not carefully calculated when making her snap decision to send Sarah to London. Now she would be in a position to breathe financially without her mother's help. She lifted her eyes to the ceiling and whispered, "Thank you, Neal."

But now there was a problem she had to face. It was only fair that Neal Landau's daughter, her daughter, know her real heritage. She was sure Marty Spears could help put together a list of any genetic family health issues that could be of concern to Sarah as she aged. Laurie had always known that at some point, when her daughter was older, she would have to come clean about her past, but not now.

Sarah was not old enough yet. Laurie had long decided that she would confront that hurdle only when her daughter was twenty-one, and hopefully able to appreciate the foibles of humans.

In the residence at the White House, President Thomson and his wife, Barbara, were dining alone. Between bites of his baked potato, seasoned just the way he liked with a mixture of specially blended spices, Thomson casually asked, "Have you spoken to Laurie Cosner lately?"

"Not for a while. Why?"

"Just curious. What do you think of her overall?"

"We've talked about this before. She's got a good head on her shoulders. Doesn't let anyone push her around."

"Do you think she's too outspoken for her own good? I mean if Cameron is serious about being the next tenant in this house."

"You really don't like her, do you?" It was a statement, not a question.

"That's not it. I just think she'll hurt Cameron in the long run."

"At first I had my doubts too, but now... If we don't support Cameron's choice—he is going to marry the woman whether we like it or not—there'll be rumors that we're old fools afraid of anything that's not American."

"He's still seeing her, isn't he? I mean they haven't canceled the wedding or anything?"

Barbie Thomson eyed her husband sharply. "Spill it out. What have you heard?"

"Nothing. I've been thinking that we should go to the farm next weekend."

Her husband had changed the subject abruptly. Barbie Thomson knew that it meant something was in the offing that he didn't want to talk about. Never mind him, she had her own sources of information.

On Sunday evening, Cameron Austin and Oliver Rogge again sat facing each other in the Vice President's office in his residence.

"You have information for me?"

"Yes," Oliver replied, "but you may not like it."

"Please," Austin said impatiently.

"Last week I found out that Ms. Cosner was going to Florida, so I got on the same flight and followed her. She went to see a man, a man at death's door may I add, by the name of Neal Landau. He's the man she lived with for close to a year when she was in Florida some fifteen years ago. It appears that Landau's lawyer, a Mr. Spears, had contacted Ms. Cosner on behalf of his client who wanted to see young Sarah before he died, claiming she was his child. I recorded the conversation. Ms. Cosner was very adamant that Sarah was not Landau's daughter."

"But I take it that she is his daughter," the Vice President said.

"It would appear so, sir, yes. But the point is now moot because the man died soon after Ms. Cosner's visit." No point going into any detail, Oliver had decided.

"I see. Anything else?"

"Yes. Ms. Cosner left for London this evening with her daughter.

From what I know so far, the girl will study music at the Royal College of Music."

"I see. And when will Ms. Cosner return to Canada?"

"I'm afraid that's unclear. She has an open ticket. She has told people in McPine that she would be on a book tour for her recently published novel..." Rogge consulted his notes, "... *Beads of the Sea*."

"That's not right," the Vice President said.

"Sir?"

"She hasn't finished that book."

"Then she said it to justify her absence," Rogge stated.

A long absence, Austin thought with great sadness. If she were to remain overseas, it would be impossible for him to try and win her back. From what Oliver had said, it was quite clear that the quick decisions had been prompted by a desire to shield her daughter, not by possible ramifications related to her brother's and his girlfriend's action.

Odd, Austin thought. Laurie's old lover died, and so did the man who set the dynamite at the Thousand Islands. Doctors had been unable to save him. The investigation was continuing on both sides of the border, but so far it appeared Peachee had acted alone. There would be no trial. The media would lose interest. It had become a non-issue.

Rogge broke the silence. "I can try and find out how long Ms. Cosner'll be away by contacting her mother. They're a very close family. I'm certain she knows her daughter's whereabouts and plans."

"Thank you, but that won't be necessary. I do appreciate all your efforts."

"Sir, is there anything else you need?"

"No. Not at this time," Austin replied, standing up.

Rogge also stood. "Sir, you can count on my discretion," he said.

"It's very much appreciated, Oliver."

After Rogge had left, Cameron Austin went to the window, peering outside at the fading light. Darkness was about to cover the capital which would awaken again in the light of a new day unlike the darkness that had fallen over him and would never lift unless he took some steps. Rogge had been right. Eileen Danfort was now the key. Reaching for his personal notebook from the inside pocket of his jacket, he sat back at his desk. He found the number he wanted and punched numbers. John Danfort answered. After expected banter was exchanged, he transferred the phone to his wife.

"How are you, Mrs. Danfort?" Austin asked.

"Fine, thank you. I insist that you call me Eileen."

"I will. I assume you know why I'm calling."

"I suspect, yes."

"These types of conversation are difficult on the phone. I was wondering if we could talk face to face at some point. You are not planning to come to Washington soon by any chance?"

What's a little lie? She wanted her husband to take a break, to relax. This would be a wonderful excuse. "As a matter of fact, John's going down on business in a couple of days. I could easily tag along."

He was pleased, very pleased indeed. Eileen wrote down Austin's secretary's number as he gave it to her. She would be in touch.

How fortunate, she thought as she hung up. She had an opportunity to remove the roadblocks her daughter kept insisting on finding. It was now up to her to do anything and everything to get those two together. It would be a labor of love, because she understood so well how afraid her Laurie was. Cameron Austin needed to recognize it as well.

"What exactly is my business in Washington in a couple of days?" John Danfort asked innocently, knowing full well that he would do whatever Eileen wanted. And saving Laurie from herself was what she wanted badly.

"We'll call it the Laurie and Cameron saga."

"Good. I'm sure I could make some contacts while there," John commented.

"Don't you dare," Eileen said. "I want to take in all the museums and whatever else there is to see."

John Danfort smiled. He was putty in her hands. "But what am I going to do while you rub shoulders with the Vice President?"

"Spend time with Mike. He needs to get away. We'll invite him along."

CHAPTER FORTY-THREE

Stepping out of the car in front of the hotel on M Street, Agent Lonsdale walked inside the luxurious Fairmont and soon located the bank of in-house telephones. A moment later, Eileen Danfort was telling him that she would be down shortly. Waiting was part and parcel of his duties, and today it was a pleasure because he had instantly liked the woman he was to escort to the Vice President's senate office. She was charming and had a ready smile which reminded him of his own mother.

Looking at the people milling in the lobby, he was pleased that the VP had seen fit to send him on this errand. It was another mark of trust, yet he wondered why Ms. Cosner had not been down the previous weekend as he had understood her schedule to be. And why was her mother the lady of the hour?

Stepping out of the elevator dressed in a classic navy suit that accented her good figure, Eileen Danfort was all smiles and spoke to Lonsdale as though he were a long-time friend.

"The car's in front," was all he said as he guided her toward the street.

She was seated alone in the back seat as they traveled the busy noon-hour streets of the capital. She felt she was already familiar with the city because she had taken a guided bus tour the previous evening with her husband and her son. Mike, who had visited Washington the year before with April, had been uncharacteristically quiet. Eileen had understood only too well. Losing a mate had been her children's lot as well as hers. She would never admit it, but Eileen was also grieving, grieving for her son's loss just as she had grieved when Laurie had been widowed.

Suddenly she saw the Capitol building with its majestic dome and turned her attention back to the city. Moments later she was ushered into a private dining room. She barely had time to appreciate her surroundings before Cameron Austin walked in. Dashing as ever, she thought, but his gaze was tired, sad.

"Hope you had a good trip down, Mrs. Danfort."

"Call me Eileen. I insist," she said, taking his proffered hand.

"If you wish. Please," he said, indicating a table where two place settings had been arranged. "Let's sit."

A single peach rose stood on the white tablecloth in the middle of the round table. He saw her eyeing it.

"Laurie gave me a peach rose after my first visit to McPine," he said simply.

A waiter came in and, prompted by the Vice President, she decided on a glass of white wine. Austin chose soda water.

"I want to thank you for coming down. I know it's an imposition."

"Not at all," Eileen said, smiling. "I had not been to Washington in years, and I want to see my daughter happy. The only way that's going to happen is if she marries you, so I was very motivated to come."

"I am so pleased to hear that."

"I'm sure you have lots of questions, but you have to understand that Laurie has always sacrificed a lot for Sarah's sake. Like all parents do for their children."

Eileen and Cameron remained silent as the server came back into the room and placed the drinks on the table.

"My secretary ordered a chicken Caesar. I hope that suits you," he said as the server was putting in front of each of them a huge salad on which a thickly sliced chicken breast rested.

"That looks great. Thank you."

A basket of fresh breads and rolls was deposited on the table, and Eileen eyed the many choices for an instant.

"We don't want to be disturbed for a half-hour," the Vice President told the slim blond man who nodded slightly and disappeared noiselessly.

"Laurie confides in you, doesn't she?"

"I think she shares the important happenings in her life, yes."

"Then you know she broke off our engagement."

"Yes."

"She gave me a song-and-dance routine about being afraid that the activities of your son's girlfriend would hurt me politically if they became known. I don't believe that to be the reason." His black eyes were darting Eileen's.

"I hope you appreciate that there are some things I can't talk about," Eileen replied after swallowing some salad. "As I said, she's very protective of her daughter."

"I know, but if the world is to notice Sarah's extraordinary talent, she cannot avoid being in the limelight." He had considered that this would be a safe remark. "Whatever the reason, I want Laurie back in my life." He wanted to ask, *what is she doing in England?* But chose a safer route. "Please tell me where she is hiding. She told people in McPine that she was going on a book tour. I know that is not the case. The book is not published yet because she hasn't finished writing it."

"I see you've been making inquiries."

"Eileen, please understand that I was devastated, so a few phone calls were made."

"I don't blame you. Not at all."

The Vice President was getting a little annoyed but his voice remained calm. "Where is she, Eileen?"

"She's in England. London. Sarah's attending a music school there and Laurie's with her."

"Really? That's odd because Laurie had made it quite clear that Sarah was to finish high school before devoting her time to studying music."

"I know, but she changed her mind."

"I was under the impression that Laurie and Sarah had agreed on the Peabody Institute in Baltimore for next year."

"As I said, Laurie changed her mind."

He attempted a smile. "And it's a woman's prerogative. When is Laurie returning to Canada?"

"Not sure. She told me she wanted to spend time with Sarah while the girl got used to a new culture," Eileen replied. "She's working on her book there."

"And she gave you no indication of how long she would be away?"

"No. Not yet, anyway."

"Want to know what I believe?"

Eileen nodded.

"Simply that Laurie thought that Sarah was possibly in some sort of danger. Perhaps the target of someone who saw her play the piano. It led her to take Sarah out of the country quickly. Am I close?"

Eileen Danfort wiped her lips with the white linen napkin and brought her wine glass to her lips, taking a small sip. "You know, don't you?"

He had anticipated the question. His expression did not change one iota. "Know what?"

"Laurie told me you had her investigated, so I'm sure you know her…secret," she said, trying to decipher if her remark had an impact by scrutinizing his eyes. She could not.

"I have no idea what you are referring to, Eileen. As I said, all I want is for Laurie to come back to this continent. The question then is: Is Sarah still in danger? If not, why have they not returned?"

At that moment Eileen was certain that someone on the Vice President's staff had unearthed Laurie's secret. In a way she felt relieved. Cameron was a good man; he would guard it with his life. "I spoke with Laurie last night."

"Did you tell her you were coming here today?"

"No. And my husband's sworn to secrecy. I talked to her because I wanted the latest, if you will, but got nowhere. I asked her when she plans to come back, but she didn't give me an answer. My opinion is that she's sorry she moved Sarah so abruptly, and now she's a little confused as to what her next step ought to be."

Eileen paused for a moment before continuing. "You're right. She fled because of Sarah. The reason's not important and no longer exists. She could come back, but you have to understand that Laurie's very much afraid that she won't be able to support you properly in your political aspirations because she's Canadian and not as familiar with your history and your politics as an American would be. She loves you and wants to marry you, but she's having serious second thoughts. And you have to agree that your job is somewhat… unusual, shall we say. No one else on this continent has a job like yours."

"Laurie and I did discuss my job in great detail and had formulated a plan that was best for us. I don't understand why she would have such doubts at this point."

"But the reality is that she does. I think you're the only one who can change her mind, so you can take it from here. You have her cell number. But I want you to know that on the way here, John and I were toying with the idea of going to London. See what's really going on."

"I would like to talk to her first, if you don't mind. Is she living in a hotel?"

"She's rented an apartment. On a weekly lease, I believe."

"You mean if she left, Sarah would be all alone in an apartment in London? No wonder she doesn't want to come back. Sarah is so young."

"The school took Sarah on as a student but could not provide for her room and board."

"Poor Laurie," Cameron Austin said so softly that Eileen almost missed it. His voice was normal when he spoke again. "The Senate will be keeping me busy the rest of the day, but I've arranged for someone to take you and your husband around, answer your questions."

Two hours later, Cameron Austin was in his office punching in Laurie's number. The answer was immediate. "This is Laurie. You know what to do." Disappointment made him frown and he saw the wisdom of not leaving a message. Instead he made plans to call during the night to catch her at breakfast.

CHAPTER FORTY-FOUR

*A*ustin knew it would be past midnight in London, but he reflected that no matter the time, he had to keep trying to reach Laurie. In the back of the limo on his way to dinner at his mother's house, he punched the number again. The previous night, he had fallen asleep while waiting for the right time to call, quite annoyed at himself. She answered on the second ring. A sleepy voice.

"I'm sorry to wake you up, Laurie, but reaching you in London has been a challenge."

"Cameron?" Her mind went blank for a moment.

"Your mother told me where you were. I forced it out of her at gunpoint."

What could she say to him? What should she say? His call was so unexpected.

"Laurie, are you there?"

"Yes. Of course. Sorry. I'm quite surprised to hear your voice."

"Why? Did you think I would simply write you off because you ran away? Your mother says Sarah is studying music in London. Why won't she be studying music in Baltimore as planned?"

Why did she think he would simply accept her decision without fighting back?

"Laurie, I understand you were afraid that Sarah was in some sort of danger, however your mother tells me that it's no longer the case.

Since I take it that was the reason you broke off our engagement, is there any reason for you to remain in England?"

"Not emphatically, no."

"Then why don't you come back? It's difficult to talk across an ocean, and I have a ring here that belongs to you."

"Cameron..."

"Yes?"

"I don't think I can go back at this time."

"Why not?"

"Perhaps you should ask your boss."

"My boss? You mean the President?"

"Exactly."

"Tell me why."

"He sent some people to McPine to spy on me, on my friends. I'm not sure what he wanted to find out exactly, but I'm certain he hoped to discredit me in some way. The President may be your friend, but I can assure you that he wants me away from Washington, away from the White House. And since I can't fight the President of the United States, I think it's better for all concerned if I stay away for a while."

"And what about what I want?"

"Come to London."

Maybe Laurie had been right all along. Were it not for his job, were he simply Joe-SixPack, he could be ready to hop on a plane at a moment's notice and have breakfast with the woman he loved. As Vice President he was not afforded such luxury. But then again no one, least of all him, had expected his personal life to be as bumpy as it had been. "I wish I could."

"So do I, Cameron. So do I."

Grace Winfield Austin was all smiles. All her children and grandchildren were around her this night. The house was a bedlam of activity, conversations, and laughter. Cameron joined in. Forgetting his worries he kissed his two sisters, shook hands with his brothers-in-law and had a warm hug and/or word for each of his five nieces and nephews.

"Where's your girlfriend?" David, a lanky seventeen-year-old, asked him.

"She's in Europe at the moment, I'm afraid."

"You mean she won't be there when you dine with the Australian Prime Minister on Saturday?" his sister Patricia asked.

"No."

"You know Washington. People are going to talk."

He shrugged his shoulders. "Let them."

After the meal when the family was lingering over dessert and coffee, Grace Austin stood up. "I have things to discuss with Cameron, so please excuse us for a moment. It's a warm night, let's step out on the patio," she invited.

The Vice President followed his mother into the late summer evening. The moon was a sliver in the eastern sky. "What is it, Mother?"

"I heard you say that Laurie Cosner's in England. What is she doing there?"

"Mother, I fail to see how this concerns you."

"But it does, my dear, because it concerns you. I hope she hasn't run away."

"What makes you say that?"

"The fact that you'll be alone at the reception on Saturday although she promised to be there with you. And also what I heard being insinuated."

"And what is that?"

"Things I didn't like, my dear. That the President wants to discourage Laurie from marrying you."

Cameron Austin controlled the anger he could feel rising. "And you listen to this type of gossip? Frankly, Mother, it is a little beneath you."

"Well, considering the source, I can't dismiss it."

His expression said: Well?

"Barbie Thomson." Grace did not miss the slight drop of her son's jaw. "I had lunch with her today. Just the two of us."

"And did she tell you this as a fact?"

"I believe so, yes, otherwise why would she have bothered? She never invited me to lunch before. I think she wanted me to warn you. She's playing for you."

This was the second time in as many days that he was hearing about the President's shenanigans where Laurie was concerned. He was puzzled. Andrew Thomson had more important things to worry about. Why was he bothering? What was Laurie to him? "Did the First Lady say anything else?"

"It seems Thomson is still peeved that you didn't see fit to choose an American, and also something about Laurie's relatives posing a danger of some sort. He wields a lot of influence, so you don't want him against you."

"Mother, even if you tend to forget, I'm a big boy. I can take care of myself."

"I know, dear, but it's always nice to be clear about the enemy's plans!"

"I appreciate your unending efforts on my behalf."

"What are old mothers for? Cameron, just between us, has Laurie run away?"

"Yes, but don't despair. I intend to dance with you at my wedding in the not-too-distant future."

"You'd better. I've already bought my dress."

He bent down and kissed her wrinkled cheek.

It had been raining for two days now, and Laurie could feel it bringing her spirit down. Or perhaps the weather was not the culprit at all. She missed Cameron so much that she now found smiling to be a chore. She and Sarah reached the restaurant and walked in, shaking the water from their umbrellas.

Once they had removed their coats and were seated at a booth, a kohl-eyed young waitress with a mount of black curls provided menus. Looking over the fare offered Sarah asked, "Mom, why did we come here?"

"This restaurant?"

"No. England."

Laurie eyed her daughter. A lot was hidden behind that question. She had to tread lightly. "You wanted to study music, remember?"

"Yes, but why so suddenly?"

"I just thought that while the planning for the wedding was going on, you should be away. I didn't want you to be a target of the media."

"I'll be eventually anyway, won't I?"

"Yes, but I wanted to avoid it as long as possible. We discussed all this before we left. Is there a problem now?"

"Well, I don't really like it here. And I have trouble understanding people."

"That's to be expected. Your ear'll get used to the accent in no time."

"And I don't like the food," she said looking over the menu. "Bangers…it almost sounds obscene."

"Then order something simple like a salad or an omelet," Laurie said.

The waitress approached. "So, luvs, what'll it be?"

Laurie ordered a mushroom omelet, and Sarah followed suit.

"See what I mean?" Sarah said as the waitress was walking away. "They call everybody 'luv.' It bugs me."

"Not everybody does it. Sarah, it's not like you to be so negative. What's really going on?"

She remained silent for a moment, then blurted out, "I miss my friends in Medford. I miss Emily."

"I know, but you'll make new ones over here."

"When you got engaged to Mr. Austin I told you that I wanted to stay with Auntie Rita while I finished high school in Medford, and you said it'd probably be okay."

"I thought about it and didn't think it was a good idea that we should live so far apart."

"Is that why you pick me up here at school every day? I'm not a baby, you know." Sarah's cheeks were now the color of pink tomatoes.

"I realize that, but I can't have you walk the streets of London alone."

"I'm going to have to do it one day, won't I?"

"Is the fact that I meet you every day the reason you're so upset, or is it something else? The school, maybe?" Laurie urged.

Sarah folded the white napkin she had unfolded earlier.

"Out with it, Sarah."

"I thought it would be fun, but it's not. The other students are much older than me. They treat me like a kid. Even the teachers. I told them about the piece I wrote and I've not been allowed to play it for them. They've decided it's no good before hearing it."

Laurie's heart went to her daughter. "Why don't you give it a little more of a chance? You haven't been there that long."

Tears appeared in the girl's eyes. "Mom, I want to go back home."

The food was served. Sarah wiped her eyes and Laurie was dumfounded. Because every day Sarah had said things were great at school, the surprise was total. She needed to make the girl think of something else

After a few bites, Laurie asked, "Did you enjoy your visit to Albert Hall yesterday?"

"Of course. Very interesting."

"You'll play there one day. I can feel it."

"Maybe. I hope so."

"There are a lot more things to see in London. I was thinking that tomorrow we could go to Buckingham Palace, maybe see the Queen. Maybe she'll have us to tea."

Sarah smiled, and it made her mother feel temporarily better.

"Or we could spend the day shopping at Harrods. What do you say? I'll get you a couple of new outfits."

"That'd be great, but I still want to go back home."

"I know."

CHAPTER FORTY-FIVE

Cameron Austin called several times in an effort to reach Laurie, but without success. He consoled himself that she would have turned off her phone to go sightseeing or shopping with Sarah, then made a point of arriving at the White House promptly for the reception in honor of the Australian Prime Minister. The guest of honor had not arrived yet, and Cameron was greeted by the President.

"May we talk privately?" Cameron asked.

"Certainly," Andrew Thomson said, guiding him to a corner of the large room. "What's on your mind?"

"I would like to know why you found it necessary to have Laurie Cosner investigated."

Thomson's expression did not change. "Nothing personal. And you know it. In this day and age, we can't afford to take any chances. Especially with that brother of hers."

"Let me assure you that McPine is not a mecca for terrorism, and that her brother is not a terrorist."

"What difference does it make anyway? She has to get used to being scrutinized."

"I appreciate that you don't like the fact that she's not an American, but that is not going to change. Or perhaps you do not appreciate that she talks honestly and frankly. Hell, just like you do, in private."

"You're a good man, Cameron. I want you to succeed me as President and I intend to do everything in my power to make it happen, but

I must warn you that Ms. Cosner will cost you votes. I worry that she may cost the Party the presidency."

"You are making too much—"

"I'm not," the President broke in, "but perhaps this is all for naught. She told me that associating with you could be a moot point. What did she mean exactly?"

His expression remaining unchanged, the Vice President replied simply, "I'm afraid I have no idea."

Andrew Thomson knew Austin was avoiding the issue. He said, "I was going to talk to you on Monday, but here it is. A few days ago, I asked for a poll. You know what the results were?"

Cameron Austin felt irritation looming. "Please tell me."

"I only did it for the good of the Party. Right now, the women in this country will not support you. When asked if the fact that Ms. Cosner was not an American played a role, a good percentage said yes."

Austin was now irked. "Mr. President, may I ask why you did not feel I should have been informed that you were taking this survey?"

"Because I was sure you would have vetoed it."

"Of course I would have. My record speaks for itself. My choice of a spouse is nobody's business."

"But it is. That's the point. In marrying you, even if Ms. Cosner is not an elected official, she'll be a Canadian at the heart of the American decision-making process, something our voters don't like."

"I can assure you, Mr. President that I will not give up Ms. Cosner because it irritates some voters. If I have to make a choice, I will choose her over the Party."

Andrew Thomson eyed his Vice President. The man had guts and he was in love. A Herculean combination. "Let's not make rash decisions," Thomson said, touching Austin's arm in a friendly gesture. "We'll talk again."

He had seen his wife approaching, the Australian Prime Minister at her side, and the focus of the evening changed. Cameron Austin was very pleased to have an opportunity to discuss a joint project the U.S. and Australia had set up to study ocean life in depth.

After a day on her feet, Laurie Cosner was glad to be relaxing, stretched out on the sofa. She and Sarah had spent the day at Harrods, and what a day! Laurie had been almost as impressed as her daughter with the array of exquisite articles to be had. They had tried on tons of clothing of all types, each finally choosing an outfit. Sarah had fallen for designer jeans Laurie would never have been able to afford had she not been expecting an inheritance. The girl was also treated to a few tops that were sure to be the envy of her friends. For herself, Laurie decided on a black designer suit that could take her anywhere at any time. It had been a perfect day. Sarah had not mentioned going home once, though the girl did have a point.

Laurie was reevaluating her stay in London. She looked around the 'executive' furnished apartment in a modern building she was leasing by the week. It was not bad as far as rented apartments went, but it was expensive. This was London after all, but it was Spartan, without soul. Basic sofa and easy chairs in the living area, and a round wooden table with two chairs in the dining area. A couple of not-especially memorable pictures on white walls. The size of the kitchen was laughable. She figured the fridge could fit twice into the model in her McPine kitchen. The bedrooms were comfortable, but it was not home. After checking her watch, she decided that she would chance finding Bernie at the greenhouse.

He answered on the second ring, surprised to hear her voice. "You're really calling from London? You sound like you're next door."

"Modern communications, Bernie. You've heard about them, I'm sure. Tell me what's been happening. How's business?"

"Pretty good, actually," he said, then spent some time expounding on *Only Roses* and telling her about his progress in growing new varieties of roses.

"Have any other 'writers' come around?"

"Not that I've heard. Any fallback from the President?" he asked, still impressed by the way she had talked to the President of the United States on the telephone when the men calling themselves writers had visited McPine.

"I'd rather never discuss that again, Bernie, if you don't mind."

"Sure."

"Listen, I may be coming back earlier than planned."

"Good. Then you'll be here for the Oktoberfest at the Opera House Thanksgiving weekend. Annabelle says the music's going to be out of this world."

"Wouldn't miss it. Bernie, are you using the house at all?"

"Well…yes. A friend is staying there this weekend."

"The divorcée with the two boys?"

"How do you... Never mind."

"Things are going well, I take it."

It took him a moment then he said, "Yeah. They are."

"I'm very happy for you."

"You were right, you know."

"I am most of the time. About what exactly?"

"About Clare. Letting go, I mean. I've made my peace now. When exactly are you coming home?"

"Probably within a couple of weeks."

"Really?"

"Upsetting your plans, am I?"

"No, that's not it. Why did you go in the first place?"

"We'll talk when I get back," she said, and he had to be satisfied with that.

Late Saturday evening—early Sunday morning in London—Cameron Austin punched a number on his bedside phone and found Laurie at home. The voice was sleepy, not surprisingly. "Sorry to wake you, darling, but this seems to be the only time I can reach you at home. I tried in vain a few times yesterday."

"I turned my cell off for a while. Sarah and I went shopping."

"Did you have a nice time?"

"Very nice. How was your dinner at the White House?"

"I missed you."

"Did people ask why I wasn't there?"

"Yes, of course. I told them that you had been unable to come to Washington and left it at that."

"And what did President Thomson have to say?"

"His methods might not be the best, but his intentions are solely to work for the benefit of the Party."

"And I am not good for the Party because I rate quite high on a scale of pissing-off the politically savvied. They can't grasp the concept of having a non-American married to a U.S. President, and they believe the voters won't either."

There was no point in telling her about the results of the poll. "A few people think that way, yes, including the President, but we can work together to change their minds. But you have to be here if we are to accomplish this. Have you given any thought to coming back to this continent?"

She told him about Sarah's disappointment in London then said, "She's so young. It was wrong on my part to take her away so abruptly. I'll wrap things up, but as long as we're here, we'll do some sightseeing and then head home. After we travel in England and Scotland, I was thinking of flying over to Paris for a couple of days. Sarah really wants to go and I would love to see the Eiffel Tower and all the rest."

"Good for you," Austin commented. "I'll be waiting. With a ring."

"About that," she began.

It was nearly an hour later by the time they said their goodbyes, but not before she had invited him to the Oktoberfest in McPine. "No Germans in our neck of the woods, but we do celebrate the bounty of the earth. Don't forget that it's on Thanksgiving weekend, in October in Canada, not November."

He smiled. "I know."

After hanging up, the Vice President was smiling contentedly. He let his head fall on the pillow and, moments later, sleep was carrying him away for a few hours of carefree dreaming.

By early October, the fact that Laurie Cosner had not been seen in Washington in several weeks, did not go unnoticed in some quarters. The expected wedding of the Vice President was a definite newsworthy item and everyone in the media was bending an ear for rumors about the preparations, the guest list or any other choice tidbit, but so far, nothing. One freelance journalist, Eva Menninger, had made the upcoming nuptials her mission. She wanted to be first in announcing its details to the world, and at the same time publish a lengthy piece on how citizens on both sides of the border viewed U.S.-Canada relations.

She had worked hard on it, and once it was ready to go, she knew the article would be picked up for wide distribution. Her share of wedding news was not so certain however. She had been forever hitting a brick wall. Either no wedding was being planned, or people had decided to discreetly guard the privacy of the Vice President. With her track record, she knew that the latter seemed improbable because she could always find someone—if one was willing to touch each rung of the ladder—willing to talk, if only to convince himself or herself of his or her worth. This time, nada. She was determined to find out why.

Eva sat in on the White House briefings and press conferences, forever searching for new angles, and had managed to publish some interesting pieces over the years. This September morning she had decided to push her own agenda.

The White House Press Secretary, Jason Stonebanks, a handsome forty-something with dark hair, briefed the media in his usual efficient manner. It was a slow news day with little new being offered to the news-hungry reporters in the room. To Eva's mind, the questions that followed did not provide the fodder she was looking for. At the appropriate moment, she raised her hand smiling warmly at Jason. It was always a pleasure to play the man who considered himself the soul of the Thomson administration.

"Yes, Eva," Stonebanks called, as she knew he would.

"There's a rumor going around Washington that Vice President Austin and Laurie Cosner are no longer engaged. Can you comment on that?"

Stonebanks took a second or two to respond. "It's really a slow news day, I see," he said, and the audience chuckled briefly. "I'm afraid I can't answer because I don't keep tabs on the private life of the Vice President."

Eva was waving her hand again vehemently and spoke before being invited. "If they're still engaged, when can we expect the date of the wedding to be officially announced?"

"Again, this is the Vice President's private life. You'd have to ask him," Jason said, signaling to someone else and hoping for a question more in line with the purpose of the briefing. He was successful.

As he was gathering his papers and preparing to leave the room, Stonebanks asked his assistant in a low voice, "Are they or are they not getting married?"

"The rumor is that they've split up," the aide replied. "That's what I heard."

Eva made it a point of walking towards the front of the room as soon as briefings were over. At times, she heard interesting remarks. Today's was especially juicy.

CHAPTER FORTY-SIX

It was mid-afternoon when Air Force Two landed at the Canadian base north of Lake Ontario on a warm October Saturday. The trees were beginning to dip into an autumnal palette of rich red, yellow and pumpkin-orange hues. Cameron Austin transferred to a waiting black van belonging to Green Lodge, and he and his Secret Service detail were quickly on their way to McPine.

He loved this time of year when the summer heat had been quashed and the icy winter winds were still far away. He could see himself as a child playing in the fallen leaves, enchanted by their lightness. He would delight in helping his parents' gardener pile the leaves on top of the rose bushes to protect them during the winter months and listen as the man, ancient in his view at the time, would explain that the leaves were rich nutrition for the soil. He suddenly felt sorry that he would never see his child experience the same simple pleasure.

The van pulled up in front of the greenhouse of *Only Roses*. Two agents jumped out and kept an eye out as the Vice President entered the house by the side door. Laurie's arms were waiting for him.

It was dark by the time Austin propped himself up on one arm and looked at Laurie lying next to him in the bed. She opened her eyes and smiled. It was all he needed to crown the ecstasy they had just shared. "At what time is the party getting underway?"

"Around eight," she replied, "but we can be late. How about a bite to eat?"

"Yes. I'm famished."

"It's all that exercise!" She commented.

He bent to kiss her lips lightly, then reached for her hand and felt the ring on her left hand.

"I promise to never take it off again," she promised.

Eva Menniger had gotten nothing more from the White House Press Secretary, but there had been plenty of people to call for comments. A wedding may have been a better story, but this wasn't bad as far as peripheral news was concerned. She reread the article one more time then went peddling.

No one really knew for certain where the Opera House moniker for the McPine Hall had originated. It had been built some twenty-five years earlier as a gathering place for all sorts of events, from craft shows and fund-raising bazaars to Christmas caroling and dances. It was also the venue for the odd play when the artistic group from Medford could be convinced to extend their horizons to pine country.

The Hall was made up of two tiers, somewhat like a split-level home. The top tier, half a floor up on either side, was used mostly to sell drinks and food when the event taking place warranted it. Tables and chairs were set up as needed. The lower tier served the main event. There was a stage at the far end, complete with dressing rooms at the back. Folding chairs and tables were stored under the side tiers to be set up as necessary.

Earlier in the week, someone—Laurie never found out exactly who—had taken the trouble to set up rows upon rows of chairs in the hall after she made a remark to Annabelle to the effect that perhaps it was time to let the people of McPine know exactly what was going on in her life. Before she knew it, she was on stage in front of the dozens of people in the hall, telling them that Cameron Austin would be at the Oktoberfest dance on Saturday. The applause had been thundering.

"You'll all have a chance to meet him," she said cheerfully.

"I thought you were supposed to get married this month. What happened?" A strong male voice asked from the back of the hall.

She was prepared for the question. "Cameron's schedule is so hectic right now that we've decided to wait until the New Year. We don't have an exact date at this time."

"Can we ask him to dance on Saturday? I mean, it would be okay, wouldn't it?" Martha Pasnak, the forty-something wife of a local farmer, asked.

"Of course. Cameron wants to meet all of you, and get to know you. Don't be shy, but remember that there'll be all sorts of Secret Service people around to protect the Vice President. So I implore you, leave your guns at home."

Laughter took over the hall.

It was almost nine o'clock by the time Cameron and Laurie arrived at the McPine Opera House. The dance was in full swing, and the talented trio on stage made up of a guitar, a keyboard and a sax were, at that particular moment, filling the air with lively sounds that had everyone clapping their hands. Decorations with a fall and harvest motif had been strategically placed around the hall and in the large windows on two sides of the building. Large round tables with chairs around them had been set up all along the walls of the hall, and the large empty space in the middle of the wood floor was for the dancing pleasure of those in attendance.

Her smile radiantly reflecting her mood, Laurie began introducing the Vice President to all those on hand. Agents Lonsdale and Dunlop kept a close eye on the pair while two other agents were alert at the door. People began filing in, one behind the other, for a chance to meet the man himself. It proved to be a long process because no one wanted to be left out and everyone had a camera. Cameron willingly obliged to have his picture taken time and time again. When he was finally able to dance with Laurie to the sounds of a classic slow tune, everyone applauded.

"Quite a group," Austin commented.

"They're very happy to meet you personally at last. It's a big deal for them," she said. "They're making up for not intruding on you in all the years you've been coming up to McPine."

"I've always appreciated it so much."

"They're great people. I'm going to miss them," she said.

"We will come back, you know," he said, kissing her cheek.

More than two hours later the party was still going strong, but Cameron and Laurie saw the wisdom of leaving. As they stepped into the cool night air, he said, "It has been a long while since I danced so much. Ladies seldom ask me to dance!"

"Think of it this way. You made a lot of women very happy tonight, and they'll be able to talk to all their relatives and friends about this for a long time to come. You deserve an award!"

"The people in there deserve the award! I am so glad you asked me to come this evening. Thank you."

On his return trip to Washington aboard Air Force Two, Austin was immediately apprised of the wire article.

No Wedding for Vice President Austin

Sources close to the White House have confirmed that the expected wedding of Vice President Cameron Austin and his fiancée, Canadian Laurie Cosner, has been canceled. The exact reason for the break-up was not given, however many Washington insiders are speculating that opposition to the wedding was strong in certain circles because the bride-to-be is not an American.

Perfect, he thought. He didn't bother with the rest of the article.

He picked up the phone and called Grace Winfield Austin. What would the old lady think of his plan?

"It's a great idea," Grace said after he had explained what he and Laurie had in mind.

"I do not want you to be inconvenienced by this," he said.

"Don't you worry about me, Cameron. I am so very, very happy."

"So am I," he said, smiling. "Laurie will call you."

"I'll be looking forward to it."

A day later, President Thomson took time to visit the Vice President in his office. He closed the door behind him.

"Cameron, I've just heard," the President said. "Tough."

The Vice President looked straight into the eyes of the President. "You of all people know that not everything you read in the newspapers or online is true."

The President's look was quizzical. "What are you talking about? I'm told that Ms. Cosner has moved to England."

Austin wanted to ask how much of a close eye the President was keeping on Laurie, but refrained. "She did, yes, but not forever. We are going to get married, even if you do not approve. And to make things quite clear right now, in order to spare embarrassing the Party, I will not be seeking the nomination for the Presidency. I will serve my country in other ways."

"You can't be serious," Thomson exclaimed somewhat too loudly. "We're all counting on you. You can't just disappoint us like this!"

"I'm afraid that's my decision."

"We've all been through a lot, Cameron. You can't just throw it away on a whim!"

"You mean, on a woman, don't you? Since I cannot give up Laurie, the choice is quite clear."

"I hope for your sake that you don't come to regret that decision!" The President warned.

"I don't see how that would ever happen."

"When's the happy day?"

"It's not decided yet."

"Well, do keep us informed. Barb and I don't want to miss it," the President said.

CHAPTER FORTY-SEVEN

The air was late-autumn crisp, but the sun was shining brightly on a November weekend when Laurie Cosner and Cameron Austin exchanged vows. The ceremony was very simple and no one outside the invited guests was aware that the event was taking place.

The wedding was held at the elegant home of Grace Austin outside Baltimore. The radiant bride wore a simple ecru lace suit with a calf-length skirt and carried a bouquet of peach roses. The groom wore a dark navy suit of the finest wool, tailored for the occasion, and wore a peach rosebud in his boutonnière.

The guests witnessing the ceremony from chairs set up in the large living room of the mansion were few. The bride walked in on the arm of John Danfort, who was as proud as if she had been his natural daughter. Eileen Danfort sat with her son, Mike and her granddaughter Sarah. Also on hand was the bride's closest friend, Rita Payne, who was accompanied by her daughter, Emily, her husband having been unable to attend. The out-of-town guests had been flown in by private jet from Toronto, the Vice President having decided that it was too important an event for guests to travel by commercial airliner.

In addition to his mother, the groom's guest list was made up of his sisters and their families. Steve Marsh, owner of the lodge at Green Lake outside McPine, and his wife, Esther, were among those flown in for the occasion.

A husband and wife team hired to take still photographs and to record the event on video —and sworn to secrecy—were surprised that no one from the Washington political scene was on hand to witness the event. Not even the President. The only other witnesses to the action were Grace Austin's regular staff who watched the exchange of vows from the opened door to the dining room.

The Vice President's Secret Service agents were on hand as well, as they were whenever Austin visited his mother. Standing at the back of the room Agent Lonsdale watched the exchange of vows. He was pleased, very pleased, at being able to witness the exchange, but most of all he was very pleased that he had been chosen to guide the detail of agents assigned to the new Mrs. Austin. He liked her, and his new duties meant that he would be able to return to pine country from time to time. All was well with the world. He smiled.

After the ceremony, the guests shared in toasting the newlyweds with champagne and in a wonderful buffet prepared by one of Baltimore's most renowned chefs. Eventually Cameron Austin got up and addressed the group, thanking them for being present. He had a kind word for everyone, thanking Eileen Danfort for having raised such a wonderful daughter which made Eileen wipe a stray tear from her eye, and told Sarah he would make a point of sharing as much of her life as he could. He ended by expressing his gratitude to his mother for overseeing the preparations and sharing her home.

The carpet in the den had been removed so the dancing could take place on the oak floor. One of Austin's nephews was in charge of feeding a sound system and had chosen a soft melody for the bride and groom's first dance.

Eventually everyone joined in and, as promised, Grace Austin danced with the Vice President of the United States. What a perfect day, she thought. At last her son had found happiness. In her earlier daydreams she had imagined that when Cameron married, it would be an elaborate world-class wedding to be remembered as the social event of the year, if not the decade. Yet, today, as Grace was witnessing the antithesis of her fantasy, she could not think of a more perfect wedding. The newlyweds had found each other against all odds and were guarding their love from the public eye as if it was a negative film being protected from filtering light.

What the world thought of their union was of no consequence. Their inner joy was all that mattered. And because she knew it would be a long and happy union, her old heart was warmed.

The very next day, Vice President Cameron Austin advised the White House that he wanted to visit the President for a few minutes. He reached the residence just as Andrew and Barbara Thomson were finishing their lunch and having coffee in the sitting room.

"Hello, Cameron," the First Lady said. "You look well."

"Thank you," he replied simply.

"What's on your mind?" The President asked. "Sit."

Barbara Thomson offered Austin a cup of coffee, but he declined and remained standing.

"Sir, I wanted you to be the first to know," Austin began, handing a large envelope to the President. "These were taken yesterday."

President Thomson fished in his shirt pocket for his reading glasses and removed photographs from the envelope. He looked at each briefly then stared over his glasses at Austin for a moment. "So you went ahead."

"Yes, sir. The immediate families were the only guests."

"Guests to what?" The First Lady wanted to know.

The President handed her the photographs.

"You got married," she exclaimed, smiling. "Congratulations," she said, and getting to her feet kissed Austin's cheek briefly.

The President also stood and shook hands with Austin. "Congratulations. You may doubt it, but I'm glad for you. You deserve a second chance. A bit later we should talk again about your future."

"Certainly."

President Thomson asked Austin to wait before announcing that he would not be seeking his Party's nomination. "I think one major announcement at a time would be wise. There'll be plenty of time later to debate your decision," he urged.

"If you say so, sir."

"When is the world going to know about it?" The President asked.

"My office will issue a statement tomorrow morning."

"We'll have a party," Barbie Thomson put in joyfully.

"Laurie and I would prefer to keep a low profile at this time."

"Of course. We'll just have a few close friends in. Otherwise, people will feel they were snubbed," she said.

Austin had expected some comment from the Thomsons for not having been invited to the wedding, and this was a nice not-so-subtle rebuff. He agreed with the First Lady that a party was a great idea.

CHAPTER FORTY-EIGHT

*I*n late September the following year, the anchor on the news network began to read a statement as the picture of Vice President Austin and his wife, Laurie, were an inset in the corner of the screen.

The White House has just issued a statement: Laurie Austin, wife of Vice President Cameron Austin, gave birth to a healthy baby boy at six o'clock this morning. The baby weighing in at seven pounds arrived a few weeks early, but mother and son are both doing well. This is the Vice President's first child. He has a sixteen-year-old stepdaughter. The new baby will be christened George Winfield, both family names.

Laurie Cosner had been keeping a very low profile for some months because the doctor had warned her that a pregnancy at her age was always cause for concern. She had been very happy puttering in the gardens of the house in suburban Baltimore, Cameron's house, which he had reopened when they were married. She enjoyed saying to her family and friends that she had simply switched her country life from McPine to Maryland. Whenever she stepped out during the summer, she had worn flowing summer dresses, and no one seemed to have noticed that she was expecting. The birth had surprised everyone, except the President and the First Lady.

Response to the news was immediate and positive. Congratulatory messages and gifts poured in from all over the country, indeed the world. For Americans, it was a ray of sunshine in an otherwise bleak year when they had to face a series of terrorist attacks. People were drinking the positive news.

For the next few weeks, pictures of the happy couple with their new son appeared everywhere. In McPine, when new magazines arrived at the variety store next to the post office or at the local pharmacies, there was a rush to see how many sported the new baby and his parents on the cover or in inside articles.

One morning, President Thomson accosted Cameron Austin in a White House corridor. "Americans seem thrilled that you're now a father. And you've got to remember that not since Kennedy has there been a young child in the White House. I think the people are looking forward to another Camelot to take their minds off their troubles."

And, amazingly, no one seems to remember that my wife is not American, Austin thought. "That in itself does not guarantee a victory come Election Day," Austin warned the President.

"Maybe not, but it's a good start. We asked for another poll to see where you stand in the minds of voters, and the majority, not only assume that you will be seeking the Party's nomination, but that you'll win and then become President next November. We need you, Cameron. The Party needs you to continue the work that must be done."

The White House was within reach. With Laurie at his side, it could be an exciting journey. One thing he found attractive about his wife was that she welcomed new experiences. She had married him and she was a new mother past forty because she had envisioned it as a marvelous adventure. Why would she not be thrilled to be the wife of the President of the United States? After all, she had a mother-in-law ready to guide and support.

The real question was: would Americans allow their President to escape to McPine? A thought occurred to him. Could he arrange some sort of treaty with Canada so that McPine could legally become American soil? Or better yet joint territory.

It was worth looking into. The people of McPine would joyfully dance in the street.

THE END

ABOUT THE AUTHOR

After being a newspaper and magazine editor, D.B. Crawford now devotes all her time to writing in a variety of genres. She lives in Montreal.